Praise for Return to Sender

"In Return to Sender, Mindy Halleck writes about family and neighborhoods and the ways our roots define our lives with the assured vividness of Dennis Lehane and the unflinching edge of Gillian Flynn. An old school, can't-put-it-down read."

Larry Brooks, critically-acclaimed bestselling author of four psychological thrillers, in addition to his work as a freelance writer and writing instructor. www.StoryFix.com

Mindy Halleck's Return to Sender has it all: a protagonist, Theo Riley, with a psychic wound that caused him, as a child, to kill three other human beings, then become a priest in an effort to find redemption for his soul, and a serial killer antagonist who makes Hannibal Lecter look like a choir boy. And add to that a fast-paced plot that slows down only when Theo periodically stops for a reflective moment that takes one's breath away in its profundity. You'll find yourself pondering your own redemption as you accompany Theo on his quest to save the woman he loves, his beloved beach town, and himself in this novel that will haunt you long after you've put it down.

Gloria Kempton, Writing Coach and author, including *Write Great Fiction: Dialogue,* and *The Outlaw's Journey: A Mythological Approach to Storytelling.* www.gloriakempton.com

*Mindy Halleck's **Return to Sender** is a deeply evocative novel wherein the protagonist, Theo Riley is a Roman Catholic Priest who carries a dark cross and earns redemption through blood and tears. This is a novel that explores what it means to have faith in a world torn by conflict.*

Bill Johnson, Author *of A Story is a Promise & The Spirit of Storytelling,* www.storyispromise.com.

"Monsters don't just happen." In her debut novel, Mindy Halleck creates a monster--Genghis Hansel--who needs a warrior-priest to release him from his demons. "Return to Sender" is a big book with a cast of edgy characters. It is a deep love story and a thriller rolled into one.

Jack Remick, Author www.jackremick.com ~ Montaigne Medal and BOTYA Finalist.

The vivid imagination of a born story-teller comes to life in Mindy Halleck's new novel, Return to Sender, starring a warrior-priest as reluctant hero—he waits for death, he prays for mercy, he hopes for the miraculous return of his fighting skills—as he faces a stone killer, the ruthless dragon-antagonist rising up from the mists with vengeance in his heart. Set against a backdrop on the picturesque—and often quixotic—Oregon seacoast, Return to Sender blooms with a sterling cast and some peachy plot-twists.

Robert J. Ray, The Weekend Novelist
www.RobertJRay.com

Return to Sender

Mindy S. Halleck

Cover Design by Loretta Matson

Cover art Clark Kohanek

Publisher BETTER LIFE PRESS
www.BETTERLIFEPRESS.com

This is a work of fiction. Names, characters, places, brands, media, and incidents are either the product of the author's imagination or are used fictitiously. Any resemblance to similarly named places or to persons living or deceased is unintentional.

PRINT ISBN 978-0-9909514-8-3

EPUB ISBN 978-1-62015-449-6

Library of Congress Control Number: 2014918810

Return to Sender

Mindy S. Halleck

Cover Design by Loretta Matson

Cover art Clark Kohanek

Publisher BETTER LIFE PRESS
www.BETTERLIFEPRESS.com

PRINT ISBN 978-0-9909514-8-3

EPUB ISBN 978-1-62015-449-6

Library of Congress Control Number: 2014918810

This book is dedicated to the remarkable men who inspired my protagonist, Theodore Riley; my husband Joe Halleck III whose faith and love never wavers, my gifted brother and story-telling mentor Clark Kohanek, who with skilled understanding of the human psyche guided me into the mind of a sociopath, and my father, Oscar Kohanek, the true buried treasure of Manzanita, whose PTSD gave me a soldier's story. And my grandfather, Frank Eli Meyers who, during the depression had to abandon his writerly dreams and box in the streets to feed his family.

Furthermore to my mother Connie Meyers, and my grandchildren Dominique and Davis Sitton-Law who inspire me to write stories with a moral compass hopeful that in the dark passages of their lives my words may resonate with their sense of humanity.

And finally a debt of gratitude to an unlikely source, my ex-father-in-law from thirty-five years ago, Lee K. Sitton who told me about the war orphans who stole his hard heart during the Korean War. His sixty year old forgotten photographs were found in my attic and served as inspiration for the backstory of Theodore Riley.

Prologue

I RECALL we took the shortcut we weren't supposed to take and, as fate would have it, the three McMurtry brothers stopped us in the middle of the alley– *their alley*.

My fists clenched. My older brother Kiernan held his hand across the front of me and said, "Be still." My fists remained knotted and ready but "still" for the time being.

The three McMurtry hoodlums were the regrettable sons of a wealthy Protestant gangster, our Da's political rival. None of them over eighteen, and all with faces as cheerful as dead hamsters. First, one of them shoved Kiernan and started yelling about our Da, his politics, our being Catholic, and something about Da having a "floozy" at the pub. Kiernan, a tall, slender agent of peace who was headed for priesthood, tried to reason with them. "Not our business," he said, holding his hands up, real calm. Then the fat drug-head brother, who had cheeks like boiled cabbage, threw a punch, took Kiernan off guard. I kicked the biggest brother in the nads, but the pervert dropped me to the ground and pinned my arms. I couldn't move and lay face-down screaming for them to stop beating Kiernan and for that hamster to get his fat *arse* the hell off a' me. "He's no fighter," I shouted. "Off me, you *prigs*! Let me up! I'll fight ya all!"

But they didn't stop their punches, blows, and kicks to his ribs even after he'd passed out.

"Kiernan!" I called out. "Kiernan?"

Then they turned on me and just as they started in an old lady at the end of the alley screamed, "Guard! Help! Guard!" They ran off. I scrambled to the ground at Kiernan's side. "Are ya alright?" There was blood all over his coat, his shirt, his face, but none on his fists.

I lifted his head onto my lap. "Ah, brother… " His eyes were open, but he wasn't breathing. I rocked back and forth, holding his lifeless body, and cried, "Sometimes you have to fight, brother. You have to fight."

*　*　*

The next Friday, my tenth birthday, Kiernan's body lay wrapped in Da's best tweed suit in a fancy casket in our sitting room. As we waited for the wake to begin, for the people from church, Da's lace factory, our pub, grocery, and school to come give their bests, bring their casseroles, and say their prayers and goodbyes to my brother, I slipped out the back door.

Just the Friday before I'd waited for Kiernan to come home and play. I was splayed across a dirt trench in our backyard stacking tiny sandbags, setting up a battlefield, forming hills and rock walls, digging trenches and valleys. Mamaí hollered to me, "Theo, watch yer sister. And remind yer Da to get milk on his way from the pub," then slammed the front door and left.

I said, "Okay," but kept playing. Da left. I forgot my little sister Imogene and continued to set up for our backyard battle, lining up my tin soldiers, the Irish Defense Forces, with green arm bands that would soon battle Kiernan's British Forces, with red arm bands. It was my fault we had to go out for milk. My fault the battle we ended up in was real, not play.

I didn't know much about politics, and didn't care much about the difference between Protestant and Catholic, but did know what I had to do for Kiernan, who always had my back, defended and protected me. I understood that. It was a brother's sacred contract. And I understood battlefield strategy and that a good one was needed against these *blaggards* that were all twice—make that *three* times—my size.

*　*　*

I sneaked inside McMurtry's store without their Da seeing me, hid under a counter and watched the *gouger* count his pinched riches and open his big safe, full as a Gypsy's bra, then stuff that money inside and lock up the store. He secured every window, double-checked all the doors, and left. Then outside was the rumble of his posh car; finally, he was gone.

When I came out of hiding, right next to me was the sweeties shelf lined with boxes of my favorite, Baby Ruth bars. I was tempted to snitch one but recalled Kiernan saying to me another time a candy bar looked good to my itchy fingers, "Rileys are not pinchers." So I left it and went on with my preparations.

My knowledge of the McMurtry boys' legenday, riotous Friday night card games in the back of the store made them sitting ducks. While waiting for them to arrive I gathered my battle supplies, gasoline and matches, then poured a ring of gasoline around the back room, up and down the aisles— then climbed up onto a rafter to wait. It wasn't much of a wait.

About ten minutes later they showed up, half drunk, oblivious to the smell of fumes I thought for sure would give me away. They entered the small, windowless back room where they had a table, chairs, and their secret reserve of whiskey and cigarettes. Above the door rested a high wooden beam sturdy enough to hold me. From that beam, with matches in hand, I watched as they settled up to the table. Their other thieving friends would show up soon, so there was little time—and in combat, timing was everything.

They laughed, talking about how they'd taken the new kid Grady's lunch money, *as they had mine a hundred times*, and how after they did that, they did something to his pretty sister and how funny it was that they left her crying in the park with her knickers torn. They'd been bad to the bone all their lives— nobody'd miss 'em.

I dropped from the beam, lit a stick match and said, "You shouldn't a' picked on Kiernan, he wasn't a fighter."

"*Jasus!*" Joe McMurtry said. "Ya scared the piss outta me jumpin' down like a chimpanzee."

"And that Grady girl," I said, "too good for any of *ya pissers.*"

"Go home to *yer Da*," Joe said. "That *provo* piss-head. And that brother a' *yers*—a fighter? No, he was a *poofer*. Now go, ya *rossie* shit, get the hell outta here 'fore I get up and beat—"

"No need gettin' up," I said. "I'll see myself out." I then tossed the flame to the floor.

A wall of fire exploded across the room. They all leapt up; their chairs flew backward. I latched the door, high-tailed it out the front, and never looked back.

* * *

At Kiernan's wake, Mamaí, whose face was now like that of a disappointed Madonna on a vicarage wall, tucked his Bible into the coffin with him. She said I smelled of smoke and told me to go wash my hands and face and to be a good boy. I did.

And as a good boy I stood next to Kiernan's casket all night. As the sound of the fire truck siren rang out six blocks away, I tucked a prayer card and a tin soldier, one of mine, in Kiernan's pocket, then tucked one of his in mine, and said, "I took care of it, brother. You rest in peace now."

Imogene stood about waist high next to me, crying. I took her tiny hand in mine and said, "Don't worry, sissy, I'll watch after ya." She finally lay down in a cozy chair and went to sleep.

The church people brought lamb stews, soda breads, meat *boxty*, and sweet potato *fadge*. Mamaí slid a Baby Ruth candy bar into my pocket and said, "You're a good boy, Theo. A good boy to sit with yer brother." Her eyes were swollen and heavy. She looked half-asleep. She hugged me tight. "You still smell of smoke." Just then a neighbor rushed in and said the McMurtry store had burned to the ground and the three sons were dead.

Mamaí's swollen eyes bulged. She stared at the man as he gave details to the gathering crowd of mourners. Then, slowly, she looked down at me, that sleepy look gone, her green eyes full of questions. She reached into Kiernan's coffin, snatched up his Bible, handed it to me and whispered, "Alright then, boy, just understand." She shoved the Bible into my hand. "There's a price for revenge, and it will be paid. You'll take his place now."

I looked down at Kiernan who had always protected me, and in that moment, for the first time, it really sank in deep, deep into me that my big brother was gone and that both our life paths were irretrievably altered by my actions and one of Mamaí's unbreakable sacred contracts. The weight of his well-worn white Bible crashed down upon me. My eyes burned with tears.

"There'll be no tears," she said. "You chose your path, now walk it. And don't say a word, boy." She whispered, "Not a word . . . I've already lost one son. Now quick, go find your Da. The dye is set. We must act fast. No time for boyish tears."

                              *   *   *

That weekend my birthday came and went without notice, without cake or gifts. Instead it came amidst tears and rumors of old man McMurtry's quest for revenge. He threatened the Grady family, whose daughter was raped by his sons the same night of the fire—and threatened our Da, who he figured had something to do with that fire, and threatened our shrinking group of friends, who, fearing his wrath, distanced themselves.

With Kiernan buried, we sold everything we owned and boarded a train, then a steamer and headed out of Ireland for America. In America, Mamaí had a good friend, Constance Beaumont, who lived in a small town on the Oregon Coast. There, she said, we'd be safe.

From that day forward Mamaí forced me to attend church every Sunday, say my prayers, wear a rosary—carrying it in my pocket wasn't enough; she wanted it on my body so Christ Our Savior would protect me from myself. And from that day forward in Mamaí's eyes was that fear when she looked at me, fear when she held me, her precious lone son, whose soul was tainted by a sin so dark she would only whisper it in prayer, red rosary in hand, face lowered in shame.

Da's dread of what may become of my "violent tendencies" led him to believe that a good beating on Saturdays would keep me in check, then church on Sundays. But as we settled into our new home and got to know our new neighbor, an American Indian, once a chief and warrior, Mamaí, despite her stern Catholic manner, decided Da's beatings were not the way. God had sent us an angel, she said, an archangel maybe, but one of God's angels none the less, and that angel's name was Solomon.

Mamaí decided Solomon would teach me his ways of hunting, fishing, hiking, and most of all, his ways of finding harmony in this world. Harmony, she said, was the deep well that would be the source of my salvation. She figured with her prayers, red rosaries, and constant vigilance over my blemished soul, along with Solomon's training, that my aggressive inclinations would take a healthy, new direction. But a blemished soul is a blemished soul.

PART I

Chapter 1

TWENTY-THREE YEARS LATER – SEPTEMBER 1956
THEODORE RILEY

THE CONCRETE TOWERS of the Oregon State Penitentiary rose high, a doomed cathedral against the wide blue sky. I parked my '39 De Soto, took another swig of Murphy's, put the bottle back under the seat, and climbed out of the car.

Next to the front gates lay a bird—a sparrow. Smashed, rusty brown-and-white feathers flittering in the breeze. I wanted to scoop it up, take it home, bury it on Neahkahnie Mountain. Instead, I walked by it and through the overlapping, locking metal gates. I was late.

Guards stared down from their twenty-foot towers of providence past the barbed wire, the cement barriers, and their rifles—.30 caliber M1s. I felt the ghost of mine slung over my shoulder. Theirs were aimed at me. I looked up. They nodded and I opened the second gate.

Inside the office was the check-in desk. Behind that desk sat a fat man with a pelt of black hair, stern puffy eyes, and a nameplate over his silver badge: *Officer Stamboli*. He had sausage-like fingers, furry knuckles, and an aroma like liverwurst. I'd never seen him before.

"Father Riley?" he asked.

"Sorry I'm late," I replied, though in that place time was a relative thing. "Where's Charlie?" I took off my watch and gave it to him.

Officer Stamboli put my watch in an envelope, handed me a pen with his hairy hands, and said, "No Charlie today."

"Okay," I said, and signed in.

He checked my signature against his paperwork. "Keys?" he continued.

I handed over the car keys and emptied the contents of my pockets: my red rosary and Kiernan's tin soldier with a chipped red arm band.

"Interesting companion for your rosary, Father," he quipped. "Okay, sleeves."

I rolled up my black shirt sleeves to reveal no knifes or razor blades taped to my skin.

"Nice tattoo," he said studying the angel on my forearm, his eyes tracing the bloody sword in my angel's hands. "Fancy yourself a fallen angel, huh." He then nodded to roll my sleeves back down as he thumbed through my Bible. "Officer Timmons, show our toy-soldier-totin', tattooed fallen angel to the chapel, will ya."

Officer Timmons—we'd met before—was a towering, hard-boiled officer with a square jaw, crew cut, and watchful eyes. He opened the door that led down the linoleum-floored corridor past the locked gymnasium where prisoners worked at the prison's main industry, wooden furniture. He didn't speak; gave the impression he didn't care for priests. That's okay, neither did I. We were both just going through the motions. Hell, had my family not left Ireland when we did I'd likely be an occupant in a penitentiary much like this one, with a guard much like him.

Our footsteps echoed off bare walls all the way to the windowless chapel. I laid my Bible on the shelf, sat on the padded bench in the confession booth that looked more like a poor man's crypt than a place of secrets, and waited for my first confession. Most weren't much more than guilt-ridden claims of virtue and pleas for clemency; they had little to do with true repentance. True repentance was rare.

*   *   *

"RIOT!" Muffled screams and shouts arose from somewhere outside, then a gunshot. "Riot in the yard!" someone yelled. I stepped out of the coffer. Two guards rushed into the chapel, kindly demanding my company. They ushered me down the hall, then shoved me into a six-by-six holding cell. The stench of bleach and vomit made me nauseous.

"I'd rather not be locked into—"

"It's for your safety, Father," one of the guards said. The clank of the metal door slammed behind me. Sirens rang out. The officer bolted away. A door somewhere far off sealed shut, sucking the air from the room. A brittle stillness fell over the long, government-green corridor. There was hushed silence except for the muted uproar outside the narrow, ceiling-high windows. Sweat covered my face, dripping from my forehead to my black cleric shirt. I blinked away images of chicken wire and sludge in my cell in Korea, the stench of urine and blood, the sound of roosters, women screaming, and gunfire—and took a deep breath, reminding myself I was in a comfy U.S. prison and would soon leave *at will*.

*   *   *

"A man of the cloth." A faceless voice curled around from the bars of the adjoining cell; a concrete wall divided us. His resonant tone was menacing, controlled—a patient cougar's rumble. "Locked up, eh... Well, welcome to the dark side of Eden, Padre."

I looked along the row of cages, cages painted a polluted milky green. My eyes and ears landed on the one to my right. His large hands hung limp outside the bars. One hand was long and slender; the other knotted, twisted, and gnarled with imperfections, yet sporting a large gold ring, as if he celebrated the defect. *But why did a prisoner still have his ring?*

"Father Riley!" blustered one guard with a just-past-puberty face and anxious blue eyes as he rushed down the hallway. "Are ya alright in there?"

"I'm fine," I said as I stood from the padded cot. "Thank you."

"I'm fine, too," my nameless neighbor announced. "Thank you."

Color drained from the guard's cheeks and his face turned to stone. He yanked the club from its holster and whacked it against the bars of my neighbor's cage. "Shut the hell up!"

Then he looked back at me. "Don't waste time on this one, Father." He hammered his club against the metal again. "There ain't no redemption for a man who hungers for children. We're processin' him in today and he's here for a good long time... aren't ya, buddy... We're gonna break that ugly-ass hand a' his to get that ring off. Should be a good day."

Another shot outside. The guard trotted off, the clank of his crowded key ring and his footsteps ricocheting off the hall into silence.

"Redemption?" My neighbor's gravelly voice pierced the quiet. "Fool."

"Is that what you want?" I asked. "Redemption?"

"Well, maybe a little salvation," he said. "Not too sure 'bout redemption."

"Anyone can be saved," I offered, "but not everyone can be redeemed. So which is it?"

"Ah, a man who knows the difference," he pondered. "They don't understand."

"Understand what?"

"Understand what I *do*."

"What do you do?"

His feet shuffled. The bars creaked with the weight of his body leaning against the gate.

"I illuminate," he said, a trace of the South in his tone. Arkansas, or maybe Missouri?

"Illuminate?"

"You wouldn't understand."

"Try me," I said.

"You… you're just another gatekeeper to my salvation."

"I'm no gatekeeper," I said tilting my head, pressing against the bars again, to see what I could see of him, his twisted hand, his ostentatious ring. "Then is there anything I *can* do for you, brother? Any prayers?"

His hands appeared outside once more, clasped together.

"*Prayers*, Padre . . . to you? Why, did you ride in on some proverbial pale horse? You that rider named Death? Should I hold my breath, speak in tongues amongst the dying, all vying, crying, lying. Should I, Padre? No… no plea for clemency shall be. The Grim Reaper holds no dominion over me."

"Okay, poet—what do you want then?"

"I want out!"

"Besides out, what do you want?"

"A cigarette." He took a deep breath. "And to go to the Kansas City Fair, ride some rides, dance, see people… cotton candy, kids," he laughed.

My stomach seized as his laughter released his dark essence. It filled his cell.

"You from Kansas?"

"Did ya know, Padre, it's tradition with German Jews, when death occurs, open a winda' so the soul can fly away like a bird… 'Flee as a bird to your mountain,' they say."

"So, Jewish then?"

"'Bout as Jewish and Kansas as you, Padre. Saw ya when you *limped* in. Saw your face in the newspaper, you're that war-hero-boxing-champion-turned-priest, from the coast. You're what, thirty-three years old? You walk like an old man."

I remained silent.

"Strange career path," he said. "*War hero.* What is it *you* want in this place, Padre? Didn't you get enough prison after that bug-infested Korean cell? And why do you smell like a Baby Ruth… and whiskey? Man of contradictions, eh?"

The weak scent of dried cloves didn't mask his sour sweat. I slouched back alongside our adjoining wall and listened to his deep, struggling breaths—the raspy noise of asthma teased his lungs, and he sounded like a sluggish Grizzly groaning in anticipation of hibernation.

"I can pray with you, or for you," I said. "That's what I have to offer." My jaw tensed again at the thought of making any request for redemption on behalf of this pervert.

"You mean prey *on* me?" he chided. "That's what your ilk does, right? Lay hands, seek some lever of power, find that crack in a man's soul, something he feels bad about. Always collectin' secrets in that little booth, black mailin' with the threat of a fiery future, strong armin' poor, dumb folk into bein' 'better men.'

But for whom, Padre?" He took a deep breath and continued. "See, this is the funny thing 'bout jail. In here, I'm a free man. Free to rest, think, do as I please. Out there in *your world*, if you had your way, everyone would be a slave to some higher power. You come here selling salvation, freedom from the future. Funny thing is, you're the one who's damned. At least we *know* we're damned. I know I'm burning... my daddy made that clear to me... but, I'm curious Padre, what are you trying to buy with your so-called *virtue?* War hero? I got a feelin' you killed more folks, *more kids*, than me. People you didn't even know. So who do you serve? Uncle Sam? Or was that just another dose of God's mercy? War HE-RO! Now that's divine comedy, there. Always got to keep your eye on those 'higher powers,' priest, murderer priest... slave. You and me, Padre, we're both slaves. Rats rotting in a cage. Thing is, I can get out."

Murderer priest reverberated off the walls, windows, bars, and silence. Through the faded green wall I felt the sneer on his face. How had this snake sensed the crack in my soul?

"Was that a confession?" I asked as two gunshots were fired outside the window.

"You familiar with the Chamber of Guf, Padre?"

"Chamber of Guf?" I repeated. Then, recalling my religious studies I asked, "Jewish mysticism?"

"Jewish mysticism," he laughed. "Finally, an educated opponent. Got a cigarette, Padre?"

"No cigarettes. What about this Chamber of Guf?"

"Alright... salvation, then," he decided. "Or some of that redemption you carry in your pocket with your fancy prayer beads. Not that I haven't done enough to earn my way into that glorious seventh heaven."

"We receive salvation through grace, not works. When we perform good deeds, it's out of gratitude to Jesus and to spread His kingdom, not to *earn* our way into heaven."

"Well, that's your take," he said. "That's fine. Absolution, then."

I should have begun the prayer of absolution right then and there. A real priest would have, a rational man would have, but I remained silent, lips clenched, jaw hardened to stone, picturing him offering pink cotton candy to a child, then sweeping that child into his dark hell. I'd seen a country full of stolen and thrown-away children. Sometimes death was better.

"Then justice," he chose. "I want justice."

"There is no justice."

There was a thud as he dropped to the floor. "So... you're a priest who doesn't offer a condemned man redemption and doesn't believe in justice?" He laughed, then his voice grew angry, his breathing heavier. "*You* dare deny *me* absolution?"

"I have nothing for you." I spit out the words with no compassion, hope, or comfort.

"They don't see the art in what I do," he said, his voice now smooth and low, deceitful in its remorseful tone. "I just want someone to see the beauty. *You* would see the beauty."

"Again, what is it you do?"

The metal door crashed open and the guard reappeared. "Father," he said as his many keys clanked against the bars. "It's time to get you outta here." He swung the door open.

As I walked by my dark neighbor's cage, I stopped. He lay hunched in the shadows of the cell; Lucifer, trapped in a hell of his own making. He turned his large, shaved head into the painted green corner. I didn't see his face. He didn't want pardon, forgiveness, or to confess his many crimes. No, he wanted respect, to be appreciated for his *art*. And no, I didn't offer him absolution. Instead, I longed to reach through those bars and beat the life from him with my bare hands. Another place, another time, I would have.

"Who's in a prison, priest?" His guttural voice emerged from the shadows.

"Perhaps," I proffered into his darkness, "perhaps the days of reckoning *are* at hand, for both of us... *Poet*." I turned and followed the guard out. Maybe that guard was right—there was little appetite for salvation behind those towers of doom, the hollow corridors, doors of steel, and windows where no light was allowed to shine through, and where birds lay dead at the entrance.

*   *   *

Outside, the bird's body was gone. All that was left were a few blood-stained feathers. Garbage trucks were at the side gate; the air reeked of the compost from the thousands of lost souls behind those walls. Clouds rolled in from Tillamook Valley, carrying the smell of farmland, cows, fresh-turned soil, a hint of rain, moisture in the breeze. I popped the top on my convertible, got in, took a drink from the bottle of Murphy's, then started the car. That hint of cleansing rain trickled light against my skin. I put on my hat, let that rain fall, and left the flat, grey parking lot to drive through the evergreen hills and wind-shaped trees of the Oregon Coast, out to a sweet world just two hours west: Manzanita, a little piece of heaven the angels saved for those few folks who work and struggle to make a life. Not the reeking souls who don't think twice about what it means to take one.

Chapter 2

THEO

THE ROAD, a ribbon of black along the Pacific Ocean, tunneled, wound, spiraled upward to the top of Neahkahnie Mountain then down the sloping highway to Manzanita. The lilac sky flickered with black birds. It was a quiet fall afternoon as I returned from the prison and down Laneda Avenue, at the end of which the silver-blue sea glimmered under the afternoon sun. I drove past the Bouvre family's summer cottage—sea-haggard white, blue shutters, windows dark, a cold and empty skeleton, as it had been for years. A ghost. I'd heard the father passed away and the cottage was sold. But still, there it sat, lifeless. *Would she return?*

Next door to the Bouvre's, Mrs. B sat on the veranda of her large log cabin painting at her easel, an oil canvas of her rustic lodge with red shutters. Sunflowers towered over her fence and her roses were in full bloom. She wore her straw Chinese conical hat. She waved. I tipped my hat and rolled the remaining two blocks home, watching her watch me in the rear-view mirror. The streets were cluttered with early hunters, fishermen, and the likes—flannel-clad locusts who fueled the economy of the Rounders (those of us who lived here year-round).

Several cars were parked along the quarter-mile stretch of Laneda Avenue, among them my sister Imogene's Plymouth Woody, Mr. Gandel's Ford truck with a bobbing hula dancer on the dashboard, and the Army jeep of the two soldiers who'd been in town on leave the last couple of days. Those two young soldiers who'd met two pretty girls over the weekend and who'd stayed at Bud's family Inn, where Bud's sister-in-law, Pearl, fawned over them during their stay, knowing they were off to an unknown fate. Those soldiers still smiled and fooled around like boys who hadn't yet seen a battlefield—fresh out of training—unscarred and unafraid, still comfortable in their own skin, confident their girls would remain faithful. Now with their duffle bags in the back of the jeep, they drove by, returning to wherever they were stationed and wherever they'd be sent beyond that—and there would be a beyond, a place they couldn't fathom just yet. They tipped their caps as they passed. I saluted. They looked startled but quickly saluted back, then drove on.

Imogene waved from the window of our family store, the Manzanita Market. I waved back with a forced smile, not in the mood for polite conversation, questions, and pointless concerns. I'd been home three months and still she and Mrs. B watched me the way mothers watched a wounded child, fearing another fall. Imogene's neon sign sputtered OPEN on and off, shorting out again.

Solomon sat on the bench in front of the store carving a small piece of wood with his hunting knife. Our old shaman's flannel shirt sleeves were rolled up, revealing his deft hands and muscular arms. I pulled into my driveway across the street.

A three-foot-tall pelican stood on the grass next to the house and watched me park. He waited as two marauding raccoons rambled toward Solomon's hundred-year-old tree hut behind Mamaí's cottage—well, my cottage now. Our family home was a small white house that had seen a thousand storms and only two coats of paint in its forty some years, with a sprawling brick-red porch and a weary white picket fence; every bit of it sported a healthy coat of moss.

The fresh warmth of an Indian summer day filled the De Soto Mamaí left me, yet the car still smelled of her gardenia perfume. I pulled the convertible top up and latched it down.

Imogene's screen door opened. Wearing her work clothes – a gingham dress and Saddle shoes with bobby socks—her big green eyes fixed on me as she prepared to dash across the street and ask her barrage of questions: *How are you? Are you hungry? Does your leg hurt?* I loved my sister, but sometimes she was just too much, too many questions, always a battle. Whoever said, "The hardest fought wars were often encountered on the home front" was right.

Thankfully, Solomon waved her back into the store where she instead watched me from the window. He then glanced my way and nodded. I went inside.

*   *   *

Mamaí's Persian carpet, with its many hues of red, lay beneath the dining table where we had done homework, eaten family meals, and played Yahtzee under candlelight during the storms off our portion of Oregon's Coast. That table, witness to our early lives, good lives—so long ago—was now cluttered with the paperwork of life: sermon notes, Mamaí's obituary (needing to be tucked into the family Bible), her estate papers, and a stack of dirty white U.S. Army envelopes held together by a blood-stained string. All but one marked *Return to Sender.*

Despite the glow of sunset sifting through the window, glistening particles settling on the white tablecloth, the room seemed cold and empty minus its family. I'd recently exchanged two dining room chairs with Da's old leather armchair and ottoman, placing them in front of my glass aquarium so I could drink in peace and watch my three new orange-and-white-striped clown fish interact with the sea anemone, making sure they connected and became family. This dance was as critical to their survival as it was mine. The timid clowns struggled against the current as the water filter surged and foot-tall sea grasses rippled, but they were settling in.

Over the hutch Mamaí had hung my Navy Presidential Citation and the photograph from me at seminary—her tainted ray of hope for our doomed Irish family. It's exhausting to be someone's hope. Exhausting. Those souvenirs of the cracks in my soul had red rosaries looped around the frames. Mamaí placed rosaries on my boxing championship photographs, on awards and medals— none on Kiernan's or Imogene's—and not as blessings, protection, or pleas to God to keep me on a virtuous path, but out of fear. Fear that I may become my worst self again. She always looked at me as though she saw a shadow— something she loved but was afraid of. The blood-stained fists of a ten-year-old Irish lad who defended his own, who to her smelled like smoke until her dying days. I picked up the stack of letters. They also smelled of smoke: napalm, to be exact.

Chapter 3

THEO

FOR FIVE YEARS I carried those letters in my duffle bag, waiting for just one message from Andréa Bouvre to unlock the mystery of her silence. Five years waiting for her to read my words, my apologies, my heart, my heartache—*five years*.

I dropped into the chair, broke the seal on a fresh bottle of Murphy's—the spicy smell of warm whiskey filled my head—and stared at the letters that now just served as another reminder.

Had she written a "Dear John" or "Never write to me again," or even the unimaginable, "I've met someone else," though crushing, it would be something. But she did nothing, and that resounding nothing was too deep a wound for me to remain a rational man.

I'd written and then carried the letters through war, through Korea's T'aebaek Mountains, burned out villages, the nightmares of warfare. I mailed them when I could; some came back to me in Korea, but mostly I figured she was getting them, that she was on that journey with me, she and I, together. But when I finally landed in Germany, there they were, all of them, with an additional letter from Mr. Bouvre telling me Andréa had married. I was totally alone. And though it was too late, I still clung to them, hid them under my pillow in the hospital in Germany, hid them in my room at seminary. Half-disheartened, half-foolish, half-hoping, I carried them. They were part of me, like the bullet lodged in my hip, the scar on my throat, the recurring bruises on my fists—they were my wound.

Mrs. B said read them. Solomon said burn them. I hadn't brought myself to do either. I wanted to bury them in *our* place, Destiny's Perch, high atop Neahkahnie Mountain, but grounded with this bullet in my buggered hip, there was no climbing to such heights.

The string around the letters was dirty and tied in a knot that hadn't been untied in years. I poured a drink and loosened the knot. On the bottom of the stack was the letter from her father.

I felt for the chain around my neck that held my dog tags and a jade ring, the ring I gave her in college, which she gave back to me the last time we breathed the same air. Memories of her, us, that ring, rested against my heart like some stagnant holy land between two worlds—not heaven, not earth, just the chafing dust of memory against my skin. I took it off and laid it on the table next to the full bottle of whiskey and the letters and thought about how angry I had gotten every time another letter found me in Korea. Another rejection, banished from her touch forever. Every returned letter launched me deeper into hell.

The letters, small pages filled with huge expectations, waited to be read, but I was paralyzed in the last time we spoke. All the sweet moments leading up to that disastrous night, that grievous decision; paralyzed by the memory playing in my subconscious, searching for a different response, different words, a different outcome, a different past. To be washed clean, made more deserving of her. But then, I knew better… redemption was a rare thing.

*   *   *

I woke in my leather chair, her jade ring in my hand, the hiss of burning wood out my kitchen window, and the low, guttural sounds of Solomon's morning incantations. The whiskey bottle was empty. As I rose to my feet a gremlin named Murphy pounded my skull with a two-handed mallet. The unopened letters fell to the floor. I left them there and put the chain around my neck, rinsed my whiskey glass, folded Mamaí's obituary, and finally slipped it into the family Bible.

Chapter 4

THEO

IT WAS SUNDAY MORNING. It hurt to put my hat on my head, but I had a sermon to deliver in two hours. It was just my luck that this would be the day planned for a strong lecture about how the overuse of alcohol leads a man astray from the light of the Lord. *And some say God has no sense of humor.*

Walking to Saint Mary's I spotted a white car, a Thunderbird parked in the driveway of the Bouvre cabin, trunk open, full of boxes. Figured they sent the brother to clean things out, but then, a glimpse: blonde hair pulled back, sunglasses, straw hat, indigo jacket, white blouse, a shapely calf-length skirt, sandals, and effortless poise—looking like Grace Kelly in *Rear Window*—even in that disguise and from two blocks' distance, I knew it was her looking at me, a ghost. My ghost. Andréa Bouvre.

She hesitantly raised her hand to wave, then quickly lowered it as if she'd just realized I was a stranger, not who she thought. My heart leapt to my throat. I couldn't move. I'd pictured her, thought of nothing but her, dreamed of her every day for the last six years, and now, there she was, Andréa.

Last time I saw her was in that very same driveway; it was a Friday. She wore her new white trench coat, her hair down around her shoulders, and she was crying, begging me not to go. But then her brother David came out of the house and lambasted me up the side of the face, shouting, "Get away from my sister, you stupid *Mick*!"

I hit back, then him, then it was full on. Don't know why I lost it the way I did, but I did. Andréa's father gripped my clenched fist from behind and yanked me off her bloodied brother. She stood in the rain with a look of horror on her face that's never left me. Her father lifted his son from the ground and helped him to the porch. He turned and said, "Andréa, say goodbye to your hooligan once and for all… let him go."

She slid off our ring, placed it in my hand, kissed me and said, "Go," then went inside.

*   *   *

The Bouvres never forgave me for when Andréa and I turned seventeen and were arrested buck-naked and drunk on the beach. Mr. Bouvre came to the Tillamook jail, bailed her out (ten dollars for lewd behavior), and left me there. Mamaí and Father Gants picked me up the next day. The lectures, rumors, town snickers, and price to be paid for our "sin" was steep. Andréa was sent to Paris that summer, and it was seminary classes instead of boxing camp for me.

Now, there she stood, hand on the car door rim for a moment longer. And there I stood, frozen, unable to believe my eyes—the mirage I'd imagined a thousand times, there in front of me. Andréa, an unrelenting magnet, me, just a piece of damaged metal with no religion big enough to save me.

Tired of waiting, she turned, climbed into her car, and backed out of the drive. I finally raised my hand to wave. Too late. Always too late. I called out, "Andréa!" and started after her but made it only a block before a sharp pain in my hip stopped me. Her tail lights disappeared at the edge of town. She was good at that. No one could vanish like Andréa Bouvre.

Chapter 5

SIX YEARS EARLIER – 1950
THEO

WAVES RAILED against the cliffs of Pirate's Cove. At dusk Andréa and I hiked the moss-covered trail to the top, Destiny's Perch, where overlooking Elk Flats to the right and the ocean to the left, we settled our blanket under a canopy of sloping junipers and unpacked a bottle of wine, meat loaf sandwiches, and lemon cake. It was her birthday.

Andréa unbuttoned her dress and lay back, her long hair feathering across the blanket. We made love and then held one another. Crashing waves and weeping winds whispered through the pines of our secret place. Secret because our parents, who disagreed in politics and religion, did agree on one thing: Andréa and I were to be kept apart. She, according to Mamaí, was no good for me, and I, according to her father, was a "dirty Irish Mick" and no good for her.

From Destiny's Perch we ruled the universe between those hours ripe with promise, hours made sweet by her touch—twilight, what Andréa called the blue hour. She loved it so much that in high school she took to wearing only blue. I admired that about her, how when she loved something she loved it completely. In happier times Andréa read poetry to me or talked for hours about how she longed to return to Paris, paint like the Impressionists, and roam the museums as she did every winter when she visited her grandma. As an art student, she had been asked to give a speech in a few days about the Impressionists at the Portland Art Museum.

"Practice your speech," I said.

She nestled into that soft spot where only she would ever fit and said, "Why?"

"Because I won't be there and I want to hear it." I lay back, waiting.

"Okay… " She cleared her throat and began, "Twilight is a restless time between sunset and dusk." Her fingers traced my jaw line. "It's when the surface of the earth is neither completely lit nor completely dark. Sunlight radiates behind the upper atmosphere, delicately illuminating the lower atmosphere. That ambient light covers half the globe. I don't know why you want to hear this now—"

"Go on," I said.

"*Okay*, well… Some call it a gift from the vaults of heaven, the eternal light of God, dividing day from night, turning the shadow of death into morning. French Impressionists called it the blue hour because of the quality of light scattered toward the earth… " She stopped, then looked into my eyes and said, "I don't care about my speech."

It was our last night before I shipped out for Japan, then Korea. A dark shadow quickly cast over her blue eyes. "Don't go," she pleaded. "Stay with me."

"I have to," I said. "It's my duty. Even if it wasn't, I've been drafted. What else can I do? We've known this for months. Why so upset now?"

"It's not fair," she said.

"I know. And I don't wanna leave you, but listen, when I return it'll be easier for Mamaí to see me as something other than her son, the priest. Easier to accept you, us… it's pretty black and white. Either I go, not that I have any choice, or stay, make her happy by finishing seminary, then break it to her. Either way it's two years."

"Black and white?" she asked.

"Let's face it, I wasn't supposed to be drafted or in love. I was supposed to be a priest."

"Only your mother sees you that way. I don't understand."

"It's a family thing."

"Still, nobody else sees you as a priest. *You* don't even see you as a priest," she went on, caressing my knuckles, still bruised from the boxing match the week before.

"I know. I just need to break it to her slowly," I reminded her. "This is a good way. And you've got another year at OSU… heck, I'll be back before you know."

She stared at the pre-dawn light flickering across the water but said nothing.

I whispered, "What are ya thinking?"

"About my speech," she said with a long exhale. "How the Impressionists tasted the world through their eyes… seldom seeing black and white… they said no true shadow is ever all black. Nature has many colors, many options. The only difficulty is in the choosing."

"I have no choice," I said. "Even without being drafted, you know Mamaí wants me to take Kiernan's place; it's a sacred contract."

"*You and your family* … Anyway, that was years ago."

"Someday you'll teach at a university," I diverted. "I could listen to you forever."

She glared at me.

"Alright. When I return *in uniform*, she'll see me as a soldier. It'll change everything. Then, soon after, we can get married."

"Theo, I love you. Always will, but you're so blinded by your 'duty' you can't see what's right in front of you."

"I know this is hard," I said. "It hurts. But it's what I've gotta do."

She pulled her hair back into a ponytail and folded up the picnic basket.

"Don't be mad," I said. "It's just eighteen months."

"Loved you since I was ten years old," she mused. "I know you. And one thing I know for sure is never ask you to do something you don't wanna do, or try and stop you when you do."

"It's just eighteen months," I said again, smiling, pulling her back to the blanket, "but it will be eighteen *long* months."

"Just know I love you," she said. "No matter what."

"I love you, too. I'll write every day," I promised. "Well, when I can. You'll hardly have a chance to miss me." I loosened the ribbon from her hair and let it fall.

She lay her body down, took me in her arms and said, "I miss you already."

Chapter 6

THEO

MY EARS and splitting skull were acutely attuned to every creak, stomp, and cheer of my parishioner's entrée. The Gandels, mister being the tallest man in the valley, and the missus the stoutest woman in the valley, crashed through the heavy arched doors of Saint Mary's first. Everyone else rushed out of the sudden downpour through the doors, shaking the rainwater off onto the stone floor of the cramped vestibule.

They parked their umbrellas in the holder, hung hats on the wall hooks, and pulled themselves together. They then filed one family per row into the twelve oak pews of the church, dropping to one knee, genuflecting, and moving on like a well-rehearsed, portly chorus line; most nodded to greet me. The six Church Ladies filed into their row. All widowed, most childless, they, too, a family of sorts. Last into their row were the twins, seventy-eight-year-old Sibbie and Ibbie McFall, who just finished teaching our Sunday school. The Church Ladies were dressed in their funeral black from head to toe (there was a funeral over in Wheeler later that day). Funerals were their hobby. They waited for people to die like a kid waits in line for a turn on the Ferris wheel. Two teens entered, holding hands. Young love, so innocent, so naive. The boy was Gandel's eighteen-year-old son. He was gentle with his girlfriend; you could tell they were lovers by the soft glances that sometime, very recently, had shifted from inquisitive hunger to knowing. Both blue-eyed blondes, who soon would make blue-eyed blonde babies, sat in the back pew in a dreamlike state, intoxicated by one another. The Gandels had always been as lucky in love and plump, blue-eyed babies as they were in farming. One had to wonder where all that luck came from and why God would allot so much to one family and so little to so many others.

Wavering for a moment, I braced myself against the pulpit, still nauseous, still shaky, with an excruciating headache. I glanced at the door wondering if Andréa would show up again, or if I'd actually seen her, or if it was a wicked, wicked mirage.

Permelia Hinkle, still shapely and fit at age seventy-nine, sat poised on the organ bench to the right of the pulpit. She wore her blue dress with a white corsage. Freckles the size of raisins covered her skin; her crinkled eyes, the shade of a copper penny, smiled with kindness. Forever understanding and forgiving of my headaches, Permelia knew the fires of hell were engulfing me as I clung to that righteous pulpit. She whispered, "Shall I begin?"

I nodded. She leaned forward with all her petite might and pressed her tiny foot on the pedal to play an austere chant from her list of five liturgical songs. Organ pipes moaned to life; nails on a chalkboard inside my head. Then to pour on the hurt, Effie Grimm began to sing.

In the crowd of thirty or so, Toreck Sealy's wife and son were seated in the back. She had another black eye that, against her alabaster skin, beckoned like Imogene's neon sign in the fog. Her withdrawn seven-year-old, Andy, clung to her arm. He stared straight at me. The fear in his bloodshot eyes woke me from my hangover.

"Good morning, everyone," I said. Andy's eyes suddenly cast down. He leaned into his mother, his head just above her hip. "Blessed are the meek, for they shall inherit the kingdom of heaven. But at what price?" Mrs. Sealy stared straight up at the light pouring through the stained-glass window of Jesus with his lambs. Then her sad eyes settled on me as if I were hope itself, not a hungover priest clinging to a pulpit. "What do you think?" I continued, "If a man owns a hundred sheep, and one of them wanders away, will he not leave the ninety-nine on the hill and go to look for the one that wandered off? Of course he will."

*　*　*

After the sermon, and after shaking everyone's hands (hiding the shaking in mine), I turned to find that Mrs. Sealy and Andy had slipped away.

A spurt of sunlight filtered through the wet trees and spiderwebbed across the side of the church where Solomon sat in the courtyard. In the center of the pond was a statue of Saint Francis holding a basin for birds. Water trickled softly from the basin. Solomon handed me a bottle of seaweed-green liquid and said, "Drink. Feel better."

He gazed down Laneda Avenue watching the reclusive old woman who lived on Neahkahnie Mountain enter Imogene's store. Her long-absent daughter and a small child waited in her rust-covered pickup truck. I looked the other way, wondering if Andréa was coming back. But she wasn't. She was never coming back. I knew that. I always knew that.

"The boy's arms are black and blue," Solomon said. "His mother's eyes, bruised." He turned his gaze back to me, his hazel eyes as sharp as the dagger on his belt. Then he stood to leave and said, "Someone should do something." He walked away.

*   *   *

The following Sunday, Mrs. Sealy and Andy weren't in church. Andy's teacher said he wasn't in school all week. I asked Bud if we could take a run out to the Sealy place to check things out—thought showing up in the sheriff's car would be an effective deterrent.

"What a man does in his own home isn't the law's business," Bud declared. "Not the dealings of a priest, neither. 'Less that man confesses or asks for help."

"Asks for help? Confesses?" I said. "You're far more optimistic than me."

"I know, Theo. But my hands are tied. I have to deal with the justice system as it is."

"In my experience there's often a cosmic gap between justice and what's just. But with a little jostle, push, and shove, justice can become a simple, understandable thing."

"You scare me sometimes, Theo. You really do." He lit his cigar. "If we don't hear anything by Friday, I'll check it out."

"Friday is a long way off," I said. "Besides, Fridays are bad luck."

Chapter 7

IMOGENE RILEY

DAILY SPECIAL
Fried Egg & Cheddar Cheese Sandwiches .50¢

It was Monday morning, almost nine—always a quiet time in my store. I lit the candles on the black shelf behind the cash register. The three red glass holders glowed to life in front of the framed photos of Da in his tweed suit, our brother Kiernan in Dublin, Mamaí in her favorite dress and hat, and of course, my Christina, though I hadn't lit her candle yet. Not ever.

The door's bell scarcely jangled as Toreck's wife came in with little Andy in tow.

"Mornin'," I said, noticing she'd cut off her hair and left blunt edges at the back of her head as if she'd grabbed her ponytail and hacked it off with a knife. Poor thing. Given she was married to the likes of Toreck, she probably had.

"Mornin'," she responded, not looking me in the eye. She reached her hand out for Andy whose shadow trailed his rail-thin mother's. Her fingernails were bit to the nubs, red and swollen. As they disappeared around aisle two I saw she wore mismatched shoes and no stockings even though it was cold and rainy outside, and Andy wasn't wearing a coat; his bony body was soaked to the skin. My heart sank.

They returned to the register and set a carton of eggs, a jar of peanut butter, and a loaf of bread on the counter. "Good choices," I remarked. Andy's eyes were glued on the peanut butter jar as if it were a huge chocolate cake. "I like peanut butter, too," I whispered.

Mrs. Sealy, who wasn't from here, was younger than me by at least five years, maybe was twenty-three. I didn't know her first name. She took a dollar bill from her coat pocket, carefully uncrumpled it, and gently laid it out flat on the counter. She stared at that crumpled dollar bill like it was the last one she had or would ever have. My heart sank again.

"Well, lucky you!" I said. "Peanut butter, bread, and eggs are free before nine o'clock. But don't go tellin' everyone in town, or I'll go broke." I smiled, shoved the groceries into a paper bag, and slid the dollar bill back across the counter to her.

"No," she whispered, eyes cast down to that dollar bill. "We can't—"

"Yes, you can," I said just as the clock began to chime. "But ya better take it now, cause it's gonna be after nine in about thirty seconds."

I quickly handed Andy the bag. He smiled big, wrapped his arms around it, headed for the door, and called, "Come on, Mom!" She folded that crumpled dollar bill back into her coat pocket, finally looked up at me, her eyes a pool of watery red, and forced a smile. They left.

A huge bubble of air let out of my lungs; those were the saddest eyes I'd seen in a long time. Clearly having her husband, *asshole that he was*, locked up last month for gold digging had dropped the financial weight of the world on her already wispy body. And now that he was out again, well, I just didn't know which was worse… *Yes, I did.*

I flipped the BACK IN 5 sign on the door and rushed across the street to ask my brother if there was something in his all-knowing Bible, or if he had a plan for ridding our town of a wife-beating bully. A real plan—one that included the welfare of a woman who'd probably never worked a day in her life and a little boy who loved peanut butter.

Chapter 8

THEO

THERE WERE NO traffic lights in Manzanita; people just knew when to go and when to stop. Most people had a sense of right and wrong. When they didn't, someone needed to do something. I pressed the gas pedal harder and forged ahead.

* * *

Just before I left for Korea in '50, Toreck Sealy was arrested twice for beating his wife when she was pregnant. Both times he was let out the next morning, only to beat her again for calling the police. Doc Maynard had asked me via Mamaí to stop by and have a talk with him before I left. I did. It didn't go well. We'd had the same "talk" when he was in high school and once went after Imogene. So, eight bruised knuckles later, him licking his wounds and thinking twice about hitting his wife, I left for Korea naïve enough to think a man like him could change.

* * *

The ten-minute drive from Manzanita to Toreck's ramshackle house in Nehalem, Oregon was filled with indecision. But, after the visit from my sister Imogene who described more bruises and the disheveled look of the Sealys, I decided not to wait for Bud, for the law, or as late as next Friday. *Someone* had to do something. This would be the third time I "talked" with him about his abusive ways, and this third time would be the charm.

Common sense tried to seep into my thoughts, but when I considered turning around and abandoning my plan I saw the bruised arms of his son Andy, who needed someone to fight for him, and pushed the pedal to the floor.

When I left, a hot autumn sun had broken through the clouds. The beach would be busy today. Bud's patrol car was at the end of Laneda next to the shore; he was walking his beat and would be for some time. I'd need him later in case, well, *when* things got out of control, which I planned on. I stopped at the junction to use the only pay phone for miles.

"Netty?" I cleared my throat. "Bud there yet?"

"No, Father Theo, he—"

"Do me a favor, tell him to stop by Sealy's place in an hour, four o'clock. Will ya?"

Ozzie's deep-throttled voice was in the background.

"Ozzie wants to talk—"

"No, no. I don't need to talk to him… just tell Bud—"

"Father Theo?" Ozzie's cavernous voice came on the line, "Is sumthin' wrong?"

"No, no. I—I'll stop in later for pie just like always." I hung up before he could respond.

Was one hour enough time, or too much?

The rusty metal and glass door had to be jiggled a couple of times to open; I stepped out to the gravel roadside. The surrounding maple trees had a striking hint of scarlet as the leaves prepared for their fall from grace, spiraling in the wind, and then, with a gust, landing in the back seat of my convertible.

I climbed back into the car and noticed the headline on the daily paper in the rack next to the booth. It read, 7-YEAR-OLD SUZY WU, MISSING – 3 DAYS. I'd just seen her last week at a church birthday party. *Surely she'll turn up.*

That grainy snapshot of her—ink-black hair, dark, almond-shaped eyes—brought it all back: three hundred, sixty-seven days of straight-on battle, seventy-six days in a hell-hole POW camp, the children, crack of gunfire, one… two… three… bodies sagging, falling, dropping, crying out, "Teo!"

I squeezed my eyes shut, reached under the seat for my bottle of Irish courage, and took a burning swig. Then I lifted my shirt, tightened the bandages Solomon wrapped around my ribcage. I tucked my dog tags and the ring under my collar, kissed Kiernan's tin soldier, took another drink, muttered, "Here's to ya, brother," and slipped the soldier back into my pocket.

* * *

It was a sultry fall afternoon. After the heavy rains the air smelled of ripe blackberries. I slowed at the driveway of a house so dog-eared it drooped from exhaustion—the Sealey's. Toreck's work truck was full of his gold-digging equipment (he was frequently arrested for honeycombing Neahkahnie Mountain in search of the long-rumored pirates treasures); otherwise, tires and dilapidated cars littered the front of the parched half-acre yard. In a fertile valley of hills and trees, their land was a flat, dry, blackened landscape leftover from the Tillamook Burn. I crept up the pot-holed driveway and parked the car. My footsteps crunching on gravel were the only sounds. The rancid tar smell of burning engine oil hung heavy in the air.

A deafening screech roared from the barn where Sealy tinkered on cars. His wife stepped out to the porch, drying her hands on her apron. Her head was wrapped in a bandana, brow furrowed. She wasn't happy to see me. I tipped my hat, pointed to the barn, and walked past her, happy not to see Andy around. He was probably down at the river like any country boy; hoped he'd stay there awhile. Mrs. Sealy nodded, hung her head, and nervously ran her hand along the door jam. Did she want to say something? I paused. She slowly made the sign of the cross and then retreated inside the house, the door screeching, then slamming behind her. The sad, doe-eyed girl wore yet another fresh black eye.

My stomach growled with apprehension. Toreck's engine sputtered, stopped, and rendered the place eerily silent. I grabbed the barn's wooden door handle, stood there for a moment, made the sign of the cross, and yanked on the handle.

"Son-of-a-bitch!" he shouted. The door creaked. The barn reeked of smoky petrol and sweat. Toreck was hunched over a truck about twenty feet away. He was a scrawny gnat with a pack of Camels rolled into his t-shirt sleeve. Both sleeves were knotted up over his Sailor Jerry tattoos of naked women and pirate ships. His head jerked up from where he worked. His narrow, lusterless eyes fixed on me the way a cat zeroes in on a wounded bird.

"Fuck off, Priest! I'm tired of you people calling, stopping by." He banged on the hood of his truck with both fists. "Get off my property." The wall clock behind him read three thirty-five.

I held my hands up in protest, intent first on talking sense to him. "Now listen, son—"

"Ain't *my* father," he said, with tobacco planted in his cheek. He had a face like a bulldog chewing on a wasp. "You ain't nobody's father." He sauntered around me, sizing me up. A thick vein pulsed up the side of his shaved head. "Nobody here needs your fuckin' help, *gimp*."

"Like it or not, *son* …, " I said, "we're talkin'." I was in a boxing ring again, my wiry opponent circling me. "Now, we both know that only a weak man beats a child or a woman."

Toreck twitched in a menacing prowl. He spit the tobacco at my feet. I stood still. When he was behind me, I didn't turn. "Let me help you," I said, listening to his thick-soled black boots thud about in the sawdust. He boomeranged to the front of me and glared into my eyes.

I continued in a calm, steady voice. "I'll take Andy and put him in a good home—"

"Good home?" he cackled. "Good home!" He flailed his tattooed arms. "What the hell do you think this is? I work my ass off fer that boy and that witch woman. They don't know how lucky they got it." His pock-marked face burned red. He jabbed me in the shoulder with the force of a slingshot rock. "Gimp." He poked again, *harder*. "How's that pretty sister o' yours?"

My temptation boiled at the thought of smashing him like the parasite he was, but my hands remained tight-fisted at my sides. I'd fought better men and won. And I'd win this time. I let him work up a fiery rage, adding words that infuriated his blaze like gasoline. "You should come to church Sunday," I said.

He flicked my fedora. It fluttered to the dirt. He stomped on it and seethed, "Go to hell."

"Pray for forgiveness," I suggested. Another ounce of fuel. It was three forty-five. Given his temper and our many squabbles as of late, this shouldn't take long; *short man, short fuse.*

Within moments, Toreck's face heated to vein purple. His fist exploded against my chin.

"You son of a bitch!" He struck me again. My jaw throbbed, but I resisted my southpaw urge to strike. "Put 'em up, Priest!" He pranced from foot to foot like a clumsy first-time boxer, fists improperly positioned, ready to deliver blows.

I stood steady. Feet at two o'clock, core muscles tensed, ribs wrapped. Bud would be there at four—I needed to string things out until he arrived. "Sunday is Communion, and then—"

"*Commune* with this, cripple!" Toreck said as he swung again. This time his fist rammed into my bandaged ribs. "Come on *gimp*, let's see what ya got!"

He struck again, then again. This time harder. *Bloody hell!* Ribs wrapped or not, it hurt. He kicked me where I carried the bullet, ramming his thick boot into my hip.

"Not so tough now, *boxing champ!*"

A jolt of pain blazed from hip to toe, nearly dropping me to the ground, but thankfully his fist slamming against my face stopped me from falling. Toreck lost the patience to egg me on and loosened his full rage as he'd surely done a hundred times to his war-weary family.

His ring slashed my brow. Blood thick as maple syrup dribbled into my eyes. A buzzing bee was trapped inside my skull. I crumpled to the dirt floor.

A shrill scream jolted me to my senses. In the corner of the barn stood Toreck's wife, hands over her mouth, eyes filled with terror. He darted toward her. I lunged at his ankles.

He plummeted to the ground, fists flying, feet kicking. Then, in the middle of our fracas, I saw Andy clinging to his mother's grey dress. She shouted, *"Please stop!"*

I pushed Toreck away and scrambled to my feet to face them. "I'm sorr—"

"Daddy, no!" Andy shouted.

I turned in time to catch his bony knuckles to my face again. I touched my aching nose and looked at my blood-coated hands. My face throbbed. It was only three fifty. *Damn!* My knees buckled. I slumped to the ground, and the contents of my pockets (coins, rosary, and Kiernan's soldier) spilled out on the ground. My face hit the dirt, and I lay there in a fetal position, holding my head and staring at that tin soldier. The bee buzzed louder. The sound of car doors outside the barn gave me hope. Then, shouting—more hope. Toreck stammered to his feet, grabbed a two-by-four with rusty nails, and raised it over my head. Gasping for air, I lifted my arm to block the blow.

The click of a .38 revolver's hammer being cocked garnered Toreck's attention. Through the blood I caught the shine of Bud's silver badge.

Toreck, mid-swing, halted all motion.

Strappy six-foot-four Bud towered over him, and in a calm and possibly gleeful tone, whispered, "Move a freckle on your maggot-filled body and I'll happily execute my authority."

Toreck, lip quivering, lowered his weapon.

My head sagged to the dirt floor again. The board dropped from Toreck's hands to the ground in front of my face. That nail was a good four *rusty* inches long.

"Ten minutes early," I sighed, and let out a deep, painful breath. *"Thank God!"*

"You can thank God... but I'd thank Oz," Bud said, nodding to Oz and Solomon, who ran in behind him. Solomon's jagged knife was poised—an ever-ready extension of his arm.

Bud, always a quarterback and now sheriff, was five years older than me and always five steps ahead. He'd arrived in the nick of time. One minute later and I'd have a nail in my head.

Andy and his mother cowered in the corner, avoiding eye contact with Toreck as he spewed his venomous words. "You bitch!" He thrashed about as Bud tried to get him handcuffed, then he glared at Andy and shouted, "You stupid little fuck!"

Bud shoved him to his knees and warned, "Shut up!"

"You dumb-shit kid!" Toreck hollered. "It's your fault!"

Solomon rushed over and braced himself in front of Andy and his mother, blade ready. Bud wrestled Toreck back up to his feet.

I'd never have picked that fight knowing Andy was home. It's not right he should see his father, even when that father was Toreck Sealy, handcuffed and hauled away. He's too young to understand that this was a good day in his life. A very good day.

Oz, Oswald Jefferson, a coal-black mountain of a man I'd known all my life, lifted me as if I were an eighty-pound child.

"I can stand," I said, gently pushing him away. "I'm alright." I brushed off the dirt. "I'm fine." I stood, my head spun, and I dropped back to my knees.

Oz took a white hanky from the pocket of his overalls. "Here," he said, "you's done bleedin' on that there white collar, Father." His face, though usually expressionless, softened. A stiff denim collar separated his broad head from his expansive shoulders. He winked. His murky brown eyes had a saffron glow. He towered over me, shaking his head, and said, "Guess you'll be needin' two pieces o' Netty's pie, and some ice for that leg. She be mighty upset seein's how her Bible-lovin' priest got hisself all beat up for some crazy-ass reason or 'nuther. *Um-hmm.* Yes, sir. Mighty upset. Callin' your sister in no time. *Um-hmm.*"

"I'm fine," I said again, finding my footing.

Across the barn Solomon stood strong, eyes locked on mine. A faint conspiratorial smile curled up the side of his craggy face. Had it been up to him, he would have cut Toreck's heart out and left his carcass for the wolves by now. Though not a bad idea, the consequences would have been undesirable. Had to admit his look of endorsement felt good. It had been a long time.

"Fuckin' bastard kid!" Toreck shouted from face down in the dirt, Bud's foot in his back.

Bud grabbed him by the arm and yanked him to his feet. "Theo?" he said.

"Yeah, I'm fine," I answered, holding the blood-soaked hanky against my nose.

"I know you're fine," Bud said. "Dammit man, why did you—?"

"You fuckin' whore!" Toreck screamed at his wife. "You did this!"

Bud shoved him into the barn door.

"Never mind," Bud answered himself. "The *why* is pretty evident." He looked at me, cautioning, "Just don't—"

"Nope," I said, crossing my heart. "Won't do it ever again."

"Prick!" Toreck shouted.

"Theo," Bud said. "Pressin' charges?" He kicked the door open and shoved Toreck out.

"Yep." Bees buzzed in my skull. "Let's press those charges."

"Hell no!" Toreck shouted. "It's my property. *I'm* pressin' charges!"

Bud thrust him into the back seat of the police car, *accidentally* banging his head on the rim of the door, and said, "For what, you pissant? Far as I can see you beat up a priest." He slammed the car door in Toreck's face, hitting his head again.

Oz picked up the board, eyed the rusty nail and said, "Coulda' been hurt bad, *dead* kinda bad. That *sqeez* of a prick woulda' —"

"I know," I interrupted. "I know." Life had taught me there were worse things than dying. I figured I'd already died once, in a manner of speaking. I could die again. "But I wasn't hurt ... well, bad, anyway."

Oz leaned down and picked up my pocket change, rosary, and tin soldier.

I stuffed them all back in my pants pocket and asked, "Ride to Portland? Tillamook?"

He handed me my hat. "I assume you don't want no hospitals?"

"I've got nothin' that won't heal on its own."

"Jus' them newspaper offices, then?"

"You think you know me that well, do you?"

"Uh-huh," Oz said. "And I think for Toreck, beatin' his family bears little cost. But by the time them newspapers get wind 'bout a drunken wife beater who just bloodied the local priest, them judges ain't got a choice but send him away for a long time."

"You think?" I brightened.

"Uh-huh, and I think you done *thunk* that out all ready."

"Maybe," I said. "And maybe sometimes justice needs a little help."

"Uh-huh."

Chapter 9

SOLOMON

SHADOWS SLIPPED IN and out of hemlock trees. Soft moss and pine needles shielded my bare feet from jagged rocks. I climbed Neahkahnie Mountain each day before sunrise, when Moon fades and Sun appears. There I see spirits of both worlds—between light and darkness—and hear voices of Ancient Ones hover over great waters of Pacific, calling to me, *"Ts-ull-ULL-leel, Solomon. Ts- ull-ULL-leel."*

Once I moved like cougar up rocky paths. Now, great Ocean blows her wind at my aging back, pushing me forward to my destiny. The ground trembles. The mountain wakes. Every movement, smell, sound of its ancient forest, like my skin, burns with fever. My spirit guide, the great Wolf, has long been silent. Now, since Theo's return, he stands at edge of our path. He knows the dark spirit also returns; trees rustle when there is no wind, birds fall silent. "The hunt is on," Wolf tells me. "We must be warriors one last time."

At the crest I stretched my aging arms to the heavens and called upon Wind. "Great Grandfather... Our time as a people, the great Nehalems, has ended. My bones are weary. The young Rounder, Theo, was once child warrior whose dark spirit I brought You many years ago. Here on this blessed ground we altered what his mother feared was his fate. He now wears white collar, calls himself "Priest." He has war nested in his soul, a heavy broken heart blinds him from his path, deafens him to his Raven spirit. Owl shows me Theo has two final journeys. One for broken heart, the other, a true blood battle. We must remove old battle from deep under his skin, make room for new battle that comes. You see all, Grandfather. I ask You to see him again. I ask You, when blood settles, help him find his way. Breathe Your spirit into his sleeping soul. Guide me with Your wisdom. Thank You, Great Grandfather. Thank You."

Chapter 10

THEO

MORNING STREAKED THROUGH my bedroom window. It took a minute before I realized I hurt like hell from head to toe. When my feet hit the cold wood floor a jolt of pain burned in my hip. I limped to the bathroom and looked in the mirror—yep, another broken nose. I popped it back into place, screaming words a priest shouldn't scream, then washed the blood from my face, looked into the mirror, and smiled, which also hurt.

In my closet hung my black robes, black shirts, black slacks. My aching body sank; I just couldn't wear that costume today. I stared at my olive green duffle bag standing in the corner. RAKKASSAN – RILEY was in black block letters along the side, with 187th AIRBORNE INFANTRY in smaller block letters below that; the rope tie was still cinched closed at the top. I hadn't opened it since 1954, two years. It bulged with my coat and boots like a withered body packed tight inside. I thought about where all I'd walked, run, climbed, and swum in those boots, always moving forward with intent. And that coat that kept me warm, protected me from the elements, carried ammo, identified me as a U.S. soldier in the air and on the ground. Knew who I was and what I was doing at all times. I untied the bag, pulled out my navy-blue sweatshirt with RAKKASSAN in white letters, re-tied the bag, and closed the door.

I made two ice packs—one for my nose, the other for my hip—and grabbed the papers off the porch step, plopping them on the dining room table. Mamaí's dining room was a serious room. A room of proper china displayed in a hutch and an oil painting of the way the beach should look: sun glistening off the sea, kites flying, kiddies playing. Not the grey sky, lone footprints along a deserted Oregon shore reality, but her sunny vision of it. In a bout of activity I took that sunny painting down, packed up her china, and restocked the hutch shelves with books—tiny rebellions against a departed women who continued her reign.

Now in the dining room with fresh ice packs, feet propped on my footstool, I opened the morning paper, the special edition *Tillamook Tribune,* to a large picture of me: black eye, fat lip, torn clothes, and a bloody white collar. *Perfect!* It's a good day when you can act with purpose and actually achieve something worth achieving. Right a wrong. Real good day.

The radiator in the corner sizzled and sputtered to life. The room filled with a wisp of steam that settled on my arms and face. I fed my saltwater aquarium. The thing was the size of a huge beer cooler and held forty gallons of water, seven tropical fish of all shapes and sizes of azure blue and bright yellows, oranges, and reds, wafting grasses and sea life, a sea anemone the color and size of my fist, and tiny, coy seahorses that only came out at night—they, I understood. The aquarium filter released a rush of bubbles just as the phone rang. I knew it was Bishop Doyle, so I didn't answer. But it rang again.

"Father Riley?"

"Yes, your Eminence," I said, steadying the telephone against my shoulder. "I'm here."

While he talked I added a touch of red model paint to Kiernan's tin solder's arm band, set it by the window to dry, then unfolded the morning papers. Both the *Oregonian* and the *Tribune* had the same headline: NEHALEM MECHANIC TORECK SEALY LOCKED UP FOR 5 YEARS. I should have felt shame or remorse. I smiled. Lip split again—it was worth it.

"The telephone here at Saint Patrick's has rung off the hook all morning," he said.

"Sorry, sir."

I moved my golf clubs, which had been collecting dust in the corner, and dropped into my chair. The radiator moaned as he said, "Funny, a repentant tone seems absent in your voice."

"Sorry about that too, sir."

"Who is Toreck Sealy, anyway?"

"No one who matters now, sir."

"This isn't Ireland, Theo. America is a litigious country and growing more so by the day. You're not in a boxing ring, and you're certainly not an Irish street thug."

"It won't happen again. And sir, I was ten when we left Ireland—hardly a thug," I said glancing up at Mamaí's rosary around my high school picture.

"What won't happen again? I understood *you* to be the victim here. Is that correct?"

"No, I—"

"*You are* the victim here, understand? I'll have the newspapers do a story about a war hero who refused violence. That'll make things clear."

"Sir, I'm no hero, I just survived for some incomprehensible reason. That's all. I'd like to stop bandying that term around. It makes me—"

"Semantics," he stopped me. "I work hard to keep any stories about the church above reproach. This isn't going to be easy to overlook, but… perhaps we can use it to our advantage."

"Advantage?"

"You're needed here this week… I'll arrange a dinner honoring your courage."

"Not up to travel just yet," I said. "Maybe next week." A promise I didn't intend to keep.

"I see," Bishop Doyle replied. "We pay a price for our ethics, Theo, especially when those ethics are not in alignment with the values of the church. Do you understand this?"

"I'm painfully aware that when we make the wrong choice for the right reason, or the right choice for all the wrong reasons, there will be a toll exacted. Painfully aware, sir."

"On to other business then," he said.

I retrieved the aspirin from the kitchen and downed four with another shot of Murphy's. Blood trickled from my nose to my white t-shirt. The red stain spread like blackberry juice.

Finally he spoke. "Your sweet mother, Fiona, was a dear friend of Saint Patrick's."

"Yes, one of your greatest admirers," I lied.

"Indeed… but, she had provocative ideas about that Indian and Mrs. Beaumont."

"They're family."

"I'm well aware of your mother's friend Constance Beaumont," he said. "Your 'Mrs. B'. I helped her deliver letters to the governor of Oregon while you were confined in Korea."

Confined? I said beneath my breath. That's one way to put it.

"She demanded your return, as if the governor himself was your jailer."

"Yes sir, I appreciate it," I said, staring into the aquarium, where something was wrong.

"However, the church is your family now," he coaxed. "I thought you were happy here."

"I was… *then,*" I said, opening the freezer. I broke ice free from the metal tray, wrapped it in a towel, settled back into my chair, and pressed it against my swollen, throbbing nose.

"Well, Fiona is missed," he said. "However, it's come to the attention of the church that her good nature fell under the sway of heretical influences in her dealings with those people."

"Heretical, sir?" His disappointment that Mamaí left nothing to the church was palpable.

"Yes, Father Riley, heretical. Non-canonical, outside scripture, morality, holy divinity… I'm sure you recall these concepts as part of your devotion."

"Vaguely," I said. "What are these influences and why do they concern the church?"

"Is it true that that Indian lives in your backyard?" he asked. "In a tree?"

"Well, that's the short story, but yes. This house sits on his family property. After Mamaí found out, she deeded that back portion back to him. It was the right thing to do."

"It's too late to argue *that* point. The problem is that we can't have a Catholic priest living so closely with an Indian in this modern era."

"That doesn't sound very modern, sir. Is this the church's opinion or yours?"

"They are one in the same, Father Riley, and that Indian *shaman* creature belongs on the reservation. And that woman, all the rumors and stories … well, she's another case in hand."

"Mrs. B's a harmless old woman," I offered, though rumors about her were often true.

"Harmless?" he challenged. "Wasn't she a rumrunner during prohibition?"

Mrs. B, now in her eighties, was a stout woman with rounded shoulders and a bulging belly. But in her day she was a "real looker," my Da said. Her skin was so white it was almost luminous. Her aqua eyes sparkled like gems beneath her wrinkled lids. Da also said she was not to be buggered with; she *was* a rumrunner and had *barmy* friends who were true pirates.

I bent closer to the aquarium glass, peered inside, and said, "Mrs. B doesn't actually like rum. Besides, she was our school teacher and Solomon's just an old man."

"Right… an old medicine man," he said. "Well, I understand the funeral, mourning, and the need to take care of things. But it's been three months."

"Who else would run Saint Mary's with Father Mark retired?" I half-asked. Then, there it was… something in the rocks moved. *Damn!* A bloody hermit crab.

"There's always someone waiting in the wings," he replied.

I lifted the aquarium lid and dropped in some food. One of my new clown fish was dead, and I took its tiny body out with the spoon-net, set it aside, and quickly looked for what killed it.

"It's time you return to Saint Patrick's," came the dreaded request.

"I can't leave." I closed the cover. "There's fifty parishioners, a Saturday class of ten teens, regularly attended Mass, and five women in the valley who are due any day now—"

"You're not a doctor, Theo," he said. "Those people can go to Tillamook."

"That's a forty-minute drive! Most don't have cars—"

"They'll figure things out."

"This is a mistake—"

"Are you questioning a decision of the church?"

I paced back and forth in front of the aquarium. "And the children here?"

"They'll find their way."

"With no guidance or help from the church?"

"It's for the greater good."

"Whose greater good?"

"Enough! You don't understand the economic realities, Father Riley. Suffice to say we need you here in Portland. Beginning next week. Is that clear?"

My body hardened to stone. "Perfectly, sir."

As an Irish-born Catholic priest with "war hero" status, I was a golden-egg-laying goose; a carrot to dangle at Portland fundraisers. And Saint Mary's was just costing them money. I understood alright. God, I hated being used that way.

"Let's face it, Father Riley, you have many, *many* skills. Running a small town parish isn't the best use of them. Oh, and I received your paperwork to terminate your prison ministry; it's denied. God be with you." He hung up.

I slammed down the phone and kicked my golf bag. Golf balls dribbled across the floor.

*   *   *

Bishop Doyle was never more wrong than when he talked about Solomon. I'd long since given up the argument and reconciled that his disdain for Solomon was partly because he was threatened by a man people considered divine in a way he himself could never conceive. Doyle could talk for hours in sophisticated circles, using thousands of lofty words and never arriving at a single truth. Solomon found truth every day using no words at all, his beliefs beginning where Doyle's ended. He perceived the world beyond the senses that filtered it for the rest of us. For this offense Doyle saw him as an intolerable iniquity, a blight on society needing to be scraped from the earth like dirt and muck from a tire.

However, he was right about one thing: I had been content at Saint Patrick's, where my tight schedule and cloistered surroundings kept everything inside of me in check, at bay. Here in Manzanita at Saint Mary's, I was reminded that being a soldier, *though Mamaí proudly displayed the medals*, was beneath me, boxing was beneath me, Andréa not good enough. Mamaí hated anything that interfered with her sunny vision of a son who was a priest. In Portland I felt I'd failed at everything else, so may as well don the robes of Saint Patrick's, keep busy, and keep my promise. Be good for something. But here... here was different.

Upon my return to Manzanita a few months ago to attend Mamaí's estate, it was as if I woke from a long, dark dream, felt my pulse again, breathed fresh ocean air again, and wanted to live for the first time in years. I was home. I could never return to Saint Patrick's.

Chapter 11

GENGHIS

USED TO THINK that in prison I'd at least be in good company: broken heroes, twisted knights, and righteous kings of the damned—the keepers of dark underworlds, that sort. But no!

In prison it's mostly just a bunch of fools who did foolish things, guarded by other fools with guns who ultimately will do foolish things. Can't suffer fools. There's no excuse for 'em.

Just want out—out of this plaster hand cast, out of this cell, this prison, this puke green hell hole where one glance, one wrong word, one secretive tug can release an alchemy of hell on earth. Alchemy. That's a good word; something *his* God would say. Still, hell on earth because, like I said, they're all fools, and a foolish man doesn't know to just shut the hell up and do his time, or bide time until he can get out, unnoticed, real quiet-like.

Rain pelted against the tin shingles outside the unreachable window near the ceiling. That pinging sound and the absolute boredom got on my last nerve— needed a distraction. I squeezed my face between the corner bars to see the guard and shouted, "Rain, rain, rain! Frickin' rain."

"Shut up, Hansel." The fat guard with the moral fortitude of a hedgehog shouted back from the end of the corridor. He sat feet propped up on the desk, clipping his fingernails. Another sound I couldn't abide. He kept watch over me and the six *empty* cells in lockdown.

"Let my teachin' fall like rain," I called back. "Like my snake-wielding evangelical Baptist preacher father always said, man needs preachin' whether he wants it or not."

"That's enough, Hansel."

"Like showers on new grass. Like abundant rain on tender plants."

"Shut the hell up!"

"Well, that's a bit harsh," I said backing away from the bars, away from his view. I raised my voice, "Don't you know God's law? Give and you shall receive; smile and others will smile back. It's the law of reciprocity." I sat down on my soft-as-cardboard cot.

"I mean it. Shut up, Hansel, nobody here cares about your preachin'."

"Tisk, tisk, officer, I don't sense you're smilin'. Nope, not smilin' at all. Haven't got the Good News, have you. Well, just remember: Give kindly, and you'll receive in like measure."

"Hansel!" he shouted, then slapped his billy club on the desk.

"It's that *like measure* part you gotta watch out for, sentry. But other than your downright shitty attitude, it's a remarkable spiritual principle, don't ya think?"

"Shut the fuck up, Hansel," he said again. "Or I'll break that other hand."

I looked down at the cast on my hand. Who breaks a man's hand just to take off a ring! These penitentiary grunts thought someone might bust me up to take my beautiful ring with the snake coiled around a precious ruby. It's just plain rude to take a man's ring from his crippled hand. Fools. Can't stand fools. But, this is a place where foolish men end up. Well, and sometimes smart men who made one slight mistake.

Shoulda never tried to visit my little friend in that state hospital, Damashe; what a name for a container for the mentally disturbed. Do the government idiots who named it not realize it rhymes with damaged? What idiots. But it's funny, and they're still idiots, and she wasn't worth a broken finger and all this monotony.

"Give me my charcoal so I can draw," I requested.

"Pray for some!" The guard retorted.

"Ok," I said. "Let me go to confession… I have things to confess."

"No priest today, Hansel."

"Well, that just don't seem right," I said. "Shouldn't there be a priest in the house of sinners, on hand and at the ready, every day?"

"I'm tellin' ya, Hansel, shut up!"

"What about our war hero friend?" I asked. "Now there's a man who knows the heart of a sinner." I pictured that war hero priest who denied me absolution and whose judgment seeped through the cement wall into my cell, crawling along the pee-stained floor, right up to me, rearing up, a judgment snake, coiled and ready to jab-jab-jab at my skin, bite, hiss, and extract that which it was sent to kill, from my body. That war hero dick sent that judgment snake after me just like my daddy did when I was a boy. When I poisoned his favorite pet, the one that crippled my hand, he told me in no uncertain words there ain't no redemption for one like me. No prayers, not enough deeds to be done to get my rotten soul into heaven after killin' one of God's precious creatures.

"That priest," I said, "he don't realize he casts a shadow long, dark as his own judgments. Daddy use to say, 'He who deceived them will be thrown into the lake a fire with the beast and the false prophet; tormented day and night forever, for what they done... for who they is.'"

"So does that make you the beast or the devil?" The guard asked.

"Oh you know who *I* am. It's that priest, that false prophet that don't know who or what he is. He don't even know he's mortal. Funny how similar we really are. Yes sir, I know that man. He's the kind of man needs to be shown."

"Hansel, I'm begging ya, shut up!"

"I'm hungry!" I called out to my fat friend. "I like Italian food... slippery sauces, noodles that wiggle and squirm... I like things that squirm. And wine, lots of red wine."

"Shut the hell up, Hansel."

"Or better yet, fried catfish, hush puppies, grits, greens, black-eyed peas and corn bread, fried okra, pork barbecue, sweet potato pie, and sweet tea, the dinner of the gods. Yes, sir-ee."

"Shut the hell up, Hansel."

"Do you just have that recorded?" I asked. "And you sit there and hit the button, shut up, Hansel... shut up, Hansel... shut up, Hansel?"

The thick metal door burst open. "New prisoner!" another guard shouted.

My fat friend dropped his fingernail clippers and jumped to his feet.

Pressed my face against the bars to see as far as I could see. A guard and another prisoner; his feet were chained. Young guy, shaved head. But then they shoved him to the left side where I couldn't see anything. Heard the clank of keys, the sound of a heavy cell door sliding open; the bars clattered as they passed one another like a metal train on metal tracks. I heard keys again as they unchained the new guy's bracelets. Then the door banged closed. Then more keys. The sound of keys in this place made me crazy. Keys. All the wrong people had keys.

The two guards whispered at the end of the hall, then both disappeared out the door.

It was quiet. I smelled the fresh scent of lice shampoo—this new guy just went through intake where they would have hosed him down before they threw his prison blues at him and told him to dress. That smell meant his skin burned from head to toe, that the water was still plugging up his ears, that his skin was stuck to the uniform because those rude shits don't give you a towel—you just dress wet and air dry.

Intake was a process of disinfecting prisoners and protecting others from communicable diseases until the powers that be decided—for research's sake— to then infect inmates with communicable diseases to see how fast and far they spread. I felt a kinship with those researchers. Fun job: looking at a crowded yard, a sea of blue, and seeing only a fertile field of human skin to corrupt beyond anything those prisoners' crooked little minds could imagine. I felt a kinship, a real kinship with those researchers.

"You got a name, hombre?" I asked my quiet neighbor who smelled of chemical spray.

I heard movement from his cell, but nothing else.

"Okay," I said. "No name, then." I pressed my face against the bars, watching the door; the guards never stayed gone more than a few minutes. "So hombre, do you like Italian food?"

More movement; he stood up and walked to the bars. "Toreck," he said. "Toreck Sealy."

"Nice to meet you... where you from, Toreck, Toreck Sealy?"

"Who gives a shit where I'm from?"

"Oh... well... I guess nobody does."

"Manzanita," he said. "Down on the coast."

"Ah, yes, I know the place well. Just spent some time fishin' in Nehalem. So what brings you here today, Toreck, Toreck Sealy?"

"I beat up a dumb-shit know-it-all priest."

"Well... now, that's not a crime, is it?"

He let out a laugh and said, "No, not in my mind. But the judge saw different."

"Why'd you tune him up, Toreck, Toreck Sealy?"

"He thinks he can tell me how to raise my son; thinks he's smarter, better than everyone."

"Why you hate this priest so much?"

"They're all liars. Full of empty vows and more secrets than a city whore. When I was a boy they'd tell *me* to bow for *my sins*... after what they did? God damn them. Damn them all to hell! I hate priests. What do they know? They sure don't know what it takes to be a real man. That's for damn sure. And this one, he sure as hell can't even put up a fight."

"Sounds serious," I said. "So are you a good father, Toreck, Toreck Sealy?"

"It's just Toreck. And yes, a better father than that boy deserves."

"All children deserve good fathers. When they don't have good mothers and fathers they's far better off bein' sent back to the House a Souls."

"*The house of what?*"

"How old's your boy?"

"Seven."

"He's still pure in God's eyes."

"What?"

"At twelve the world just really comes after ya. He can still be saved."

"Saved? He don't need savin', cept from his ugly-ass ma and that meddlin' priest."

"Will you be a better father when you're freed, Toreck Sealy?"

"Sure… yeah, I probably will." He sounded drained.

"Not having a good day, Toreck Sealy?"

"Good day? Shit no. No, not a good day," he said.

"You need a good meal. When I'm havin' a bad day I like to think 'bout real food."

"Food is food. So why are you here?"

"Food is food? You're missin' out on life, boy. Food is not *food* till it's cooked in lard: chicken, pork, beef, catfish, squirrel… cooked in lard, man. Now that there's food."

"I don't give a shit 'bout your weird ideas 'bout food. What are ya in for?"

"Well… that's a fun story… Did ya know the Oregon Trail started in Missouri?"

"Man, you don't make any sense."

"Well, let's just say God sent me down that trail to lead his fallen children out of hell."

"Ah, shit… " Toreck dropped to his cot. "Another preacher."

"Not exactly… So tell me about this meddlesome priest you hammered up who fancies hisself a savior of children. I think we could have some fun with him—show *him* the light."

Chapter 12

IMOGENE

DAILY SPECIAL
Rhubarb Pie with melted Tillamook Cheddar .50¢

The mahogany door to Mamaí's cottage was open; bread crumbs were all over the porch. Everything was a mess. Mamaí's precious Persian carpet had fish food on the corner by the aquarium, the china cabinet was now home to books and *socks*. I stepped in and called, "Theo?"

"In here." He strolled into the kitchen from the back porch—no shirt, dabs of iodine on his chest, holding an ice pack to his wavy brown hair. The screen door slammed behind him.

On the dining room table was the *Tillamook Tribune* with his picture prominently featured on the front. I snatched it up and said, "Why didn't you knock that pissant out?"

He pulled his sweatshirt over his muscular frame, quickly covering the scar above his heart and that tattoo that was forbidden conversation, and tilted his head at me. "Immie—"

"Oh shush! I'm so mad I'm thinkin' 'bout beatin' up a priest myself!" I threw the ice pack in the sink. There was dried blood on the counter. In the window was Kiernan's tin soldier. It looked so small, no bigger than my ring finger. It had fresh red paint on its arm, but every other bit of it was chipped or rubbed bare, down to its grey cast iron. My heart sank.

"You coulda really been hurt," I said, moving a stack of books and plunking down on a dining room chair. "You make it through Korea and now you're pickin' fights?"

He stood, quiet and confident, waiting for me to calm down. Despite his façade of patience, there was something unsettling about him these days.

Behind his drooping, sleepy green eyes there'd always been an alert intelligence, but now there was something more, something deeper, darker, something lost, something irretrievable.

"Do you have anything at all to say for yourself?" I asked.

"I know that fighting with you is like thinking an umbrella will protect me in a flood." He smiled and tucked his chain with the dog tags and our grandmother's jade ring beneath his shirt.

"True," I said. "Shit, Theo." I tugged my pack of Salems from my dress pocket and put one in my mouth, a thing never dared while Mamaí was alive. I looked around as if she'd come barreling around the corner and slap them out of my hand—then, staring at Mrs. B's portrait of her, I lit up.

He reached across the table and said, "I'm fine," then yanked the cigarette out of my mouth and continued, "but you still can't smoke in this house."

I took it back and said, "Toreck's not sane. He won't just 'forgive and forget,' ya know. When he gets out he'll come lookin', wantin' payback... So do ya plan on not fightin' back? Cause I'd like to have some notice—gotta call the ambulance in Tillamook, or the *coroner*. Then, well, pick out a dress for the funeral, and then there's the food for the wake, and the—"

"Alright, alright," he said. "Let's just jump off that bridge when we get to it, shall we."

I opened the bandages and handed them to him as he patched himself up. "This is war... He hates you, anyway."

Theo tore open a bandage and said, "It'll be fine."

He had a familiar look in his eyes. He tended to zero in on an injustice with single-minded abandon until the issue was rectified. He had that same distant gaze now.

"You're a war hero, for God's sake! And was there nothin' in your vows about fightin'?"

His smile faded and he said, "It's all a fight. Everything's a fight. Hell, I wake up every morning fists clenched, ready for something. Anything. It's all a fight. But it's a rare treat when you actually know what you're fightin' for. And I'm no hero, Imogene. Just a survivor."

"Maybe. And maybe I don't understand," I said. "Maybe because you don't talk to me 'bout anything real."

"Real? Okay, here's real," he said. "Saint Patrick's was no challenge. Swallow the dogma, keep my head down, just keep moving. No different than that North Korean prison camp, no different at all. But here, with our beach, the ocean, Neahkahnie, Rounders, Solomon, you... every place, every person knowing me, demanding truth. Here, it's impossible to deny who I am. Impossible to keep my head down and not engage. And when I engage, Imogene, when I engage, it's always a fight."

It was the first real thing he'd said to me since he'd returned. His expression was harder now, older than how I see him in my mind. Korea had darkened the radiance of his eyes and sobered him like a cold slap to the face. I let out a deep breath and said, "Thank you for that... maybe I don't understand. Heck, how could I? But one thing I do understand is that Toreck would have *happily* gutted a priest yesterday. I understand that." My tears suddenly welled.

"Alright," Theo said. "But he didn't. And I'm fine."

"But he wants to now, doesn't he?"

"I'll burn that bridge when I get to it."

"What's with all the jumping and burning of bridges? Can't ya just peacefully cross one for once?" I said, taking a drag and blowing the smoke away from him, toward the window. His precious golf balls were all over the floor. Mamaí's sacred shrine to him—his military awards and medals—were missing from the wall. "Love what you're doin' with the place."

"Thanks," he said as he wrapped white first-aid tape around his hand.

"You ever gonna talk about anything?" I asked. "I mean, you know... what happened?"

He looked up at me. "Cut that, will ya?" he said holding out the tape.

I cut it in half. "Fine then."

He skillfully patched himself up like he'd done it a million times before.

"I remember Da saying, 'Yur not an Irishmen 'til yur muzzle's been busted a good many times,'" I said. "It's your third broken nose. Aren't you bloody Irish enough?"

"Hope so," he said with a half-laugh.

His unopened red-white-and-blue-rimmed letters were on the table, the string untied.

"Andréa stopped by the store," I said. "Said to say hello."

He sat quiet for a minute and then said, "Will she be back?"

"Don't think so," I said. "Her family's finally sellin' the cabin. She just picked up her things. She's had a tough year, losin' a parent and all... You okay?"

He forced a smile and said, "I'm fine... She okay?"

"I guess," I said. "Hard to tell with her—she always looks like everything's perfect."

He didn't speak, just stared out the window across the street to the Bouvre house. Did that cold slap happen before he went? I never understood what happened between them.

"Okay, off limits," I said. "Let's chat about that fight then... I know Mamaí said you were God's warrior, but she's gone now."

"I gave her china to Oz and Netty," he said.

"Can we ever have a straight-on conversation? And I know 'bout the china."

"I'm no warrior."

"Oh yeah, forgive me. You're just a punching bag now."

"Exactly."

"So you're schemin', then? Cause this couldn't a been the whole plan, right?"

His tan face went pale and blank for a minute—lying wasn't Theo's forte.

"Thought so," I sighed. "Since you don't have much of a plan, I do. We're takin' money from our inheritance to send Toreck's family far away from here. Five hundred dollars should help them get a start somewhere. And you need to let them know that *today*. She came into the store this morning and looks about to break in two. We can help a little more."

Theo stared at me like he'd never seen me before.

"And you," I said, "need a long, hot bath."

He smiled and leaned forward, closer to me. "I love you, little sister."

"Yeah, well, you still need a bath."

"Didn't have time last night." He sat back in the chair and secured three bandages over the cut on his clean-shaven chin, plunked the ice pack on his knuckles, and smiled at me. "See," he said and held up his hand. "I'm fine." A trickle of blood dropped from his nose.

I handed him a hanky. "Shit, Theo... I thought your bloody nose days would be over."

"The road to heaven often passes through hell," he said. "And, apparently, Manzanita."

"Yeah, but who said to knock down the door and shout, 'Hello Satan, I'm home?'"

Chapter 13

THEO

GUNSHOTS—not from Brownings or grease guns, but the rifles of hunters, echoed from the mountain. Was it hunting season already? I stepped outside as Imogene crossed the street and returned home. As he did every morning, Solomon sat in meditation on the bench in front of her store. He reminded me of the immense stone Buddhas settled into the green Korean countryside waiting for sunrise—unscathed by inhumanity, looking upward, waiting for a better day. Behind him the chronic sound of gunfire ricocheted through the windswept pines and ancient spruce trees on Neahkahnie Mountain, which overshadowed the town. Scarlet and amber leaves dotted the otherwise verdant hillside. A thick mist rolled in. If there were stone Buddhas and temple peaks rising out of that mist, I'd think Manzanita was somewhere in the valley of *Dowon-ri*. Though haunting and dangerous, parts of Korea reminded me of home—a home I was grateful Mamaí did *not* deed to the church upon her death. Grateful indeed.

Birds squawked and fought along the wires. Stoic Raven, who Solomon says is still my spirit guide, was twice their size and perched on a red branch of the madrone tree; his black marble eyes watched them as if he were a disgruntled guard in a winged prison. He waited as I tore bread into chunks and placed it on the balustrade of the front porch, where twisted vines of wisteria spiraled up the thick, round posts to the roofline, trailed over the brick stairs to the other side, and wound back down. As soon as I left he would take the bread, bury it out of site of the other birds, cover it with a leaf or plucked grass, then look at it several times before being satisfied it was disguised. When it came to food he was covert as the Chinese Communist Forces, or CCF, at dawn, when they were most active. Just then a gun-loaded truck full of anxious elk hunters careened to a stop at Imogene's curb. Dressed in camouflage greens and greys, they jumped out, shouted "Beer!" and hurried past Solomon as though he were invisible. As they rushed by him, Solomon's eyes remained closed while the essence of their two worlds collided.

I understood Raven, understood my aquarium, those hunters, Solomon, even what happened in Ireland and Korea, more than I understood why I was back in Manzanita being told what to do by another power-hungry bureaucrat, and why again the painful hope, the endless ache for answers, the longing for a glimpse of Andréa had awakened after trying so hard for so many years to put that fire out.

Chapter 14

THEO

THE NEXT MORNING Suzy Wu's eyes gazed up from the paper on my doorstep: GIRL MISSING DAY 10. I laid it on the table—*Where was she?*

Outside, Solomon sat thirty feet away, hunched on the stump next to his fire, his hunting knife at his belt, his back to me. His grizzled hair hung to his shoulder blades and was matted from mist against his flannel shirt. He was alone, speaking Nehalem to himself—that mysterious language of his elders; guttural sounds that to me were poetry.

He stood and threw his knife into the black painted circle on the faded board against the side of his hut. As a boy I'd tossed my knife there a thousand times, aiming straight and steady, funneling my anger into that target. His skilled hand landed the blade dead center, as always.

He turned toward me and said, "We are archers. Each of our days is an arrow." His crinkled eyes squinted against the sun. "Yesterday you aimed high and steady. Good."

I felt like a ten-year-old boy again, receiving my mentor's approval. "Thank you."

He pointed to Raven in the tree above us and said, "Ravens dwell beyond realm of time and space; they are bringers of messages from spirit world." Above us the coal-colored raven with jet-black shaggy feathers around his neck made a throaty rattle sound.

"Raven is omen of change," he said. "You soon will gain wisdom and courage needed to enter your darkness; the home of all that is not yet in form. Those letters, your darkness?"

"I suppose ... "

"Burn them. Let it go." He went inside his hut and closed the door. Raven took flight. The size of a red-tailed hawk, he hovered and circled over our adjoining yards. Solomon's incense smoldered; the burning wood crackled.

Let it go? Thought I had. Thought I let "it" go while lying shot and dying in a God forsaken chicken wire cell in Korea. Thought I let it go when I put on this white collar. But then, there she was again. And then, gone… again.

I thought about the last time we were together, Andréa telling me about the Impressionists and the blue hour, and how I didn't know then that I'd spend years trying to recall, imagine, internalize. Make her words, the sound of her voice, part of me—poetry in my darkness. I memorized her words like I once did Keats, Browning, or Kipling. And now all I wanted was to un-ring that bell, erase the sound of her voice, forget her sweet whispers. But all I could do was remember when she traced my body and face with her soft fingertips, casting every bit of our time into memory. Everything she ever said, breath to my lungs, resurrection for my body.

Chapter 15

THEO

IT WAS a quiet fall morning with only the sound of my footsteps on the gravel flanks of our single-lane tar road. It started to rain. Softly, evenly, persistently. I headed out for my walk, feeling each of Toreck's blows with every step. A year ago I'd been told I'd never walk again, then were the six months of crutches, then just a cane, and now a mere limp; all I wanted was to walk until I couldn't walk anymore. Then I'd climb Neahkahnie.

As I passed I nodded good morning to Pearl in her garden. Her bicycle with the basket leaned against the gate of the nineteen twenties boarding house that had been in Bud's family since the late eighteen hundreds; ever-pregnant baskets of geraniums and ivy dripped from the window ledges. Not even five feet tall, she wore a yellow raincoat with a matching hat and tended her pumpkin patch, humming undecipherable tunes filtered through her Korean-English. Her always sun-kissed face, dark almond-shaped eyes, and boundless energy were now, after ten years of living here, also part of this windswept landscape that teetered at the edge of our shore. She waved. I waved back. The rain stopped.

*   *   *

The beach survived yesterday's sand castle contest and now had half-washed-away fortresses along the shore. Waves thundered in grabbing at the wet sand with frothing fingers; castles tumbled, fortresses fell. Barefoot, I stepped inside one of those sinking castles. The foamy tide was warm, soothing as it swirled around my feet, reclaiming its terrain. Above me a dark mist engulfed Neahkahnie Mountain, shrouding pines so twisted and warped by this world their reach for heaven was thwarted.

Then I heard the unmistakable rumble. The Church Ladies' glossy black 1940 Packard lurked like a hearse at the top of Beech Road, searching for me. I leaned into the large rocks and tugged my hat down, hoping to blend in. But it was too late. They spotted me. Their car inched forward one block at a time, watching as if the ocean would reach out and snatch me away. The only thing that kept them out of my business was a funeral—anybody's, whether they knew them or not. I'd check death notices in the paper and find something, other than me, for them to attend to. A crab burst out of the sand at my feet and skidded along the beach, dragging and boosting his shell to the next hiding place. "Sorry, fella," I whispered.

The car stopped. The back doors flung open. Twig-thin Ibbie and beachball-round Sibbie McFall spilled out of the car, then scampered down the sandy mound at the end of Beulah Road. "Father Theo!" they shouted. "Father Theo!" They held their hats and gripped their dresses in the front, revealing thick beige knee-high stockings with elastic garters—an image I'd sooner erase. They navigated down the sandy mound. The Packard containing the other ladies skulked at the top of the knoll. They all waved as Sibbie shouted, "We heard about your valiant battle to save that poor Sealy woman and her child. Victorious in virtue. Praise the Lord! Are ya alright, Father?"

"Yes, fine ladies, just enjoyin' a moment to myself here on this once-lonely beach."

"Let us give you a ride back to town." Sibbie and Ibbie, whose faces were like plump apple pies, each with two black cherries for eyes, and who were remarkably the same despite their Laurel-and-Hardy-like shapes, looped their arms in mine. They smelled of rosewater.

"No," I said wriggling out of their grip. "That's fine, I'll be there in thirty minutes."

"But Father?" Sibbie cautioned. "You shouldn't be walkin' so much."

"I need to walk. Doc's orders... good for the hip, ya know."

"But Father?"

"No, no, you go now. I just need a few more minutes... communing with God, here," I said and waved them off. They finally relented and marched back to their car.

Water filled the space around my feet; sand bubbled and shifted as eyes bore into the back of my head, then Ibbie shouted, "We need your opinion on a new Bingo night. Sister Sibbie thinks Thursday would be best before the weekend, but I think we need to consider Friday before evening prayers, more of a weekend festivity of sorts. Don't you agree, Father?"

"Thursday's great," I said. "Not Fridays." I had my own festivities on Fridays that included my good friend Murphy and our usual staring contest with my aquarium that often took all night, and often left me with a Saturday morning headache—from the staring, of course.

I lifted an alder branch from a pile of driftwood to pull away what looked like a fishing net. A crimson-stained crab emerged from the dark strands, gripping a twig with one claw for defense and towing a small severed finger in the other.

"Oh God!" I jumped back. My hip seized. I dropped to the ground, back-peddling up the embankment in shock. It wasn't a fishing net. It was hair—long black hair.

"Father Theo?" Sibbie called out as I lay sprawled in the sand, staring at the twisted mass beneath the driftwood. They ran toward me. I extended a forceful hand. "Stay back!"

"What? What... is it?" Ibbie slowed, a vague, pale recognition overtaking her features. Behind her, Sibbie stopped cold, covering her face with her gloved hands.

"Get the sheriff," I ordered trying to stand. But my hip gave out with a crippling spasm. I sank farther into the watery sand next to the small pale body, naked, but mercifully wrapped in seaweed and tucked beneath the half-burnt log. The crab vanished with its fleshy treasure.

The Church Ladies began to shriek at the sight of the little girl face down in the surf.

"Ibbie!" I shouted. "IBBIE!!! Get Bud, now!"

They all made the sign of the cross and then scrambled back to the Packard. All four doors popped open then slammed closed. The engine roared. Mrs. Scovelli slapped her hand on their dashboard Bible and Ibbie hit the gas. Dust and gravel billowed.

With my arm strength I pulled myself up on a rock, fist pounding my hip for release from the cramp—I regained control of my leg. Free of the spasm I took a deep breath and noticed tattered strands of pink fabric a few yards away, gently swaying on the foam of an incoming tide. It was a high tide, marking a change in seasons. A tide sent to swallow the crippled and the dead.

Chapter 16

THEO

SUZY WU'S BODY was cradled in sand, the tide ebbing it back and forth. Her body was bloated, her hair matted like black seaweed across her face. Ink-black eyes open, glossy, staring through strands of black, at nothing... or maybe something. Either way, staring. Her alabaster skin was bruised all over, and the smell of her rotting corpse was a thousand times worse than sour vomit. Seagulls picked and pawed. I waved them away, took off my jacket, covered her body, and ran my hand over her icy brow, closing her lusterless eyes. *Oh, little girl.*

A few weeks earlier in Sunday School she'd shared her drawing of Adam and Eve in the garden with her class, many of whom had done the same drawing but with stick figures and little to no color. Suzy's was full of color: green, yellow, a big red apple, and an Adam and Eve with thick black hair, slanted eyes, and broad smiles.

I sank back to my knees, numb. The images I fought daily, nightly, to keep in the shadows surfaced like an ice pick to my brain: murdered children, my little orphans, their tiny bodies strewn about like garbage—the pungent smell of death everywhere. But I never had to go tell their parents the news. They had no parents. They had only me.

How would I tell Suzy's family? What words would possibly matter?

While watching the road for Bud's car I tried to say a prayer, but all I could come up with was *why? why? why?* Then I noticed her hands.

* * *

Bud's patrol car lurched to a stop at the bluff. He was so tall that behind the bottle-green visor on the outside of the windshield all I could make out was his broad shoulders and the flicker of light off his badge; he looked headless. He was on his car radio.

The Packard rolled to a quiet stop behind him. He stepped out of the car, closed the door, and slapped his cowboy hat on his head. The Packard doors burst open. All the Church Ladies scurried out. Bud motioned for them to stay put, then headed down the path. They followed. He turned twice to tell them to stay put. Both times they waited a minute then rushed to follow.

Then Bud stopped cold. "Ladies!" he shouted without turning around. Brows creased, his eyes locked on me about twenty feet away. He removed his gun from its holster, held it high, and pulled the trigger. The ladies jumped and clung to one another. The shot reverberated through the air. They stayed put. He re-holstered his gun, marched over to me, and said, "Whada we have here?" Then his face dropped, he let out a deep sigh. "Shit."

I pointed to the other side of the log and said, "Look at her hands."

Chapter 17

THEO

AFTER BUD WROTE his reports and took pictures and the coroner took the body, I went home, dropped into my chair, drank two shots of Murphy's, and stared at my fish and the Navy Citation that Imogene had hung back up on the wall. That Citation had once represented a good day's work; now it just made me feel helpless. I didn't like helpless. I yanked it down, shoved it in the drawer, grabbed a fresh bottle of Murphy's and headed back to the beach.

The police cars, coroner's wagon, and onlookers were all gone. The sun and the tide also had come and gone. It was muggy and approaching sunset. I plopped down a few feet from where I'd found her body. The log was still there, but there was no evidence she ever was.

"Alright God," I said. "How many times do we have to have this talk? It's not like I'm praying for a football team to win some championship. Hell, you gave your own son the boot, supposedly for our sins; still don't understand how that one works. Though I'm *told* it works on the back end, blind faith, blood and all... and that's what I tell others." I downed half the bottle in one long gulp and then stood. "I tell them that, even though personally I've even given up on anything man does, evil or good — it rarely makes sense. And I certainly can't make sense out of the things I've done. You know all that. But you... you're supposed to know better, at least that's our hope. Are we all just slaves like that prison poet said, waiting for the scraps of fortune, grace, peace... love? It'd almost be funny, that 'Divine Comedy' he mentioned, if it weren't so frighteningly true." I slumped back down in the sand and took a drink. "I didn't know about Divine Comedy when I was ten years old, but I get it now. Joke's on me.

"Why do you keep dropping dead children at my feet? What do you want? I meant my vows when I took them. I want to be a man of peace, a man who turns the other cheek, who makes amends for having taken lives. But, forgive me Father, how can I? If Andréa hates me so badly she can't even speak to me, if there's no forgiveness, and if all those kids I tried to save are in heaven now, if there even is a heaven, then why not just take us all, get it over with. Why not take me?" I shouted, then yanked my white collar off and threw it in the ocean. "Take me!"

* * *

Woke at sunrise to Solomon standing over me, my shoes tied together and draped over his shoulder, a blanket on his other shoulder. "Here," he said, and tossed my shoes to the sand next to where I'd slept.

My head spun. I struggled to prop myself up against a driftwood log.

"What are you doing?" he asked.

I darted a look around the beach. It was early morning. My jacket was twenty feet away, my wallet in the sand next to me, shirt *gone*, pants soaking wet, and no socks. I felt for the chain around my neck making sure the ring and my dog tags were still there. They were.

"Not sure," I said, picking sand from the corners of my mouth. Then I spotted the Church Ladies, all six of them standing next to their black Packard at the top of the hill—crows on a wire—dressed in black, holding their black-gloved hands over their brows to block the sunlight and get a real good picture of me sleeping on the beach with half my clothes gone. I waved. They scrambled to their car as if the boogeyman had said *boo*. Their engine hummed to life. Mrs. Scovelli, a woman who weighed no more than ninety pounds but had feet and hands the size of a man's, slapped her big hand onto their dashboard Bible and held it there as they all craned their necks to watch me. The car drove slowly down Beech Street. I waved again.

Solomon squatted down and said, "There was nothing you could do about the child."

"Good to know nothing's changed," I replied pulling a strand of seaweed from my hair.

He tapped his finger on my tattoo and said, "Winged soldier with sword is a warrior."

"*Was* a warrior," I said and wrapped the blanket around my shoulders; my head throbbed and my stomach flip-flopped into my throat. My lips trembled from the cold.

"Your drunkenness has nothing to do with dead child," he said. Then he stood back up blocking the sun. "Are you the Theo who was my student?"

"No," I said. "I'm not. I'm a gimp, a throwaway, a cripple." I shoved my feet into the wet shoes. "I'm good for nothing but bein' a punchin' bag."

He glared at me and said, "This is true. You act like punching bag, you are punching bag; a beat-down warrior... not worthy. This is the truth you make."

"Make? It's just the way things are."

"Inside each of us two hungry wolves fight."

"Wolves?"

He frowned down at me and said, "The wolf is a tracking predator."

"Oh great! Wolves now? Okay, let's have your grand tale about wolves."

"His eyes," he said, "are large and piercing, on the front of his skull. He sees everything. Those eyes shine like embers from bonfire. Both wolves with hungry eyes desire different things: one seeks anger, regret, greed, self-importance, guilt; all these are hungry things."

"Sorrowful things... hungry wolves... what are you talking about?" "You, sorrowful thing who should listen," he said pulling me up by my arm. "The other wolf hungers for peace, love, and compassion. This same fight goes on in you, me, every man, some women." He motioned for me to walk.

I walked; my teeth chattered from the cold. "Alright... alright. So which wolf wins?"

"The one you feed most."

"Still my teacher."

"Still student?" he asked, now walking ten feet ahead of me. "Read your letters, Theo. Learn from your pain. Must open wound to heal it. Then burn them. Let fire cleanse your wound. Learn to stand on your two feet again, root them in ground where you live. Feed hungry wolf who wants peace." He leaned down and picked up the empty Murphy's bottle from the sand. "Not this hungry wolf." He threw the bottle into the black ashes of a cold fire pit. "That hungry wolf dies here."

Chapter 18

THEO

DRY TOAST was all I could keep down for the better part of two days. Two days hiding from the uninvited light filtering through the blinds, two days to feel human again.

When I did, I took my duffle bag from the corner and dumped the contents out on my bed: a Webley .38 caliber revolver, jump gear, log books, and the aviator sunglasses I'd bought in Germany. I hung my leather Rakkasan jacket in the back of the closet, piled the jump gear in the corner with my black boots, put the gun in my drawer, the glasses in my pocket.

It felt good to unpack that part of myself, get it out, let it breathe. Real good. It never seemed appropriate or safe to unpack in my room at Saint Patrick's, where, except at fundraisers, my soldier past was hush-hush, nothing my brethren could ever understand, nothing they wanted to discuss. But here I could let it out of that tight canvas bag, unfold the clothes, shine the boots, sharpen the knife. It felt good, like being in my own skin again.

The phone rang.

"Good morning," I said.

"Father Riley, this is Bishop Doyle's assistant," he said. "We have you scheduled to return to the Oregon State Penitentiary next month on the first and third Fridays."

"Of course you do," I said. "Thank you for calling."

Fridays. I hate Fridays. Nothing good happens on Fridays.

Would I run into Toreck? Was prison just adding bad habits to his repertoire?

I picked up my knife and immediately pictured the slanted eyes of the first man whose life it took—not even a soldier, just a frightened farmer-turned-warrior by order of his government. His soul left this world, taking with it what was left of my innocence. Part of *me* seeped out of him that day, a red stain on the earth altering my perceptions of all I'd held sacred. Soldier or not, to take life was a sin. Remembering myself then—blood on my palms, primal instincts awake—made my skin crawl, my heart skip a beat. Not so much at what I did in the face of war, but that *it* existed within me all along. I never thought twice about the fire, the dead McMurtry brothers. Still didn't. It was a just thing that had to happen, and even at ten years old, I was willing to pay the price. But hand-to-hand combat awakened a different animal altogether. Solomon says we all have those instincts. So, I wondered, what did Toreck have hidden that the battlefield of prison may bring to light?

I opened the box of .38 slugs—it was full—slid it into the drawer with the gun, grabbed the empty duffle bag, and opened the front door. The Tribune stared up at me from the welcome mat. BODY OF MISSING GIRL, SUZY WU, FOUND – CORONOER SAYS 'FOUL PLAY': HANDS WERE TIED.

                                     *   *   *

Flat grey clouds cloaked an invisible sun generating a painful haze my eyes weren't ready for. Taking shelter behind my forgotten aviator glasses, I stepped over the paper and down the steps, empty duffle bag and folding shovel in hand.

The tide pools steamed as I marched past them, bag in tow. At the north end of the protected beach, Neahkahnie raised high out of the mist and plunged into the sea. I imagined climbing that winding trail to the top as I had climbed it a thousand times, my bare feet in the rich soil, feeling the vibrations of Neahkahnie, feeling like a flea on an enormous sleeping beast. I dreamed of Destiny's Perch, our secret place. Dreamed of taking my letters there, leaving them, burying them, burning them—every imaginable version. But every version of that dream took place at the top of Neahkahnie—out-of-reach Neahkahnie.

I secured the canvas strap over my shoulder, leaned into the wind, and continued toward Smugglers Cove. Shiny jellyfish and sand dollars littered the shore, the sweet scent of blackberries and pine trees filled the twisting breezes. At the foot of Neahkahnie I flip-locked the shovel and filled my bag with sand. It was the darkest sand on the shore and the very sand where Solomon taught me to fight with a stick or my bare hands. It was where he said the Black Pirate who planted the Spanish treasure deep in Neahkahnie Mountain lost his final battle, and where his body fractured into a million pieces and disintegrated into that sand, staining it black forever.

Then, according to Solomon, his spirit fled to the mountain where he protects the prized beeswax and gold from the onslaught of treasure seekers. I filled my bag with that dark, spirit-filled sand and hefted it over my shoulder, carried it back to my cottage, and hung it on the back porch where my punching bag once hung.

Chapter 19

THEO

WITH THE TAPE from my old boxing kit I made the figure-eight strap between my thumb and forefinger, wrist and palm, again and again. Solid hands, solid fists. The boxing ring was a sacred place to me, a world you couldn't take for granted, where a bell asked the questions, lies died—truth oozed out of every pore— answers stood bleeding but alive. It's not unlike bowing before the altar, signing the cross, and the silent prayer. Kneeling beneath the ropes, praying to keep your chin tucked, hands up and feet on the floor—a sacred appeal. I had a sick love, a reverence for the place; the boxing ring, a house of pain where you left your problems for the day. I guess that's the way some people feel about church—wish I did. What I did know was that the ring was the only place I ever felt any control, and as a kid surviving Da's love one punch at a time—culminating in a boxing scholarship—I learned to stand firm on my own two feet.

With wrists wrapped snug, I tore the tape with my teeth, tied my gloves on for the first time in years, and let loose with an increasing rapid-fire barrage of strikes until sweat covered my body and the cartridge lodged in my hip throbbed like it wanted out. My adrenalin surged. When I looked up, Solomon stood next to his fire watching me. He nodded.

* * *

It was a long cloudy morning of calls and visits from parishioners. Some wanted to add their two cents about how they'd have beaten Toreck up, not realizing how short-sighted that solution was. And others congratulated me, forcing me to give my lackluster speech about how violence was no answer. Others asked about Suzy Wu, though few knew her very private family.

The Tuesday Bingo ladies, who consisted of the six Church Ladies and two other women from Nehalem, finished shouting "Bingo!" at noon, which they did so I would think they were actually playing Bingo and not poker. Then they cleaned up the basement recreation hall, set out flowers, strung garland for a wedding that was to occur that afternoon, and left. I stood on the steps trying to get rid of Mrs. Voigtle, who wasn't much taller than the four-foot statue of Saint Francis of Assisi in the quad.

"Soon as I saw the paper," she said as she handed me a pie with burnt crust, "knew you needed a homemade pie... I hated that bastard's father, and Toreck's just like 'im!" She clenched her bony, wrinkled fist and held it high. "Good on ya, Father Theo... *Wham!*" She threw her breathless punch into the air.

"*Ohhkay*," I said. "Thank you." It was the fifth apple cobbler delivered that day. She pivoted around, threw another fantasy punch, and prattled off to her rust-covered 1933 Dodge pick-up, where her balding cat waited on the dashboard. Just then a grey 1950 Buick pulled into the parking lot. I turned to see a man in the driver's seat watching us. Didn't recognize him. He turned off the engine. When Mrs. Voigtle pulled out, he opened the door, stepped out, slipped on a wrinkled sports coat, and sauntered toward the church steps.
Cop, maybe?

"Afternoon, Father Riley."

"Afternoon."

He climbed the stone steps and reached his hand out to shake. We shook, turned, and entered the rectory. He smelled of vinegary aftershave.

"Can I help you?" I asked as I placed the pie on the hall table, dipped my finger into the baptismal pool, crossed myself, and entered the chapel. He followed but didn't take off his hat.

He cleared his throat and said, "Well, it's about that Chinese girl you found—"

"You know I can't comment on that."

"Well then, it's about your fight with a Toreck Sealy. You were a boxing champ, then a war hero. How'd the likes of Sealy get one over on ya, Father?"

"Read the papers. Make your own conclusions." I set out six candles for mass.

"I have... and I think you're a hero, *again*."

"Who *are* you?"

He tipped his hat, his face eager and hopeful, "Hugh O'Neill from the *Oregonian*, sir."

"I've said all I have to say." I grabbed the box from behind the pulpit, tore it open, unpacked the new hymnals, and asked, "Bishop Doyle send you?"

"Listen Father," he said. "I'd like to do a story on you, your war background. What happened in Korea? What was it like?" He held his cheap ballpoint pen over his pocket-sized pad of paper, hovering, waiting.

"Can't say," I said. "Guess you had to be there."

"Did ya get that limp over there?"

I stacked the books and set out the unity candle for the wedding.

"Oh, come on," he said. "There must be some comment, somethin'; some battle, some memory, somethin' you can give me?" He slid a folded newspaper clipping out of his pocket.

"Something I can give you?... Hmmm," I said, tightening my fist, swollen knuckles cracking. "Let me see... No, nothing. Thank you just the same."

He unfolded the newspaper clip. *What now?*

"This is a picture of you, right?" he asked, and then read, SERGEANT T. RILEY FROM OREGON ESCORTS CATHOLIC NUNS AND KOREAN WAR ORPHANS.

He held it out to me. I'd avoided that photo for years. My spine stiffened.

"This nun, these kids," he said studying the grainy photo, and then glancing up at me, holding out the clipping. "You helped them. Where are they now?"

The children's dark eyes emerged from the grainy picture—for a moment I swear they all moved. We were in Pusan. I in uniform, my M1 strapped to my back, tying shoelaces for two sisters. One was seven, and the other five years old. They had never seen shoes that tied. One of the girls held up her foot smaller than the palm of my hand for me to lace. "Teo," she called to me, (all the orphans called me Teo) "tie shoe." Then she smiled and placed her tiny hand on my shoulder. The following day we were ambushed, she and her sister killed.

I grabbed a church pew to balance myself. My stomach rose to my throat.

"Father—"

"Good meeting you," I said catching my breath. "Take a pie when you leave." I nodded to the rectory table where the other pies were lined up like offerings at the altar.

"Father Riley, I think you did the right thing. I think—"

"You know what I think?" I said, turning to face him square on.

"No," he said, eagerly pressing his pen to his expectant pad. "Please, tell me." His brows arched high above his hungry grey eyes. The newspaper clipping was already tucked away.

"I think you should take the pie on the far left. It's from Mrs. B. She makes the best crust in town. She adds rum to the apples. It's good."

His eyes narrowed and his brow knit into one thin line across his forehead. "So, Father," he said as he glanced at his notes. "You went to Korea in 1950, flew with the 187th, you did some serious shit, then for some reason you were charged with protecting a group of Korean orphans, then ended up a POW, then in a hospital in Germany for a year, then home in fifty-four. How'd a war hero end up taking priest vows and hiding out in Portland for over a year, and how'd that same war hero end up in a podunk town like Manzanita?"

"Long story."

"Well, I got the dates, but I need that long story to go with those dates."

"When I understand that *story*, you'll be my first call."

"But Father. You should be careful." He slapped his pad closed and shoved it back into his pocket. "Some stories find a way of writing themselves."

"And so goes the history of the world," I said, continuing to stack the books. He flicked a speck from his hat, yanked it down on his head, and stomped out.

As soon as the heavy wood door slammed shut, he came back through. "Rum, huh?" he said and grabbed Mrs. B's buttery tart. He tipped his hat, said, "Thanks for the pie, anyway," then slithered out the same way he slithered in.

He wasn't unlike that photographer in Pusan who was there that day to photograph dead bodies, eager for the paycheck they represented.

A reporter—most certainly Bishop Doyle "taking advantage" of a situation. He'd write what served them both. I didn't care.

The chapel went quiet. The stench of the reporter's aftershave lingered near the altar. *Did I have a comment?* What *comment* could sum up how I didn't recognize what mattered in life until meeting the children in that photograph? And how none of it mattered until I wrote about it in my letters to Andréa. How nothing had any value until I told her? How Toreck was an easy problem to solve. And how on some days apple pie was the only answer that made any sense.

My hands trembled as I organized the pulpit, dusted the gold cross on the altar, opened the Bible on the lectionary, placed a black ribbon where I'd be reading for the wedding, and closed the cover. Weddings were the worst part of my job; all that transitory bliss. Funerals were easier—well, not easier, but at least unspoken, because there really are no words for the loss of a love. And unlike the transitory bliss of a wedding, a lost love was etched into faces at a funeral, a truth that would live inside those left behind forever. No words required. I could relate to the unspoken foreverness of it all. I could relate to funerals. But I couldn't relate to weddings.

The image of that news article burned inside me as did the images of many dead or discarded children of Korea—all the ones I couldn't help, couldn't feed or protect. I felt as helpless then as when the McMurtrys held me down while they murdered Kiernan.

I set out the bread plate and wine chalice for the Eucharist liturgy, then turned and twisted with a right step on the wrong nerve, which sent fire through my hip; spasms ran up my back and down my thigh. I dropped into the chair behind the pulpit, my collar drenched in sweat. It took two years to get that image out of my mind. But there it was again.

Chapter 20

SOLOMON

OUR NEHALEM MYTHS die with me, the last storyteller. Owl gives vision; my final student will be white female child of lost woman with red shoes. She, at last, is my final journey.

For a thousand years Manzanita was home of my family, my ancestors. When I soon go with my wife Ruby, there will never be another Nehalem in this valley. Our language, dust.

I raised my arms to morning heavens. "Great Grandfather," I said loud to His blue sky. "Three weeks ago, You sent Grandmother Owl to perch on oak tree that shadows Theo's home. She brings him her medicine, her teachings to see beyond shadows of fear and darkness, through to other side that promises light, happiness, and knowledge. She says if Theo wakes he will obtain her medicine, hear Raven again, and return to life where his true journeys wait. If he does not, he will be lost. Will You wake him from this slumber where he lives a half-life in cage built by his father and foolish hopes of his mother, and where his heart is broken in two?"

I dropped my arms to my sides. The sun rose waking the creatures of light, signaling to darkness it was time to rest. I stood on the crest soaring above the seashore; cold, raging winds slammed against the mountain's flanks. My spirit power filled me. I saw fifty miles north, then south. Black Bear, Elk, and great Eagle woke in rustling leaves behind me. I closed my eyes, took in the salt smell of Mother Ocean, the squawking of her hungry birds. "*Ts-ull- ULL-leel, Solomon.*" My Ancient Ones said, "*Ts-ull-ULL-leel.*" The tide comes. They call me home.

Chapter 21

THEO

IT WAS LATE SEPTEMBER when a man from the town of Wheeler came to Saint Mary's for confession. He'd been home a year from his tour in Korea, which also included a six-month hospital stay in Germany—same circuitous journey as mine. He said, "Father, I can't sleep."

His body leaned against the confessional wall. His breathing was shallow; he spoke softly, the way one talks when the exhaustion of grief has overwhelmed him.

"Sleep can be a gift or a battle of spirit," I said. "Why do you think you can't sleep?"

"Why do ya suppose God allows war?"

"Well, I think God allows war so men will see with great clarity what sin really is. Before Korea I thought lightly about sin and was optimistic about human nature."

"So, you *were* a soldier?"

"It's why you drove to Manzanita instead of your own parish, isn't it?"

"And now … since Korea?"

"And now … well, I'm not as optimistic about human nature. War forces us to examine our frail humanity. Maybe in examining that frailty you'll find the antidote to your restlessness."

"Thing is, I'm not even sure what I need to confess; it's just, I see them everywhere."

"Whom do you see?"

"One night," he said, "at a farmhouse, me, my best friend, and two other guys from our troop found the farmer and his family in the barn … beheaded."

He told me the graphic and violent nightmare. One I'd seen a hundred times. In the end his friend was killed.

"I shot the guy who killed him," he said, "but another grenade blew me off my feet. Landed face down next to my buddy. His eyes were open, staring at me... from where? His soul? His dead soul? He just stared like he was askin' why. The other guys dragged me off to shelter. My hand was gone. Now I'm worthless. Can't work, can't sleep, can't even talk to people I known my whole life. Can't face his mother, his girlfriend. Can't tell her I was a coward."

My hands shook. I sat forward struggling with *my* memories, trying to do my job.

"Son... The souls of men survive the dissolution of their bodies and have an immortal subsistence." My hollow words, vapors against the mesh dividing us. "Work then, on your soul," I said, barely able to utter the religious speak when I, too, was lost, asleep between death and resurrection, awaiting some judgment day here or in the hereafter, for all I'd done, all I'd seen.

"Thank you," he whispered. "Thing is, dying woulda been easy; livin's what's hard."

The weighty lament in his voice concerned me. Knew it well, knew where it may lead.

"It is hard," I said with a sudden clarity about what he—what *any* soldier—needed to hear. I leaned in and said, "Give thanks you had the power to shepherd evil from this world back to God for His swift judgment. Give thanks you were able to do something about the tribulations brought forth by evil men. Be thankful knowing God *chose* you, and that now you will be healed through His mercy. You shot an animal who killed the blameless. Take comfort that that animal never took the life of innocence again. Because *you* took action. Be proud, son, for that's not cowardice." I sat back from the screen and straightened my collar. A quiet calm washed over me.

He took a deep breath. "Thank you, Father... thank you. My penance?"

"Your penance... Read Romans 13, about governing authorities being God's servants, agents of wrath, bringing punishment to the doers of evil. Understand that the Lord uses man-made authority to rain retribution onto the wicked. So, read and find peace in understanding. That's your penance. Then sleep like sleep is your reward."

Chapter 22

THEO

DAMP SHEETS CLUNG to my skin. It was four in the morning. It had been two years—still wasn't accustomed to sleeping alone, no snoring men, no bombs in the distance, no crying children. I dropped my feet to the cold, wood floor and studied my jump gear piled in the corner—folded, stacked, ready. Army-green pants and shirt, black boots, cartridge belt with canteen, headgear and gloves, pocket compass, medical kit, Ek Commando Knife, toggle rope, water purification tablets, and notebooks with jottings of Korea's bewildering Karst Caves. Thing is, everyday, wearing all that gear, I knew who I was. Had clarity, never wondered why I was there or what I was supposed to be doing. Not once. I wrote it all down when I could, every bit of it.

After two years of solitude, two years of thinking, pondering, and examining every detail of my life like a madman with a jigsaw puzzle, I realized writing it all out gave me a safe place to put the undigested sights, sounds, and images. Then sealing them away shifted the burden so I could move on and be a soldier, do what I had to do. But now what would I do with this Pandora's box, these letters containing my puzzle, my nightmares?

With sunrise approaching I grabbed the stack of letters and went out back. The wicker chair on the porch moaned against my weight. The full moon hung like a pearl over Manzanita—its milky light played with the shadows of my yard and filtered through the screened-in overhang of the porch. I imagined that full moon shimmering off Andréa's hair. *Living was the hard part.*

Solomon's hammock rocked in the breeze next to the carved cedar totem that towered over his work shed. The orange hue of sunrise filled the mist. His sunflowers tilted their sleeping heads upward to the waking sun, like him, always seeking light.

I propped my feet on the banister and switched on the old torch lamp with a cut glass shade; its vanilla glow cast down. The letters were heavy in my hand.

The top letter, postmarked Kimpo AFB, would be the first letter—after eight weeks' training—I wrote about finally being a Rakkasan, a paratrooper with the 101st Airborne Division. The Japanese called us *Rakkasan*, which meant "falling down umbrella men." It stuck. Thought she'd get a laugh. Mailed that letter the day we shipped out for Seoul, September 3, 1950.

I set the letters down, unable to read, then strapped on my gloves, had a go at the bag.

Ten minutes later the telephone started to ring. By the time I took off the gloves, wiped my face, and made it inside, the ringing stopped. I picked up the bottle of Murphy's on the kitchen counter, took a good long whiff of the spicy liquor, then re-corked the bottle and put it back on the shelf. The phone rang again, then again. I finally picked up.

"Father Theo," said Lucy, who managed most calls from in or out of town from the switchboard in her house. "Can you hold for Bishop Doyle?"

"Yes, I'll hold." *Now what?* I looked at the kitchen clock; it was eight- thirty in the morning.

"Father Riley?"

"Yes, your Eminence," I said. "I'm here." I took a clean pair of socks from the hutch.

"Father Hugo is not well," The Bishop told me. "We need you at the prison today."

"But—"

"Ten a.m. sharp… And wear your robes. The mayor will be there for a dedication ceremony. There will be reporters. It would be best if you are seen shaking his hand."

"I understand," I said. "And how is Father Hugo?"

"He'll be fine. He thanks you. Now, God be with you." The line went quiet.

I doubted that our elderly Father Hugo was even expected to go. The Bishop's desire for favorable press and forever pushing his fundraising agenda was what mattered. I dropped food into the aquarium, put my white collar on, did *not* change into my robes, grabbed my hat, and slammed the door. Guess I'd be dealing with Toreck again, sooner rather than later.

Chapter 23

THEO

AT NINE FIFTY-FIVE A.M., hairy-knuckled Officer Stamboli checked me in, took my rosary, tin soldier, and car keys, and motioned for another stern-faced officer to guide me down the halls to the dimly lit chapel. We passed through the only window-lined corridor in the building. Outside in the tiny courtyard was that news reporter, Hugh O'Neill, with a camera; the mayor; several business dignitaries; and the warden, all shaking hands. I walked past following the silent guard, preferring to sit alone in a small pine box than shake hands with the Bishop's wealthy disciples.

Inside that pine box I placed my Bible on the shelf, dropped down on the bench, and sat in silence for nearly an hour thinking about the last letter in the stack. It was cast into memory, word for word because I'd written it over and over again.

Dear Andréa,

This will be the last time I write you. I've heard your silence; my eyes are open now. No doubt you've found another. Hope he takes you to art galleries, buys you flowers and looks into your deep blue eyes and is mesmerized, as any man would, should be.

I was too young, too dumb, too full of the expectations of others to see you were, or should have been, my everything, my destiny. I should have given you everything you desired, because within your desire is where I am alive. I want you to know I love you, always have, always will. I may die here; hope this letter finds its way to you because it is my last wish in this life, that you be happy. Roam museums in search of your soul, bathe in the twilight, your blue hour, write poetry, love, and be happy, my dearest Andréa Bouvre, heart of my heart. I love you. Good-bye.

— Theo

Chapter 24

THEO

SUDDENLY SOMEONE OPENED the door, entered the other side of the confession booth, and said, "Forgive me Father for I have sinned. It's been four years since my last confession. I feel a heavy burden. Too much time in a cage plays on a man's mind some."

"Do you wish to confess your sins?" I asked.

"I could confess it a thousand times and never be at peace."

"If you believe confessing again will bring you peace, then go ahead."

"I murdered a man," he said and then paused. "For killing my two children in a drunken rage. He came into our store and shot them, my boys, ten years old… confessed it a hundred times, doesn't matter, still can't wrap my mind around being a murderer, and you're just gonna tell me to do some Hail Marys. He's still dead, kids gone, wife gone, and me, unforgivable… condemned."

"Exodus 20:13," I said. "A more accurate translation would be, '*You shall not murder.*' This commandment doesn't forbid the taking of life under certain circumstances."

"What?" he said.

"Do you feel remorse for your actions?"

"Well… yes."

"Then you are forgiven. Now the hard part begins… Forgive yourself."

He sat silent for maybe three full minutes. I, too, remained silent, recalling that passage I'd read a thousand times.

"Okay," he finally said. "You're the first one of you guys to say something like that."

"You should do some Hail Marys, though," I said. "Can't hurt."

"Thank you… I will, Father." He genuflected and left the booth.

Within a few minutes someone turned the door handle of my side of the booth.

"Other side," I said. Then the rickety entrance on the other side of the confession booth opened. A short, thin man sat down behind the mesh screen, his breathing quick and shallow. He had his grey denim hat twisted in his hands, wringing it like a dishrag. I could make out a broad, eager smile on his bony face as he rocked back and forth.

"Ah... ah... bless, yeah, yeah, that's it... bless me, Father—" he stammered, grasping for long-forgotten words. "Yeah, bless me with my sins... that's it."

"*For* your sins."

"What?"

"Fine," I said. "I absolve you from your sins. In the name of the Father, the Son, and the Holy Spirit. Amen." I lacked the patience to hear him list them out.

He rocked back and forth on the bench, wringing his hat, then said, "Yeah. So, Father?" He stopped rocking, leaned his face against the mesh and smiled. "Father Riley, right?"

I stared at the thick wire screen that separated us. "Yes," I said, straining to pull his face into focus; didn't know the guy.

"So... so, I'm s'posed to... a—"

"Supposed to what?"

"S'posed ta read ya this note." He unfolded a piece of paper. "A... *Ya can't enter a strong man's house 'less ya first bind him*... yeah, that's it."

"What is that supposed to mean?"

"Dunno... Oh yeah, s'posed to say ya have a pretty sister... yeah, a real looker, man."

I stood, hitting my head on the shelf. "What's your name?"

He bolted from the confessional. I shoved my side of the door, but it stuck. Something was jammed against the outside. I shouted, "Who's out there?" and jostled the door, but it wouldn't budge. Rammed my thumb into the button to turn on the red light for the guard to come. No one came. Pounded the door again. "Is anyone out there?"

Then the guard yanked it open and said, "Something wrong in here, Father?"

"Who was that prisoner who came in a few minutes ago? Where were you?"

"I stepped down the hall for a minute. Didn't see anyone."

"Then how did he get in here?"

"Well, he wouldn't have. I have a list."

"There *was* a guy who came in and—"

"I think you're finished here, Father," he said as he reached inside the booth, grabbed my Bible, and handed it to me. "Let's get you on your way then."

"What? No… who was that?"

"Told you I didn't see anyone, and nobody gets in or out without my say-so." He shoved the corridor door open. "Now, you have a good day." And then slammed it shut.

*   *   *

"Where's Stamboli?" I asked a young sergeant who now sat behind the front desk.

"Don't know for sure," he said. "Think he's gone for the day."

He handed me my keys, rosary, and tin soldier. I shoved them in my pocket.

"I need to know the name of one of the prisoners who came into the chapel."

He picked up the telephone, pressed a button and said, "Would you check the list for who visited the priest today?" He soon hung up. "You had one visitor today… big surprise."

"There were two," I said. "I want a name."

"Sorry, Father, I just do as I'm told here."

*   *   *

Somehow it was Toreck. I was sure of it. He'd gotten some lackey to deliver a message. But the guards? How could the likes of Toreck garner their alliance? How could he possibly have known I'd be there today? But then, prison walls have ears and eyes, and while prisoners often make promises and threats they can't keep, I wasn't willing to underestimate this one.

Chapter 25

IMOGENE

DAILY SPECIAL
Liver & Onions, with Gravy & Buttermilk Biscuits .75¢

It was three years ago now, but I remember it like it happened last night.

When I woke, three, maybe four days later, I was in our apartment, not the hospital. I struggled to get out of bed. My stomach and legs cramped like a thorny pincher crab was trapped inside me, fighting to get out of my body. I hunched over and made my way to the door where, clinging to the wood frame, I braced myself.

Across the hall her bedroom door was closed. I sank to the hardwood floor and stared at that closed door and all it meant. Then the lower half of my body stopped cramping. It went numb and limp instead—couldn't move my legs, so I dragged myself across the hall, reached up, turned the glass door knob, and opened her door.

The window was open, the air crisp. Her pink chiffon curtains I'd made on her one-month birthday floated in the breeze. The top of Thomas's head raised over the rim of our rocking chair, the chair where I nursed our sweet daughter all the months of her life. He sat up, slowly turned his head, and looked at me. He looked older in the grey evening light. I sat on the floor in the doorway. He stood. *She's gone*, he said and then lifted me up into his arms and carried me back to bed. *Now sleep*, he said.

At four o'clock in the morning I woke to the sound of her crying. Then a terror bolted through me—she was cold and alone! Leapt from our bed, where Thomas was sound asleep, rushed into her room, reached into the cold crib and rustled through the blankets for her tiny, warm body. *Christina*, I said. *Christina!* She was gone.

That thorny crab kicked and pinched inside me again. I plucked her blanket from the crib. It was a small quilt that Pearl, Mamaí, and I made during my pregnancy, stitching every square of pink and yellow together, talking, laughing, and waiting for Christina's arrival. I took that quilt and ran down the apartment stairs and out the back door of our store. I ran for an eternity through the black tar streets, then backyards, then driveways and dirt alleys of Manzanita. Clutching her quilt I ran through the night until my bare feet hit gravel, then stopped.

The leaning black sign with chalk-white letters read *Cemetery Road*. I'd seen that sign a thousand times in my life but had never felt its heaviness before that moment. *Cemetery Road.* Another closed door. I ran again.

Ran until my feet felt the cold edge of the lawn at Neahkahnie Graveyard — squeezed my eyes shut — didn't recall being there just days before. Though I must have been. Had no memory at all. I buried my face in her quilt and trembled at the lingering sweet smell of baby powder.

Opened my eyes. The full moon emerged from behind black clouds. It had a milky halo and cast a translucent light over the graveyard, bringing life to the tattered, faceless statues of winged angels, praying children, and the unkempt stones of fallen veterans from forgotten wars.

Marble headstones leaned in the often-waterlogged soil like old friends supporting one another to the bitter end. I went up and down the cracked, stone pathways where trinkets of love lay forsaken. Some graves were clean and well tended, others swallowed up by weeds, thistle, and the passage of time. Hugging her quilt close to my chest, I walked. Moonlight danced and shimmered off the hard surfaces like it did in the waves in the ocean. Felt I was drowning — kept walking on those cracked stones that now felt like rushing waters. Rising, sinking, floating… rising again.

Then, there it was: a fresh mound of earth and a tiny statue of an angel with wide open eyes of cold grey marble. The world spun. The waters rose. My limbs were heavy. I held the blanket closer and read the brass plaque: *Baby Christina – May 1954 – September 1954.*

The wind whistled through the leaves and gravestones. Then I heard it. The wailing; my wailing — crying, the slow click of footsteps on that very crumbling pavement, whispered prayers. The Church Ladies dressed in black, holding their gloved hands out to me. I saw Christina's tiny casket lowered into the ground. I heard Mamaí gasp. I squeezed my eyes shut. Didn't want to see it. *No!* I screamed. *No!*

Just then the rains began, cold and soft. Leaves shook as the drops landed. The graveyard glimmered like a precious stone for a moment, then the moon slid back behind the clouds. Darkness wrapped around us… I grabbed my stomach, feeling as if that crab had nearly stabbed and dug its way out. Dropped to my knees and covered her grave with the blanket. I lay down next to her, my sweet child, and cradled my arm over the cold soil. She was warm now. I fell into a deep, deep sleep.

Woke in the early morning light to shadows; Thomas and Bud stood over me.

She's gone, Immie, Thomas said, kneeling down, trying to lift me from Christina's grave.

No! I said and flung my arms and body over the mound of dirt.

He tried again to pick me up. *No,* I said. *Go away.*

Immie, Bud said as he leaned down close to me. *Honey, your feet are bleeding and you're nightgown is soaking wet. Let us get you home.* Bud scooped me up into his arms and carried me to the car. Thomas followed.

For several weeks Thomas refused to let me visit the graveyard. He watched me closely. I resented his eyes on me, watching me, preventing me from what he felt was wrong or perverse in some way. *In his way,* his "we just have to move on" way. A few weeks later I was able to drive again without cramping, without crying, without wanting to drive the car off a cliff. Convinced him I was fine, whatever fine meant. He finally returned to work.

After that, each week when I went grocery shopping in Tillamook I turned off the bend on Highway 101 and slowly drove down the old gravel lane to Cemetery Road. I parked, sat in the car, and cried, and then opened the door and put my feet on that cracked and crumbling ground. My legs went numb and that old pincher crab fought and clawed inside me every time, so I hunched over and walked that broken stone path to Christina's grave.

The first week I planted two hyacinths, pink and purple. Colors I thought would have been her favorites. Then I put some of the soil from her grave into a small, canvas flour bag and put that bag in the back of my Woody with the groceries. My disapproving husband never knew the flour bag he carried in with the groceries contained the dirt from his daughter's grave. I gently placed that precious soil in the garden patch outside the back door. I did this every week for one year.

Chapter 26

THEO

BUD'S SHERIFF'S OFFICE was located in the Tillamook Courthouse building. On the way home from the prison I swung by to chat about the prisoner's threat, or whatever it was—*sounded like a threat to me*. Inside the building police officers had the lobby on lock-down while they transported a man in cuffs.

I waited next to the courtroom doors over which a colorful fresco titled "Building of the Morning Sun, 1950" hovered, surrounded by walls of limestone and cold linoleum floors. I often stopped and took in that rare fresco, painted on the building's twentieth anniversary by a nun who tried to bring light to a place of darkness, a place where time held still for no man and justice often pulled a veil over freedom. Thought about my nuns in Korea, devoted women who tried with all their might to bring light to that dark place but instead lost *their* freedom.

* * *

The wide, marble staircase to Bud's second-floor office echoed with each step. He was seated at the back wall—his desk by a large window, his size-fourteen cowboy boots propped up on that desk—talking on the phone. Compared to the other ten sheriffs in the noisy office with twenty-foot ceilings, he was bigger than life. His designations and awards were haphazardly thumb-tacked on the wall behind a shelf with a framed photo of all of us: his brother James, Bud, Solomon, and me, fishing in Nehalem the summer before James died. Such a sad death—after surviving gunfire wounds in Korea, he died here from a lung infection he'd gotten over there in that far-reaching, endless war.

In front of the photo was an old rabbit's foot lucky charm Imogene had given him when he went to Germany; it was encased in a glass box.

Bud covered the receiver and said, "You look like shit, old man, gettin' any sleep?"

"Back at ya," I said, dropping into the oak swivel chair in front of his desk.

He finally hung up, dropped his feet to the floor, and said, "Let's grab coffee."

I followed past several beige-clad officers at beige metal desks with metal ashtrays and spirals of thin, white smoke. Beige walls with Wanted posters and lists upon lists of names and photographs of victims and crime scenes surrounded us; such heaviness hung on those walls of government beige. The huge office smelled of cigarette smoke, and even though it had high ceilings and high windows, it was dark—despite all the light that painting nun tried to deliver.

Bud grabbed his hat and said, "Got an open detective desk."

"Not looking for a job," I said as we descended the stairs to the small, crowded cafeteria, where we poured our coffee and spotted a table out of earshot.

"I already got the call," he said as he dumped sugar in his coffee. "We're on it."

"What call?"

"A guard, *who shall remain nameless,* called from the pen. Said you had a visitor."

"Why nameless?"

"You more than most know some politics need to stay in the shadows to be effective."

"Okay. Spies. I get it. Good."

"*Spies* is a bit strong; I like to think of them as wartime allies."

"So does your *ally* know who—"

"Soon as I know, you'll know... Remember that game against the Nehalem Crusaders?"

"Forty-two," I said. "Same year you shipped out. I still have a chipped tooth."

"Yeah, sorry 'bout that, but you ran interference just as planned."

"Yep, you set me up to get steamrolled by that haystack, Withers."

"Touchdown, though. Right?"

"Right," I said. "You trying to tell me I'm a decoy, or that someone's gunning for me?"

"Little a both." Bud stood. "So that quote your mystery visitor repeated— Bible?"

"Yes, but he's too stupid to have picked it, or even understand it. So is Toreck."

"For a preacher," Bud said, "you sure look on the world with an icy stare, my friend."

"That's what highly trained soldiers do." I stood to leave.

"I thought you were a priest now?" Bud grinned.

"Anyway, there's something else going on here. I just can't put my finger on it. And though I don't mind taking a hit, it's the mention of Imogene that worries me."

"Immie'll be fine," Bud said. "And I'll have eyes on you when you're at the pen."

"Whose eyes?" I asked.

"Nameless."

"Oh, right, *he who shall remain nameless.*"

Chapter 27

THEO

THE SECOND LETTER in the stack was thick—five or six pages, dated November 1950. I turned it over and over again, looking at her name, her address, the red stamp across the unopened, sealed back: *Return to Sender*. The heavy envelope smelled of war: dirt, blood, sweat, and the ubiquitous rolling black clouds of napalm—smells that never leave me. I closed my eyes and felt every flashing image.

November 1950 – that letter would be about the parachute assaults on Pyongyang. How we roped supplies and delivered light-armor vehicles, artillery, and troops. And how in November, the Chinese intervened and all hell broke loose. How the frigid morning light always revealed dead soldiers from both sides, tangled in the defensive wire, hanging in a hard-earned, easily shattered silence. *Difficult image to shake.* And I'd have written how memories of her kept me sane; wrote that in every letter.

I wanted a drink but showered and got dressed instead. It was a thorny day for Imogene, so I picked some flowers from Mamaí's garden and put them in a jar of water to take over later. I needed to devise a plan to keep Imogene safe without her knowing what was going on. *Was that even possible?*

Chapter 28

DAILY SPECIAL
Fresh Corn and Red Pepper Chowder and Crab Cakes .75¢

The sun came out of hiding. Rays of gold illuminated the red Folgers cans along aisle two, then danced off the glass freezer doors in the back of the store, reminding me I needed to restock Olympia beer and mudworms. I wrote .20¢ on the cardboard sign in front of the cigarette rack. I swear, when smokes get to thirty cents I *will* quit for sure! But for now, I needed one.

I tucked a pack of Salems in my pocket and stepped out back to sit at my patio table. Birds flocked and chirped at the feeder, sun poured through the lattice, sparkled along the English ivy, then settled softly on Christina's soil. The smell of dirt from my flowerless garden caused a tremble. I was suddenly cold. She would have been three years old today.

In the middle of that soil a tiny twig with a green bud, not an inch tall, had burst through the dirt. I didn't have the energy to yank it out. "What do you want, little twig?"

Then Mrs. B's shutters banged open; wood against wood echoed through the sleepy streets, pulling me back. Soon she'd pass by waving like a silent town crier doing her duty, announcing the day had begun. I gazed at the soil one last time and said, "It's just a day like any other day." Doused my cigarette and went back inside.

The Coca-Cola clock on the wall chimed seven times. Amber flecks of sun struggled through the windows. Theo crossed the street, returning from his walk, half-limping. His beach walking was as obsessive as when Andréa left to spend time with her grandma in Paris. Whatever draws him to beach walk these days didn't matter—I was just glad he was home.

Bud's mushroom-brown patrol car — still boasting two bullet holes in the side door over the insignia TILLAMOOK COUNTY SHERIFF — bolted to a stop at Theo's curb. He got out, slammed the door, leapt the stairs, then disappeared inside. What were they up to?

Frank Sinatra played on the radio. I dusted, shook out the checkered curtains on my two front windows, and lit my memory candles. Usually my mornings were spent cleaning the store and prepping food in the deli before lunch rush, but since Pearl was working with me, there was little to do. It was also nice not to have Thomas watching my every move, saying "You okay?" Real nice. Especially today. I glanced at our lackluster wedding photograph on the corkboard next to the counter. *Imogene and Thomas 1949*. After all we'd been through, now he was like a stranger.

It was tea party day for Mrs. Scovelli and her granddaughters. I set up for them — placed mason jars of daises on the two tableclothed picnic tables, one small jar on the children's table by the back door. Then I opened the bag of party supplies: a new coloring book, some paper dolls, and a box of crayons. I held the crayons close to my face taking in the waxy smell, then set the box down and stared at the small table and four white chairs. My girl would have spent a lot of time coloring and playing at that table. The pink-frosted cake I made last night was in the center of the table next to the dozen pink cupcakes I decorated. I lit one candle in the heart of the cake, stood back, stared at it, and said, "Happy birthday, darling." Then blew it out, no wish — licked the sweet frosting off that candle's end and smoothed the rippled topping with my fingertip so the cake looked untouched. I moved it to the other picnic table for later and set out pink plates for the girls. Two separate events, so closely linked...one table set for death, the other for life.

I took a long drag off a cigarette but the sugary taste lingered.

Across the street Bud and Theo strolled down Theo's steps. Even with his limp Theo moved with the natural, laid-back manner of a trained athlete whose eye was always on some unseen nemesis. Bud in his sheriff's uniform and hat, sunglasses, and cowboy boots was still a confident Marine. Amazing how two different wars on two different continents had shaped the two men I'd known all my life into two men I now wondered if I knew at all.

The rich aroma of fresh-brewed coffee filled the store. I quickly straightened my apron, cinched my hair back, switched the OPEN sign on, and dropped two sugar cubes in Bud's mug just as the screen door squeaked open. "Mornin'," he said. "Mornin' guys," I said opening the register drawer. The "no sale" sign sprang up. I checked the money and pointed to the coffee pot. The light was green, their cups ready.

"Mornin', sis," Theo said setting down a jar of picked daisies—weeds Mamaí tried so hard to kill every year that now grew like wildflowers in the backyard. Then he glanced at the lit candles and photos on the wall shelf, took off his fedora, ran his fingers through his hair, and nodded to our dearly departed.

"I'm fine, guys," I said, because they both stood staring at me. "Just fine."

"Good," Bud said taking off his wire-rimmed sunglasses. In those glasses he looked like a hardened police officer, even to me. But once he took them off, those steely eyes turned to soft cornflower blue, and his tan, skinned face crinkled slightly when he smiled. I nodded toward his and Theo's cups. Bud grabbed his, tucked his glasses into the shirt pocket beneath his badge, and beelined for the coffee pot. Theo followed.

Bud's sandy hair had been newly cropped so close to his skull that his square jaw and wide forehead were even more prominent than usual. "Fresh cut?" I asked.

"Yep," he responded, returning to where I stood counting pennies. "Ole Frank over in Nehalem's chargin' forty cents for haircuts now; that's too rich for my blood." He leaned on the counter, his face not ten inches from my hands, watching as though studying my skin.

I felt his eyes on me and smelled his zesty aftershave. His rough, square hands, nearly the size of a shovel, cupped his steaming coffee mug.

"You look good." He smiled. "Hair's gettin' long, like when you were in high school."

"Thanks... Thomas doesn't like it long, though."

"Right," he said, then stood up straight, clearing his throat. "How is the old guy?"

"Who knows. He used to call in the mornings."

"He'll call today, kid," he said. "Sellin' timber's hard work. All that travel."

"Yeah, I guess," I said. "But these days he's just gone, then he returns— no pomp, no circumstance, no nothing."

"Right," Bud said. Just then Solomon's bench banged against the wall as he plunked down on it. Bud poured a cup of coffee and took it out to him.

Theo stood by the window, reading the newspaper. Pearl rushed through the door with her arms wrapped around a bouquet of gladiolas the width of her entire upper body. "Mornin' Teo," she said as she raced behind the counter to give me a long, one-armed hug. She smelled of spices and wore her favorite polka dot shirt with her same old plaid pants.

Mrs. B came through the door wearing her best cheongsam, the green one, with her ivory combs in her hair and several rings on her fingers. Bud and Solomon followed her inside. They all gathered near the other picnic table.

Pearl put the flowers in a large vase and joined them with her two cups of tea. The clock chimed nine times. They all sat silently on the benches.

"It's a beautiful cake," Mrs. B said.

Everyone nodded. Pearl quietly set out plates and forks and handed me the knife. I cut into the cake, one piece at a time, and laid each piece on a plate. Theo passed the plates down to the others while Mrs. B, whose hooch cane had been hollowed out during prohibition, and was now a constant companion from what she called the "dark years" dispensed brandy into everyone's coffee. Then I put the knife down, sat on the bench next to Theo, and stared at my piece of crumbling pink cake.

Bud cleared his throat and said, "It's delicious. Cherry?"

My eyes burned. "Yeah," I said. "Cherry. But this is the last birthday cake. I'll set up a candle and be done with it."

Theo put his arm around me, kissed my head, and whispered, "It's a beautiful cake, love. And grief... it takes however long it takes. You be done when you're done."

"Well," I said. "It took three years. I'll light that candle today. Set her, us, free."

Everyone held their glasses up and said, "To Christina."

Chapter 29

THEO

PEARL AND IMOGENE prepared for the tea party that would ensue at ten. Both childless, they made those once-a-month tea parties major events.

Mrs. B sat down next to me and said, "We were plenty worried about our girl after the baby died. Somethin' just cracked. Then living with that glummy-gus Thomas only made things worse. I think now he's gone, *and I hope he's gone*, she's finally on the mend. She's lookin' and actin' like Imogene again, don't ya think?"

"I do," I said. "Wish I'd been here then."

"You are now."

"I'm glad *you* were."

"Couldn't of kept me away," she said. Mrs. B still had a stunning face, a certain undeniable, regal grace: white hair, tan skin, and sapphire eyes. Her ivory combs were a crown—fading vestiges of a tattered queen.

She stood and gave Imogene a long, silent hug, patted her back, then grasped both her shoulders and kissed her forehead. Mamaí said Mrs. B was at Imogene's side daily for two months after the baby died—no better comrade in a battle. And now a great ally in resurrection.

* * *

After everyone left I looked for Imogene's Winchester.

"Where's that gun you usually keep behind the counter?"

"There," she said pointing to the rifle butt that peeked out from beneath her apron. "It's empty, though. Why?"

"You should have cartridges," I said picking it up and checking the loader. Empty.

"I do, they're at your house. Mamaí kept them in her jewelry box."

"Your shells are in her jewelry box?"

"Yes, and your socks are in her hutch," Imogene said as she stacked the dirty cake plates.

"I'll bring them over later."

"Your socks?"

"The cartridges for that gun... *I see you're feeling better.*"

"I don't like to have loaded guns—"

"I know, but while I'm doing the prison ministry I think we should all step it up a bit. Some of those thugs get out, you know."

"And head straight for Manzanita?"

"Yes, of course," I said. "They're handed a map to here as soon as they're released."

She laughed, lit a cigarette, and said, "You know those are weeds, right?"

"What?" I looked at the drooping daisies. "They look like flowers. Anyway, seriously... Yesterday, a prisoner made some comments. We need to be careful."

"Okay," she said. "Go ahead, load it... I like the idea of shootin' somethin' right now."

"How many nips did you have?"

She held up her hand to gesture "Just a little," and said, "You see Toreck yesterday?"

"Actually I did see hi... he's fine."

"Oh good, I was worried. Nice to know he's in excellent hands."

"Yep. He's in good hands."

"Was it him who said what was said that made you want to load my Winchester?"

"No, that's what worries me. I think he's makin' friends."

"Toreck make friends?"

"Prison's a different kind of world," I said. "Friends come more in the form of allies."

"Well, I'm glad we helped his family, but will that good deed come back to bite?"

"Maybe, but I can handle it."

"I'm sorry you had to get beat up and all. Then Suzy... Losin' a child is so hard."

"Save your sympathy for the Wu family," I said.

"Did you see a lot of dead bodies in Korea?"

"Well, it was *war*," I said, watching Bud outside checking in on his car radio.

"It's just all so awful," she said, pouring another daub of brandy into her coffee. "Why do you do what you do? I just don't get it."

"Not again, Imogene."

She glanced at our brother's photo on her shelf and said, "He faithfully went to mass with Mamaí, prayed to a God on a cloud somewhere just waitin' to grant sacred prayers—but you didn't go. So why do you still try to fill his shoes, bein' *two* sons for parents who lost one? The shelf's full. Everyone's gone. Why now? I sure as hell don't care."

I showed her the *Tribune* and said, "Did you see this? First the Soviet Union's sending dogs into space; now *we're* sending monkeys."

"Hey," she said. "Let's send Toreck up with those monkeys... *That's* a good idea."

"I think you're onto something."

Bud came inside. "It's quiet in town."

"No Toreck," Imogene said.

"Well, no need to worry about him," he said.

"What's he gonna do when he gets out?" she asked.

"Ah, honey, that's five years down the road," he said. "Now, what's for lunch today?"

Chapter 30

THEO

THE SHELLS for the rifle were in Mamaí's jewelry box just like Imogene said. There was also paperwork and a faded photograph of Solomon standing in front of his home in our backyard. In the photo his crooked chimney sprouted up like a chimney sweeper's old top hat from the sloped, shingled roof on his hut—a thing of much curiosity in my younger years. Carved out of a still-rooted, mammoth Sitka spruce that had been felled sometime in the mid-eighteen hundreds. That massive tree trunk had been his family's abode since. Like the many Leprechaun stories firmly planted in my imagination and carried across the sea from Ireland, here was a man who actually lived inside a tree in our backyard. Of course "our backyard" was once his family's property. Still, it didn't get much more fantastical to the mind of a child.

The date in the corner of the photo read nineteen thirty-five. I slipped the relic into the envelope of papers, set the envelope on the dining room table in the pile of all the other papers I still hadn't dealt with, and headed back to Imogene's before her lunch rush began.

Solomon was seated on his bench in front of the store waiting for the Great Grandfather to give him wisdom for the day.

"Mornin'," I said.

With his head tilted back and eyes closed, he said, "When you look into eyes of archenemy, you see your destiny—then it creeps along your spine until it is fulfilled."

"Okaaay… "

"You have seen your destiny."

"I lived."

"No," he said. "Not Korea, not that bullet in your leg. This destiny comes soon."

"We're keeping a lookout for Toreck."

"It is not Toreck."

"Who, then?"

"Toreck is trouble, but he is small trouble. The other enemy, large man with spirit black as pirate's sand. He is more than trouble—he is evil."

He then waved his wrinkled hand for me to leave and immediately slid back into his ruminations. His head tilted back; the sun glistened off his high cheekbones, illuminating the map of a thousand journeys on his craggy face. His weathered hands lay on his lap; his fingernails, the soft goldenrod color of grain and thick as an eagle's talons, had dark soil permanently ground beneath them. Scars covered his tawny forearms, every scar, every bit of earth on his skin part of his journey through this world to the next. I envied him for knowing who he was, what he was here for, and where he was going. How he lived in constant awareness of his own mortality with a gentle knowing that he was part of something bigger than himself. But what destiny did he see for me?

* * *

Inside, Imogene recuperated from her morning, sat at one of the tables with Mrs. Scovelli and her five- and six-year-old granddaughters and their friend for their tea party.

"Morning, ladies," I said.

"Morning, Father Theo," they sang in their little girl voices.

The smell of maple syrup wafted through the store. Pearl was in the back kitchen sloshing pots and pans in the sink and murmuring to herself.

The little girls sat with pink cloth napkins on their laps, pink cupcakes on their tiny pink plates, and miniature pink teacups with actual tea. They wore ribbons in their hair, strands of pearls, and ruffled dresses. Imogene gently patted their curly heads, offered cakes, milk, and honey, fluttering around them like a protective butterfly afraid to land.

Behind the counter I grabbed the Winchester, held it out of their eyesight, cocked it open, and quietly loaded the shells. Pearl's dark eyes watched me from behind the kitchen curtain. She nodded and kept rolling dough on the chopping block. I locked the magazine and stood it back up in the corner, hidden behind an apron, hoping neither of our girls ever needed to use it.

Chapter 31

THEO

THE BEACH WAS ABANDONED. Silver waters shimmered; word of Suzy's fate and no suspects sent the late-season tourists packing. I skipped a pebble atop the waves looking for Solomon's White Sea Otter to bob up and down in the water. Early winter is when she returned, searching for what remained of his people, to guide them to the next world. They believed that her gift, *to see her*, was to set a pained spirit free. I studied the flickering waves like an Irish fisherman searching the sea for a beautiful Selkie.

The first time Da had seen the beach, he stood at the edge of Laneda Avenue, flung his arms into the air, and shouted, "Dammit Fiona! Ya brung us to the bloody end a the world, woman!" He'd looked at the Pacific Ocean as if it were a prison far from his dreams of Ireland.

Mamaí had tightened her grip on my hand. I'd tightened mine on Imogene's. In that moment, and forever more it became the three of us against him, against the world. What for him had been the end of a narrow globe became for me a vast, colorful center of the universe, a cosmos wherein Korea was a black- and-white hell; Ireland, a tumultuous moss-green heaven; and Solomon, an earth-bound god with spirit guides. And a White Sea Otter that, like a Selkie, traversed two worlds.

In my gut I felt that soon all those worlds would collide and that Solomon was right: I needed to be ready for a fight. But if Toreck was trouble, and of course he always was, who was the evil one? I headed home to prepare.

* * *

The walnut grip of my Ek commando knife was worn, nicked, and sturdy as ever. As I held it, a release, a feeling of readiness filled me. More than any gun, a knife made me feel capable and prepared. As I shined its double edges, a thousand images came to life—shook them off, took my leather sheath from the drawer, secured it to the side of my left boot; with my right hip buggered, it would be easier to grab my knife from the left side.

My black army boots hadn't been worn in a couple years. Took them and my shoe-shine supplies to the back porch. As the sun set I finished my spit-shine and put the waxy-smelling brush back into the wooden box; Solomon came up the stairs. "Evening," I said.

He sat, gazed out over our shared yard and his hut where a thin, grey smoke puffed from his chimney, and said, "Read letters?"

"I'm close," I said, breathing in the vanilla smell of burning ponderosa pine. Smoke hovered close to the earth. Against the orange sunset the oak tree's shadow overwhelmed our orchard of three trees; red apples scattered on the ground beneath them.

"Which wolf do you feed?" he asked, glancing down at my leather knife sheath.

"Not sure yet. Can't tell if the letters make me angry, sad, or numb… can't even come up with a prayer. When I hold one in my hands, it's heavy, and then the dates… images attached to those dates come to life… rushing back. Everything that happened, that I did, saw, smelled, experienced. It all comes back."

"Your whiskey, prayers, and church ceremonies won't help *this* pain," he said. "Burn them. Fire ceremony will cleanse wound. You remember ceremonies?"

"I remember."

Chapter 32

THEO

DURING MY FIRST YEAR in America, nineteen thirty-three, I was a good student of Solomon's.

The Saturday just before my eleventh birthday I hurriedly did my chores, then sprang off the back porch and ran to his hut. Most summer days were spent with him, but this day was to be a special one. It was the day I was to become a warrior, announce my warrior name.

Anxious as I was, he made me sit at his hickory table and wait. Wiggling my legs, tapping my thumbs, looking around while he fidgeted with his baskets. His cabin was filled with shipwreck memorabilia—beeswax, oars, ship odds and ends. He was rumored to have found gold from one of the lost Spanish galleons. I never saw a sign of it—*and I looked*.

Finally, we set out for our ritual climb up the sixteen-hundred-foot peak of Manzanita's sacred mountain, Neahkahnie, which means "place of the deity." We made a circle of rocks and built a small fire. He lit his rolled tobacco leaves, the length of a corncob, and placed them on a log causing the fire to spit, spatter, and crackle. We looked out fifty miles over the shimmering blue-grey waters of the Pacific Ocean. Three eagles soared above the ancient Sitkas.

Below us, shrouded in red maples, zigzagged the long dirt path to Manzanita. Behind us, jagged old-growth spruces dripped with moss. In the shadows of one tree I saw the dark eyes of Solomon's spirit wolf watching us—above him, a black raven. I'd seen them together before. Right then I decided to alter the warrior name I'd thought long and hard on.

The evergreens swayed to the whispers of Solomon's Great Grandfather, who I knew as the wind, or my Catholic mother's God. We stood in silence. Tobacco smoke filled my senses. He motioned for me to sit on the ground. I did, folding my legs like his; waited for him to speak.

"Eagle flies high," Solomon said as he pointed to the three eagles that circled in the cloudless sky. "Sees farther than all creatures… Eagle is messenger to Creator. To hold or wear Eagle feather causes Creator to take notice… This feather honors Creator in the highest." He took a large eagle feather from his suede medicine bundle—it was from the hallowed headdress of his father's father—and with both hands held it up to the sky; a sacred offering. Then he lowered it, smoothed the tip with his sinewy fingers, and said, "This gift honors receiver with great love and respect." He looked me over; my spine stiffened. "First step to become warrior." Prisms of gold light flickered in his dark eyes. "When man becomes warrior, warrior heart drums in that man, rest of his days." He set the feather down on his medicine bag, took a burning ember from the fire, and held it in his hand.

"Do you remember your lessons… what it means to be a warrior?"

"To seek truth," I said. "Protect the weak, honor the pain of others, respect the earth and all living things, fight for justice, atone for death, and understand the cost."

"And the cost?"

"A life for a life."

"The price?"

"Eternal vigilance, sacrifice so others may have peace, love, and family."

"A warrior's duty?"

"A warrior is responsible for the garden of life."

"The reward?"

"Hope, internal vision, a better future."

"Good," he said, then placed that hot coal in my hand. "That fire now burns in you."

Without flinching I stared at my blackened palm, felt the burn on my skin marking me.

"Know who you are," he said. "Know that fire in hand now grows in your heart and lives in your blood. A warrior owns his soul. No man can take your soul or poison your mind; silence your heart. A warrior is forever fierce, forever awake, forever alive in his task. Now, close your eyes and call on your spirit power; announce your warrior name."

I closed my eyes tight, tilted my head to the sky, and called out, "I am Raven Two Fists! A warrior!" Then opened my eyes. That raven now perched on a tree limb tilted his head toward me, took flight and circled, swooped down, and then perched on the log at my side.

"*Duh-HOOTS-nuh* … Good name," Solomon said, holding the white-tipped feather.

Thunderstruck and trembling, I bowed my head, raised up my hands, and accepted the grand treasure, understanding that what I did in Ireland, what Mamaí was so afraid of, was not a thing of shame or something for which to be forgiven, but a warrior's act. I held my head high.

"Sacred tobacco must be burnt." Solomon blew into the tobacco bundle. White smoke spiraled to the sky. "In this way Eagle and Creator are notified of name of new holder of feather. Creator," he called to the sky. His hair fluttered in the wind. "This boy Theo is now warrior, Raven Two Fists." He closed his eyes and laid his strong hand on my head. A bolt of intoxicating energy spiked down my back, taking my breath away.

"It is done," he said and abruptly removed his hand. "Creator watch over you now."

We smothered the fire with dirt and damp leaves and prepared to descend the path home. I wanted to run, anxious to tell Mamaí and Imogene. Da wouldn't have cared.

Solomon pointed up to the tree and said, "That Raven... he waits for you." He wrapped a rag around my bleeding palm. "There are many things beyond our knowledge. It is power of the unknown at work. That Raven, he is your spirit animal. He sees your long journey. Day will come; he will lead you back to this holy place."

Chapter 33

THEO

THE BLUE GULL CAFÉ was shaped like a railroad car with windows along one side. Six booths overlooked the busy parking lot of the Tillamook Cheese Factory. In the center of the narrow room were four two-person tables and a long stainless steel counter with five swivel stools. From there diners had a view of the perpetually red-faced cook pulling tickets off the wheel, shouting, "Up!" and slapping plates of greasy burgers on the shelf for the waitress to pick up. The blonde bombshell waitress, whose nametag read Betty-Jo, poured me a cup of coffee and said, "Mornin' Father."

"Morning. Seen Bud yet?"

She turned over the other coffee cup, poured it full and said, "He's pullin' in right now." She nodded outside to his patrol car and walked away, straightening her hair. She put the coffee back on the burner; behind the counter she looked into a small mirror, quickly dabbed red lipstick on her lips, smacked them together, and dusted her bangs to the side.

The cook pounded on the bell and shouted, "Order up, Blondie!"

The bell on the café door sounded. Bud came through, took off his hat, smiled, and nodded at Betty-Jo. She smiled, pointing to my booth.

"Ham slams, side a scramble," the cook barked hitting the bell three times. "Gonna give you a wig-wallopin' you don't get these out, *now!*"

"I don't wear wigs, ya old goat," she mumbled as she grabbed the orders.

"Mornin'," Bud said dropping into the booth; he immediately spooned sugar into his cup. "What's got you in town today?" he asked taking a sip, his eyes watching Betty-Jo carry two "ham slams" to the booth behind me.

"Just up," I said. "Couldn't sleep; needed a drive and some coffee, a good bacon hash."

Betty-Jo came to our booth, took out her pad and pencil, and said, "Mornin' handsome," to Bud.

"Mornin' sweetie," he said. "We'll take two bacon hashes and one of those cinnamon rolls I smell. Or is that *you* smellin' all sugary sweet?"

I squeezed my eyes shut, unable to bear witness to the hackneyed flirtations.

"Officer Grearson... You're just a crime waitin' to happen," she said, then flipped her pad closed, turned, and walked away. Bud watched.

"So is it Betty-Jo, Blondie, or Sweetie?" I asked.

"Just call her Betty-Jo. Like her name badge says. She hates those nicknames. Of course, she loves it when *I* call her 'sweetie,' but given your tight collar and all, it might not be appropriate for you." His grin was wide and sarcastic.

"Why don't you just ask her for a date and get this torture over with?"

"Date?" he said. "Why would I do that?"

"Well, hate to worry the winsome or jangle the jaded here, but the way you two go on—"

"Why ruin a perfect relationship. Besides, she's married to the cook."

"Well... " I glanced at the cook, who sneered at the customers seated at the counter. "Okay, then."

"Case you haven't noticed, I'm not the datin' or marryin' kind," Bud said. "So, what brings you to the big city, Father Riley?"

"Just breakfast, finding out what you've heard, then back to town."

"I think it was just a well-played prank. Probably Sealy gettin' some lackey to do his dirty work. I wouldn't worry about it."

"Yeah, probably," I said. "It's just he mentioned Imogene—"

"I didn't say *I* wasn't gonna worry about it, I said *you* don't need to. I'll be followin' this till it's over. Whatever *over* means."

"Okay, but you'll keep me posted, right?"

"Sure," he said. "You look like hell, man, like you haven't slept in days."

"Sleep comes and goes."

"Maybe it's that job a yours. All those confessions, people's secrets, funerals and crap. It's depressing the shit you have to deal with."

"This from a man who deals with crime and criminals all day, every day."

"Yeah, but I have a chance to do something. You pretty much come in after the fact."

"I like to think I make a difference."

"I know ya do, little buddy."

"*Little buddy*?"

Betty-Jo laid our hot plates on the table, took Tabasco sauce out of her apron pocket, and set it in front of Bud's plate. "There ya go. It's hot. Don't burn those lips, now." She winked and sashayed away. Bud leaned out of the booth, watching.

"I'll pray for you," I said grabbing the Tabasco and dotting my eggs.

"Pray for yourself, little buddy."

"Okay, as a kid I hated it when you called me 'little buddy,' and I—"

"Yeah, I know. But should a priest really *hate*?" He smiled and dug into his breakfast.

"Hatin' you right now," I said, digging into mine.

"Oz says you carry a tin soldier in your pocket," Bud said. "What's that about?"

"Long story."

"I got time."

"It was my brother's," I said. "But that was a long time ago. Doesn't matter now."

Betty-Jo dropped off a warm, sugary-smelling cinnamon roll the size of a dinner plate.

We both glanced out the window at a sudden ruckus—a rowdy group of Tillamook High boys piled out of a glossy red 1953 Chevy Bel Air.

"Those boys there, lookin' for trouble on this fine sunny day," Bud said. "On the prowl, just like you and my little brother in high school. You boys were into four things: boxing, cars, booze, and girls. And pretty much in that order."

"Good ol' James," I said, watching the boys climb into a blue convertible with some girls, then squeal out of the parking lot. "We were kids. Things change."

"Maybe," he said, glancing at my knuckles. "How's those knuckles?"

"They're toughening up."

"Your old buddy, Murphy?"

"We're seeing a lot less of each other these days."

"Your mom's car looks shiny and new like the classic it is."

"Yeah, so?"

"Yeah, so number four, who's the girl?"

"What girl?"

"The girl I see written all over your sleep-deprived face... your early morning walks, the way you box the shit outta your bag. That girl."

"Oh, that girl."

"She in Korea?"

I shook my head no.

"She dead?"

"*Dead*... no."

We finished our breakfast in silence. Betty-Jo brought more coffee and took our plates.

"So," Bud said, lighting a cigarette. "I heard the Bouvre girl came to town and packed up the house. Heard that asshole lawyer Mr. Bouvre died and the family finally sold it."

"Yeah, I heard that, too."

"Did you see her?"

"See who?"

"The girl you couldn't take your eyes off every summer since you were ten years old. The girl you fell in love with but for some dumbass reason broke it off."

"I saw her."

"Did you talk to her?"

"I'm a priest now."

"Yeah, well, I've seen you talk to women."

"She's married now."

"Heard she's divorced," he said. "Still a real looker, that one."

I took a crisp two-dollar bill out of my wallet and said, "This one's on me."

"You gonna tell me about that tin soldier?"

"Not today," I said.

"The girl?"

"Not today."

"What *are* you gonna do today?"

"Drive back to town with the information you *didn't* give me."

Chapter 34

GENGHIS

THE YARD WAS FULL. Muscle-bound fools with prying eyes, everywhere. I spotted Toreck; two new black eyes (fresh out of solitary confinement after pitchin' a screamin' fit at a guard). I took my tray to his table, sat down, and handed over my piece of corn bread. I hated corn bread; besides, it's important to feed your pets.

One-eyed Joe looked across the table at me like I was crazy. "Boo!" I said. He looked away and minded his own muddled-up business.

"Thanks," Toreck said tearing into the offering. His knuckles were split and bruised. I figured he'd finally got the piss beat out of himself and could maybe listen to reason.

"That priest a yours should be here today," I said.

"He's not *my* priest. He's not my nothin'," Toreck said through his food — *disgusting.*

I glanced away and said, "You know Nehalem well?"

"Shit, man, grew up there, why?"

"Met a guy there, lets me use his cabin."

"Who?"

"Gary somethin'."

"Gary Hiccurs?" Toreck raised his brow. "That old geezer shot at me once — don't let nobody come near his place. Why you?"

"Oh, we just have an understanding," I said, picturing the shocked look on Gary Hiccurs's face when I shoved his own knife into his belly.

"Hiccurs used to dig for gold up on Neahkahnie, 'fore my time, but he said he found some. Never seen it, though."

"Gold, huh," I said real low. "Well, we could use some of that. Was it pirate's gold?"

"Yeah, and I was close... real close to findin' it," Toreck said. "Hiccurs don't like cripples." He glanced at my hand. "Don't see him takin' to you."

"Oh, that hand works jus' fine now that cast is off. It jus' don't look so good." I wiggled the three fingers that wiggled and said, "It's more like a strong hook. I can make a fightin' fist, drive a car, and do just about anything else you can imagine." *Not that I thought Toreck had any imagination.* "It's just my ring and pinky finger that's all folded over."

"How'd that happen?"

"Snake bite," I said. "I was a kid; pigmy rattler, very rare snake. Destroyed the nerves in the left side of my hand. Anyway, we can use that cabin when we get out."

"We? Out?" Toreck mumbled as he gazed around the yard for guards or prying eyes.

"Yeah, out. I could use a partner like you. We'll find that gold," I whispered. "Now, let's be sure to be cooperative, not rebellious or otherwise foolish, till your time's done."

Toreck rubbed his bruised knuckles and said, "These dicks—"

"These 'dicks' have the power fer now. Don't be misled; bad company corrupts good character. Are you of good character, Toreck?"

"Soundin' like a preacher again," he said, still surveying the room. He sneered at one-eyed Joe, then looked at me and said, "Okay. I'm in. How?"

"You'll get out on good behavior... a shortened sentence. After all, it was just a fight."

"*With a priest.*"

"Yeah," I said, "but he'll forgive and forget. It's his job."

"What about you?"

"Oh, don't you worry, I'll orchestrate somethin' divine. Don't ya worry 'bout me at all."

Chapter 35

THEO

ON THE FRONT PORCH was the *Tribune*. NO SUSPECTS IN SUZY WU CASE. "Her two front teeth were missing and she loved rainbows," the article stated. I couldn't read it.

Down the street, Mrs. B, out for her morning walk, was already past Pearl's. We Rounders set our clocks by the rhythm of her life, the pounding of her lopsided footsteps and her cane hitting the ground mid-stride, clip, clip, hard against our one paved sidewalk. When she walked, it was time for Imogene to turn on the OPEN sign. It was time for coffee, for newspapers, for mail— for the welcome noises of day.

In Korea I'd often close my eyes, terrified. I couldn't grasp the concept of God watching over me, but I could imagine the sound of Mrs. B's cane, daydream that bombs dropping so near my life were not bombs, but instead were the pounding of her steadfast, booze-filled walking stick: click, click, click. The sound of life, not death. Even in the jagged mountains or marshy lowlands of Korea, when the grazing fire from machine guns filled the night, I closed my eyes and envisioned all of Manzanita: the tiny stone church where, on Sundays, fifteen or twenty parishioners' voices raised in song until the tiny chapel vibrated in holy harmony. Hidden in foxholes, the world ablaze around me, I'd nod my head to the beat of their hymns until that cadence took over the sound of helicopters that pulsed through me. Then, I'd move my hand up and down, feeling the meditative strokes of my paintbrush on all my summer jobs when I was seventeen: the fence, motel, laundry, Mamaí's, now Imogene's store; and imagined Solomon keeping guard of our universe. Those things I could imagine.

* * *

Mrs. B disappeared down the beach path. I closed the door.

The last week there'd been a rash around the scar in the palm of my hand and around my neck from the white collar bands, so I put some salve on both, secured the collar very loosely, and walked the two blocks to Saint Mary's.

Rumpled brown leaves drifted earthbound to the ground, settling in heaps and mounds around the mud puddles at the edge of the gravel-flanked road. The sugar-and-cinnamon smell of pumpkin pie drifted through Manzanita. Trees were nearly bare. I took a deep, energizing breath and walked on, trying to think of how to console the Wu family and recalling the whispers of that prisoner with the twisted hand whom I denied absolution. Why, when I think of Suzy Wu, does he come to mind? I'd pictured him several times since that day; couldn't shake his voice. And that prisoner who said "pretty sister"? Couldn't shake him either.

To purge my disenchantment with mankind, I cleaned the rectory shelves while the Church Ladies played their "Bingo" and gossiped.

Ibbie McFall shuffled the cards and, with her spindly fingers and papery-skinned thin arms, skillfully handed out the "Bingo" cards and chips. Mrs. Scovelli picked up her cards with her large hands and smiled. She wore a pink sweater with a plunging neckline and a hanky tucked into her wrinkled cleavage. On days when there were no funerals, she wore red lipstick on her thin lips—lips that, when parted, revealed huge tar-stained teeth.

I preferred them in their funeral black. At least then everything was covered up.

Emma Whittle didn't smile at her cards; instead, her brow rutted; the skin on her skeletal face dripped like candle wax and settled in soft pink puddles beneath her chin. She folded her cards and laid them on the table. "I'm out," she said, glancing at the clock.

"That's the same kind of Bingo we played in college," I said.

"Is that so," Permelia said as she set a red chip in the center of the table. "Imagine that."

"Mm hm." I went back to repairing the shelves.

Soon their talk turned to bitter gossip about the Wu family: her grandfather had been "*Chinese*," Sibbie whispered, as if Chinese were synonymous with syphilis.

Ibbie nodded, "Yes, one of those filthy boats." Her round, dark eyes bugged out from her gaunt face, and her long neck was roped with sinews. "Those yellow women are immoral." She lowered her voice and said, "They're raised as concubines and have s–e–x with anyone they want. And they're lazy thieves, too." They all nodded in conspiratorial accord.

"That's it!" I shouted, jumping down from the ladder. "What is it, the eighteen hundreds? Get out!"

Sibbie's portly face dropped, "Father Theo—"

"No, you're done here," I said, scraping all their "Bingo" crap into a box. "Game's over."

"What happened?" Permelia grabbed her purse and stood.

"I've had it with your gossip. You talk about anyone whose skin's not as white as—wait a minute, let's look at some facts *for once*. Sibbie, Ibbie." They clutched onto one another. "Wasn't your grandad a murderin', thievin' Irish gangster? And Emma Whittle, your mother a Russian saloon girl who landed a rich German refugee, Mr. Whitenstein? Whittled that name down. Easy to alter the truth, isn't it? And you," I said turning to Mrs. Scovelli, who reeled back. "Where do I start? Scovelli? *Italian?*" She flinched as I yanked the last "Bingo" card from her hefty hand. "A *spik?*" I stopped myself before saying Permelia's grandmother was black.

Their jaws collectively dropped. I crammed their "Bingo" supplies into the cupboard. "So there's your gossip, ladies," I said and slammed it shut. "The thing is, nobody gives a damn! And if I ever hear you speak of a child again, dead or alive, with your narrowminded ugliness, I'll bloody excommunicate you myself!"

Sibbie's hands drew to her mouth in horror. "Father Riley!"

Ibbie tugged on Sibbie's arm to leave. They plucked their belongings from the floor, ran from the church as if the building were on fire, and piled into their Packard, locking the doors. I followed them out. Their engine roared. Sibbie slapped her hand on the dashboard Bible. Their faces pinched, puckered, and shriveled like rotting apples, giving me their collective evil eye. The car rolled out of the parking lot in slow motion. They all gawked at me through the windows like I was a derelict just let out of prison. I shouted, "And no more POKER in church!"

Chapter 36

THEO

THE WU FAMILY lived on a small chicken ranch outside of Nehalem off Northfork Road, which ran parallel to the Nehalem River. The thick pines and once colorful maples, now exposed, reached their spindly branches to the darkening sky: unfinished sculptures begging their maker to complete them, all hugging the highway to Nehalem.

As I turned to go up their gravel drive, I saw Mr. Wu, a local fisherman, in his rowboat in the middle of the Nehalem River. He wore a black suit and was hunched over, holding his head. Beside the boat his black hat floated in the water. His grief-stricken posture was that of a man laden by undeserving guilt—because Suzy went missing while he was in China visiting family. They had to wait a few weeks for him to arrive home before they could have her service.

The stairs to their porch were lined with flowers and baskets of fruit. Many of the drawings Suzy had done in Sunday School were hung on the porch rail. My gut twisted as I recalled her handing me those drawings each Sunday. Now, like my clown fish, she and her vivid colors were gone.

Suzy's grandmother, Bao-yu, had no creases on her face, but her hands were wrinkled and grey; she rocked in her wooden chair on the porch. Stone-faced, she stared at Solomon, who sat silently in the yard. Their Chinese custom dictated that elders grieve a child's death in silence because they aren't to show respect for anyone younger.

Solomon had been a good friend to her husband before he died many years back. They worked the railroad together in the early nineteen hundreds. The Wu family honored Solomon with a bowl of oranges, sweet cakes, and a glass of rice wine. He wore his mourning blanket around his shoulders. Beside him two peacocks had settled in, their iridescent aqua-colored feathers folded beneath their plump bodies, beaks buried in their wings.

Their house smelled of a honeyed green tea—reminded me of Korea. The Wu family sat in their small living room in front of a carved redwood altar with a statue of Buddha, a picture of Christ, a large school photograph of Suzy, burning incense, and plates of oranges for their deity.

Silence was all I had to offer. I never found the words to console them.

Suzy's mother, Mrs. Wu, kept patting my shoulder and saying, "Thank you." Thank you for what, I didn't know. Two hours passed. Women kept handing me plates of piquant food. Though not hungry, I ate their offerings of fried rice, crab dumplings, grief, and misplaced gratitude.

The cuckoo clock on their wall announced with a loud rooster's screech that it was five o'clock. Solomon stood, came inside, and placed his hand on Mrs. Wu's shoulder. She silently nodded, then closed her eyes. He motioned for me to take him home.

Mrs. Wu stood, wrapped her arms around me, and said, "Thank you."

"Mrs. Wu, I appreciate it, but thank you for what?"

"You will find the man who took my child," she said, "and you will kill him."

"Mrs. Wu, I'm a priest, not a police officer. I'm sure they'll do everything they can—"

"No, is you. Burden of righteousness lives in your heart," she said patting my lapel.

She disappeared into a kitchen full of mourners; a handful of guests gathered at the table of food. Many of them watched me, smiled, nodded, and spoke in Chinese to one another. I felt they could see through me: where I'd been, what I'd done, how many with faces like theirs I'd killed. I wasn't a priest in Korea; I was a soldier.

The air grew stagnant; the house swelled with mourners. Towering over them like a tree that had sprung up in their den—and suddenly feeling naked in a room of witnesses to my guilt, shame, and incapacity—I grabbed my hat and quickly drifted through the shrinking, crowded house to the front door where, once outside, I gasped for air.

Solomon was seated in the car; the two peacocks stood in full regalia at the bumper. A bottle of Murphy's teased me from the glove box, but this wasn't a time for weakness. I quietly got in and started the car. For the ten-minute drive home, neither of us said a word.

I parked. Solomon got out and went inside his hut.

That reporter, Hugh something, was seated on my porch banister, cigarette pinched between his fingers, waiting. "Father Riley," he said as he stood. "May I—"

"Not today," I said, slamming the door behind me.

* * *

There was no fire that night; no incense, no incantations. Just Solomon's closed door. The osprey was on her perch outside his gate. The owl in the oak tree, no hooting, eyes closed. The air vibrated from the silence. I sat on my porch until night fell and kept picturing Mr. Wu hunched over in his boat in the middle of the river, holding his head. When the ink-black night consumed Solomon's totem, I went inside.

Before dawn I leapt from bed, trembling and confused. For a moment I was surrounded by CCF. Straw-colored faces emerged from a mist. Angry, peering eyes and knifed bayonets. I reached for my knife, then jarred awake. I fully came to, then loaded my .38 for the first time in two years.

Chapter 37

THEO

SUZY'S REAL GRAVE was now filled with a pool of water and delicate sea anemones. Silver-blue waves whipped into a foamy white fury just inches away. I'd never pass it again without seeing her face. Life, so fragile. How did her tiny body end up there?

Heat from the sun blazed against my black pants. The .38, which I hadn't carried in years, was heavy, yet comfortable in my waistband against my back. Winds rustled through the soft grasslands that protected the beach, the sweet smell of blackberries permeated the air, butterflies whispered—hushed angels on a cloudless late October day.

I settled on an immense rock, squinted my eyes against the sun's glare, and searched for answers in the glass-like waters. Answers to how to erase the images of those sweet children in Korea that looked so much like Suzy Wu, or how to extract the sounds of them playing and singing their songs in my waking memory. How could I silence it all? I searched for answers, a way to bury the image of those hushed angels deeper inside, or somehow toss them into a gentle sea of forgetting. I searched. No answers. No forgetting. Not today.

* * *

As I returned to town, Bud was leaving. He rolled down the window and said, "May finally have a lead in the Wu case. I'm off to Tillamook. You armed?"

"Yeah," I said. "I'll stay in town all day."

"See ya tonight." He drove off.

Solomon was on his bench, sharpening his hunting knife on a palm-sized grindstone. He looked up at me and said, "Your fists, sore?"

"Yeah," I said, looking down at the fading bruises on my knuckles. "But stronger."

"You're a southpaw," he said. "'Bobber and weaver,' newspaper writers said. Your coach said your head was 'elusive target' and that was your strength, no matter what weight you fight."

"That was a long time ago," I said. "Most of them tried to convert me from my southpaw ways—turn me around and have me take a right-handed stance. But I'm a southy all the way."

"Yes," Solomon said. "Leopards do not shed spots."

"I guess not."

"You are leopard with deep, dark spots… since you were a boy," he said, and then looked me in the eye. "He was your blood. You defend your blood."

"It cost my family everything."

"What was your warrior pledge?"

"To be vigilant," I said. "Protect the garden of life."

"Sometimes this means life for life."

"Right. Life for life."

"You are southpaw, leopard, warrior. Time of grieving is over. Time to honor your wounds, let them be wisdom, guides for next journey. I see shadows on the mountain. Trouble comes. Time to get ready."

"Ready?"

"You are holy man with knife in his boot and a gun secure at his back. I think you remember *ready*," he said, then dropped the sharpening stone into his medicine bundle and wrapped the suede strap around it. "The Ancient Ones tell me the battle that comes unfolds slowly. Begins in hunting season. At sunrise."

"What begins at sunrise?"

"You read letters?"

"I wrote them, I remember what's—"

"Every day you must battle dark sand in your warrior bag until fists are strong and no longer bruise. Read letters, heal old wound. Then burn them. Bring back spirit of ten-year-old warrior. There will be fire again. Fire is cleansing tool."

"Fire," I said. "Alright, then what do I do?"

"You will know what to do… because you will be ready."

PART II

Chapter 38

THE NARROW HALL WINDOW that looked over the prison yard was enclosed by a metal screen. Over the last months I'd seen Toreck roughly six, seven times—smoking, lifting weights, always alone, always scowling, a phantom on the periphery. Today he stood up from the weight bench, tipped his grey prison cap, and smiled at me as I passed. *What was he up to?*

I closed the door of the confessional, laid my Bible on the shelf, unlatched the knife sheath on my boot, and for two hours listened to every sound, every door, every footstep. But after my obligatory time and no visitors, I left to meet Bud at the Blue Gull for a late lunch.

*   *   *

Always on guard, Bud (who wasn't exactly a "view" guy but was more of a "keep an eye on things" sort) invariably sat in one of the vinyl booths at the window, watching the passersby as if he may recognize a criminal, a crime, or a potential situation.

"Afternoon," I said, flipping a coffee cup over and signaling Betty-Jo for coffee.

"I noticed," Bud said still staring out the window. "You wear your boots these days."

"Yeah."

"Been hearin' ya *at the crack a dawn* poundin' the shit outta your duffle bag on the back porch," he said as he dumped half a bottle of ketchup on his fries.

"Just trying to get back into shape."

"For what? Another local dirtball wife beater you thinkin' 'bout visitin'?"

"Dirtball... No, nobody I can think of today."

"Right," he said. "Maybe I should fill *my* duffle bag with sand." His eyes drifted to Betty-Jo, pouring our coffee. He winked. She smiled.

"Nah," I said. "It's too old. It'll just fall apart. Besides, I'd hate to see a man of your advanced age do something as extreme as exercise."

Betty-Jo stifled a chuckle and then walked away.

Bud sat back in the booth. "I'm wearin' a gun, ya know. Not afraid to use it."

I laughed and said, "So shoot me... then tell me why I'm here."

He shoved his plate aside. "Got some news late last night."

"News?"

"Toreck."

"Just saw him."

"That's just it." Bud cleared his throat. "He's gettin' out on early release, eight months and good behavior."

"Never thought I'd hear his name and the words 'good behavior' in the same sentence."

"You don't look surprised."

"Figured something was up... I've been to the prison sixteen times in eight months, every visit seeds an uneasiness under my skin."

"Yeah," Bud said as he motioned for the check. "Combat boots, duffle bag, bruised knuckles. Figured you were sensin' somethin'." He laid some cash down on the table.

"So, Toreck?" I asked.

"Got tabs on him," Bud said as he slapped his cowboy hat on and winked good-bye to Betty-Jo. He'll likely risk another dig on Neahkahnie for gold but then smarten up and hit the road."

"Yeah... That might work on Imogene, but you and I know he'll go home, find his wife and kid vanished, house sold. Alone, broke, and nowhere to turn. And we both know that'll go over without a ruckus, don't we."

Chapter 39

THEO

IT WAS JULY. A black panel truck was parked on the edge of Beech Road. I descended the sandy path for my morning walk; kept my eye on that truck. The cab was dark.

After months of going to the prison twice a month, feigning interest in the lies of culpable men, and listening with intent for the voice who threatened my sister, I'd grown increasingly paranoid. And now Toreck was free. It was an old familiar friend, that anxious wait for the moment I stepped into the ring, when that imminent bell that can't be un-rung, rings.

*   *   *

Along the shoreline logs and driftwood had been tossed and piled like toothpicks by the night's storm. I wanted to take my walk but couldn't shake the feeling someone was watching me. I glanced back up to the road; the truck was gone. Swift shadows of clouds moved about the ground as I rushed up the sandy hill. The truck was now parked at the end of Fourth, and this time someone was in the cab. Maybe a poacher getting a two-month jump on elk season? Maybe. Maybe not. I kept walking toward town with my eye on that mysterious visitor.

Aside from the faint hiss of the outgoing tides, the only sounds were the low tootles of an owl and the crunch of my footsteps on the pavement. There was a red glow inside the truck. Cigarette, maybe? I didn't have the patience or luxury to wait and see, so I turned and headed toward it. The driver started up the engine, flashed his headlights, and drove up Beulah Road—evidently he didn't want company. He disappeared around the bend.

In her school-bus-yellow hat, Pearl bobbed up and down behind her picket fence as she yanked out weeds, turned soil with her trowel, and cussed in Korean. I stepped across the street and said, "Morning Pearl," still watching for that truck.

"Morning, Teo," she said. "I like dis garden… but so much work."

"Mm hm," I said and nodded toward her fresh-plucked pile of weeds. "Well, at least you know who your enemies are."

Pearl sat back on her knees, wiped her black licorice hair from her brow, and said, "Yeah. Apids, weeds, slugs, frost, spiders. I no like the black spiders."

With dirt smudged on her face and hands calloused as a shoemaker's, she looked like a Korean farmer tirelessly working in her rice paddy fields. But here alone, she was a good target.

"Today, rhubarb pie," she said.

"Good, good," I said as the truck slowly appeared again at the end of Beech.

"I see him before," she said.

"Who?"

"That truck," she pointed.

"Don't point. Where have you seen it?"

She jabbed at the dirt. "Two days, he jus' sit there. He bad, like black spider."

"I'm sure it's nothing."

The truck idled at the corner of Beech.

"You not good liar, Teo."

"Yeah, I'll work on that," I said. The stranger backed up, turned, and tore down Second Avenue, disappearing around the corner. I looked for it to reappear like the telltale nose of a coyote sneaking around a chicken pen. But there was no sign of it. There was also no sign of Bud's car. "Bud gone already?"

"He go in early today," she said.

I scanned the street from corner to corner. "Okay…," I said. "How about you go inside and get an early start on that pie." Then I rushed home and left a message for Bud to call.

*   *   *

Solomon was in his yard chanting, low and muffled, but I couldn't see him anywhere. Then he materialized like a ghost out of darkness—a vision of his younger self, as he had done many times when I was a boy. He appeared shadowy, though the morning was now clear blue, and sat on his tree stump next to Raven totem and Frog box, eagle feathers in his long, black hair, bare back in his buckskin pants and moccasins. He carved a piece of red cedar,

Young Wolf by his side. He started his mantra low and rhythmically. Dragonflies and hummingbirds flitted about. I stood at the kitchen window listening, sharpening my knife.

When I was a boy I told Mamaí that I'd seen him disappear and then reappear, like a ghost. She looked at me so matter-of-factly that I knew she'd seen this apparition herself. "Son," she said, burning her moss-green eyes into mine. "Do you honestly think that all the Irish who swear upon their loved ones they've seen the good Mother Mary or Saint Joseph himself, floating over some or another town, that they be crazy? Do you doubt them, boy?"

I shook my head, *no-no-no*.

"Do ya think there's only holy magic in Ireland, child?" she said, offering a Baby Ruth. "Now go sit quietly, listen to Solomon. Don't be questioning a wise man till you are one." She had shooed me out into the world, ever shaped by the sharp edge of her words.

Then, before my disbelieving eyes, Solomon dissolved; vanished into the shadows. I shut my eyes, and then opened them again. Solomon, ever free from the laws of this universe, was gone. And in that instant I knew that whatever he prophesized had begun with that lurking black spider at the end of the street. It was time.

Chapter 40

GENGHIS

THE SHIVE WOUND in my ribs burned. Upon our well-planned exit, one-eyed Joe tried to take me out. He wanted to be a brave fella so I left him alive, barely, but with that shive's marks up and down his face for all his cell mates to see how worthless he was in his valor. Makes me smile when I picture our good-bye; one-eyed Joe now has no eye.

It was hotter than a billy goat in a pepper patch, and to top it off, Toreck spent the morning droning and pacing at the river's edge outside the cabin. I stood on the porch with my coffee, listening. Irritated.

"Where'd they go?" Toreck asked. "That bitch wife a mine sold the house and disappeared? Hell no man, she ain't smart 'nuf to do it on her own. *Priest* musta helped her."

His whining was tiresome. "So, tell me about the priest," I said. "And the town."

"Riley... real Ivy Leaguer," he said lighting a cigarette. "Went to college, boxing champion all through school, then got shot in Korea, got some fancy medal. He's always been everybody's golden boy. Pisses me off. Now he's a fuckin' priest."

"Warrior priest," I said. "I like it."

"Huh?"

"Nothing. Go on... What about his family?"

"His hottie sister's always been a little queen bee, everybody's princess. Sheriff's a square—real punk with a gun. That chink woman is the sheriff's sister-in-law, she's one a them war brides, came in forty-six, with his brother."

"His brother?"

"Sheriff's brother died a couple years back. I'd a sent that witch woman packin' back to the rice paddies, man. But, they're all tight." He tossed the match to the water. "Like family. And that Indian and the old lady, Mrs. B, especially can't trust those two for nothin'. Thick as thieves."

"Good to know," I said, and dumped my cold coffee in the dirt. "So, this queen bee sister, she razzes your berries, does she?"

He laughed. "Yeah, I'd like to rattle her cage."

"Now there's an idea."

Chapter 41

THEO

SOLOMON SAT on his bench, eyes closed. I didn't want to disturb him so I quietly opened the door to Imogene's. Then, for no apparent reason, he said, "You cannot kill the white-faced Sea Otter—it angers South Wind."

"South Wind," "Everlasting Man," and "Great Grandfather" were all his names for God. He gazed off at a distance that held images for his eyes only and said, "Father followed her once to her home underwater." The gold flecks in his eyes sparkled. "She gave him three magic arrows… said she will return someday." His words suspended in air like dust particles at dawn. Then he looked at me and said, "She returns soon," and handed over a jar of salve. "You hold that bullet long enough."

"Thanks. What do I do with it?" I asked. He turned his face away, closed his eyes, and slipped back into that other world. I opened the door to Imogene's and left him to his meditation.

* * *

"Damn-and-blast!" My sister's voice crackled through the nearly empty store.

She stood with her hands on her hips behind the counter. Her pale skin burned red.

Bud ran his fingers over his razor cut and said, "Nothin' I could do to—"

"There was nothin' you could *ever* do about that bastard!" Imogene's voice pitched. She fumbled under the counter for her cigarettes, lit one, and threw the match in the trash.

"Mornin'." I crept in, happy I wore my collar—armor against a petulant Irish lass.

"Toreck's out a prison... *four years early*," she said, pounding out her freshly lit cigarette in a metal ashtray. It vibrated against the wood counter like a spinning top. "I suppose you knew that already? Never mind. Bud, tell him the rest."

"Look at this," Bud said, and handed me the *Oregonian*.

OREGONIAN NEWSPAPER July 1957

Salem, OR – On July 15th, the Oregon State Penitentiary experienced the most destructive riot in Oregon's penal history. Convicts gained control of the building on Saturday, setting fire to cell blocks and shops, vandalizing property, looting, and taking several hostages. Negotiations between the convicts and state officials took place late that night and well into the next morning. The instigator of the riots is not yet known, but the convicts' demands, including a new warden (Hoyt Culver), medical care, and expansion of the work release program, were reluctantly met by dawn. During the two weeks leading up to the riot there were a number of hunger and work strikes, which coincided with much political and public discussion about prison conditions. The violence took the lives of three guards. A final body count on missing prisoners has not yet been provided. It is estimated that at least seven prisoners were also killed. The riot caused one million dollars in structural and water damage.

Chapter 42

THEO

IMOGENE LIT THE CANDLES in front of the four framed photos of our dearly departed. The glass containers glowed red. She crossed herself and lit a cigarette. Solomon came inside and helped Pearl lift flour bags to shelves in the back kitchen.

"Rumor has it," Bud said, "Toreck let it be known he ain't too happy you helped his family disappear. And apparently he kept some interesting company in the pen."

"And?" I said. "I mean, Toreck's happiness wasn't ever part of my plan."

"Right, no problem. We can handle Toreck," he said, giving Imogene a reassuring look.

She rolled her eyes and said, "You two always think you can handle everything."

"Loosen your girdle, Nancy," I said, feigning a smile. "It'll be fine."

"Huh! I don't wear a girdle, and things are seldom fine if he's involved," she said. "You plan on fightin' back this time, now you've rammed a stick into that hornet's nest?"

"I plan on fighting if there's a fight," I said as my gut twisted, telling me there would be.

"Alright, you two." Bud laid last weekend's *Oregonian* on the counter. "Remember this riot at the pen last week?"

"Yeah, I saw the paper," I answered as Imogene's eyes scrutinized the grainy pictures.

"Well, it was the same day Toreck was released. They thought seven prisoners died in the fires, but apparently not all seven bodies were accounted for. Far as we can tell, a prisoner named Genghis Hansel somehow escaped, not sure how. But my source hinted they're buddies and are headed our way."

Chapter 43

Genghis

GARY HICCURS'S SHACK hadn't been touched in the months I'd been *confined*. Looked like nobody on this earth missed the guy. The cabin smelled of dried fish and dust. It appeared our Gary didn't know cleanliness was godliness. It was a pig sty but better than that damned cell.

I started his pick-up truck. It roared to a rumble; looked like it wouldn't go over ten miles an hour, but that was fine. Besides, I didn't want to use the black truck I'd pinched in Tillamook except for special trips.

The Nehalem store was five minutes away. We needed supplies, so I headed out while Toreck slept on a cot in the back room. He sleeps a lot, and late; seven, even eight a.m.—me, if I slept, then up at sunrise every day, clockwork, the early worm, all that sort of crap. I figured in a fishing town the store would open early, too, so off I went in that old bald-tire, sputtering contraption, poor excuse for a truck.

This Nehalem was my kind of town; right out of another century. The sidewalks were wooden railroad planks like in some Western. I glanced up and down the sleepy street to see if any podunk sheriff was lurking. There were five weary buildings: store, café, tavern, an out-of-business logging office, and a barber shop with one of those red-white-and-blue barber shop doohickeys hanging by the window. But no sheriff.

Nehalem lacked a proper restaurant. No little old ladies in a local antebellum house serving up breakfast; no full course of biscuits and gravy, fried bacon, eggs, maybe even some sweet corn fritters. My stomach growled as I entered the Two Table Café where the sign above the counter read *God Bless America*.

Personally, it looked to me like they had room for three tables. There were no customers, nobody serving anything, just a young guy in a flannel shirt hiding behind the counter. "Cook's out sick," he said, pointing to the coffee pots and donuts. Now, I had a real hankerin' for some good old fried taters, slaw, green beans cooked in pork, and fried okra. Oh my good God, hungry, hungry, hungry. Tried hard not to think about honest food the last few months, but now, well, hungry.

Bitterly disappointed I bought a cup of hot, weak coffee and a sugary donut and waited on the dock for the store to open at eight. The fresh air was invigorating after the smoky riots, and that maple donut went a long way in reawakening my taste buds after that godforsaken salt-lick grub in the pen.

After I bought Portland's *Oregonian* newspaper (with the headline AUGUST 1ST— CONVICTS STILL ON THE LOOSE!) and some provisions, I noticed a truck with California plates parked next to the Riverside Tavern, and a little girl inside, her head propped against the window, asleep. Who would leave a child in a car this time of day? Or maybe she'd been there all night.

Dropped my bags into my truck and walked across the street to the Tavern parking lot, looked inside the cab window. She was a little red-headed child with freckles, about seven, and alone. Looked up and down the street; not a soul in town. My hunger rekindled.

The truck door was locked. Behind the window she was so close. I touched my fingers to the glass where her tiny head rested on the other side. I could almost feel her. Smell her.

I marched up the stairs and went inside that weathered watering hole. At one end of the bar sat an old wrinkled woman. Looked like a tumor that'd grown out of that bar stool, like she'd been planted there for years. Probably had. She smoked a cigarette and stared straight ahead at the collection of deer heads and antlers on the wall behind the bar. Most of their glossy eyes stared back; one old buck didn't have eyes, just empty sockets full of dust. The place smelled of stale beer, mold, and dirty ashtrays. At the other end of the bar were two other people: a thin, weasel-looking guy, maybe twenty-eight or -nine, wearing black snakeskin boots that looked to be my size, and a young, bleach-blonde woman who looked ridden real hard and put away wet. Short skirt, tight blouse, red shoes. She whispered in his ear and bit at his neck like a harlot. He put his hands on her breasts like nobody else was in the room.

"Be watchful, friend," I said approaching them. "Be wary of the seductive words of a promiscuous woman."

Her head lifted; a mannequin raised to life. She glared at me, anger in those half-lit eyes. Real anger. "Who the hell are you?" she asked.

"The poison of vipers is on those lips. Nothin' but unfaithfulness 'tween those breasts, boy. That woman's a desert where men die a thirst. Mother who abandons her child at a pagan's alter will surely rot in hell."

"*What?*" the young man asked through his drunken haze.

His hair was coal black and his skin olive colored; clearly not the red-headed child's father. But he was wearing a ring that caught my eye. *I needed a new ring.*

"Mind your own business," she said, her red lipstick smeared across her filthy mouth.

"Is that abandoned child out there yours?" I asked.

"Tula May?" she said. "She's fine. She's sleepin'. Leave us be."

A fat bartender came out of the back room and asked, "Any trouble here?"

"No trouble," I said looking to the ground. Didn't need him seeing my face or calling any police. Turned and went back to my truck. I waited an hour, patient as a cat at a mouse hole, watching the girl, making certain she was safe. When they finally stumbled out around nine-thirty, she'd been awake for twenty minutes, sitting up in the seat, not surprised to be there. She sat quietly and waited for them to come back. A child deserves better parents than that.

Their truck swerved out of Nehalem and all the way into Manzanita. I followed. Then they drove up a hill alongside a mountain behind town and up a dirt drive to a small broken-down cabin. I parked and hid in some bushes. They went inside, forgetting about the child.

Within a few minutes Tula May climbed out of the truck and carried her blanket inside. She was a cute little thing, real cute. Still pure. She deserved better. I knew right then and there I needed to save her soul from that wretch and her wretched ways.

Loud music blared from a radio. I slowly climbed one rickety stair at a time. Inside they laughed and shouted at each other, then laughed some more. I peered in the dirty window. They were half-naked, her still wearing her cheap red shoes, beer bottles everywhere like they'd been partyin' for weeks. The child was nowhere in sight. I shoved the door open and said, "I warned you, brother." They looked surprised to see me again so soon. "Never trust a whore who neglects her child."

Chapter 44

SOLOMON

MY TRAIL wound through land of old woman Marge. Her cabin sat on north side of Neahkahnie. Marge died from exploding heart many weeks ago. Her wild daughter returned and lived in cabin. She was bad seed. As I passed cabin I heard a cry. Small child was inside, behind curtains. I left her basket of blackberries like I used to do for Marge.

"I am Solomon," I said loud. She did not come out. Then I hid behind the oak. She came out, looked around like scared animal, snatched up basket, and rushed back inside. She was alone. I stayed and waited for her mother to return. She did not.

Under night sky, the face of my Ruby was in the stars, Fiona's voice in the rustling trees. Those talk-too-much dead women wanted me to help that child. They said she was a gift.

"I am old," I said, "tired of children and their children ways. I need no gifts." They shushed me and said she was my last journey. "Be awake," they said. They say a lot.

The child watched out the window. No bad-seed mother returned. No light came on in cabin. I felt her fear, heard her cries, moved to porch, and said, "I am Solomon. You sleep now. Do not be afraid." I laid my old body down on hard stairs. Her cries stopped.

"This child is a gift," my Ruby said again in the treetops. Fiona whispered in the wind, "This child out of the shadows is salvation."

"I accept," I said to the sky. The child was my journey. The great Wolf stood in the far-off trees, waiting while the talk-too-much dead women worked their plan through me. Wolf is patient.

* * *

For three nights I returned, slept on hard porch. She slept inside. Every day the basket was empty. Every day I filled it with berries and smoked salmon. Three nights is long time. I am old. I tapped on door and said, "Child."

She slowly opened door. She was no taller than Imogene when she arrived from Ireland. This child from darkness had brown eyes of a lost doe and wore rags. She was dirty and smelled of a dead woman's house. "Come with me," I said and held out my hand for her to take.

She looked at my hand, my face, my clothes, my hair. Then she pushed the broken screen door open and whispered, "I'm Tula May." She stepped out on porch, looked right, then left, then slipped her hand into mine. "I hided in Grandma's cellar. A mean man took my mommy."

Chapter 45

THEO

IT WAS LATE Friday morning. Bud called and said he had something he wanted me to see, so I hung around the house, cleaned the aquarium, fed the fish, and cleaned off the dining room table except for the bottle of Murphy's and the stack of letters. I picked them up and thumbed through them as I did occasionally. In the middle of the stack was the thinnest letter to Andréa, dated September nineteen fifty-two. Fifty-two was when all the real difficult choices started. I'd carried a letter from Imogene in my pocket because the ridiculousness of her letter cheered me in the middle of Korea's bedlam. She'd ordered a "new- fangled electric skillet," couldn't wait till it arrived. She sent me the recipe for ginger shortbread; said all my new friends would like it. Every time I read it I thought, *Dear God, where did my baby sister think I was?* What the hell did she think I was doin'? *Gotta love that girl*, I'd think, then laugh every time. Then cry.

Sometimes I'd sit down in the middle of a burnt-out village, read Imogene's letter, force my eyes, my mind off the carnage onto something sweet, innocent, trying to save what was left in *me* that was sweet and innocent. Her letters reached me occasionally, and in reading them I always wondered why Andréa's didn't. I asked Andréa that question, in this short letter. I didn't need to read it to know what I'd written in this one, the thinnest envelope.

I secured the string around the unopened envelopes and put them in their place next to the fresh bottle of Murphy's; thought how good a drink would taste, *feel*, but thought better of it and stepped out to the front porch for fresh air. Bud had just parked at my curb. He opened the car door and said, "Let me check in and grab a file." Then he picked up his receiver and, as he spoke to sheriff dispatch, rustled through a box of files on the passenger seat.

While he gave his whereabouts, I watched Solomon walk toward Mrs. B's cabin, his long, grey hair, brown leather vest, red shirt, and Levi's, carrying his annual three wool blankets that Imogene ordered. Each year she folded and packaged them together with string tied in a knotted bow. He held the hand of his new protégé, Tula May Hildy, Marge Hildy's granddaughter. Her mother had gone missing *again*, and Tula May was left behind *again*. Her mother abandoned her repeatedly to go on drunken trips with different boyfriends, but there'd always been Marge—hermit though she was—to fill the void. But with Marge gone, Tula May spent her days with Solomon and her nights with Mrs. B. We were all confident her drunken mother would show up at some point with some sort of story. Then we'd figure out something more permanent for the child. Tula May said a man took her mommy; we figured that happened a lot.

Bud answered a muffled voice that croaked from his car radio. "I'll be in Tillamook in an hour," he said. "Then I'll check on that truck." He stepped back to the sidewalk, handed me a paper with the Oregon State Penitentiary logo and a murky black-and-white photo of a man.

"What truck?" I asked.

"Seen this guy?" he asked, motioning for me to look at the photograph.

"Who's this?"

He took a pencil from the pocket beneath his badge. His mood turned a corner—lines in his tan face deepened and his thick brows constricted over his eyes. He said, "Toreck kept with that bastard there. He likes young girls. *Real young.* Usually those kind get shivved the first five days—some mysterious shower accident that was never investigated. But not this guy." He slammed the file down on the kitchen counter. "He's as slippery as one of your hermit crabs."

I handed him a cold bottle of Olympia from the refrigerator. "Why's that?"

He stared at the notes. "He's linked to some gruesome stuff, but nothin's ever stuck... just a few months in jail here and there." He looked up. "Is that bacon I smell?"

I pointed to a plate left over from breakfast. "So, what are you telling me? What's he got to do with Toreck being released?"

"This is the guy who escaped—one of those missing bodies after the prison riot. Toreck'll be worse for the wear after time spent behind bars, sure, but this ugly guy here, he's a real problem. Look there." Bud turned the file toward me and shoved a piece of bacon in his mouth. "Now, our Toreck's a slimy snake who's never been smarter than his own anger. I can deal with him. But his friend here... he's a hungry predator. Anger's easy to deal with, but hunger's a different thing altogether. He's a rabid dog, and rabid dogs need to be put down."

"Toreck doesn't make friends," I said.

"Neither does this guy. He makes disciples."

Bud studied the file and read, "This Genghis Hansel... *Who names a child Genghis?* Anyway, he's thirty-eight. Went to prison for kidnapping and rape of a minor when he was twenty-two. Been arrested seven times since but never served much time since the victims wouldn't testify."

"What do we know about this guy," I asked, "and why wouldn't they testify?"

"Fear," he said. "One young girl, *twelve years old*, is in Damashe State Hospital for a breakdown." His thick barrel chest visibly sank. "They busted him tryin' to break in to see her. He said he wanted to visit her; I say he wanted to finish the job."

Bud tipped his cowboy hat back on his head, leaned his body against the kitchen counter, ate bacon, and read, handing me pages and photographs.

"In the pen," he said, "he grew his hair long, like it is in that photograph, there." He motioned to the picture in front of me. I stared at the dark eyes of the man with shoulder-length hair holding a metal plate in front of his chest, number 209666.

"*666!* Is that a joke?" I asked.

"No joke." Bud continued, "And when Toreck was set free under Oregon's new Rehabilitation Act—rehabilitation my ass!—anyway, our boy Genghis here disappeared. Oregon's had five prison breaks in two years. This makes six."

"How do you know they were friends?"

"I have a source who says Genghis and Toreck did everything but sleep together. Our Toreck hung on every fiery word Genghis preached. Whatever lights his match was lit in his childhood. The real sick shit is like that, happens when they're young. Like that hand of his, it's apparently crippled by a snake bite from when he was kid. He nearly choked to death, then had lung problems. And it says here the doctor said his hand needed to be amputated, but little Genghis's father said he wouldn't have been bit if he was free of wrongdoing. He said he could live with his 'sin.' Genghis was seven." Bud shook his head. "Yep, too late for rehabilitation. These kind just need to be stopped. The only remedy is a nice shiny cartridge through the skull."

"I should probably say something about redemption right now, right?"

"Yeah, but you won't cause you pretty much agree with me, right?"

I tapped the file in his hand. "Crippled hand? That's that guy I met at the pen. Read on."

"Right. So, this Genghis drew snakes with charcoal that coiled up along the walls and the ceiling and around the floor, coiled snakes around his toilet, his bed, and sink. He has a snake tattooed on his forearm. Says here he's also a preacher of some sort."

"A preacher with tattoos?" I asked.

Bud looked at me and said, "Why… does that sound odd to *you*, Father Riley?"

"Just keep readin'."

"He worked in the prison library; a smart guy. High IQ," Bud said. "They're the worst." He rolled up his neatly pressed long shirt sleeve. The eagle on his forearm held a crumpled American flag in its talons with "lest they forget" scripted along a banner. A grey scar slivered through the middle of the flag where the cartridge from a Parabellum, a Nazi Luger, tore through his skin. The same kind of shell was now lodged in my hip.

"I gave a photo to Oz," Bud said. "He's on the lookout, too."

"Well?" I asked.

"Says here since they were no trouble, guards left them alone. They said Genghis 'had no soul.' *No soul.*" He looked up from the file. "What bullshit! Those pansy-ass guards wouldn't know evil if it stared them in the face." He slammed his half-drunk beer down on the counter. "Nazis, now there's a wicked bunch. And this Genghis here, must be German with that name."

"I don't know about this guy," I said, "but Toreck's served time. Maybe he just wants to lick his wounds and get past it all. Maybe we should just—"

"You are *not* going to say forgive and forget, right?"

"What," I said, "no room for rehabilitation? Redemption? Isn't that in *your* manual?"

"This is me ignoring your religion crap. And he hasn't served *all* his time. Just enough to piss him off. You can help or not. Your choice. But I guaran- damntee you these two are double trouble."

"You know it's in my job description to offer those options, right?"

Bud glared at me and said, "Yeah, helpful. Thanks."

"If he's headed anywhere," I said, "it's probably to his family's old homestead."

"Maybe." Bud guided a toothpick from one side of his mouth to the other, then smiled, closed the file, dropped his empty bottle into the trash beneath my sink, and said, "So, you gonna be a priest or the old Theo when this trouble comes knockin'? And it'll be knockin', so as I see it, you have three choices: you can be forgivin', forgettin', or packin'."

"I'll be and do what I have to when the time comes."

"You shoulda gone into politics, Theo."

"Since I hate politicians and politics I'd say I made the right choice." "*Really,* cause you don't seem to care much for the church or other priests, either."

I handed him his hat.

"Since you put that contraption on your neck," he said, "I jus' figured you'd taken a bullet to the skull that nobody'd found yet. Takin' those crazy-ass vows—just another casualty of war."

"Good to know how you really feel."

"Well, I'm not too worried that you'll drop to your knees in prayer when trouble hits."

"Oh I don't know, a little prayer can't hurt."

"How's that .38 fittin' in your belt?" he asked. "That knife in your boot; that for cleanin' your fingernails? Jus' keep yer eyes open." He yanked his hat down firmly and headed outside.

"Speaking of eyes open," I said following him out to the porch, "this morning I saw a strange truck. Pearl saw it too."

Bud stopped on the steps and turned to me. "Strange how?"

"The shape of the truck, and the driver's behavior. He just sat there staring straight ahead, not like he was watching the sunrise, more like he was watching me, us."

"Was the truck black?"

"Yeah," I said. "Someone sat in the cab, watching or waiting or something — kept vanishing then reappearing. Something wasn't right."

"Was it a black *panel* truck?"

"Yeah, black panel. Why?"

"It's stolen, maybe used in a crime… Just stay far away from it, and let me know when you see it again. Plates?"

"Gone. What kind of crime?"

"I'll get back to you on that. Jus' keep those eyes open."

As Bud's car pulled away from the curb, I looked up the street to the vacant Bouvre house. If it sold, the new owners had not shown up. Could someone be hiding inside? That's where I'd hide — in plain sight. I closed the door and headed across the street to take a look.

Chapter 47

THEO

THE BOUVRE HOUSE hadn't been lived in for a long time and, other than the couple of times Andréa appeared and disappeared, hadn't even been visited since Mr. Bouvre's last heart attack, from what Imogene said. I hadn't seen him, *them*, since the night before I left for Korea. Hadn't stood in the driveway since that night either.

I checked all the windows, the front and side doors; all locked up except the back door. I went inside. Everything was in boxes, the mirrors covered with black cloth, the furniture covered with white sheets, the many oil paintings gone from the walls. It was a ghost of the house it once was. It seemed so much smaller than I remembered.

Each of the three bedrooms was packed up; so was the small basement. Nobody hiding, nobody living, nobody returning. The only things that seemed out of place were the toy trucks and coloring books on the dining room floor.

* * *

It was dusk. Solomon rhythmically chafed his knife on a hide as I stood at my kitchen window mindlessly eating Imogene's blackberry pie. I thought about Andréa and the summer we built the wall between our home and Solomon's. That summer, when we were twelve years old, Mamaí said to build a three-foot stone wall between the two properties. She said it was to remind her of the mottled-grey limestone fencing that, like jagged zippers, crossed the valleys and climbed the hillsides of her war-torn Ireland. She said Solomon was a lot like Ireland: war-weary, scared, and more powerful for it. Andréa helped me get each of those stones into place, then we ran to the beach, stripped down to our skivvies, and jumped into the ocean. How could she so easily forget those sun-drenched glory days?

Outside, Solomon sat on his stump next to his Raven totem; he was a tireless mentor with Tula May, who now sat cross-legged on a blanket at his feet. At the Raven totem's base was the faded green Frog. Solomon pointed to Frog and said, "Frog's task is to send souls to next world. Frog is a being, lives in two spheres—water and land. Respect him. He passes through two worlds, natural and supernatural. Frogs are spirit helpers of shamans." Tula May's eyes popped, then she wrote something down on her tablet as Mrs. B taught her to do. Solomon waited to go on with his lesson until she finished.

The wood-carved Frog clutched a small Soul Box with its frog arms. The tiny box had a removable lid and a deep drawer. Inside were three sharp arrowheads and a newspaper article. I only knew this because, to my great shame, I once snuck a peek. The newspaper article was about his wife, Ruby. It was to go with him when he crossed over. The article never mentioned her name. It said only that an "Indian woman" died, "accidental death." The truth was, Ruby had been beaten and raped by a local recluse who had just returned from a drunken hunting trip. It took three days for her to die.

For this brutal murder that hunter served one year in prison then disappeared. Some say out of guilt, some say shame. Some believe otherwise. I've heard hundreds of confessions from guilty men—true remorse and shame were rare. I tend to believe Solomon had a hand in the rumored "otherwise." There would have been no other way for him to find peace than to avenge.

Solomon continued his lesson, "Is only through trouble we learn strength of our spirits."

He had overcome a world of pain, destruction, and utter hopelessness, but still smiled, still loved. His spirit glowed brighter than any of the gold sepulchers surrounding the bishop. There was nothing in my small stone church more divine than the hallowed ground where he worshipped, and no sermon ever spoken more sacred than the whispers he heard in the wind. He was busy right then saving a child. I was once that child.

Solomon's voice hushed, his evening incantations completed. The back stairs to his hut creaked; the door closed. Tula May would soon be asleep on the small cot in his hut, and he in his outside hammock, the same as he and I had done many times when I ran away from home and got as far as the other side of that stone wall— fifteen feet away—with all my earthly belongings wrapped in a rag and tied to the end of a stick. I knew he'd sit in his chair next to the cot while she dozed off beneath the dream catcher. He'd whisper to her, "Follow the way of your heart. It is hard way, but good way." Then he'd brush his rugged hand over her eyes, closing them; he'd say "Dream a good dream." And she would.

Chapter 48

THEO

IT WAS a slippery slope, Tula May staying with Solomon when Mrs. B was too tired; it would be good tidings for the bishop. He'd twist it into a plan to rid our town of our "savage heretic." I decided I'd make arrangements for her to stay with Imogene until we could find out what happened to her family. A child could do Imogene some good. Besides, the authorities would have just tossed her in with strangers. At least with us, she had Solomon. She was a troubled little girl, sweet, but sad. I'd like to say all she needed was God, but I think God knew what she needed, and what He sent was Solomon. No one knew better than I what that meant to a lost child.

As night fell I dropped my white collar, tin soldier, and rosary on the dresser, then picked up the phone and jiggled the brown cord. "Lucy?" Clicked twice. "Lucy?"

"Yes, Father Theo," she yawned. "I'm here."

"Connect me to Imogene's, would ya, love."

"Hello?" Imogene said, picking up on the first ring.

"Immie, what do you know about Tula May's parents?"

"They're crazy," she said. "I know that much."

"*I mean—*"

"I know what ya mean."

The crumple of cellophane came across the line as she opened a new pack of cigarettes.

"No," she said. "We don't know where they're off to this time, and since Marge died, they have no one to babysit the kid. Stupid people."

"What a mess," I said, picturing Marge who'd lived in that log cabin for the last half-century. Solomon had taken her elk meat. She made him blackberry preserves—doubt two words ever passed between them. After Marge's daughter dumped Tula May, Marge had lugged her around. But Marge up and died about six months ago. Bad heart, doc said. Afterward, Tula May's parents—her mother and some guy—came back for awhile.

"Anyway," Imogene chimed back up. "Solomon asked if she could stay here for awhile. I said yes, starting tomorrow night. I need to... well, you know, make a place."

Her words hung in the air. She hadn't opened the other bedroom door for years. The baby's things were in there and hadn't been touched. Who knows, having Tula May stay with her may be healing. Or devastating. Either way, a child was in need, Imogene had a big heart, and as usual, Solomon was two steps ahead of us all.

"Thanks," I said, downing two aspirin. "We'll chat tomorrow then."

"Theo," she caught me before I hung up, her voice a whisper. "It won't be for very long, will it?"

"I don't think so, love."

"Okay," she said letting out a deep breath. "What do you plan on doin' about Toreck?"

"He's done his time," I said, opening the jar of Solomon's ointment, which smelled of rotting eggs and burned my eyes.

"What did you do in that war," she said, "wait for them to knock on your grass hut, invite you to a duel? NO! You laid in wait till they were right on top of you, and then BOOM! You surprised them. Didn't you? You weren't a priest then, you were a soldier. Try to remember how to protect yourself for God's sake."

"*Grass hut?*" I said. "*Duel?* You're watchin' too many Bogart movies."

"Well," she said, "our lives are changed now. Can't you finally live yours?"

I rubbed the awful-smelling balm into my hip. "Not havin' this conversation *again.*"

She took a long drag. "I think your penance has been enough. Kiernan wanted to be a priest, but you, you're just payin' a tab you don't owe."

"Trust me, Immie, it's my tab... Now, how can I help you with that room?"

"No," she said clearing her throat. "I'll take care of it alone."

I recalled the letter from Mamaí telling me what had happened with baby Christina.

"Sis, remember what Mamaí used to say?"

She remained quiet on the other end of the line.

"When God leads you to the edge of a cliff," I said, "trust Him fully. Let go! One of two things will happen. Either He'll catch you when you fall, or He'll teach you to fly."

There was another long silence. Had I said the wrong thing?
"*Ohhh* Father," Lucy whispered, "that was beautiful."
"Lucy?"
"Yes?"
Then I heard a soft disconnect. "Imogene?"
"She hung up, Father. Did Fiona really say that?"
"*Lucy!* Dammit, girl, get off the line!"

Chapter 49

THEO

IT WAS TWO in the morning. I sat in the dining room with the lights out. The pale night lamp cast a radiant pastel glow throughout the aquarium reef and throughout the house. My three sea horses bobbed in and out from behind the rocks; cleaner shrimp and black urchins busily cleaned algae off the glass, and the sea anemone, closed as a fist, had tucked both clown fish safely inside.

Across the street, under the weak blush of our one street lamp, Imogene's store was dark, locked up until morning. I thumbed through the stack of letters, trying to remember what I had written—visited ghosts most of the night. Fell asleep with them in my hand. The telephone rang and startled me awake. The kitchen clock read three thirty a.m.

"Hello?" I answered. The letters dropped from my lap to the floor. I heard breathing on the other end. "Hello?"

"You think you can go to war," the caller said, his voice a low murmur. "Battlin' an enemy you can see. But you don't know what true warfare is."

"What? Who is—"

"You know your Bible, Padre? 'These signs shall follow them that believe,'" he said raising his voice. "'In My name shall they cast out devils, speak with new tongues. They shall take up serpents, and if they drink any deadly thing, it shall not hurt them; they shall lay hands on the sick, and they shall recover.' Mark 16."

I recognized that voice with the slight Southern tinge. "What do you want?" I asked.

"You think you can kill," he said in a near whisper, "and then tuck that part of yourself under that clean, white collar… tight, secure, no threat. *War hero priest.*" He took a labored breath and said, "Well, you're wrong, Padre. Some men get into fights they're destined to finish, no matter what the cost, no matter who pays. Is that you, Padre? Padre with an archangel burned into your arm? Is that you?"

I turned on the lamp and said, "We've been close personal friends now, for what, five minutes? I think it's time you tell me what you want."

"Got ma'self a nice shiny ring. Course it's not as good as the one I lost, but it'll do."

"How about you come into town, I buy you a coffee and you show me that ring?"

"Did ya know, Padre, sparrows see the soul's descent. That's why they chirp so joyously."

The phone went dead. A chill rippled up my spine. I pictured his twisted hand hanging outside his cell and recalled him wanting to give a child cotton candy again... how he called me "Padre." *Genghis Hansel.* He and Toreck, *buddies*? Was Imogene in real danger?

I pulled on my sweatshirt, grabbed the rifle from behind the bedroom door, my .38, the box of cartridges, and went back to the dining room. I turned the leather chair to face the window and opened it to hear the night sounds: wind shivering through leaves, insects chirping, dogs, cats on rooflines, and wolves. Listened for human sounds like car engines, hushed voices, whispers, muffled footsteps, but the only sounds were the aquarium's humming and the chamber of my gun as I checked the six-shell barrel.

Darkness whispered and shifted. Night is a living thing full of rich, dank smells. Soundless lightning helixed from cloud to cloud; bold daggers of light illuminated the street in flashes too quick to capture. In every spark, thought I saw something but was left staring into obscurity.

Soon morning sunlight danced across the crystal glasses in Mamaí's hutch. Rain drizzled on the sidewalk in front of Imogene's. An abrupt and deafening downpour pelted off the roof, then stopped as suddenly as it started. There was nothing—no one, no footsteps. Just a rainbow stretching across the morning sky and two looting raccoons standing on their hind legs in my front yard, staring at me from behind their bandit masks as if *I* were the intruder.

Chapter 50

THEO

PINK GLOW from Pearl's bedroom lamp twinkled against incoming fog. Mrs. B's shutters were still closed. Two blocks away Mr. Forester's '39 Buick rumbled to life for the ten-minute warm-up before he headed to the Wheeler rest home for breakfast with his wife. The only other sound was my U.S. flag fluttering against the wind. The aquarium night-light clicked off; the blue day beam clicked on. It was six o'clock; I'd call Bud around seven. The smell of coffee filled the house. I poured a cup and sat back down by the window.

I recalled Bud telling me how Pearl gets up every morning, goes into the kitchen, takes out two cups, then stands at the counter and stares at them. She fills them with coffee, takes them to the table, and sits James's cup where he always sat. She looks intently at his chair, as if he were hidden in its wood slats. Her jaw slacks, her thick lower lip droops, her face goes pale, her eyes tear up. She stares at that chair. But then it's as if she wakes from a deep sleep. Head snaps up, she sips her coffee, goes on with her day. Bud said now *he* looks at that chair sometimes as if James were really there, smiling over his morning paper, telling him about the football games. Laughing. It was creepy, Bud said. Just creepy.

Just then their kitchen lights snapped on. She was up. I went back to the kitchen and picked up the telephone.

"Sorry Lucy, it's Father Riley again, Manz-203, please."

"Yes, Father."

"Mornin' Pearl, can I talk to Bud?"

"He jus' leave," she said as his car drove up Laneda and past my house in a hurry. I'd just missed him.

Chapter 51

THEO

PATIENCE WASN'T MY FORTE. I secured my .38 in my belt and headed out to look for signs of either Toreck or anything out of place. Signs of life where there shouldn't be. This Genghis Hansel was, as Bud said, a *real* problem. I felt him creep along my spine as if he were a shadow close behind me, whispering, waiting.

*   *   *

White sand dollars, many in pieces, were scattered along the shore like the trail of a broken plate. Sea lions bellowed in the distance. The wind carried a seaweed-smelling mist that settled on my skin. From the narrow end of the beach I looked straight up Beulah Road to the north side of Neahkahnie Mountain, where the old Sealy homestead was now boarded up. The mountain was awash with an oppressive, thick fog. The tops of pines reached through the dense vapors. Eagles and owls perched on their lookouts. That side of the mountain was where wolves roamed, roads were unpaved, yards were unmowed, and hundred-year-old log cabins weren't boarded up, but were still lived in. Spirals of grey smoke rose up through the tree tops from the fireplaces of the few deeply imbedded cabins. The smell of smoke hung heavy in the air.

Was Toreck in his father's tumbledown shanty? I studied the mountain but couldn't see the house through the trees and barely recalled where the overgrown gravel road was that snaked up that side of the mountain. Nobody had been in it since his old man died.

Mist turned to summer rain. A thin red line etched the bottom of the heavy sky. I headed home to get the car. When my feet hit the tar, I saw that same black truck slowly emerge from the fog two blocks away and approach me. As it got closer the driver rolled the window halfway and tossed out a lit cigarette. He was almost close enough to hit me. On his forearm was a tattoo of a snake coiled around a naked woman. His eyes bore into me. His face, clinched like a fist, was full of hatred. I nodded. No response. But I got a good look: white, broad shoulders, head shaved, tan skin, hollow eyes, deep scratch marks on his cheek. *What would leave those marks?*

The truck moved past me in slow motion. I nodded again. He glared. His eyes were red; the icy crimson of a man who *never* slept. A wave of heat flushed from my neck to my face, head, and ears. Then he sped up and disappeared around Fourth Street, only to quickly reappear on the corner of Third. I rushed to Pearl's gate. She came out on her porch in her bathrobe. He turned left onto Laneda, red taillights glowing. He tapped his brakes in front of Imogene's.

Pearl quickly descended her stairs. "Same man." She nodded toward the truck now three blocks away, passing Mrs. B's cabin. His lights flashed again. Was this a threat? "Black spider," she said.

"Why'd Bud go early?" I asked, watching as the man put his arm out the window in one sharp motion—a one-fingered salute—then sped up. His red lights vanished at the edge of town.

"That spider not nice," Pearl said.

On my porch was a handwritten note on stationary from the Ester Lee Motel in Lincoln City. The handwriting was small, tight, and constricted, as if it had been typed.

Saint Michael the Archangel, defend us in battle; be our protection against the wickedness and snares of the devil. May God rebuke him, we humbly pray: and do thou, O Prince of the heavenly host, by the power of God, thrust into hell Satan and all the evil spirits who prowl about the world seeking the ruin of souls. Amen. Amen. Is that you, Padre? Prince of a heavenly Host? Saint Michael? Is that you? This is going to be fun.

Chapter 52

THEO

Bud's car reeled to a stop outside my house. He came inside and said, "So, you saw the truck and then this note was lying on the porch with a rock holding it down when you returned?"

"Yep," I said. "I just came back to get the car and go investigate the old Sealy cabin."

"Let's do that *together*, later," Bud said, squinting to read the small writing.

"This Genghis called me 'Padre' when we met… he thinks I understand him."

"Do you?"

"Him, no. But some of his twisted religious references, yes. In a way."

"Well, I don't understand all this religious hocus pocus," Bud said, "but I do understand we have an escaped convict here and for whatever reason he's fixed on you."

"If you look at that note, you'd think he wants to do battle with a religious figure."

"Worthy opponent?" Bud asked.

"Something like that."

"Like a silver bullet and a vampire."

"Right, but I don't have any silver bullets."

"That's okay," he said. "I don't believe in vampires."

* * *

We searched the mountain and around Manzanita for two hours. Nothing. Bud dropped me off by nine thirty and headed back to Tillamook to put out another warrant for the truck and its driver. Still, I felt he, or they, were right under our noses—watching, waiting.

Chapter 53

THEO

HANSEL CHOSE an interesting passage: *All the evil spirits who prowl about the world seeking the ruin of souls.* What did he want from me? *The ruin of souls?* Whose?

When I returned from the kitchen with my flashlight, Tula May's face was smashed against my screen door, peering inside; Solomon stood in the yard behind her.

"Morning," I said.

She set her bucket of friends on the porch. Solomon had said she needed something to love and gave her a salamander she named Newt and a starfish named Starfish.

"Keep girl this morning," Solomon said.

I opened the screen and said, "*All* morning?"

Tula May stood arms crossed, with an unmistakable pout on her scrunched face.

"She stay with you," he said.

"I don't wanna," Tula May said, and accentuated with a stomp of her foot.

Solomon pointed to Mamaí's doomed tulips in the garden, urging TulaMay to look, and said, "*With so much rain, so little sun, tulip remains like tight fists…Day will come when risk to remain tight in bud is more painful than risk to blossom, seek sun.*" He then looked at me and said, "*When they do not come into the flower, they wither and die.*" He turned and walked away in a hurry, his hair waving against his red flannel shirt, his bare feet gliding along the gravel flanks as if he scarcely touched the ground. He quickly passed the sleeping Bouvre house and disappeared down their back road.

Tula May stood maybe four feet tall. She uncrossed her arms and said, "Huh?"

"Sometimes it takes a bit to understand what he says," I said. "But then, one day you do."

"Okay...," she said, relenting, and came inside. She wore baggy brown pants and a clean white blouse, neatly tucked under her belt. Her freckled face was scrubbed clean, her reddish-brown hair combed and pulled back into a ponytail. She had the tiny suede purse Solomon had made for her strapped across her chest, exactly like he wore his medicine bundle. "Whatcha doin'?" she asked.

"Well, I need to get some things done while I wait for a telephone call."

"Whatcha need to do?"

"Let's finish feeding these fish here," I said lifting the aquarium lid and turning off the blue light. "And then I need to catch a hermit crab." I dropped in a lettuce leaf. The fish nibbled at the floating feast, unaware of the menacing crab.

"Why?" she asked, staring at the aquarium with a frown.

"Well, he's hurting my other fish," I said. "Have you ever seen an aquarium?"

"No," she said, her face further crumpled. "Why does he hurt them?"

"It's what they do."

"Why?"

"Okay," I said, as the radiator blew a bout of steam. "Let's do this." I handed her the flashlight and lifted her onto a dining room chair. "You wait there." I watched from the kitchen and gathered my supplies: a juice glass and a piece of raw shrimp.

She laid the flashlight on the table and yanked a small tablet out of her suede bag. "How do you spell *aquarium*?"

As I opened up the aquarium and slowly gave her the spelling, she gripped her pencil in her fist and wrote on her pad as if she were carving wood.

"What are you carryin' in your purse?" I asked, moving rocks and sand with my fingers.

"It's not a purse, it's a medicine bundle."

"Ah, right. Sorry. What ya carryin' in your medicine bundle then?"

She took out her belongings, lining them up side by side on the table, and said, "This White Sea Otter Solomon carved is my safety spirit till I get one a my own." She patted the two-inch wood carving. "And this paper and pencil is from Mrs. B so's I can do my job."

"Your job?"

"Yeah," she said. "Mrs. B says all Rounders have jobs, and... and mine is collectin' words, write 'em down, spell 'em right, and keep 'em safe. But Solomon's words don't count." She shook her head. "They're good words, but they jus' don't count."

"Yeah, good words," I said. Mrs. B was preparing her for school, and as many of us had learned, the Nehalem language—though Mrs. B said it was as rich and layered as English poetry and that Solomon was a skilled lyricist—was forbidden in the classroom. *It's a dead language,* a teacher once scolded me. "They may not count now, but they'll matter the rest of your life."

"Well that don't make no sense neither," Tula May said.

"I know. But it will someday."

"Okaaay…," she said, looking up at me like a tiny news reporter with a smileless expression and just as dire. "Are you sure that's how you spell *a-q-u-a-rium*?"

"I'm sure." I rolled my sleeve up farther and sank my hand back inside the aquarium to jiggle the rock where I knew the crab was hiding, just to irritate him. The fish scattered.

"Are you six now?" I asked.

"Yep, six," she said. "How do ya spell *fish*?"

"F-i-s-h."

"You sure?"

"I'm sure."

She closed her tablet. "Mrs. B gets grumpy when my words aren't good 'nough," she said. "Whatcha doin'?"

"Well, I need to find that crab," I said. I took the glass and slid it back inside the aquarium between the coral rock and the sunken treasure ship. "There, that should do it."

"Do what?"

"Sooner or later that crab is going to go after that shrimp in the glass there."

"So?"

"So, when he does he won't be able to get back out of the glass—it's too slippery."

"Well, why would he go in if he can't get back out?"

"Are you sure you're only six?"

"Yep, six," she said, holding up her hands, one with four fingers folded. "This many."

"Well, he can't help himself. All that hermit crab knows is that he wants what he wants. And very soon nothing else will matter to him but that shrimp."

"Okaaay." She looked at me like I was crazy.

"You see… the world's like an aquarium," I said. With my arm in the water I stirred the stillness, probing its shadows with my fingers, moving the driftwood pieces, shells, and sea grasses around; flushing him out. "In the daytime all the fish, like those orange clown fish, live their lives. Then at night they sleep inside their protector, like the sea anemone." I touched the soft finger-like tip of the anemone. It quickly fluttered and withdrew.

"Wow," Tula said. Her eyes widened. She pointed the flashlight.

"Then, when it's dark, the night creatures come out." Her yellow light peered into the shadowy tank as I talked. "But, unlike the clown fish, the hermit crab is not cute and is often predatory."

She put the flashlight down and picked up her pad. "What's pr-e-d-t-ury?"

"Hold the light here," I said, my arm fully submerged in the aquarium.

"Sorry." She dropped her pad, grabbed the flashlight, and turned it to the murky waters.

"Predatory is when a stronger creature preys on, *hunts*, a weaker creature."

"Like Solomon and the elk?" she asked.

"Well, close enough," I said. "You see, these creatures here need each other, just like people." I pointed to the bright yellow tang that scurried to the shipwreck to hide from my hand and the disturbed sands. Tula May's eyes followed the clown fish as the anemone opened and folded its tentacles over it: a blanketing hug of thick pink skin. A sea horse warily inched from behind a rock, and a shrimp busied itself cleaning the bottom of the tank around the treasure chest. Tula's eyes widened as the mysterious creatures came into view.

"See there, some need each other for shelter, others for food or cleaning; then others to kill what threatens the rest, like those snails crawling up the glass eatin' algae. But a real danger is the hermit who grows in the darkness of these rocks. If he gets big, he's a danger to 'em all."

"But," Tula May whispered, "why did you get the hermits if you don't like 'em?"

"Well, unfortunately, you can't know their eggs are in the rocks until they hatch."

She held the flashlight with both hands and focused the light inside the watery world.

"It amazes me how these fish share the same space," I said, "and yet live in two utterly different worlds. Not so different from people." I tried to be humane and catch them first. But, if they didn't get into the glass, then I'd have to find them, destroy their eggs, hunt down and kill the rest. Hoping the crab would fall for the trap, I put a blanket over the aquarium to give him the darkness he preferred.

"Did I come from an egg?" she asked.

"No," I said, not willing to go down that confusing path.

Her soft brow furrowed and she asked, "Can the hermit crab hurt *me*?"

"No darlin'," I said wiping my hands dry. "We're not gonna let anything hurt you."

I poured her a glass of milk and sat down across the table from her, glanced out at Imogene's, and rolled my sleeves back down. "Tula May, can we talk about your parents?"

Her eyes sank somewhere deep inside. She folded her tablet closed, tucked it and her pencil back into the pouch, then took out her safety spirit, the White Sea Otter, rubbed its carved head, and set it on the table in front of her. She took a long, slow drink of milk, looked around my house, settling her eyes on the basket of socks I kept in Mamaí's china hutch. Then she let out a deep sigh and said, "Okay."

Chapter 54

IMOGENE

DAILY SPECIALS

Smoked Salmon Burgers and Potato Salad + Drink .75¢
Friday's Pie - Apple & Peach Streusel .50¢

Time had come. The Coca-Cola clock chimed nine a.m. Rain turned to ice pellets that beat against the walls, the windows, and roof, bouncing upward from the sidewalk. The sky was dark as dusk. The cacophony of loud noises included Pearl beating bowls, pots, and pans in the kitchen making soup, baking cakes, and rolling dough. I leaned against the door frame and watched her work in a flurry of activity between the long stainless steel counter and the wood butcher's block. Burlap bags of flour and potatoes were piled against the wall at her feet. The smell of maple sugar frosting coated the air. The headache I'd had all night returned and pricked at my brow. "Pearl," I shouted. "I'm gonna be upstairs making room for Marge's girl, okay?"

"Okay," she said as she mixed and measured with her hands, tossing in fists of cinnamon, throwing flour, and smashing berries with her bare fists.

I hung my apron on the door hook and climbed the stairs to my apartment. In the mirror at the end of the hall I took myself in, recalling the many nasty things Tula May's mother said about me through the years. Her with her tall, lean body and plump breasts that men stared at, in awe, watching them float about beneath her tight cotton blouses as if they came from another planet. I arched my back, thrusting what little I had forward. It didn't help. I recalled her bright pink lipstick and hair so ratted in the back it looked like a nest. No wonder that child looks at me, who her mother called "plain as a pancake," as if I were an alien. Suppose to her I was.

Oh well, I'd make room for her just the same. That wild witch of a mother has dumped her for the last time. Theo would find her a good home. A few nights with me would be fine.

The glass doorknob to Christina's room was cold. I ran my other hand along the rim of the door, the edges of the molding I'd painted while still pregnant. I swallowed hard and then turned the handle, opening the door for the first time in three years. Then I sank to the floor, out of breath, my headache now like an ice pick at my temple. I reached up, pulled the door closed, leaned against the wall, and tried to catch my breath.

Suddenly Solomon appeared down the hall at the top of the stairs, an apparition slowly coming into focus. He had his medicine bundle in his hand. Pearl stood behind him. He dropped to the floor at my side. Pearl nodded and went back downstairs. He took my hand, breathed in deeply, and closed his eyes, my hand clenched tightly in his. He remained silent for a few minutes. I, too, closed my eyes, then felt a warm calm wash over me. He stood, reached his hands down for me to take, and said, "It is time."

I took his old, strong hands and pulled myself up. He wiped my tears with his leathery thumbs and gripped my hand in his. He opened Christina's door again and led me inside. I closed my eyes and followed into the pink-walled tomb.

Solomon had wanted to go inside her room with me for some time, he said I needed a ceremony, to grieve, but Thomas said it was nonsense, to just get past it, let it go. But I couldn't let her go, so I closed the door and never opened it again. Then Da died, Theo went missing in Korea, and Mamaí got sick, then died. In the last three years, I'd never really said goodbye.

Solomon sat me in the chair Mamaí gave me for rocking Christina. Rain pummeled the roofline. The heaviness of the room pressed down on me. I sank into the chair; every bone, every muscle, every cell in my body ached—that thorny pincher crab pinched inside me again.

Solomon sat on the floor, opened his medicine bag, and took out bundles of sage and incense. The rain stopped. I watched him, avoiding her room and the many pictures, dolls, blankets, and soft pink clothes—all those tiny pink things, so heavy with longing.

He lit his incense, closed his crinkled eyes, and prayed to his Great Grandfather in that language I never understood but that soothed me just the same. I closed my eyes and fell into his voice—his incantations, his song of sorrow, his prayers to one greater than we. Solomon's voice, like a hot bath of sea salts, gently tugged and pulled the sorrow from my body.

Chapter 55

THEO

"**THEY SAID** they had to go to California," Tula May explained. "They gived me cookies and said they'd be back in a couple days. Mark—that's mommy's new boyfriend—says I was too ugly to go outside, said animals would eat me. 'Stay put in the house,' he said." Her shoulders hunched. She stared into her milk glass, then back at that basket of socks in my hutch. "They were gonna leave in the mornin', but then that big man came. I hided outside in Granny's hidin' place." Her brown eyes were dull, not playful.

"Tula, I—"

"Oh," she said, sitting up straight, "it's okay." She then tapped the top of her spirit guide. "Solomon said it was a lie. He said I'm beautiful, and nobody can change what Great South Wind has maked," she proudly announced. "Mrs. B heard him, and she agreed. And you know that don't happen much. So I figure, must be true." She somberly looked down to her glass.

"Well, sweetie… Solomon never lies." I reached down and gently touched her chin, tipping her face up. "And yes, he was right. Look at you! You're a very pretty girl."

A smile tickled the edges of her lips but, like the morning sun, was too weak to fight through the clouds and make an appearance. "I'll bet the day you were born your mother said you were as beautiful as the tulips in May, and then decided that must be your name."

Her eyes glistened. "Ya think?"

"Of course she did. How else could you have the name of God's favorite flowers? I'm sure you were named for the red and pink tulips of May."

Her face flushed. She sat quietly, taking in my words, then said, "I know you call South Wind 'God.' Solomon told me. It means the same. It's jus' God's so big he needs lots a names." She carefully set her empty glass on the table and wiped her mouth with her arm. "Mommy said there's no God. She jus' don't know yet. And Mark said God didn't care 'bout ugly kids."

"Seems Mark says a lot," I said, tightening my grip on the tin soldier in my pocket.

"Yep. Mark said Mommy should jus' leave me with Granny and go to Frisco so she can sing in nightclubs. He said I jus' got in the way."

I ran my hand across the stubbles on my chin, gripping my mouth shut, stifling anger. "Sweetheart," I said, "you're not in anybody's way, not ever." I handed her another cookie and asked, "Now, can you tell me what the big man looked like?"

"No, I hided my eyes and crawled outside. I didn't like his voice. He was loud and mean. He scared me. Then they all started yellin' so I covered my ears like Granny taught me to do when they's fightin'. Mommy fights with people *a lot*."

"That's okay," I said. "You're safe now."

Despite it all, Tula May was curious about her surroundings, playful with her new bucket companions, and she listened to anyone who spoke to her with a keen interest. She had been left alone so much in the small house on Neahkahnie that I supposed the sound of someone talking would fascinate her the rest of her life.

"Solomon came at night," she said, "and slept on the front porch so I wouldn't be a-scared. Then when they didn't come home," she let out a labored breath, "he said I needed to come to his house cause his old bones can't sleep on that hard porch no more." She reached over, pointed at my white collar and asked, "Why you wear that?"

"Well… it's a… it's my uniform, like Sheriff Bud wears a badge, I wear a white collar."

"So you can talk to people about your God, right?"

"Yes, but he's everybody's God, not just mine. He's yours, too."

"Nope," she said. "I don't know God, but I'm close to havin' a *real* spirit guide." She scooted out of the chair and grabbed her White Sea Otter, securing it in her pouch. She then straightened the strap across her chest so it settled at her belted waist, glanced at her notepad, nodded to herself as if to approve of her notes, and slid it back into her bag.

She was smart, loving, and intensely observant; a sponge absorbing Solomon's world, like I had. A carved spirit guide, two creatures to love unconditionally, and schooling: Solomon spinning a restorative web. He more than anyone could eradicate the venom that had sunk into her spirit. I'd learned the hard way that there were times to battle the darkness and other times to surrender and just let in the light. Perhaps in God's divine wisdom, He knew this village needed a child. In that instant I knew Tula May, like Solomon, must remain in Manzanita. Needed to spin a web of my own.

"Soon I'll have a spirit inside me," she said. "Solomon says yours is that fat raven."

"Oh," I said, looking outside where Raven watched from the madrone tree. "Well, yes."

"Can I clean my friends?" she asked. "Solomon said I could."

"Of course," I said and opened the door. The rain had stopped. I ushered her out and turned on the garden hose. The sun splashed and sparkled over the wet yard. "Here's a bucket and a scrub brush. You warm enough?" I asked. She nodded and fervently got to work scrubbing her loved ones, whispering to them they'd be alright. I didn't want her to be alone in the yard with the black panel truck lurking, so I stayed outside with her.

"When I don't wash 'em they stinks to high heaven, Mrs. B says. So it's my job to keep 'em clean. All Rounders have jobs, ya know."

Even at her age she knew having a job meant belonging. She never belonged before, never had something of her very own to love and care for—so she washed those creatures as if they were the crown jewels.

"And you're doing a good job," I said. "A real good job."

Certainly nothing could replace the love of a good mother, but that wasn't what she had. Some parents didn't deserve children. The women in this town could lavish love on her. Of course if her mother came back, hearts would be broken. But, then, no real love is ever wasted, and rumor had it, sooner or later broken hearts mend.

Tula May was in the right place. If thrown into foster care, she'd be lost. If Bud knew, he'd insist we turn her over to the authorities. But the ironclad laws of Bud's world could assert themselves over and over and never make things right. Manzanita was a separate, private part of God's cosmos, where the impossible was still possible and where Solomon always knew best.

Sun quickly gave way to a blanket of clouds. From my porch I heard the waves and foraging seagulls and looked around at the morning—looked also for that truck. Across the street the clatter of Imogene's sign clanked against the glass window on her door as she flipped to OPEN. The smell of donuts in the deep fryer perfumed the air. My gaze landed, *as it always did*, on the still-vacant Bouvre house.

Out-of-season rifle shots blasted through the trees somewhere off in the distance, toward Elk Flats. Black silhouettes of birds scattered like ink spots against the sky.

"Tula May, let's get a fresh donut, shall we?" I said reaching my hand out to hold hers. She didn't accept but walked close by my side, clutching her suede pouch. Solomon emerged from Imogene's back door.

"There were three shots on the flats," I said. "Did you hear them?"

He nodded, leaned down to Tula May, and said, "Clean your friends?"

"Yep," she said.

"Good. *Duh-HOOTS-nuh*," he said patting the top of her head.

She darted a look at me and said, "That's a dead word, but I like it. Means *good girl*."

"It's a good word, honey," I said. "I like it, too."

"You go inside with Imogene," Solomon said.

"But… I been waitin' for you."

He leaned down again, knife at his belt, medicine pouch at his side. "You go now."

"Okaaay," she whined and stomped into the store.

"I be back soon," he said, nodding to me to still keep an eye on her. He then hurried down the alleyway and cut through backyards, zigzagging to the trailhead up Neahkahnie. I knew he'd follow those shots to see who was hunting out of season. Not that he cared much for man's law, but he did care about strangers not respecting Mother Nature.

One year he tied three "early"' hunters to their rig and left them on the flats for two days before Bud followed up on reports of people screaming and found them there. They had killed two mother deer and their fawns; *someone* had spread their victims out in front of the men. The "city boy" hunters were lucky *someone* didn't cut their throats.

When Bud brought the poachers back into town, the then eighty-two-year-old Solomon sat on his bench in front of Imogene's and glared at them. Bud asked the city boys if that old Indian there was the one who got the drop on all three of them. None of their egos could reconcile the long, grey hair and wrinkled skin with the "crazed warrior who appeared out of nowhere" who jumped them in the middle of the night. As Bud expected, no one pressed charges.

Chapter 56

THEO

WITH TULA MAY settled at Imogene's for the night, Bud in Tillamook until late, and the Church Ladies' Rose Contest in the church courtyard finally over, I poured a hot tea, minus the Murphy's, and sat on my back porch with the letters, determined to open one.

One letter postmarked October '52 was heavier than the rest. I closed my eyes, held it in my hand, and tried to recall why it was so heavy. October? Oh yeah. October. Before sunrise, we Rakkasan were charged with dropping into the Happy Sun Orphanage in the mountains to move some kids, a Catholic priest, a Frenchman, and his Irish nuns to a convent near the T'aebaek Mountain Range. Seemed simple enough.

I asked the sisters why the children were in danger. One nun explained they were the unblessed of mixed race, the undesirables. Half-breeds. Half-Chinese, Korean, Mongolian, or half-white, half-black. Either way, undesirable bloodlines. And undesirable bloodlines had to be cleansed, she said. One of the many gruesome plans of the North Koreans, who we called the NK, was to enter every orphanage and slaughter those helpless kids.

This heavy letter was where I wrote the details of that night, that evacuation of twenty-seven motherless children with sad brown eyes, the brave and peace-loving Father Answar, and six faith-filled nuns. Away from dropping bombs, bayonet slayings, and an unfathomable hatred.

Just holding that heavy letter I heard their voices, saw their round faces, full of curiosity. How they touched our uniforms, stared at our revolvers, boots, my belt of knives, grenades. Their eyes full of questions: Why did my field jacket have so many pockets? What did the insignias on my uniform mean? When would they see their parents again?

Father Answar and five of those Sisters of Mercy didn't make it that night. The remaining sister said the fires of hell had risen up and consumed their peaceful valley and that a flood from heaven was needed to cleanse it of its lack of humanity.

A dark curtain closed in on me. I couldn't breathe. I slid the weighty, still-unopened letter marked *Return to Sender* back into the string and set it down.

* * *

Just as the sun fully set Solomon stepped up to my back porch and said, "It is awake."

"What's awake?"

He sat on the banister and said, "Neahkahnie fighting spirits."

"Well, I'm not sure what we can do about waking spirits until they—"

"Tire tracks of a truck go up, then disappear," he said. "There is disturbance. Is not good. I go again tomorrow."

"Should I drive up to Sealy's?"

"You will not find him there."

"How can you be sure?"

"I am sure," he said, then stood and walked back to his yard.

His soaring fire snapped and spit, casting a golden radiance that emanated off his silhouette and throughout his yard. He took items from his Medicine Bundle and laid them on his log bench. The smell of sacred herbs he'd sprinkled into his fire filled the night. He raised his arms to the sky, calling upon his spirits as he began his incantations. A full oyster-colored moon settled into the sapphire sky. Creatures flitted—frogs croaked, crickets chirped. I eased into my wicker chair. Solomon chanted, low and rhythmically, breathing in his burning white sage in his nightly ceremony to purify the sacred ground. He sent out prayers and called on the wisdom of his Ancient Ones, meditating on the battle to come.

The firelight grew smaller, the moon brighter. His rhythms lulled me. He stopped, placed his prayer feathers back in his large abalone shell. Each feather symbolized something different: trust, honor, strength, wisdom, and many more easily misplaced virtues. He then doused his smoking sage. Then, as always, he tapped three times on the head of his carved Frog, letting the creature know it wasn't yet time to carry his soul to the next world. That way, when he slept, he needn't fear Frog would think him dead, and take his soul home. He often spoke of Frog's powers to live in two worlds.

The tree creaked as he climbed into his hammock. The animals hushed. Beams of a Hunter's moon washed eerily over our adjoining yards. It had a luminous, pearlescent ring around it, which, though hauntingly beautiful, meant heavy rains would follow, the sea would thrash against the shores; two worlds would collide, and flooding waters would overwhelm our valley.

Chapter 57

SOLOMON

THE LATE-DAY SUN sagged toward horizon. Soon Theo would open church doors after ladies played their games; shouting, laughing in basement. My body was tired from searching for waking phantoms on Neahkahnie, even more tired from talk, talk, talking of this small child, Tula May. Her mother wanders lost, under a dark cloud—gone seven days now. Like ashen seagull whose bill stained red by blood of Wild Woman, she was scarred by bad deeds of another; could not get free from poison. There was no help for the mother. The child did not know this yet.

"There," Tula May said as she laced Eagle feather into my hair. "I put feathers in your braid." Her hand, size of sparrow, patted my shoulder like my own daughter once did. "When I grow up I want my hair to be long like yours—except soft, like girl hair, not boy hair. Can we dance now?"

I stared at the trees, waiting for drums of my elders. They did not come.

"South Wind blow energy into my spirit," I whispered, then stood. Ruby wanted me to stay, help Tula before crossing over to next world, but I was tired. My Wolf remained faithful guide. He was tired, too. He waited patiently for our last journey.

Tula May jumped up, raised arms high in air, and asked, "Is this how?"

She circled church's garden pond, flailing like baby bird who struggles to fly.

"Yes," I said. "Very good. *Duh-HOOTS-nuh.*"

The pines swayed above; their branches touched, waking Ancient Ones. Drums whispered from far away. A car sped down alley. Tula May stopped and looked up. Then her face fell to earth. She waited for her mother's stolen spirit to return. It would not. The stain was too deep; she was gone into darkness. The Great Spirit breath finally filled my lungs.

"As you dance," I said, standing, "call all the world's creatures to surround you and aid your vision quest." I reached tall, outstretched my arms. The drums grew louder, filled my aging timbers. I felt eyes of Ancient Ones—Ruby's eyes. Many summers passed since I smelled rose petals in her hair. Even then, her scent filled me. I took deep breath. She was close.

We circled pond like a tribal fire. Ruby urged me to teach Tula May, as she had done seventy years ago when she begged me to teach our own, now-departed children.

"Send forth voice from mind," I said, pointing to the sky. "See sound beams travel out through the winds... through everlasting time... Feel wings brush against your body." I moved my arms like eagle's wings. "Do you sense presence of animal powers yet?"

"I... I don't think so." Her arms, color of white seashells, drooped. "Maybe." She struggled to lift them higher.

"Hold arms closer to body... Your spirit power maybe is not bird."

Her eyes fixed on me.

"Listen," I said. We circled pond, my arms spread wide, she small, but steady. "Listen to hear Birdsong, howling Wolves, Horses neighing, scream of mountain Cougar—all sounds of South Wind's animal kingdom. Listen, little one, listen."

Old Osprey chirped its short whistles, swooped through courtyard, joining dance. Theo, in black robes, watched from doorway. Shadows draped courtyard of stone place of worship.

"I hear them!" Tula May's spirit eyes glowed. "I hear them."

We kept moving. Ancient drums rumbled in my chest, I smelled the smoky fires of long ago, felt and saw one hundred Ancient Ones dancing with us. "As you move in circle," I said, "surrounded by animal powers, watch your dancing footsteps change. Be alert. Watch your hands and arms." The drums in my soul thundered. "You will slowly see change, from deep inside. It shows in your way of dance."

She curved her back, bowed forward, leaning low. Weaved footsteps around pond; intentional and strong.

"Movements," I said, "are traits of your animal, whose presence you will now feel."

"I feel something," she whispered, her round face serious. She moved with cautious steps, fixed on her dance, watching her bare feet and hands. "I feel something!" Excitement spread across her face. "I tingle!"

"*Duh-HOOTS-nuh!* Good girl! Now, when animal fully climb into you, let it celebrate in your spirit for while." My old arms grew weary of eagle wings. "Now, stop dancing," I said and collapsed arms to my sides. The Ancient Ones fell silent and vanished. "Stand still now. Let breathing be slow and rhythmic once again. Close eyes." We stood next to pond, panting. I closed my eyes and faced vanishing horizon where Wolf stared back—his dark eyes, razor sharp, gazed into mine. He looked into my soul. His deep breathing echoed inside me. Then he turned and walked path ahead of me. He, too, is old. His back hunched, his hair matted. He limps from too many battles. We are same.

"Welcome your animal into your soul. This animal will be friend—guide on journeys and when troubles come. Each animal has unique medicine. Their gift to you." My Wolf paused on path, looked back at me. He is ready to go home, but he waits. "Our tide is coming," I told him in my mind. *Ts-ull- ULL-leel, my friend.* He knew it was Ruby's mother spirit wanting to help white child. I told him when I am finished, we two warriors take final journey. I opened my eyes.

Tula May's eyes also opened, burning with joyfulness. Her face sparkled, sweaty. It was good dance. "Solomon," she said. Stretched out her arms and wiggled her fingers, looking at them like they were new. "I think my animal is… is a mouse."

I looked up from my haze. My Wolf disappeared into mist.

"*Hmm?*" What could small grey animal do to save child? "Mouse is good," I said. "Mouse runs and hides very well." So this is the power the Ancients feel she will soon need.

Tula May smiled at me like my young ones did long ago.

"Yes," she nodded with great motion. "A mouse named Nancy Little Feet."

"*Duh-HOOTS-nuh.* Mouse is great travel spirit. Very good!" Smell of Imogene's blackberry pie found me. "We take Nancy Little Feet to have pie now."

Theo smiled, motioned her to enter room where Rounders have pie after he speaks from pedestal. I let go of Tula May's hand, nodded to him. He handed me whole pie.

I walked alley along side of church to my hut; Ruby's dark eyes looked down on me. Scent of her hair filled my spirit. My time was short. Soon Tula May, Nancy Little Feet, must go her path alone.

Chapter 58

THEO

FAT DROPS OF RAIN pelted my shingle roof. By four a.m. thunder forked across the sky. I tossed and turned, wondering who left the fresh tire tracks on Neahkahnie. Opened the bedroom window to let in the humid smell of wet soil, grass, and trees, a reminder…

*   *   *

It rained hard the night we evacuated the children from their orphanage, harder than I'd seen, even on the Oregon Coast. The smell of wet dirt, trees, and napalm. That's the smell I remembered most, the chemical and petroleum of burning napalm. We scrambled with the kids up the dominating T'aebaek Mountain—the mountain was nearly the same height as Neahkahnie but had limestone caves tunneled deep within. Massive stalagmites hung heavy throughout the corridors. Ancient bamboo-roped bridges built across chasms linked the vast rooms of the caves to one another. It was otherworldly. But the surviving nun knew the place, the Karst Caves, and said we'd be safe. Water spouted from innumerable cracks and seeps; the sound of rain and falling water was everywhere.

We clawed our way up the hills and out of the valley of death. The CCF had entered the war that week and were as ubiquitous as the rain. The NK were ruthless and bloodthirsty and wanted those kids—and now us—dead. The kids and dedicated nun were too vulnerable for us to abandon for slaughter, so we, my buddy Lieutenant Peters and me, abandoned our orders instead.

When there was time to think—a rare luxury—I was deeply disturbed by the callousness that had grasped my soul. Struggled to regain control of emotions, tried to remember scriptural passages that might tell me what to do, but all I recalled were Bible teachings about "just wars," not about loving my enemy. Lost God's messages, words, and prayers somewhere before each brittle dawn. Sometime before the rising light, my spirit twisted and grew as barbed as that image burned into me of wire where bodies hung trapped, drained of life—there with them hung my innocence and wonderment at life. With them hung my disillusionment with mankind, with God, with everything I had stood for.

*   *   *

Rain hit harder, a thousand drums beating against everything in their path. I turned on the lamp and got dressed, recalling all the details written in that heavy letter.

Solomon once said that the raindrops of a storm were not rain at all, but the tears of his Ancient Ones, and of Ruby and his three children, who died of natural causes; none lived past fifty years. These rains, their tears, were certainly falling now; pinging off glass, rattling windows, pelting roofs as thunder boomed through the sound waves. A sharp crackle of lightning hit not far away—there was a loud thump, the street light went out; town went black.

I grabbed my flashlight and headed to the hall closet for the box of storm supplies and set them on the dining room table. Lit a candle and put it next to the aquarium—light flickered off the glass tank. Lit two more, glanced out the window to Imogene's. Her apartment was dark. I went into the kitchen to light up the gas stove. It clicked three times, then the smell of gas, and a small flame burst around the rim of the burner. Outside the window, Solomon was in his yard, shirtless, arms outstretched, face toward the sky, eyes closed, taking in those tears.

I wondered, had he been there, if he'd have said *Korea's* Ancient Ones were crying, that that was why the sound of rain was ever-present—it was *their* tears. I remembered thinking it at the time. Korea was a heartbreaking place. Even I saw too many tragedies to recall. I'm sure its Ancient Ones were, *are* crying.

*   *   *

I filled the coffee pot with water and left Solomon to his rain. It fell softer but steady as a waterfall. Weak morning light crept into the cold house. Then the electricity popped on. The house hummed with all the noises a house makes, the ones never noticed until they're gone. I blew out the candles, and just as the coffee pot gurgled to a finish, the aquarium's night-light clicked off, day-light on. Bud pushed the front door open and yelled, "Up yet?"

"Kitchen!" I said, reaching into the cabinet and taking down a second cup.

"Mornin'." He slapped a file down on the counter, poured himself some coffee, and took a deep whiff of air. "What's that—?"

"Sol's ointment."

"Right," he said. "Jeez, you stink."

"It grows on ya."

"God, I hope not."

"Little early for you, isn't it?" I asked.

"Storm," he said, taking a bite of *my* toast. His eyes drooped, baggy from sleeplessness.

"Would you like some toast?" I asked. "You know, of your own."

"No, that's fine," he said. "Little too much butter, though." He dusted crumbs from his shirt. "So… that truck you saw."

"Yeah?" I said, dropping two more pieces of bread in the toaster.

"When was the first time you saw it?"

"Couple days ago. Why? Who is it?"

"Black panel—are you sure?" Bud asked, his thick brows knitted closely together.

"Absolutely. Why?"

"Well, the owner was found in an alley behind his locksmith business in Tillamook."

"Is he alright?"

"He's not doin' too well."

I made the sign of the cross. "Is he—?"

"Yep. Dead," he said. "A black panel… not so common."

I pictured the truck moving slowly, then the crimson-rimmed eyes of the driver, then him flicking his cigarette out at the end of the street. "Do you think—?"

"I do," he said, depositing his mug in the sink. "It's Hansel." He looked at his watch and out the window toward Solomon's yard. "Old man up yet?"

"Yeah." I glanced outside. "He probably just left. Said he was going back up there early to see if he could find the vehicle that left those tracks. Why?"

He stared into Solomon's yard at the hanging hides, handmade arrows, drums, and ceremonial canoe Solomon was carving out of a fallen redwood, and then said, "Guns loaded?"

"You keep asking me that," I said. "Yes… loaded. But how can we be sure it's Hansel?"

"Look here," Bud said as he held out that gritty photograph. His voice went from old toast-stealing friend to stern Officer Bud Grearson. "That the driver?"

"It's him."

"Between Nehalem, Wheeler, and here, we have what, maybe twenty teen girls, another thirty little kids playin' in the streets, down at the river, the beach, and up on Neahkahnie?"

"At least."

"Well, for some crazy-ass reason he's set his sights on you. And *you* means Manzanita." He shoved the file in my hand and said, "Like it or not, you're in this fight now. I want you to read every detail of what he did to some of these kids. I guaran-damn-tee you there's more victims… There's no room for your religion crap here. We're playin' for real. Netty and Oz saw Toreck *with* Hansel in a black truck two days ago. Now, what we've got here is one of your damned hermit crabs hidin' out on Neahkahnie. And rumor has it, catchin' hermit crabs is somethin' you're pretty good at."

Chapter 59

THEO

THE FILE HAD TILLAMOOK COUNTY JAIL in black square letters across the cover and smelled of cigar smoke. Inside were snapshots of young girls with swollen eyes and bloodied lips; one girl's head had been shaved, and they all had a look of terror in their eyes like the concentration camp photographs in last month's *LIFE*. Words jumped off the page: *kidnapped, held hostage, tortured, ten years old*. I closed the folder. Pictures and names lodged in my throat like undigested food. How was it possible this monster hadn't been caught? But then there'd always been evil in the world, always would be. The only real question was what to do about it.

* * *

After I showered and dressed, Solomon came through the back door.

"Mornin'," I said. "Anything on Neahkahnie?"

I poured a shot of Murphy's into my morning coffee to help dislodge that undigested bit of matter, slumped into a dining room chair and said, "Just calming my nerves."

He shook his head no, gave a dark glance at the bottle of Murphy's, picked up the file from the table, and opened it.

"Can't look at it anymore," I said. "Besides, I need to get to Saint Mary's for confession."

"You need that ritual?" he asked. "For your Korea?"

"I never go to confession myself. Should, but I don't. This is for the parishioners."

"Catholics like confession," he said. "Creates change, helps stuck energy flow, lightens saddle of guilt, shame. It is ceremony. Ceremonies are good for lost, sleeping people."

"Excuse me, *you* have all kinds of ceremonies."

"I am different kind of lost... I am left behind... but I am awake."

"Never thought of you as *any* kind of lost," I said, tying my shoes.

"This not about me. Is about you. You are sleeping in your life."

"What? Is there a sign on the door that says 'come on in and nudge the bear'?" Solomon glared at me.

"I'm awake," I said. "I know who I am —"

"No," he said. "You know who you're supposed to be — you have forgotten who you are. You sleep, like Neahkahnie Mountain, a warrior who slumbers beneath dark blanket, slumbers to hide from pain, hide from true self." He placed his forceful hand on the file. "To know your enemy, Theo, is to know yourself. *You know this.*"

I stared at the file. A sudden consciousness came over me. I *had* been afraid to look at them. If I kept my head in the sand, whom would that serve? "All right, I get it. I'm awake."

"You have stone on your heart... weighs you down. You need ritual to lighten load... for Ireland, Korea... for guilt or shame?"

"No guilt," I said, realizing that the gravity of shame was the only real emotion I felt anymore. "And no, I don't need a ritual for shame."

"Shame is hard," he said, "like festering bullet in your hip. Only way to heal, return to source, cut open, drain poison before it cripples body." He picked up the letters and saw they were unopened, unread. "Then do fire ritual. You used fire before to cleanse a festering wound."

"Yes," I said. The image of the McMurtry brothers' building in flames came to life. No shame. No guilt. I'd healed a festering wound. "I have. But that was then, this is now. How?"

"A way comes... soon. I see it. Soon you, *Raven Two Fists*, will be one to nudge bear."

He set the stack of letters back in their place where I kept them like decoration on the table. Then he picked up the file and handed it to me.

"Now," he said. "You have enemies here. Right now you must wake to know *this* enemy. He grows strong. Both men, afraid of nothing on this earth, apart from you."

"Why me?"

"Toreck is fool. He wants revenge for what you took from him. Revenge is deep well more potent than fear. He cannot help himself. But the man with snakes, he is dark spirit. A demon with powers of control. He will force you to your greatest battle."

"I'm not a soldier anymore."

"Remember your lessons? Sometimes you choose peace, sometimes fight for it."

"At seminary they taught that a man of God always chooses peace."

"Man cannot walk two paths," he said. "Know this enemy. Remember your lessons."

The back door banged closed behind him.

*   *   *

The faces of the orphans passed through me again; an eternal, far-reaching shadow. I pictured their protector, Father Answar—the most peace-loving man that ever walked this earth—tearing off his robes and picking up a rifle before *all* his orphans were gunned down. It was a short, barbed distance between peace and violence—a distance a man *should* be prepared to travel to protect those he loves. Like Kiernan, Father Answar had underestimated his enemy's hatred. We all did. I wouldn't again.

I downed my last shot of Murphy's. The fiery warmth rushed through my veins. Then I took the half-full bottle and wrapped a thick barrier of medical tape—used to wrap my knuckles—around the seal. I placed it next to the letters. Solomon was right—it was time to be fully awake.

Chapter 60

THEO

MORNING CONFESSION HOUR was unattended. I sat in the booth with a flashlight, reading the police file. Rain pinged against the stained glass. Pearl came into the church, lit a candle, said a prayer, then left, leaving the sugary smell of peach cobbler behind. I was hungry.

The file was enlightening. Hansel had been tortured as a child. His father, a disturbed and twisted individual, used religion to reign his dark kingdom. A man like that does a lot of damage, more than most because his victims believe he has the authority of God behind his perverted words and deeds, and therefore give him dominion over their lives. Especially a child. Don't know what all went on, but do know he hurt young Genghis; planted a poisonous thorn deep inside him. And what I know about that is hurt children grow up and hurt things, animals, and other children trying to extricate that malicious thorn. By Genghis Hansel's age, thirty-eight, there's no help to offer. I should have considered salvation but believed otherwise—like Bud said, he's a rabid dog. He just needs to be put out of his pain.

The file had pages of notes, suspicions, leads, disturbing coincidences, but no evidence. The officers across the country who had compiled the information had no doubt that Hansel was a child molester *at least*, murderer at worst. No doubt, but no evidence, and our justice system demanded evidence. However, in the absence of proof, doing what's *just* may demand something different altogether.

Back at home I wrapped my hands, boxed for thirty, tossed my knife at Solomon's board twenty times—ten for exercise, ten for aim. I loaded both of Mamaí's rifles and set them in the corner next to where my black robes hung in the closet with my Army jacket and fatigues.

For the first year home I had been comfortable at Saint Patrick's wearing the robes that separated me from the people. But here, in this village, my home, we're different from the rest of the world—in an orbit all our own. Here, I'm also a Rounder. No black robes, white collars, or tight confession booths would ever change that.

Chapter 61

IMOGENE

DAILY SPECIAL

Ham and Swiss on Rye, Sweet Potato Salad and Greens .75¢

With Tula May sleeping in Christina's bed across the hall from me, I'd tossed and turned all night. By dawn there were five cigarette butts in the ashtray on the patio. I had to face the day ahead just like any other day. But it wasn't like any other day. There was an intruder.

Pearl arrived by six so we'd have two hours to get our work done before opening.

"Here, hon, cut up these eggs, would ya," I said handing over the boiled eggs. As my sign sputtered on, I wrote the specials on the chalkboard, then hung it over the window by the new Rit Dye case. Theo's car backed out of his driveway, top down. He waved and headed toward Highway 101, summoned to Portland. It was no surprise the bishop beckoned him to Saint Patrick's for events—the wealthy women of the church opened their tight pocketbooks when handsome Father Riley was around.

Pearl stood at the butcher's block with three finely chopped piles: celery, eggs, and onion. She was careful not to allow them to touch; never mind that in sixty seconds she'd be tossing them in a bowl and mixing them all together.

I counted the register money and watched Pearl slowly lift one food pile at a time with her cupped hands, then gently nestle them into the mixing bowl. She crowned the pile with the onions as I put a new roll of register tape inside the till and closed it.

Pearl grabbed a wooden spoon and mashed her masterpiece of finely diced morsels with a fierce beating. Faster and faster, knocking the life out of whatever she imagined lived in it. And Pearl imagined some kind of ghost or another lived in everything. Then she stopped her frenzied beating, set down the smoking spoon, and stood back. A smile came over her round face. She pushed her wayward strands of hair behind her ears, looked up, and said, "Okay, it done."

"Okay... egg salad it is," I said.

Tula May appeared at the foot of the stairs, fully dressed in her beige pants, white blouse, and suede pouch. Her hair was a rat's nest and her freckled face had crease marks from the pillow.

"Tula May!" I said. "Good morning."

When I passed Christina's room she had been snoring. I didn't have the heart to wake her, or the courage to step into Christina's room and wake another child sleeping in her bed.

"Did you sleep well, honey?" I asked.

She stood there with her hand on the door frame like a reluctant cat near a cold bath. Her brow creased. She studied Pearl and asked, "What's she doin'?"

"She's making food for customers." I motioned for her to sit at the table where I'd put out a bowl, Frosted Flakes, milk, and bacon. "I didn't know what you liked for breakfast so I—"

"This is for me?" Her eyes popped. She sat on the bench and gawked at breakfast, then ran her fingers along the checkered tablecloth, lightly touched the petals of the sunflower in the mason jar, then warily stroked its soft fuzzy center.

I sat down next to her. She scooted a foot away, still a skittish bath-fearing cat. "Okay," I said and poured cereal into her bowl. "Let's start with this."

She snatched two pieces of bacon and shoved them into her mouth like a hungry thief, her cheeks bulging. She gulped the milk, staring at me as if I'd reach out and slap the glass from her hand. I knew she'd been eating nothing but fish for breakfast with Solomon, and who knows what else—if anything—before he found her, so this kind of food was probably all a shock.

"Don't eat so fast honey," I said. "There's plenty where that came from."

She whipped her head around and looked at Pearl. Pearl nodded yes. Tula May returned her gaze to me, then to the cereal box with the big orange tiger on the front. I poured milk over her flakes. A warm rush of blood pulsed through me. I felt suddenly dizzy, so I stood up and walked to the window, lit the candles on the shelf in front of my photos, and watched her eat from that safe distance instead, as if she were one of Pearl's ghosts. That familiar feeling overwhelmed my body: muddy stones bubbled and crumbled beneath my feet—sinking, falling, drowning. That thorny crab inside me pinched a little. I hunched slightly, then stood back up, lit a cigarette, and gazed helplessly outside. She'd only be here a few days, maybe weeks, I told myself. I can do this.

Outside, trees were bare. The heavy rains knocked to the ground what few leaves had clung to Theo's oak tree. The skies brightened almost unnaturally as a rainbow arched high against the sky.

Tula May didn't look up from the cereal box, which she now gripped in both hands studying the smiling Tony the Tiger like she'd never seen such a thing.

Pearl was deep-frying donuts. Always indifferent to fashion, she wore plaid pants, a paisley shirt, and a black-and-white polka dot apron all splattered with batter. We both looked at Tula May, so small, so innocent. I glanced back out the window where the light was now a soft blush of pink against the cottages along Laneda Avenue.

"Well," I said, taking a deep breath and dousing my cigarette, "let's get to work." To lighten things up a bit I turned on a station that played Buddy Holly and Elvis. Pearl dusted and restocked the three rows of wooden shelves: C&H sugar, Ivory soap, Hills Brothers Coffee, and woolen blankets. Except for the lanterns, pickaxes, and maps of Neahkahnie, there was nothing fancy, only the bare essentials needed at the coast.

Pearl aligned the coffee cans with strict precision: all cans to the edge of the shelf and all letters facing front, like little red soldiers. Since James had died last year she'd developed interesting habits, like beating the food into submission, gardening at dawn, and always needing two cups for tea as if he'd stroll up behind her and want some.

Solomon cracked the screen door open and said, "Salmon today."

"Great," I said, handing him a cup of coffee. "I'll clear off that freezer shelf."

He smiled but never came inside in the mornings, preferring his feet not to hit hard floors before noon, instead favoring the soft ground God intended. The look on his face startled me; he looked tired, suddenly older. I shook it off. Hell, he'll outlive us all.

Tula May jumped up from the table, grabbed her sweater, and quietly ran outside.

He walked her to Mrs. B's like he used to walk me to the school bus stop, wearing his red shirt and blue jeans, barefoot, cup of coffee in his hands.

Mamaí once explained that it took him many years to appreciate the texture of the white man's world. Born in the 1860s, he grew up wearing elk hide, riding horses, and hunting when and wherever he wanted. He hated white man's clothing until Ruby gave him a red flannel shirt like the timbermen wore. To this day, it's the only kind he will wear. I supposed the fact that Ruby liked it made it tolerable to him, soothing against his skin.

"Need peaches!" Pearl shouted from behind the back shelves.

"Got it." I took the supply list from my pocket and wrote, "Solomon's shirt and blankets, peaches, corn flakes, shortening, flour." Already worn out from no sleep, I plopped down on the stool behind the counter. Solomon left Mrs. B's and headed through Theo's yard toward his hut. The morning sun quickly faded. Sunglow clouds rolled in.

Sitting there, I realized that since Solomon had gone into Christina's room with me, I hadn't felt my heart plummet when I passed her door. I looked in there twice just yesterday and didn't get woozy or cry. I hadn't had the crushing sense of loss that had plagued me, or felt that thousand-pound rock that had weighed on my heart for so long. Maybe Solomon was right: Now at peace about her death, I could have a spiritual union with her for the rest of my life. I liked that idea of a quiet time all our own. Maybe I *could* let go of that heaviness.

My clock chimed nine. Thomas hadn't called in eight days. Oh well, like Theo says, tragedy either bonds people or becomes an abyss too deep to traverse.

The phone rang and nearly startled me off my stool. "Imogene's," I said.

"Hey there, Imogene girl!"

It was our local dairy farmer whose wife never let him spend more than seventy-five cents a day on frivolities like food and who still had a tinge of Norwegian accent, though he'd been in America for over fifty years. "Mornin' to ya, Mr. Gandel," I said.

"What's fer lunch today?"

"Anything you like, but the special's ham and swiss and Mrs. B's pickle jam."

"Alrighty then." He hung up. Worried he'd miss the special and have to pay twenty-five cents more for a regular menu item, his lanky, six-foot-five body would hustle through the door at eleven sharp—with his tractor left running out front. I liked the old guy. After all, when I was in school, he always bought chocolate-mint Girl Scout cookies from me. But other than that, he and his wife were the spend-thriftiest people in town.

Thomas was also thrifty. I looked at our wedding photo. I loved him then. But soon Christina came. She'd had his big brown eyes, and when she suckled my breast, I gazed into them, feeling certain she was God's calling card as He knocked on the closed door to my heart. I let Him in again, certain He'd blessed me like no other. I had a loving husband, an adorable baby, and the life I'd always dreamed of. Did I blame Thomas for her death, as he said? Maybe.

"Imogene!" Pearl's voice pierced my thoughts. "Telephone!" She pointed to the phone.

I doused my cigarette and grabbed the receiver. "Manzanita Market."

There was no answer. "Hello?" I said. No answer. "*Hellooo?*"

"There *was* a man," Lucy chimed in. "He asked for you by name."

"Was it—"

"No," she said, "not Thomas. Sorry Imogene. I didn't recognize the voice."

"Thanks, Lucy." I hung up.

Pearl stood across the room, broom in hand, staring at me. "Thomas?"

"Let's just get our work done," I said. I went to the back kitchen to stir the soups and check on the corn bread. Honestly, I had a little cry over the chowder. A bit more salt wouldn't be noticed. I covered the soups, wiped my tears, and returned to the front of the store.

Pearl stood behind the register, wide-eyed and frozen. On the other side, motionless and staring at her, was Toreck Sealy.

Chapter 62

IMOGENE

DAILY SPECIAL
Cherry cobbler with Vanilla Ice Cream .50¢

I forced a smile and cool as a cucumber moved toward the counter.

Toreck stood with a pack of Camels in his hand. His ruddy skin was scarred from the acne he'd had in high school. He had a hunting knife attached to his belted jeans, and he wore thick-soled black boots and a brown leather coat over his white t-shirt. Had an even sharper edge to him than before prison. He seemed bigger, leaner, more muscular. His once-dirty reddish-blond hair was shaved to his head like a military cut. Sporting a shiner, he was pumped up, ready for trouble. He stood at the counter and stared at Pearl with a blank, hate-filled look.

"What you want?" she asked.

Adrenalin barbed up and down my spine. I moved slowly past the shelves and picnic tables until I stood next to her behind the register. We hadn't seen him up close in over a year, but he hadn't really changed. Mean men—and Toreck Sealy was born mean—don't change much, they just get meaner. And certainly prison had done nothing to soften the wife- and child-beating bastard.

"Can we help you?" I asked, bracing myself.

Pearl trembled. I grabbed her hand, praying Bud would burst through the door any second. Toreck remained silent, staring us up and down with hungry eyes. I sucked in my chest and pulled my sweater closed. "Those cigarettes are twenty-five cents."

A twisted smile formed on his face, and he said, "What's buzzin', cuzzin'?" My body stiffened. "We don't want any trouble here," I said. "Twenty-five cents." I held out my trembling hand for his money, trying to pull his attention away from my breasts.

Being close in age, we had gone through school at the same time. He'd been a bitter pill all my life. Face-to-face with him now I saw that his blunt nose and receding brow had tightened and tanned, but he still had the unalterable face of a tyrant.

His smile faded. "What's your problem, witch woman?" he hissed at Pearl through his yellowed teeth, leaning forward and distorting his expression. Their eyes locked. "Why the hell do you look at me like that, gook?" He leaned across the counter. "Boo!"

Pearl jumped, then quickly reached under the counter for the baseball bat. "You—"

"You nothin'," I said holding her back, reaching out my hand. "Twenty-five cents."

He threw his coins down on the counter. Two shiny dimes and a dirty nickel spun and rolled to the floor. His eyes moved to me. I felt a deep sinking sensation. No kindness was going to belay this dog of war. Pearl was right—he needed a baseball bat right upside his head. I looked down to where the bat was usually propped under the shelf. It was gone. *Shit!*

Suddenly Bud shoved the door wide open. "What the hell you doin' in town, boy?" he shouted as he marched up to Toreck, towering over him.

"I told you not to show your face for two weeks till you cooled them jets," Bud said sizing him up from head to toe. "I catch you fightin' again, anywhere, your ass is mine." He moved his face within an inch of Toreck's. "You understand me, boy? No trouble outta you." He burned his stare into him. "Or your friend."

Toreck's face tightened at mention of his friend. Who was his friend? His small, dark eyes squinted behind the bruise. He stood vigilant in his hostility, fists clenched. "Fuck you," he spewed. "I grew up in this worthless shit-town and I'll damn well come to the fuckin' store whenever the fuck I want to."

Pearl and I both stepped back from the counter. Bud didn't flinch.

"That's two, boy," Bud said calmly, staring deep into Toreck's mottled face. "Three's only a matter of time," he said, putting a toothpick between his teeth. "Just a matter a time, boy."

His tone was more aggressive than usual. *Was he goading him like Theo had?*

Toreck broke his stare with Bud and fixed his beady eyes on Pearl, then me. I felt his rage crawl under my skin and somehow seed itself there like a deep-rooted, poisonous weed.

"I wonder, Sheriff," he said real calm, as if someone whispered in his ear. His face relaxed, and a menacing smile curved up the left side of his bruised cheek. "Which one of these two broads you'd kill for." His ferrety eyes darted up and down us both. Then they settled on me.

I threw my arm around Pearl's shoulders and glared right back at him. I didn't want him to think I was afraid, but honestly I wanted to cry. The coolness in his voice unnerved me more than his words, though they were pretty damned upsetting. He slowly and confidently turned to Bud like something smarter, cooler, and more deliberate suddenly possessed him.

Bud's face turned to stone. His brow formed one grizzled line across his forehead. "Was that a threat?" he asked. His voice was so constricted I thought he'd pull his gun out right then.

"Just curious," Toreck said, grabbing a tobacco can. He flicked a dollar bill to the floor.

Bud stepped close, loomed over him, and said, "Don't come back here, ever." He poked Toreck's chest real hard. "This store," he said as he pointed all around, "off limits. Hear me?"

The screen door swung open. We all looked. Solomon stood with the sunlight behind him. He glanced at the three of us and spotted Toreck. His eyes locked on him like prey. He stepped inside, and the door slowly shut behind him. Solomon gradually slid his hunting knife from his belt and hunched like he was about to wrestle a bear. Bud put his hand up, suggesting he do nothing. Solomon remained ready.

Toreck backed away. "Gooks and redskins," he blurted. The calm Toreck disappeared with the return of the old Toreck. He grabbed the door handle, nearly wrenching it off its hinges. "That's all we got in this stinkin' town, gooks and redskins." He stormed out and the door slammed closed. All the combs bounced off the rack and hit the floor. The metal Elsie Borden Cow display prattled against the wall, then it, too, dropped to the floor.

"Everybody okay?" Bud asked. "He didn't hurt ya none, did he?"

Solomon put his knife back in its sheath.

"I no like dat Toreck," Pearl said, shaking her head like Mr. Gandel's dashboard hula girl. "He goin' to do someting someday."

"Go ahead, Pearl, honey," I said. "Finish up those shelves and let's get the clam chowder goin'. All's good now."

She disappeared into the back kitchen mumbling, "Devil eyes say die, gook, die."

"Listen," I said to Bud, who helped himself to a soda from the Junior Coke Machine. He snapped the top off and stood guard, eyes fixed out the window. Toreck started his Chevy pick-up; the rumble of his engine rattled the windows. He sped away, brakes squealing at the corner. "He scares the bajeebbies outta me. What are we gonna do?"

"Until he does something," Bud said, "I can't put him away. All I can do is watch his every step." He stared out the window and downed his Coke. "I'm tired of waitin'… I hoped he'd take a swing at me."

"Yeah, you were doing a Theo," I said as the truck disappeared at the end of the street. "But I think after today we need a better plan than to be polite and hope for the worst." I rummaged under the register for the bat. "*Polite* can be misinterpreted. Where's the bat?"

"I know! I know!" Pearl called from the kitchen.

I pictured Toreck's eyes roving up and down my body and remembered the time in eighth grade when he shoved me against the school lockers and tried to kiss me and grab my boob. I kneed him in the groin so hard he turned purple. I was willing to do that again if necessary.

"I heard a rumor about a black truck," I whispered to Bud. "What's that all about?"

"Nothin' to worry about... just a stolen truck." He scrunched his brow, looked at me, and said, "Where do you hear about these things all the time?"

"Like you," I said, "I have sources. The truck?"

"Right," he said, returning his watchful eyes to the street. "If you see a black truck, stay clear and call me immediately."

"So, it's important... maybe dangerous?"

"Maybe," he said. "So yes, be careful." His face showed the struggle that passed through him. When I was in high school—a silly young girl with a secret crush on him—he rushed to join the Marines to fight in World War II. Men like Bud faced their demons head-on, no pussy-footing around. Even though the demons take a toll, men keep fighting. They go to war, hearts full of salvation, thinking it will matter. They return with a weighty dark stain on their souls and ghosts that haunt them in their sleep.

When he returned from war, wounded, with no sign of life in his eyes, he aimlessly walked the beach and slept at his family's inn for six months. Then one day he woke, and the next thing we knew, he'd joined the Coast Guard and was in charge of the station on Neahkahnie Mountain. He was as vigilant as a lighthouse keeper, watching for Japanese submarines, airplanes, and any other affront to our shores. Bud manned the watch post on Neahkahnie Mountain for the last year of the war; Oz and Solomon at his side.

In that moment, standing at my window and holding Bud's crumpled, beige Stetson, I saw him differently: as a man, not the town hero, just a big-hearted man who needed to keep those he loved safe. I wanted to wrap my arms around him, lay my head on his chest, and bury my face in that safe place just below his clean-shaven jawline. Trace his brow, his eyes, his lips with my finger. I inched closer to his side and watched with him, listening to his deep breathing, then closed my eyes and took in the smell of his skin. It had a trace of Old Spice.

"No more!" Pearl shouted startling me from my trance. She blustered out from the kitchen curtain, bat in one hand and the pistol from beneath the kitchen sink in the other. "I no trust him." She hurried to the locked case where we kept bullets and other more dangerous things like hunting knives and rat poison. She held the bat tightly under one arm, the pistol under the other, and fumbled with the lock. "We ready next time," she said, and reached in and knocked a box of bullets all over the floor.

"Pearl," Bud said. "Sweetie." He quick-stepped over to her, took the gun from her grip, and set it aside. "Let's not be shootin' anybody. No cause for that." He gathered up the bullets and closed the gun case. "Prison's no place for a lady."

Pearl yanked her hands to her hips and stared up at him like an angry teenage daughter, then stomped off to the kitchen.

"Are you sure?" I asked, opening the cash drawer and dropping in Toreck's money from the floor. *Business was still business.* "Seems to me you and Theo are planning on trouble."

"Not sure of nothin'," Bud said. "Not plannin' nothin'. Just bein' careful."

I heard the click of the gun's barrel and looked up. He held the old rifle we kept behind the counter and cracked it open. "This is loaded?" he asked looking up at me.

"Yep," I said. "Theo loaded it some time back. So, does this mean I can shoot that bastard if he comes into the store again?"

Chapter 63

THEO

BUD'S TALL FRAME shadowed the doorway of the vicarage—a rare site indeed. He took off his hat and said, "Need to talk to you," looked around the rows of benches, realized it was empty, then relaxed. "Can we go somewhere... else?"

"Come on back," I said, laying the Eucharist candles on the lectern. "My office is quiet until the ladies get here in a few minutes. Bingo, then all hell breaks loose, as you know."

"Thought you told them no more poker in church."

"You've got the gun, you try and stop them."

"Nope," he said. "That's a fool's battle." He dropped his hat on a chair and sat down.

I pointed to the file on my desk. "Awful stuff."

"What's your take?"

"Well," I said. "Hansel's childhood was disturbing by all accounts."

"Okay, but what's this crazy's problem now?"

"Well, his dad's a preacher, mom's Jewish, from Germany... real old school. His dad, one twisted man, warped little Genghis with his manufactured religion crafted from his wife's Jewish theology and his own snake-yielding, back-hills, holy-roller Baptist roots—even on a good day that's napalm."

"Baptist and Jewish. What the hell?" Bud said, quickly darting a glance at Jesus on the cross over my desk.

"I like to pick my battles when possible," I said. "Explaining world religions to you isn't on that short list."

"Okay funny man, I know what they are... it's your point that eludes me."

"Well, it's the references he's made: Chamber of Guf and the seventh heaven."

"And you're gonna explain that whole Chamber of Guf thing to me, right?"

"I need to do more research, but the short version is that in Jewish mythology there's a Tree of Souls. When it blossoms, it creates new souls that fall into the Guf, the Treasury of Souls where the Angel of Conception watches over them until they're born and descend to earth."

Bud scratched his head and said, "What does that have to do—"

"Just stick with me," I said. "According to some rabbinical teachers, the trees are resting places for souls, and only sparrows can see those souls descend, which is why they chirp. He mentioned that to me. When the last soul descends, the Messiah will come, and the world will end. In this belief system, even a newborn baby brings the Messiah closer simply by being born. Thing is, Genghis has it reversed and twisted, believing the opposite, that the more children under the age of twelve (the age, I'm guessing, of *his* lost innocence) who are sent back still pure—therefore filling the chamber—the sooner the Messiah will come and the world will end. I see the world as his pain. His pain will end. These souls are bird-like, free to fly, to return to seventh heaven. He wants to be free. The point is, this lets us know, like you've suspected, he's not just one of your run-of-the-mill wing nuts—he may actually think he's on a religious mission, which is why denying him absolution stuck in his craw." "A religious mission, huh?" Bud said. "Well, I gotta say, I was hopin' for wing nut."

"You and me both, brother—because a man on a mission is a different thing altogether."

Chapter 64

THEO

IT'S HARD TO ANTICIPATE the actions of a crazy person, but the more information, the better. I found an old college book, *Trends in Jewish Mysticism*, and read up on the Chamber of Guf.

Weeks had passed with no sign of any trouble. I figured they were laying low, hoping everyone would think they moved on. But I suspected that was not the case and continued my research of old news articles about missing children.

I was due to cover the store for Imogene, so took the book and headed across the street.

It was early fall. A gust of dry leaves swirled past Imogene's open window. The crisp breeze tickled at the newspaper stand where a rock the size of my fist held down the papers. On Tuesdays she drove into Tillamook for supplies, usually alone. Since she refused to let me go along, I insisted she take Pearl and Tula May. For once, she didn't argue.

I sat behind the register, tore into a Baby Ruth, and in-between reading about Jewish mysticism and studying the Hansel file, manned the register for some very big retail: Mr. Kenney's cigarettes, and the McFall twins' purchase of black molasses for their constipation, which I could have lived the rest of my life without knowing.

The clock chimed ten thirty. Mrs. B pushed through the door, laid her supply box on a table, and said, "Mornin'."

"Mornin'."

She unpacked her blackberry-rum jam onto the shelf marked "Mrs. B's Secret Recipes"—those jars would fly off the shelf because everyone believed she poured a stash of prohibition rum into each batch.

She untied her scarf and tucked it into her blue-and-grey-plaid jacket. Her outer clothing was like a snail's hard shell: practical and protective of what lay beneath. Beneath were her Mandarin blouses, silk scarves, and jade necklaces—the soft underbelly of her past. Able to converse in three languages, she was like a planet in a universe of her own making with her unforgettable and unforgotten past always wrapped around her.

"Tula May go with the girls?" she asked.

"Yep, shopping."

"Bouvre house is still empty," she said.

"Yep."

"Time will tell," she said, tucking errant hairs into her snow-white braided bun.

"It always does."

"We Rounders can raise Tula May just fine, you know."

"I know," I said. "I'm working on it." I'd left messages with my old friend Judge Madsen to find out about adoption or other legal remedies to the situation.

"Well," she said rapping at my feet with her cane. "Work harder."

"Yes ma'am."

"I'm going to need brandy," she said and raised on her tiptoes to take a dark brown bottle from the top shelf. She nestled it into her coat pocket. "Put that on my tab."

"Got it," I said, writing "$1.48." Ironic, given all the rum-runner rumors that brandy was her drink.

"Looks like rain," she said.

"Yes, ma'am, it does."

"You're agreeable today. I hope that means you're up to something… Remember," she said as she cast her expectant eyes on me, "you were a Rounder before you put that contraption on your neck, and you always will be." She opened the door and looked me straight in the eye. "And Theo, this is one child you *can* save."

"Yes, ma'am."

The screen door slammed behind her. I looked at Imogene's telephone. *Why hadn't Madsen returned my calls?* Next to the phone, someone had stuck Imogene's crabbing and fishing license over her wedding photograph. I moved the license just as Imogene's Woody lurched to a stop. She shot out of the car. Pearl, who believed the inevitable impact would be less from the back and thus didn't ride in the front, climbed out as well.

I stood with the door open. "Imogene?"

She pushed past me.

"Pearl?" I said. She scurried by with Tula May in tow.

Imogene tore her jacket off and threw it on the counter, then grabbed her cigarettes.

"We see them," Pearl told me as she took off her matching jacket.

"What?" I asked. "Who?"

"You bet we see them." Imogene yanked the telephone off its shelf and anxiously tapped the connection bar. "Lucy? Lucy?" she shouted into the phone. "Dammit, girl, where are you?" She leaned down toward Tula May and whispered, "That's a bad word, honey. Don't ever say it." Then she stood back up and yelled into the phone, "Dammit Lucy, are ya there?"

"You see who?" I asked.

Pearl frowned and whispered, "Him."

"Toreck?" I asked.

"Lucy," Imogene said, "*Tillamook 222*. Bud's office." Holding the phone, she paced back and forth behind the register. Pearl stood bug-eyed, biting her lip. Imogene stopped pacing and stared at her wedding photo. "Yes, I'll hold," she said, then reached up, took the pin out of the fishing license, and hung it over the photo. "Yes, I'll hold for Sheriff Grearson."

She turned to me and said, "That master plan a yours... well, it's come back to bite."

Chapter 65

THEO

THIRTY MINUTES LATER Bud's patrol car careened to a stop in front of the store. He pushed the screen door open. "Theo, did *you* see anyone?"

"Just Rounders." I climbed down from the stepladder—the silent doorbell was hopeless.

Bud grabbed a maple bar from the tray next to the coffee pots.

"Well?" Imogene said. "What did you find?"

"Not a damned thing," he said.

"We can't say *damn*," Tula May scolded.

"Sorry there, Tula May."

"It's just Tula… I don't like Tula *May*."

"Sorry," he said, draping his arm over the canned-foods shelf. "I stopped by Gandel's, Anderson's, and Gordy's. Nobody seen or heard a thing. Even drove to Sealy's place… don't look lived in."

Imogene's face tightened. "*We saw them*. Both Toreck and another man in that black panel truck. They stopped next to us at the stoplight, Toreck stared at us and said, 'What's *yur* tale, nightingale' or something stupid like that. Then he sneered and flipped his middle finger. I don't like that, but that's not what bothered me," she said blowing smoke. "It was the way he looked at us… then pointed at me with a scary look." She crossed her arms over her chest, her cigarette fixed on her lips. "My skin's creepy-crawling. 'What's your tale, nightingale?'… What does that mean?"

I put my arm around her shoulders. "Nothing's gonna happen to anybody."

"Yeah, Immie," Bud said, forcing a half-smile. "I'll make damn sure of that."

Tula threw her arms up into the air, rolled her eyes, and slid her notepad out of her pouch like she was going to write him a traffic ticket.

"Sorry," Bud whispered. "Bad word?"

"Expect me to believe that?" Imogene marched over to Bud and yanked her hands to her hips. Jaw jutted, green eyes blazing. "Don't even know where they are, do ya?"

"Now, Immie," he said, "I won't let anything happen. You know that."

Oz swung the door open. "Mornin'!" he said. "Did ya'll hear the fracas last night? Two shots and squealin' tires in front a my place. What a night! Netty made me get the shotgun and put it by the bed." Then he darted a glance at everyone. "What?"

"The girls saw them this morning," Bud said.

"Me too," Tula insisted, closing her tablet and sliding it back into her pouch.

Oz's face grew solemn. "So did Netty. I was gonna tell ya later."

"Later?" Bud asked, yanking the seldom-loaded gun from his holster. He flipped the chamber open. "*Any* sighting is urgent. Does everyone understand?" He took the six bullets from his belt and loaded the .38.

"Okay, Sarge," Oz said, nodding his big head like a chastised soldier. "Well, she saw 'em, crack a dawn when she went out to the henhouse for eggs. They's a drivin' from Neahkahnie toward Nehalem in that black panel that looks like one a them Nazi trucks."

"And then you girls saw them coming from Nehalem toward Neahkahnie, right?"

"Right." Imogene's eyes bulged. Tula nodded.

"What time?" he asked.

"We were just gettin' in from Tillamook," she said as she looked at the clock. "Two-ish."

Bud looked at me. "At sunrise these two went to Nehalem, spent several hours there, then drove back to Neahkahnie."

"Yeah... Fishin' maybe?" I said hoping to calm everybody's nerves.

"Is your collar too tight?" Bud snapped. "Those two are fishin', Theo, but not for any fish." He slapped his hat on his head and stomped out the door, Oz on his heels.

Chapter 66

THEO

ANTICIPATION HUNG in the air in every move, every ring of the telephone, every door opening and closing, every new car that rolled into town. We hadn't seen or heard anything about Toreck, the truck, or Genghis Hansel in several days. Where were they?

Tula hadn't been sleeping well, so Imogene devised a plan. Solomon and Tula spent an hour in Christina's room chanting, burning white sage to clear negative energy, and blessing the room as Tula's now. Imogene, Bud, Pearl, Mrs. B, and I waited downstairs, playing gin rummy and listening to the evening news on the radio. The odor of sage drifted downstairs. I opened a window to let out the herb-filled smoke that overpowered even Bud's cigar.

When they finished, Tula came downstairs, stood at the landing and said, "You can come up now." Not smiling, she looked sad, resigned to the fact that she had to leave Solomon's and stay with Imogene not just a night or two, but permanently, whatever that would mean.

"Theo," she said. "Solomon says you should say a prayer."

"Let's go then," I said.

We all ascended the stairway to Imogene's apartment. Not much had changed since Mamaí bought the building in the 1940s, except that Imogene had wallpapered the hallways in jade green with cream-colored flowers and painted the dark doors a soft cream. Tula entered her new room. Imogene had originally wallpapered Christina's room with pink ballerina paper and pink curtains, but that was all gone. It was now painted the color of a spice: saffron with white curtains. Our Tula wasn't a pink kind of girl. The Humpty-Dumpty lamp had been replaced with a brass lamp. Brass and spice. That pretty much summed up our "just Tula."

"Look," Pearl said, pointing to Solomon's dream catcher hanging over her small bed. Then she opened the closet door and said, "See?" and pointed to the two dresses she'd made for Tula. I couldn't imagine our little pant-wearing newspaper reporter ever wearing a dress. "For you." Pearl then pointed to a small wool coat, red-and-brown-plaid Pendleton, matching hers and Imogene's. It was a grand attempt but, I feared, doomed to fail — ruffles and pretty coats didn't speak to this child born on and of Neahkahnie Mountain.

Pearl leaned down and hugged her tightly. Tula's eyes bulged. Her body stiffened. She wriggled out of Pearl's clutches and climbed up on the bed, sat cross-legged, and looked up into her dream catcher, then to Solomon, who nodded.

"Thank you," she said, almost forced, and certainly practiced. With one look he assured her she was strong enough to move ahead. *Listen for the whispers of your guide,* he would have said. He nodded to her bucket in the corner. She looked at Newt and Starfish. "Thank you for our room," she added, her eyes red and crestfallen.

"You're welcome, sweetie," said Imogene, pale as a ghost, as she sat beside her.

I wished Tula didn't have to leave Solomon, but the world dictated otherwise. Besides, she needed a mother, a regular home, not a hut carved from a hundred-year-old tree and a ninety-two-year-old man who spoke his dead language to animals, trees, and phantoms.

"You gonna say a prayer?" Tula asked looking up at me with those questioning brown eyes and a freckled face that hadn't yet found a reason to smile. "Of course," I said. To my astonishment Imogene didn't roll her eyes at the mention of prayer. Pearl scooted off the chair by the door and sat on her knees next to the bed, folding her hands — always the best Catholic in the room. Bud stepped out into the hall, never wanting to be in any room with practicing Catholics. "Let's say the Guardian Angel Prayer."

Tula sat on her bed gazing up at me as if I was going to pull a rabbit out of my pocket. Solomon sat cross-legged and closed his eyes. Even Imogene closed her eyes.

I cleared my throat and said, "Angel of God, my guardian dear, to whom His love entrusts me here, ever this day be at my side to light and guard, to rule and guide. Amen."

"Amen," Tula said, surprising us all.

"Amen," everyone except Solomon said in unison.

"Did you see the aquarium?" I asked pointing to the five-gallon aquarium I'd set up in her corner with a makeshift pond, some driftwood, and rocks inside for the salamander who, with winter coming, would either up and die or need a place to hibernate. "That way you can put him in his own bed at night."

"Newt has a room, too?" Tula's velvety eyes popped. She jumped down, took the salamander from the bucket, and laid him inside the shallow tank. Stroking him, she leaned close to the glass container and whispered, "It's better than the bucket."

After we all celebrated Tula's new home, during which Imogene was uncharacteristically quiet, we went downstairs. Oz and Netty joined us. Despite worrying when or where Toreck and Genghis would show up, it was good to be together with family, and the Rounders were family.

While they talked, I watched my sister with Tula. How would this end for them? Mamaí wrote to me in Korea, explaining how at three o'clock one morning the whole town was awakened by Imogene's screams. How the baby had fallen asleep and never woken up—a "crib death," Mamaí wrote. And how for many, many nights Imogene snuck out of bed and ran in the rain, carrying a blanket, to cover her three-month-old's grave to keep her warm.

Imogene lowered the snicker-doodle jar so Tula could take a cookie and ran her fingers gently along the curve of Tula's soft cheek as if she touched too hard, the little girl would disappear. "Take as many as you want, honey," she said. Her eyes watered. She patted Tula on the head, then turned to the window and said, "Look at that rain come down."

Chapter 67

THEO

AT ONE OF Imogene's tables, Mrs. B sat with Oz, correcting his spelling on Netty's new menu. Oz never made it past the fifth grade because his father made him quit school and work. He'd lived here all his life, and he was one of the smartest men I knew. He listened intensely.

Pearl sat at the other table with her two cups of ginger tea, sorting stacks of S&H Green Stamps, licking and placing them in her book. Hard rain pinged off the roof. Windows steamed.

Bud, Solomon, and I stood near the back door by Imogene's patio so Bud could blow his cigar smoke outside. I lowered my voice and asked, "Was there anyone at Sealy's place?"

"Not that I saw," he said. "No tracks on the drive yet, either. I can't figure it out." He looked at Solomon who stood next to the potbellied stove. Solomon nodded, turned, and walked out the door. By morning we'd know where Toreck and Hansel were holed up.

Netty, who was rail-thin and grew up in a juke joint somewhere in Mississippi, was dressed in her calf-length navy dress with cherry blossoms. She wore heavy stockings and black shoes and settled down next to Pearl. "That newt thing upstairs?" she said. "Deadliest thing in the river."

She turned her eyes up to me, her long lashes like butterfly wings; she smiled and continued. "I saw a big ol' mean huntin' dog take a bite outta one a year or so back." She messed with her hair, black ringlets framing her face against flawless skin. "That dog choked for near-on ten minutes, then fell over dead... But that Tula, she an angel sent from heaven. She be okay, long as she don't bite that little demon." She laughed, picked up Pearl's stamp sheets, uncurled the edges, and handed them to Pearl, one at a time.

Netty had long, thin fingers, sturdy from picking cotton—and now blackberries—faster than anyone in town. Sturdy as those fingers were, they were elegant. That was Netty: forty-five but looked twenty, strong, dependable and elegant, playful and full of grace. Pearl nodded, struggling to listen and count her stamps simultaneously. Oz kept looking up to see where Netty was. She was the center of his universe, his queen. His eyes landed on her, he smiled, then turned his attention back to Mrs. B.

"Andréa be returnin' for a spell," Netty said to no one, but clearly to grab my attention. "Says I should open the house."

My eyes locked with hers.

"She and her family be back in a few weeks, she said. Called jus' last night." Netty smiled and kept uncurling the edges on Pearl's stamps. "Never thought I'd see the two of ya in town, same time again, not in my life. But that God, he has a sense a things all his own." She looked up at me and smiled. "But I guess you knows that better'n me."

"One would think," I said, though we both knew better.

Netty had worked for the Bouvre family cooking, cleaning, opening and closing down their summer house for many years. She and Andréa had always been close.

"Have you seen her?" I asked, real low so nobody else would hear.

"Yeah, I seen her," Netty said. "She pretty as ever, an' that little boy a hers is real cute."

"Little boy?" I said. "Husband?"

"Don't know nothin' bout him… Jus' that boy."

What kind of joke was our all-knowing God playing now? It wasn't enough to torture me with a *sighting* of her now and again, but a son and husband? All of us in a town no bigger than a baseball field. *Not funny, God. Not funny at all.*

Chapter 68

THEO

ALL NIGHT I LISTENED for cars, footsteps, noises that didn't belong. All night, every sound reminded me of the Karst Caves: sounds, smells, threats hidden in every echo. I tried to recall in which letter I wrote to Andréa about the noisy bats. Was it October '52, or later?

The children had been terrified of the Daubenton bats that built colonies inside the caves. At night the scratching sounds and flapping wings were as threatening to them as the CCF running up on us at night was to me. The nun told them the bats were good luck, there to protect us, that they stayed awake at night to keep watch. The oldest boy rolled his eyes back in his head when the nun said that. In any other world he'd have been a budding teenager full of angst and attitude, not an undernourished warrior ready to fight, ready to die, not old enough to understand the meaning of either. Not old enough to fathom any of Korea's madness. But then, who was?

As the days, nights, and weeks had gone on, those brave children folded the strange noises from the waking Daubenton bats into that place where they carried the heavy burden of acceptance—they slept through the night with those mysterious guardians taking flight above them. It became part of their new existence.

It occurred to me like a bolt of lightning to my heart that when I was with the children hiding in that cave, listening to the Daubenton, writing those letters, Andréa was already married to someone else. Was that why the letters came back? All that time there was someone else and then a child of her own to take care of. I had been a fool *all that time*.

Chapter 69

THEO

OZ FINISHED UNLOADING the cord of wood I bought. The smell of fresh- cut oak now filled the house. I handed him some cash and asked, "Hear anything last night?"

"Everything and nothin'," he said, his brows arched high above his gold- rimmed eyes. This was a man whose eyes always looked bloodshot; he'd seen a world of injustice and kept it to himself. "An' dat Netty girl, she hear everythin' you can imagine. Up and down all night."

I followed him outside and said, "We're all on edge."

Mrs. B raised her cane and waved as she passed Imogene's. Solomon wasn't on his bench. He was late.

Oz hopped back into his truck. "See ya."

"Yep, see ya."

Just then Imogene's screen door screeched open. Tula slipped outside, already dressed in her beige pants, white blouse and belt, the suede purse strapped across her chest. She set a cup on the bench, looked around for Solomon, and went back inside. She soon re-emerged, carrying a plate of donuts and her bucket of friends. She positioned the bucket next to the bench and climbed up to her customary place. She cradled Solomon's coffee cup in her hands and looked up and down the street.

Imogene came out with a blanket for her shoulders and patted her on the head. She looked down the avenue, then across the street and saw me. She pointed to Tula, and I nodded that yes, I'd watch her; she went back inside.

I wished Thomas would come home, but given the way things were between them lately I knew we might not see him for a while. In a way, that was alright. Imogene was more herself the last few weeks than any time since my return. Maybe it was the absence of Thomas, or the presence of Tula, or even the obvious spark her and Bud. I didn't know. My sister looked almost cheerful; her eyes glistened again. *Why* didn't matter.

It was nearly seven thirty. Where *was* Solomon?

The phone rang. I ran back inside but watched Tula from the window.

It was Judge Tobias Madsen. He and I trained in Japan together. I was banking on a favor he owed me, hoping it would blind him to the facts of an abandoned girl and a town who wanted to adopt her. But I didn't expect much.

Solomon joined Tula as I hung up.

*   *   *

Bud pulled up to the curb after his two-block drive to the store. Solomon's eyes were closed, shoulders slumped, head leaned back against the wall—he looked dog-tired. Just as the sun broke through the dense clouds, I stepped up on the curb. "Mornin', all."

"Morning, Father Theo." Tula angled her eyes at me. She had her notepad on her lap and was collecting words. "Everything's fine now," she said.

Solomon's feet were bare, dirty from the trails. His knife was snug at his side, and I saw that his leathery hands had dried blood along the outer palms. He opened his eyes and stared straight into mine. He then nodded toward Tula so I'd keep quiet.

Bud was still inside his patrol car on his radio but finally swung the door open and dropped one foot on the walkway. "Yes," he said into the handset. "I'll be there by ten." He slammed the door, greeted us, and gaited up to the curb, forcing a smile.

"Sheriff," Tula said, sheltering her eyes with her hands to look up at Bud. "Solomon was teaching me numbers. He says you should go to... " She glanced down at her pad and read, "One, two, six, Neahkahnie Road," then looked back up. "Soon as pos-si-b... well, real fast."

Every tanned crease of Solomon's face deepened and sagged. His eyes squinted against the explosion of sun as he said, "Time has come." Then he looked deep into me; his eyes burned with what he'd seen. He abruptly stood, reached to my white collar, and tapped at my throat. "This will get in way."

"Way of what?"

"Time to be warrior again."

"What did you find?"

"Two *Un-OONS*," he said, and gently patted Tula's head.

She jumped down from the bench and gave Bud her paper. "Here, so you don't forget."

Solomon stood, motioned for her to follow, and headed for their trail.

"What did he say?" Bud asked.

"Two *Un-OONS* … two white people."

"Did you see the blood on—"

"We can assume those two *Un-OONS* aren't in good shape."

"126?" Bud read aloud. "126 Neahkahnie Road? That's Marge Hildy's address."

"Tula's grandmother?" I said.

Bud's face tightened. "Think so."

"What—"

"Whatever it is, he didn't want Tula to hear anything about it," Bud said climbing back in the patrol car. "Keep an eye on things."

Chapter 70

THEO

THE MCFALLS' BLACK PACKARD bolted to a stop at the curb.

"Father Theo," Sibbie and Ibbie said in unison. Ibbie leaned across Sibbie from behind the large steering wheel and said, "We're headed to Wheeler to that Johnson man's funeral, would ya like to come along? Maybe say a word or two at the—"

"Did you know him?" I asked.

"Well no, but—"

"Not today."

"But Father, it'll only take an hour—"

"I said not today."

"Well!" They huffed and sat up straight as corpses. The car pulled away from the curb and hurled down Laneda Avenue.

After seeing the blood on Solomon's hands I was reluctant to leave Imogene's, even to go a block away to the church. It shouldn't take Bud too long to get back. I decided to wait. The street was as quiet as an Irish fishing village in February.

Inside, Imogene was cutting onions and crying, Mrs. B was at the stove stirring chowder, and Pearl was hunched over the butcher block pressing pastry dough with her wooden pin. The three of them, like high school girls, enjoyed their Thursdays working together. They played music, drank brandy-laced coffee, and talked about movie stars, gossip, and whatever it was that they hushed whenever I entered—likely not discussing politics or religion. But their playfulness was good for Imogene, reviving a little piece of what had died with Christina.

"Immie—"

"Theo," she interrupted, "we saw Bud take off like a bat-outta-hell and we know Tula's with Sol. We know somethin's up." She tipped her head to the side and gave me her "you don't need to worry about me" look. "I've got plenty of protection. We're fine here."

I glanced at Pearl; she held the rolling pin up like a weapon. Mrs. B arched her white brows and nodded, lifting her cane to assure me she'd clobber anyone who posed a threat.

"And as you know," Imogene whispered. "Mr. Winchester's loaded."

"Well then," I said, "looks like I'm useless just hanging around. I guess—"

"Hold on," Imogene said. "We do have a wee problem that you *can* help with." She took my arm and opened the door. "See that bucket there?" She pointed to Tula's bucket.

"Yeah?"

"Well, I convinced Tula that creature should have a nap in the sunshine while she hiked."

"And?"

"Well, I lied," she said. "That Newt, there? He's dead. But… if you go find her another one, she'll never need to know that the pet she loves died in *my* house. She's already *thrilled to pieces* to be here."

"You want me to go find a new salamander? Now?"

"Mm hm…," her head nodded up and down. "And not just any salamander. One that looks just like him." She jabbed her finger toward the bucket at the dead, now greying, lizard.

We both gazed down at him. "So," I said, "he kicked the bucket?"

"Funny," she said, not smiling.

"Okay. But I can't pluck one out of my aquarium, you know. This'll take some time."

"I know. But I can keep her busy and not thinkin' about him for most of the day. By then you should be able to catch one of those buggers."

"I'll rig a trap," I said. "Leave it at the spring since this dying pet is an ongoing issue."

It wouldn't take long. I could get to the spring, put a bowl with some dirt and a plastic bag down, and drive back in less than twenty minutes.

Imogene held out her hand. "Give me the keys to the rectory."

"Why?"

"Your faithful Church Ladies'll be there about ten, won't they?"

I handed her the keys. "Just be careful."

"Cause they're such a scary group?" she asked.

"*In general*," I said. "Be careful *in general*."

I glanced down the street—no Bud, no siren from his patrol car. But also no gunshots or birds scattering on Neahkahnie, which would be a sure sign of trouble. "Okay, back in fifteen."

Chapter 71

THEO

WATER GUSHED OFF the side of Neahkahnie down the rushing stream. Pools formed and attracted salamanders. Bud wasn't a quarter mile away and would hit the siren if there was any real trouble, so I rigged the trap.

The sound of that rushing water reminded me of the day we—Lieutenant Peters, the nun, the kids, and I—trekked down from the caves in search of fresh water in the Naktong River. But in that fresh water was a dead horse and two dead CCF, splayed out on blood-stained boulders in the stream. I'd hushed the children, who no longer needed hushing. By then they knew their lives depended on collective silence. We hid them in the trees and searched for a sign of soldiers or war-faring peasants. Half the time we weren't sure what the enemy looked like—Chinese, Korean, Russian, child, or adult—all equally deadly.

I shoved those images back inside where I'd kept them quiet the last two years. Two years of being in closed quarters, seminary and Saint Patrick's, or places filled with city noises. Not the noises of streams, animals, rustling leaves. For me, those noises of the natural world, Solomon's environment, contained memories. And the more time I spent in his world, the more impossible it was to silence the other.

As I stood to head back to Imogene's, two salamanders scampered up the fallen log and started eyeing the bait—brine shrimp from my aquarium food. So I waited. A few more minutes wouldn't hurt.

Chapter 72

IMOGENE

DAILY SPECIALS
Vegetable and Elk Stew with Fresh Baked Garlic Bread .75¢
Friday's Pie - Warm Cherry Walnut with Vanilla Ice Cream .50¢

When I reached the church courtyard, the sun had begun to burn through the thick fog.

There was a red shoe on the stone edge of the fountain. It was the kind a city girl would wear, a red strappy thing wrapped in a black ribbon. How odd! I left it in case the owner returned. But who in *this* town had *those* shoes? I pictured the Church Ladies in sexy red strappies and laughed to myself.

The front doors of the church were always left unlocked. I pushed through the arched wooden entry, headed down the short hallway to the recreation room, turned on the lights, and opened the drapes. I opened the cupboards, where Bingo cards, chips, and jars of pennies were kept, set up the coffee pot, took out the sugar cookies, and dropped some wood and a match in the woodstove. The place was cold as all get-out and the ladies were late. I wasn't sure I really needed to wait, but then if they arrived and Theo wasn't here, they'd get all confused and call Lucy. *Who needs that...* So I waited to explain that their illustrious leader would be right back.

I don't know how Theo spent so much time in the place. It was damp, cold, and eerily quiet. It made me nervous. I hadn't been to mass in years. Well, except when Theo had special events—then I'd go. But even then I sat in the back and never listened. As the stove clicked to life, I roamed back up the steps to the chapel. It was dark inside. Because it got so cold Theo kept the red drapes pulled closed over the stained-glass windows: winged angels and children, Jesus on the cross, and of course Jesus with his flock of lambs. I'd been forced to stare at those flawless images all my childhood; I hated them.

While the drapes held in *some* heat, they held out all the light, so I lit one of the candles next to the pulpit and looked out at the hazy room of pews. The sound of a bird or a cat shifting about came from somewhere in the dim chapel.

I turned to the cross behind Theo's platform. I hadn't said a Hail Mary in years; not since Christina. "You here, God?" I said. "Here in this place?" My words echoed through the room.

"So, what's your plan?" I asked Christ who hung prostate above the stage. "Will Thomas *ever* return?" I settled on my knees and stared up at the wooden cross, unable to bring myself to fold my hands in prayer. I left them stiff, rigid at my sides; my gold charm dangled at my wrist. "Did you send Tula as a peace offering?" A surge of anger boiled. "Do you mean for me to love her?" My body tensed and began to shake. "And then what?" The burn of tears surprised me. "You'll take *her* away, too?"

I heard a sound again. I turned to face the darkness, focusing my eyes, glancing quickly from one empty pew to the next, until I spotted the source of the disruption. In the back pew next to the door sat a large figure. I could vaguely make it out—a man? "Hello?" I said. I rose from my knees and wiped my cheeks. "Hello?"

With a loud scratching sound, a lone flame glowed in the back pew. A cigarette blazed to life in the shadows. He took a long, slow drag and blew the match out with his inhaled smoke. Every sound echoed. He didn't rise. Even *I* would never light a cigarette in church.

"Who's there?" I asked, pulse racing.

"Very nice." A deep voice broke the stillness. "Nice to hear a woman pray like that." He placed the cigarette in his mouth. "With anger... I liked it." He clapped slowly but loudly, as if he were at the theater. He rose to his feet, still clapping, and said, "Imogene Riley." My skin crawled at the sound of my name. "You *are* a pretty girl." He stepped into the isle, not twenty feet from me. Still, in the darkness, I couldn't see a single detail about him—only his silhouette in the light that strained through the drapes. "*Much* prettier than reported."

I couldn't make out his face but felt his sinister smile. I froze. Damn. I froze! "Who—?"

"Friend of an admirer, let's say," he chuckled. "Tell your golden boy, that precious war hero priest brother a yours, we'll meet... again." He dropped the burning cigarette to the church floor and turned to open the doors to the courtyard. A sharp blaze of golden-white sunlight burst through and blinded me. "When I'm ready," he said.

Light engulfed his dark outline. He turned, faced me, stretched out his arms, took hold of the church door handles, and paused there in that inferno of brightness.

"Until we meet again, Miss Imogene Riley," he said, then slowly pulled the two arched doors, sealing them shut like a coffin and sucking the air out of the room. His voice echoed. My throat tightened. Where the hell did he come from? He knew my name. Was that Toreck's friend? Damn! I stood there, dumbstruck as a frightened five-year-old. Couldn't move my feet. Couldn't scream.

Then I gasped like someone had slapped me on the back, forcing air back into my lungs. I bolted off the pulpit, scrambled down the aisles, and stamped out his still-glowing cigarette. I burst out those doors into the graveled parking lot where I circled, spun, and circled some more. He was nowhere. No cars, no people. I looked around; nothing but a scent. His trail of smoke. It was sweet, like the smell of pumpkin pie baking with cloves—that was it, cloves.

The red shoe was gone. Did he take it? Hell, did he bring it? Whose shoe was it? I scrambled across Laneda Avenue like one of our prowling raccoons, peering up and down the street, flinching and jumping at every sound. As I reached my store, there it was, outside on Solomon's bench. That same red shoe.

Chapter 73

SOLOMON

MANZANITA CLINGS to southern slope of Neahkahnie. As we climbed, ocean's waters hurled against its steep cliffs and flew skyward like ghosts of white doves.

Tula groaned, "Solomon, are we there yet?"

"Come, Little Mouse." I took her hand. We hiked higher than before.

Down the trail's edge, winds had curved and shaped madrones and pines along cliff, just as Tula would soon be shaped by angry storm upon us. The climb was hard for her. But time was close when she would need to run farther, faster, and higher than dark spirit who will follow. I smelled fresh blackberries, knelt down and felt path.

"Child," I whispered. "When you climb, look for prints like these... If pine needles are settled on print, it is old. If not, it is fresh, like this one. Bear is close." She stared at bear print. "Come." I ushered her to hide in bushes. We listened for bear sounds.

"Okay," I said. "We go now."

In blue sky above, two young, foolish falcons tried to attack eagle. Eagle's talons stretched out, ready to strike them down. They would not survive.

"Over there," I said. "We will draw on spirit power." I pointed to grassland that sloped to open field surrounded by ancient trees. "This Nehalem place is sacred."

"Sacred?" Tula asked, reaching into her pouch for her tablet and pencil.

"Yes, sacred. Elk feel safe in open space. Once, my people hid in trees, waiting for elk to walk into meadow." I pointed to the center of the field. "And then, an arrow through its heart."

"Ew!" Tula scrunched her face.

"They cut elk open," I said, "on ground where it died. They set its spirit free and gave thanks to elk for nourishment, then sanctified ground where great elk fell."

"San-c-t-i—?"

"Blessed."

"I don't understand those words."

"It is special place. Holy," I said. In trees ahead, leaves rustled. "*Sh!*"

A mother deer and fawn entered path ahead. We stood motionless. She looked at us, then to open field. Wise Mother smelled us, decided to forgo fresh grasses. She and fawn pranced into ancient Sitka trees where forest floor was dark, full of hiding places, shadows, and secrets. Wise Mother.

"Are you gonna shoot her in the heart?" Tula asked.

"No," I said. "It is wrong to kill mother and harm child. Come." I motioned to the clearing and handed her a small blanket. She carefully placed it. I took herb medicine from my pouch. "Here, draw circle around you and bless circle with sage."

Tula stood from blanket and shook sage branch around edges.

"Like that?" she asked.

"*Duh-HOOTS-nuh.*"

She sat, legs crossed. I sat on grass next to her and said, "Take in deep breath."

We both breathed in Great Grandfather's quiet breeze. "Get comfortable," I said. "Take another deep breath. Inhale... exhale deeply."

She breathed in, then out. Her eyes watched me.

"Chase away shadows of fear," I said. "Close eyes. Begin dream of this place like forest trail, bubbling mountain stream, or this grass-and-flower-covered glen. In your mind, hold violas in your hand, smell Mother Ocean, hear her birds sing to you."

Tula's speckled face broadened with a wide smile. Her eyes, though closed, moved beneath her lids, conjuring images. If she learned to go to this place, her spirit would be safe from what my dreams say will follow. Her body will mend if seed of safe place is planted within her.

"Now," I said, closing my eyes. "Move about in this world, seeing, smelling, and feeling everything. Sit quietly. Begin your journey into spirit world with prayer. Continue with meditation. Soon, you will hear something—you will see a creature slowly coming to you. Is it your mouse?"

"Yes," Tula whispered. "It's Nancy Little Feet."

"*Duh-HOOTS-nuh.* Now, keep eyes closed. Be open to what magic lesson, what wisdom Nancy Little Feet brings you. Listen with whole heart." A twig snapped somewhere behind us. I opened my eyes. It was mother deer wondering what we were up to. Tula sat motionless, eyes closed, gazing into herself.

I closed my eyes. Soon my wolf appeared to me. *I know*, I said to him in my mind. *Our time is short.*

Chapter 74

THEO

BUD BURST THROUGH the door, turned Imogene's sign to CLOSED, and said, "We've got a problem." Then he reached across the counter, grabbed the telephone, and repeatedly tapped the connector. "Lucy?" He tipped his Stetson back on his head and looked at me with an expression I knew well: whatever he found was bad.

"Bud," Imogene said, "I saw a—"

Bud raised his finger to his lips, motioning for her to wait a minute. "Lucy," he said into the telephone. "It's Sheriff Grearson, connect me with the Portland Police, will ya."

He turned to Imogene and me, held his hand out, and told us to hold on for a few minutes.

Then he slid a piece of paper from his pocket, handed it to me, and said, "Mean anything to you?… Yes," he said to the phone. "Still holding."

"It's a confused quote from Isaiah," I said, "but otherwise, no. Where's it from?"

"Crime scene," he said. He tucked it back in his pocket.

"Someone came into the church earlier," I whispered. "Scared Immie to death—"

Bud held his hand up. "Yeah, Lucy, I'm here."

Imogene lit a cigarette. Mrs. B took a swig of hootch, and Pearl plucked the ends off green beans in a rhythmic motion, dropping them into the metal bowl beside her stool. The snapping sounds filled the otherwise quiet store.

"Yes," Bud said. "Captain… wait… Lucy, *dammit girl*, hang up." He waited a moment. "Captain, we've got a murder scene down here in Manzanita."

Imogene's eyes bulged. Mrs. B steadied herself against a shelf and Pearl stopped snapping the heads off beans.

"I've secured the scene," he continued. "Locked the house, and I got someone boarding up the windows, and posting signs." He looked at us all and mouthed *Oz*. "No, I haven't seen the truck in a few weeks now."

"No," he said lowering his voice. "I don't know who they were."

Imogene clung to Bud's arm. "They?" she whispered.

"I'll wait at the property," he said. Then he looked at me while talking to the captain. "Tell them when they get to Manzanita to go to the purple store on Laneda Avenue and ask for Father Riley." He looked at me, I nodded. "No," Bud continued. "There's only one store in town. They won't get lost. Then Father Riley can show them how to get to Marge Hildy's."

Chapter 75

THEO

"OKAY THEO," Bud said, opening the door to his patrol car. "You can usually talk a hungry dog off a meat truck, so get those girls calmed down and don't let any gossip spread. We don't know what we're dealing with just yet."

"Those are no *regular* dogs," I said, pointing to Imogene and Pearl who watched us from the window. "But yeah, got it."

"I'll be at Marge's," he said. "The bodies in that house been there a few days from the smell a things. I got Oz boarding up the front door so animals don't completely destroy what little evidence is left." He opened the patrol car door, slid inside, rolled down the window, and said, "Bring the detectives soon as they arrive." His radio buzzed like a live wire.

"Okay," I said. "Soon as they get here."

Solomon and Tula emerged from a trail a couple blocks away, walking casually despite getting soaked from an abrupt cloudburst.

Imogene ran to Bud's car, leaned into the window, and asked, "Where you going?"

"You're soaked to the bone," he said forcing a smile. "I'll take care of things. You go on inside, now."

"That was me inside a few minutes ago," Imogene said, "listening to you tell someone on the phone there are dead bodies. How do you 'take care' of that?"

"I just don't want ya worryin' about those—"

"Dead bodies!" she said. "I'm not, I'm worried about all these live ones and that bastard I just saw in church. It was him, Toreck's friend."

Bud looked up at me.

"We were just getting to that when you came in with this news," I said.

"I'll send Oz back down to watch the store while you bring the detectives up," Bud said. "Store is to remain closed."

Imogene nodded.

"Immie, go on inside," I said. "I'll be right in. Then you can tell me everything."

She hesitated but then hurried back into the store.

Bud's smile, which hung like an unhinged shutter on an empty house, dropped.

I leaned down to the patrol car and asked, "Who do you think it is?"

"Don't know," he said shaking his head in disbelief. "The stench of gasoline is so strong I can't believe the whole place didn't go up in flames. Their bodies were seated upright in two chairs, side by side. Looks like the killer set a fire that for some reason petered out."

"You suppose it's Tula's—?"

"Don't know… It's some sick shit though. There was a Bible and a box of dead rattlesnakes. Don't know who they are, who did it, why… nothin'. Yet." Bud shook the rain from his hat and tossed it to the passenger seat.

"Did you actually read Hansel's file," I said, "or just give it to me to read? Because if you read it, you'd know that all points directly to him. Snakes and Bibles; right up his alley."

The rain stopped as suddenly as it had started.

"See," he said. "You'd make a good detective."

As Solomon and Tula approached, I saw Andréa's white Thunderbird slowly pulling into the Bouvre driveway. A bolt of lightning shot through my veins.

"Old man," Bud said. "Those bodies… you think two, maybe three days?"

"Two," Solomon said.

"Do you know who they are?" I asked, watching Andréa get out of the car and run into her house with a small suitcase.

Solomon's face sagged. He looked to the ground, nodded yes, and looked up as Tula stepped to the bench. She took off her medicine pouch and stared at the wet seat.

Andréa quickly returned to the car and opened the door. She stood, hesitant with her hand on the rim, and then looked up at me. I stepped away from Solomon and Tula, intent on slowing my racing heart and heading straight to her, not hesitating, not giving her a chance to run. But then Tula said, "Hey," and pointed to a red shoe on the bench. "That's mommy's shoe!" She smiled in a way I'd never seen her smile before. She picked up the shoe, still tied with a black ribbon, and said, "Where's Mommy?"

"Yes," Solomon said. "We know who they are."

Andréa got into the car, backed out, and headed to the highway.

She did not return that day. Or any day soon thereafter.

Chapter 76

THEO

MARGE HILDY'S once-white cabin hadn't been painted in fifty years. The two-story house leaned toward the ocean like a juniper tree; the porch dipped at the top of the three sloping stairs. One good wind and a howling wolf would knock the place down. Bud had taped the door with yellow police tape; Oz had nailed wooden planks across the windows. I stepped through the barricade and entered the house. I was immediately hit with the smell of rotting corpses and gagged. I covered my mouth with a handkerchief and continued. The two bodies were seated in chairs, hands tied behind them. They were unrecognizable.

Outside the detectives from Portland got out of their cars and slammed the doors. I stepped back outside, took a deep breath, and pointed them to the crime scene. Then I returned to town. There would be no leaving Imogene and the girls alone again.

Chapter 77

THEO

ON THE PROMISE of an exclusive interview later, the *Oregonian's* Hugh O'Neill managed to keep the specific location of the murder out of the paper. GRUESOME MURDERS ON THE COAST was the headline. There was no way to identify the bodies other than the dental reports, which took weeks. But we had no doubt it was Tula's mother and her boyfriend.

* * *

The foul-smelling ointment, which I now kept on the back porch, soaked into my bruised hip. Solomon stood in his yard. The rain beat hard against his wood-shingled roof. It was muggy, and the sound of rain was everywhere, pelting leaves and dropping to the ground. He stood facing the sky, bare chested, arms outstretched. It had been more than fifty years since Ruby's murder, but once in awhile he was still moved to stand in the rain and feel her tears wash over him. I imagined he felt lost, yet found in that cleansing moment.

When the sky stopped crying, he rebuilt his fire. Tula arrived as it sparked at the darkness. The chafing sounds of him sanding and shaping his canoe filled the night.

At some point he left a small tin box on the porch. It smelled of dried lavender and was full of photographs from 1910 to 1918. These were the long-missing photos Mamaí told us about from when a photographer came to the valley to document "the last Indians."

Many of the photos were of Ruby, with her waist-length black hair and dark eyes that burned through the murky photograph. Some pictures were of Ruby and Solomon with their three children. Pictures of him in his headdress and suede clothing were proud and striking—it was another world. Why, after all these years, was he giving me these now?

I knew to quietly accept the gift, no questions. I knew also he didn't need the pictures; his memories were alive and inexplicably linked to his every step.

As he stacked wood for tomorrow's fire, I went inside and placed the pictures with Mamaí's photograph albums, one of which was Andréa and me at my graduation.

When I moved one of the old albums, a picture floated to the floor. I'd forgotten I'd sent it home. It was my only photograph, a black and white, of myself, the nun, and the orphans. I picked it up. It was the same one Hugh O'Neill had brought to church that day. That photographer outside Pusan had shoved us all together and snapped the shot for some newspaper. I'd paid him for a copy.

My captain later said that I'd been "taken in" by my sympathies. Perhaps. But when I promised to protect them, I meant it. He didn't understand why we went through hell trying to keep the children safe from the North Koreans and the CCF. He didn't understand how holding a dying child in my arms changed me— me, a man who came to question the relevance of pacifism. If everyone wasn't a pacifist. A man who no longer recognized the blurred line between war and murder and who one day realized that whoever I just killed had a sister and a mother. The captain didn't understand the chaos of that forest—how it teemed with weapons and the stench of blood, or how death waited around every hushed whisper. Leaving Korea was like being sucked up by a large vacuum. Promises broken, lives lost, blood everywhere. As they airlifted me out, I couldn't stop seeing their eyes, hearing their screams, *my* screams for them. I squeezed my eyes shut, forcing those last images out of my head, and slid the photograph back into the album. Like Solomon, I didn't need the reminder. Those images were alive, burning inside me. Always would be.

And somehow, my love for Andréa, a love I didn't realize until it was too late, was now enmeshed with those images, those memories. My longing, poured into those unopened letters, was now attached to the children. It was all one. When I thought of them, I ached for her. And given how things had become, I'd never have a chance to clean up the mess I made of our relationship. Outside, Imogene called for Tula to come home for dinner. I wondered if Tula had any pictures to remember her mother, and what her last memory would be. Would it be her eyes, her face? Or would it all be snarled, a memory of being locked in a closet with no way out?

Chapter 78

SOLOMON

WE PAUSED at final crest to top of Neahkahnie so Tula could catch her breath.

"Why do you use arrows to hunt?" she asked. "Aren't guns easier?"

I motioned for her to sit, rest. "When arrow pierces our friend the Elk, it is clean death. Bullets miss the breathing organs, leave animal to suffer. Dying in stress poisons meat, bad for humans to eat… wastes friend's sacrifice. Guns, bad for hunter and hunted."

The bushes moved. I swept Tula up and slipped into underbrush. Mother black bear and cub wandered onto plain, mother stopped, looked around, stood high on hind legs to catch scent of who or what was there. Tula pulled her hand over her mouth. Bears passed.

"Be still when you see bear with cub. Wait for her to leave before you come out."

Her hand dropped away from her mouth. "But she stood up so tall… so mad."

"She smells her environment to see if safe. Bears will not attack if you stay calm. Walk backward, eyes down, slowly. Run, they run after you. And nobody outruns bear."

"What if it comes after me?"

I took a stick, broke in half, and handed to her. "Now you have weapon you use *only* if bear comes after you." She gripped it in her hands. "Now," I said. Pointed to a cedar. "Hit tree with stick. Hard." If she never felt what it was to swing and strike, she would never use it. I picked up stick and held it like sword. "Now, fight," I said, knowing she soon would need these skills. "*Duh-HOOTS-nuh*, Little Mouse. Harder, with all your spirit power, fight the bear."

Chapter 79

IMOGENE

DAILY SPECIAL
Chocolate Cupcakes .10¢
Closed for Sunday Mass — Open again at 11:00 A.M. sharp!

The Catholic Church and I hadn't been on speaking terms for years. But maybe Theo was right about creating order for Tula. "Order out of the chaos," he said. *Fine.* For her, I'd go, begrudgingly. But no sitting up front. The back row, close to the door.

My store's specials sign would give the busybodies something to gnaw on. *Imogene went to church!* I was tired of their theories on the still-unsolved murders. It was time they had something new. I hung the sign in the window, grabbed a pack of gum, and went upstairs.

"Ladies," I said plunking down on Tula's bed. "We only have twenty minutes."

Tula and Pearl stood next to the mirrored vanity. Pearl had tried for several days to persuade her to wear the coat that matched ours. It lay crumpled on the floor in the corner. She also tried to convince Tula to wear the dress; then was the struggle with her hair. All lost battles.

Pearl wrestled to braid her wavy shoulder-length hair.

Tula turned to me, her eyes pleading and said, "Do I have to?"

I ran my hand along the edge of the untouched bed I'd made the day before, wondering when she'd stop sleeping on the floor.

"No honey," I said, "you don't have to do anything you don't want to do."

"Ouch! Stop that!" Tula yanked away from Pearl.

She'd been angrier and more distant since Bud took her mother's red shoe. It was, after all, evidence. Such a clinical word for such a gruesome thing. Evidence. Proof that something unexplainable and grotesque had taken place.

"Pearl, let her be now," I said, gently patting the top of Tula's unruly chestnut hair. "Let her choose." I motioned for Pearl to follow me.

"She look like boy," Pearl said as she marched down the hall to the kitchen.

I set a cup of mint tea in front of her at the table, then another cup for her ghost, and said, "Let her find her own way."

I thought about Tula's face when Bud put her mother's shoe in the bag marked OCTOBER 1956 – MULTNOMAH COUNTY SHERIFF: EVIDENCE. How her eyes blinked away the tears. I thought on how he had her mother on a cold slab in the morgue, unable to release her body because it was confirmation of a transgression: *evidence*. And if he could release it, there was nobody to release it to, nobody old enough to understand, nobody to care what happened to Tula's mommy. Bad mommy that she may have been, she was still a mommy. Even though Tula didn't know those things, I think she sensed them. That was enough for now. And for now she could bloody well wear whatever clothes she wanted.

"She just needs more time," I said. "That's all."

Pearl stared into the empty mug next to her tea, cupped her hand around it, and relaxed into the vinyl chair. "We be late to church if—," she started to say, but right then Tula slithered into the kitchen.

"I'm ready," Tula grumbled, staring at the linoleum floor, her hair haphazardly braided with the pink ribbon Pearl wanted her to wear, knotted in the rubber band and dangling like a hangman's rope along her left shoulder. She didn't have on the dress—her slacks and white cotton blouse, of course—but she *was* wearing the sweater that went with the Sunday school dress. Never mind that it was buttoned all kiddywampus. It was on, and we were near ready.

A smile as broad as a Moon Pie spread across Pearl's face.

Inch by inch, I thought, that's how we will discover this amazing though somewhat cranky child. Inch by inch.

"You have time for a quick breakfast," I said, pulling a chair away from the table for her. "Cereal, hotcakes, eggs?" I knew to not fuss over how cute she looked. Pearl's syrupy smile was plenty to embarrass her to pieces, maybe send her running back upstairs to tear off the sweater, yank the ribbon out of her hair, and lock herself in that room for the third time in as many days. "Hot cocoa?" I asked, real swift before she had a chance to reconsider. "We're out of Tony the Tiger, but we have—"

"Twinkies," Tula said, dropping onto the bench and trying to straighten her ruffled sweater cuffs. "And milk… *please*. Solomon lets me have Twinkies."

"Okay," I said, not wanting to put a wrinkle in things by telling her Solomon didn't know *everything*. After all, along with his fish he'd eat an entire pie for breakfast, lunch, and dinner if I'd let him.

"You so pretty," Pearl said, cautiously leaning forward and patting her hand.

Tula slid her hand off the table to her lap and offered a strained thanks.

"Twinkies?" I said pondering my open cupboard. I hadn't thought about Twinkies in years. "Hm... " I searched the shelves. "If I let you have a Twinkie, *for breakfast*, will you also eat one egg, then?" I found a box of Twinkies behind the Ovaltine and Quaker Oats.

Tula's face pinched up. "Ew!... Okay... But I need mustard. Eggs need mustard."

"Okay," I said. "Mustard on eggs, coming up."

The Twinkies had been shoved to the back of the freezer some years ago. I stared at the white box. My body tensed.

When I was pregnant with Christina I'd craved and eaten them every day for eight months. Then, when she was born, my taste for them turned to disdain, like smelling alcohol the morning after a drunken night—I never wanted another. Besides, I had all the sweetness one heart could handle in the tiny fingers and rosebud lips of my baby girl.

I opened the package, wrapped one in foil and set it on the woodstove to thaw while I scrambled eggs.

"There ya go," I said. "One Twinkie and two scrambled eggs with mustard."

We watched her devour the Twinkie. The creamy filling spread across her lips. I felt for the charm on my bracelet and massaged the letters.

When Christina died I bought several boxes of Twinkies and scarfed more than a few each day for a month, unable to get enough. I'd open the package, peel off the cellophane, smell, touch, squeeze, and pick at the apricot-colored cake. Then I'd shove the whole damn thing in my mouth. The centers split open and coated my throat with cream so sweet it reached into my tear ducts and ruptured the dam that held back what was left to spill. I'd weep and eat, starved for something, anything to sustain me.

Chapter 80

THEO

THE TASTE in my mouth was so familiar, so startling, it woke me. I had to take a drink, hoping the mouthwash would burn my taste buds, render them numb. I drank, then stood at my bathroom mirror hardly recognizing the haggard man who stared back. Brushed my teeth. The taste, a mix of juk rice with eggs and seeds from Korean pine, was still there. I splashed cold water on my face, got dressed, and headed out. It was Sunday—had to get to work.

Before heading to Saint Mary's, I walked over to Mrs. B's as she'd asked me to help her move her easel out to her porch. There was a tropical like breeze with the hint of her rose garden. I hesitated at the gate; she was in her window, unaware of me, captivated by the letter in her hand. She wore her green Chemise with the black frog buttons. Her snow-white hair, not in its usual bun, floated across one shoulder.

She was reputed to have had a lover, a Chinese ship captain, who sent her gifts and letters from afar. She held one of the tawny letters from her red basket up close to her aging eyes. She'd read them every Sunday for thirty years: her sacred observance on the day set aside for sacred things. Rumor was her captain disappeared one day and those letters were all she had left.

I felt like a trespasser at the gate and turned away, eyeing the street for real intruders—glanced at the Bouvre house. I always thought Andréa would be like Mrs. B when we grew old, sitting on the porch painting sunsets, sunrises, the mountaintop... and me, I'd be chopping wood in the backyard or building something. It was our world, in my vision. Never doubted who she was, just never knew who I was or could be. Never realized that it didn't matter as long as I was with her. "Too late" happened so fast that it, too, left an eternal taste in my mouth.

* * *

Mrs. B folded the letter back into its mysterious place to await the next Sunday and the next. I headed up the steps and knocked on the ornately painted door of her rustic log cabin. She opened the entrance, a door within a door, latched with a Chinese brass plate in the center. Ironic that her Captain sent her that door... ironic because they were fated to live on separate sides.

"Mornin', Theodore." Her eyes, red and raw.

"Mornin'," I said. "Can I ask you a question?"

"You can always *ask*."

"Why do you read those letters every week?"

She tied her silk scarf and said, "Solomon has told me for fifty years to burn them."

"Yeah, he's big on burning things."

"I read them," she said, "to feel something so deeply it nearly cracks me in two. To understand the price I paid for freedom." She pulled on her jacket. "You see, had I gone to China I would have gained love, but lost the life I'd fought and won, from my father. I'd have lived as a white woman married to a Chinese man. Hated by all the other women, confined in his palace, no work, no teaching children, no taking trips, no seeing family and friends again."

"You never told me—"

"Before you went to Japan and Korea you wouldn't have understood how different things are there... those cultures... so different from here."

"True."

"I loved him with all my being... but I loved myself more. I can live with that. It was the price I paid. And he... well, he could not move to this country for many reasons."

"I'm sorry," I said, "I shouldn't have—"

"So, those letters are a grave I visit, where I mourn, leave my tears, and then move on, remembering I was once another person, one who was loved. He said it was our fate; made me promise to go on without him, and have a happy life. I hated that promise when I made it. I hate it still. But I'll keep it till my last breath."

"You're braver than me," I said.

"It's not bravery, Theo, it's life. Grow up. The curtain of fate falls, destiny delivers, life goes on. You can't erase what's done. Let me ask *you* something; do you regret tryin' to save those poor Korean youngsters?"

"No, I'd do it again. Regardless of outcome."

"Exactly, so it's not regret you have in those letters on *your* table, it's grief. It's your suffering. And maybe some real hard growing up."

"Maybe."

"We all have grief and we have containers for our grief. Pearl has that spare cup; Imogene, her death shelf with those candles; Solomon, a Frog box; and you, my dear young man, have those letters. They're not love letters, like mine. Yours hold something you can't face."

She pulled her coat on, looked at me, and said, "I doubt it's Andréa, but she's part of it. You made a mistake there and now you have to live with that mistake. But more, I think those letters hold the horror of what you went through in war. Those bloody letters contain your grief, don't they? Bleed them of it, you must embrace your grief in order to transcend it, Theo, you know this. Then burn them, like Solomon says. Burn them like you did that building when you were a boy."

"Does everyone know about that?" I asked.

"*If you recall*, I am why you're here in Manzanita... Of course I know. Now, you regret burning that building?"

"I only regret not being able to save my brother."

"And you don't regret trying to help those children. But you do regret whatever happened between you and Andréa, right?"

I nodded.

"Good," she said. "Now we're clear on what is and what is not regret. Read them, then burn them, and then just walk away, have a happy life whether you want to or not."

"Right," I said. "Happy life. Want to or not. Grow up. No regret. Got it."

"Good. Now, leave me alone," she said, and then pointed to her art supplies. "Zucchini bread's in the kitchen."

"Thanks," I said turning to assess what needed to be moved. Without a word she was at the bottom of her stairs by the time I turned around. She tied her straw China hat over her scarf and headed toward the beach, where she would stand like a lonely heron at the edge of the shore, remembering, as she did every Sunday.

Chapter 81

GENGHIS

A HOUSE UNSANCTIFIED is a house unfit. I searched the war hero's sister's store—spotless and organized—then her upstairs apartment: not a Bible to be found. And I searched real good.

A Bible should be out where all the world can see that the one who lives there fears Him. But there was none. Not even in her dining room where she had a gold-framed painting of God's work—the ocean and one of His glorious sunsets. She also had fancy dishes displayed in a cabinet as if holy, a nice big window with a view of the ocean, and wallpaper to match the blood-colored drapes. There was a long wooden table so clean it glistened in the morning light. While they all pretended to be pious in her brother's church where he veiled his secrets and spoke his lies, she had carefully chosen and carefully placed all these things. But nowhere did I find a Bible. Without His word a house is unsanctified. Unfit.

The child's room was a bizarre place with all the trappings of the secular world. But odd even to me was the bucket with a dead serpent inside. My daddy kept a box of snakes in my room. At night, in the dark, all I heard was the hiss of them snakes, every coil of their bodies, the thump against the side of the box when one rolled over. Then some nights my daddy would open my door in the wee hours, turn on my light, and look at me real hard with his ice-cold eyes. He'd open that box and drop in a live rat. Then he'd turn off my light, laugh, and close my door. I'd curl up, holding my knees, and listen as that box came to life with the death that ensued inside. The rat squealed as those snakes ripped and tore its body. I clung to my knees and shook like a cat on fire. I knew then that no child should have a serpent in his room.

I looked inside that bucket at that dead serpent, and I knew, I just knew, this was no place for a child.

Chapter 82

THEO

IT WAS THE MIDDLE of the night. The house was dark and quiet except for the hum of the aquarium filter. I stood naked at the kitchen counter, eating the rest of Imogene's berry pie and staring out the window at the remnants of Solomon's fire.

The telephone rang—an alarm against the quiet.

"Hello?"

"Father Riley?"

"Yes, this is Father Riley." I set down the pie tin, worried someone had died or was hurt.

"Father Riley." The man's voice was low and deep as a well, but not more than a whisper. "You're a killer, Father Riley."

"Who is this?"

"A killer who fell asleep, dreamt he was a hero… but now that killer wakes again, don't he, *Father*… He wakes from dreams, nightmares, faces the stench of his own sin and the blood of innocents. He wakes. You can't leave Eden and expect to return, Padre. You done took a bite out of that big ol' poison apple, now that bitterness pulses through your veins, don't it?"

A sick feeling washed over me. "All right, Poet," I said. "I'm awake. Now what?"

"Did ya know, Padre, that the Messiah—you believe in the Messiah don't you?—well anyway, he won't be returnin' till all the souls are sent back to the House a Souls. Flee as a bird to your mountain, they say."

"Has there been a death?"

"There's always death."

"Chills run up and down my spine," I said. "Now, what do you want?"

"I am illuminating, Padre."

"Illuminating?"

"Sleep well, Priest. Your nap will end soon. Your Eden will be lost. That poison in your veins will turn to dust." The line went dead.

I suddenly *felt* naked—pulled on pants, my Rakkasan sweatshirt, and searched the house. There was something about him, like he was right there in the room, the yard, across the street, or under my skin. I looked around outside, then across to Imogene's. Nothing. But I felt those beady red eyes staring at me from the dark.

The rest of the night I was as awake as when I sat at the edge of the Karst Caves—sleeping souls behind me, my gun gripped in my hands, listening to the Daubenton bats and everything else that scratched or crawled along the surface of the caves.

* * *

At dawn the *Tribune* landed on my porch with a thud. It read TORECK SEALY – TILLAMOOK JAIL HAS REVOLVING DOOR. Toreck had retained an attorney and been bailed out of jail again. Someone paid for an expensive attorney. *Certainly not Toreck.*

Chapter 83

THEO

TRILLS OF LAUGHTER came from inside Imogene's store. I opened the door and said, "Okay, you can go shopping now." Settled my toolbox on the counter and hung my hat on the hook. "I'll fix that squeaky door while you're gone."

Figured I couldn't do a thing about Tula's family, calls in the night, or the whereabouts of a man whose hate ran so deep it oozed from him like water off the walls of the Karst Caves. But I could fix Imogene's door.

"And the bell?" Imogene asked.

"And the bell."

Pearl grabbed Tula's car coat and offered it to her; Tula shook her head no and wrapped her pouch over her shoulder.

"We're ready," Imogene said, holding her hand out in anticipation. Instead, Tula walked past and out the door. They followed, climbed into the Woody, and drove off.

Clearly Imogene hadn't read the news.

* * *

The girls had been gone to Tillamook for nearly an hour when Bud stopped by with a gift.

"Here." He handed me a bag. "Whoever left it wiped off their prints. It's useless to the investigation. It'll only get lost in the evidence room. But to Tula it's probably all she'll ever have of that mother a hers. Little as it is, *sick as it is*, it's better 'n nothin'."

"Probably so," I said, taking the shoe out of the plastic bag and placing it next to Tula's toy box. "So, no real proof then of who did it or why?"

Bud took a bottle from the cooler, flipped off the cap, and said, "I never understand the whys. But I think we know *who* did it. Provin' it's another story altogether. And I think we know it's the same person who got Toreck bailed out."

"The 'whys' are important, too," I said. "Speaking of, will you grab a book for me at the Tillamook Library? Effie Grimm has it at the library desk for me."

"A book?"

"World Religions. I'm doin' some research."

Just then the Woody screeched to a halt at the curb. Tula and Imogene opened their doors and stepped to the curb carefree as ever, watching as Pearl crawled out of the back. She held onto her scarf, holding her chest through her coat like she was having a heart attack.

Bud opened the door, stifled a grin, and said, "Pearl, you okay?"

"She'll be *fine*," Imogene said. "She's just a backseat driver, that's all."

He tipped his hat and left.

"Tula," I said, "Bud brought you a present." I pointed to the red shoe.

Without a word, she snatched it in her hands, bolted up the stairs, and slammed her bedroom door. Imogene glared at me, then we both scaled the stairs behind her and listened through the door. I placed my hand on the glass door knob but then heard her; Tula was talking. No, meditating. Or crying. We put our ears closer to the door and listened.

"I'll be a good girl," Tula sobbed. "Send my mommy back."

Imogene clasped her hands over her mouth. Her eyes pooled. My heart sank.

As I began to turn the knob, Tula said, "If you can't send her back, can she be with Ruby? Can they be watching over me?" Then she began to hum and chant like Solomon. I cracked the door. She sat holding the shoe and rocking. I closed the door and left her to her mediations—words intended to bring her mommy back in *some* way. Words that, if whispered, chanted, and deeply heartfelt in front of Solomon's dream catcher, would find their way to the Ancient Ones. Those Ancient Ones whose whispers she believed could send hope, grant wishes, proffer messages, and shelter her world, and maybe, just maybe give her an ethereal mommy who actually loved her.

Chapter 84

THEO

THE CHURCH LADIES, all donning funeral black, came over to me before Sunday service, their heads hung low. "Did you hear?" Sibbie asked.

"Hear what?" I asked.

"Mrs. Bouvre… Andréa's mother, she died after a long fight with cancer. So sad."

They all nodded, studying me for a reaction.

"We're driving to Portland today for her funeral," Ibbie said. "Would you like to go?"

"Go?" I said. "No, thank you. Please tell Andréa how sorry I am."

"She might like to hear that from you—"

"No, ladies, I can't go," I said. "But I trust you to represent us all. Thank you." I never knew her mother much. A quiet woman, Jewish but not religious, always in the background. Andréa and she had their struggles, but still, poor Andréa. Even in a strained relationship, to lose a mother was a complex and painful thing. My showing up at her funeral would only make matters worse. This explained why she, *they* didn't return for summer.

* * *

After Sunday service, after the Sunday school class decorated the rectory with Thanksgiving turkeys made from their hand prints on colored paper, and after the parking lot cleared, I headed to the rectory where at the bottom of the stairs I was met with Toreck Sealy.

He dropped his cigarette to the floor and asked, "Where's my family?"

"Gone," I said pushing past him and opening the door. "I suggest you do the same."

"Gone where?" He followed me inside the parsonage.

"Just gone, Sealy, and unless you're here to confess something or spend some time in prayer, I think you need to leave."

"I asked you where they are." The vein along the right side of his shaved head pulsed.

I held out a prayer pamphlet for him and said, "Here, some light reading for your trip."

He grabbed my robe, shoved me into the wall, and shouted, "Where the fuck are they?"

I stared back at him, smiled, and said, "Where they are, is gone."

"I beat the shit outta you once," he said, "I'll do it again, make it permanent." He backed away, then rammed his fist into my chin and hunched himself back, fists up, ready for a scrap.

"We're done here," I said straightening my sore jaw. "You've hit *me*, now hit the road."

I turned to go upstairs. He grabbed the backside of my robes and yanked. I nearly lost my footing but turned in time to take another blow to the jaw. I sucker punched him, knocked the air out of his lungs. He gasped and bent over as I cuffed his nose. It cracked loudly.

"I said we're done here." He lay on the floor sneering at me, blood splayed across his face. I reached out my hand to pull him up. "Come on, we're done with all this."

"Fuck you, Riley!" he shouted, then stood, stomped up the stairs, and slammed the door.

Chapter 85

THEO

THE DRIVE to Tillamook was uneventful. I pressed charges against Toreck, which I hoped would get him tossed inside again.

I was in no hurry to return to Manzanita for three o'clock confession hour and listen, *again,* to Pearl's remorse over killing slugs, or Effie Grimm's guilt about having said bad words about Betty because she flirted with her now-dead husband over twenty-eight years ago. Nope, no hurry at all. So on the way back I pulled over at the viewpoint, parked in the abnormally warm November sun, put the top down, and studied the sympathy card that for three days I'd carried in my coat pocket, intent on writing something full of grace and understanding, then sending to Andréa's mother's address. But I hadn't thought of what to write. Or if I should write anything at all. Or if I wrote anything if it would just be returned to sender.

I spotted Solomon and Tula about a hundred yards away in the middle of Elk's Flat, sitting on the grass surrounded by graying lavender bushes. I got out of the car and walked the path toward them. As I came nearer, I overheard what he was saying.

"North wind is power," he said. "A power that take first wife's *adzekl* deep into ocean."

I knew the story well. The tale about how his Ruby was taken from him didn't change with every telling like so many stories in a village of fishermen and treasure hunters. Instead, that particular story was cast into the deepest crevasse of his heart, memorized, transformed, and retold in sharp blades of chiseled bronze words. She'd been so beautiful, he explained, that one day when he was not there to protect her, the jealous North Wind blew down on the ocean and took her canoe, her "adzekl." She never returned.

It was a far more beautiful telling for Tula than the brutal reality. I sat on the grass. He nodded and continued. Tula, with her satchel strapped across her tiny chest, listened with fascination. Then Solomon stood, put his sturdy rough-skinned hand on her head, and patted gently. "Your mother who wore red shoes," he said as he leaned down and gazed into her eyes, "she is gone... She will not be back. North Wind took her to be with Ruby."

Tula wiped her tears on her sleeve, then took his hand and whispered, "Okay."

"We ride home with Theo," he said.

"Okay," she said. "I'm tired."

"Yes," he said. "Sadness is heavy. But you will learn to walk with its weight on you." He looked at me and said, "As we all must."

Amazing what a simple clean truth can do.

Tula climbed into the back seat and passed out before I even started the car.

"The battle that comes will follow this child," he said.

"The battle?"

"This battle needs for you to listen and watch. Much patience. It will unfold slowly then explode. You must be ready. When this battle is over, you will find peace."

Chapter 86

THEO

DECEMBER 1957, Toreck was released from yet another stint in jail. Bud studied both his and Genghis Hansel's files like a chess board wondering who'd make the next move. I wondered too, but I studied news articles across the country; missing children who, if found, commented on common things like snakes, spicey smells, a crippled hand. That sort of thing.

Christmas arrived in a flurry of snow and activity. I received a beautiful Parisian Christmas card, unsigned, mailed from Beaune, France. I knew it was from Andréa.

Imogene's Perry Como Christmas album played and replayed a thousand times during the week leading up to Christmas Eve, echoing through the abandoned streets of Manzanita. Her explosion of decorations was everywhere: the store, her apartment, my house, Manzanita's one street lamp, where she tied a large red bow with bells that jingle-jangled in the wind. On Mrs. B's front porch, tufts of white snow settled on the tops of all four China-red shutters like whipped cream on strawberries. Imogene hung green garlands of holly around those red shutters, and even her Woody wore a wreath on the front bumper. Bud said that Imogene had puked Christmas all over town. When she tried to put a wreath on the grill of his patrol car, he said "I'll shoot the damned thing, Imogene Riley!"

* * *

Christmas Eve was at Imogene's cozy garlanded apartment. After a turkey feast, we watched Tula's first Christmas. As Imogene and Pearl presented—and by *presented* I mean in the way one would the crown jewels to the Queen of England—one fancy green-and-red-wrapped-and-bowed package at a time, I thought about the orphans who'd never heard of Christmas or had new toys of their own, but played, when it was safe, with sticks, stones, and whatever else we could find.

Imogene and Pearl handed Tula one gift at a time, then sat back, waiting with expectant eyes for her to unwrap their love. Pink roller skates, a hula-hoop, a Barbie doll, sweaters, skirts, hats, gloves, and so on, for over two hours.

Of course Tula didn't know it was love she was unwrapping. That it was the long-stifled explosion of adoration from two childless mothers. But despite all odds, love it was. At first she looked like she'd hit the Christmas jackpot, but after the first hour, she grew exhausted. For Imogene and Pearl, it was an experience they'd wanted all their adult lives: a child at Christmas. And lucky Tula was the beneficiary of their broken dreams. I said a quick prayer that she'd survive their tsunami of love. Normally I'd say Imogene went so far overboard there was no saving her; but in this case, she deserved to give a child a glorious Christmas as much as young Tula needed it.

Solomon, who never understood stories about a white-haired man flying from rooftop to rooftop, fell asleep in what was once Mamaí's reading chair, the wine-red, high wing-back Victorian that Imogene moved to her apartment last year. As he slept and Tula's thank yous grew less enthusiastic, I looked at him: ninety-two years old. How long would we have him?

Outside the window snow fell light and soft. Drifts of it heaped against the northern walls of Mrs. B's cabin, and from Imogene's second-story apartment I saw beyond my cottage to Solomon's hut, so firmly rooted in the wintry earth it was completely sheathed in white. In all that white, I saw a fresh, unblemished world and wondered about Andréa; could we be made new, cleansed of our pasts? That sympathy card, which I simply signed, *With all my heart, Theo*, never came back to sender. And the unsigned Christmas card from her—were we communicating in this deafening winter silence?

Imogene and Pearl continued with the gifts and ribbons like two cats with a ball of yarn. Their playing was a good thing—a healing thing. Mrs. B made Bud, who arrived late, a turkey sandwich and cinnamon cider; the smell drifted through the apartment.

Bud handed me a Christmas cigar and said, "Merry Christmas."

"Cuban Bolivar," I said, peeling off the gold seal. "Legal?"

"Friends in low places," he said. "Enjoy."

I sensed that whatever had kept Bud from Christmas dinner—a thing he'd never normally be late to—was going to wait until tomorrow.

Chapter 87

THEO

AT THE FOOT of Neahkahnie, a quarter-mile from town, was a stream with a fallen, rotting log—a perfect hibernating refuge for salamanders—where I now had a permanent "Newt" trapping station. I found myself wandering over there and checking on the salamander situation frequently, because though they hibernated in winter, an occasional abruptly awakened Newt would wander drunk-like into the trap. We'd convinced Tula that they slept in the winter, but sometimes they started to smell—dead in her aquarium— so we replaced them with another sleeper. Occasionally I had to buy them from my friend at the Seaside Aquarium, where I got my fish tank supplies. The whole Newt state of affairs was a full-time job.

The quiet winter forest was like the Karst Caves, where even the slightest sound bounced off walls. There was no mistaking the sound of a man's body weight on those ramshackle bridges that echoed through the caverns. I always thought they were such a contradiction; caverns that shrouded ancient mysteries with bridges that couldn't keep a secret.

In Neahkahnie's forest, sounds echoed off silence, and my breath hung frozen in the air. Those sounds used to bring me peace, soothe me, make me happy. Now they were alarms, filling me with trepidation. How could I get back to that serene place where I sat in a forest for hours and felt at home? Had I gone so far off life's trail that I'd lost that part of myself?

I settled back, listening to North Wind chase away East Wind. Solomon had begun his winter incantations: *Dasc-se-lit*, the "moon's winter dance," which meant pushing away fall, making room for deep winter. I pushed away memories of blood and war and focused instead on the once-soothing stream. Then, with two sleepy Newts in my bucket, I headed home.

* * *

In the mail was a three-weeks-old Christmas card from Toreck's wife with a joyful drawing of Santa from her son, Andy. They were fine. Hidden, with new names, happy—the lopsided scales of justice balanced, for now. A child saved.

Chapter 88

THEO

THE FBI FILE on Genghis Hansel had arrived Christmas Eve—which is why Bud was late—and it wasn't all that illuminating. It was a partial file, no real meat. The FBI, Bud said, wasn't a sharing organization. "They think I'm a small-town sheriff with something to prove."

"Well," I said, "all the calls, the shoe, missing kids… him at the church last spring … "

"He's sure fixated on you," Bud said. "But scarin' Immie like that really pisses me off."

"Why won't they listen to you?"

"Think about it," he said. "We got us a town bully who keeps gettin' into shit, then we got a stranger who shows up and disappears, a couple red shoes, and a couple dead nobodies… not exactly airtight." Bud pondered the file.

"What about Suzy Wu?" I asked.

"Can't prove a thing," Bud said. "But I think he killed that poor child and was arrested on those fluke charges of breaking into Damashe to visit another of his victims. In jail by the time we even knew Suzy was missin'. Then poof! Gone before we could charge him with anything. Like I said before, he's a slick one."

* * *

The Newts began to wake and stay alive as spring arrived.

By the end of spring, we still had heard nothing of Toreck, and no one had seen or heard a thing about Genghis Hansel. We hoped they were far, far away. The murders of Tula's mother and her boyfriend remained unsolved, and since Bud had described them as "riffraff" in the eyes of the law, it wasn't investigated too eagerly—except by Bud, who remained convinced it was Hansel and equally convinced that he'd be back.

In April, Netty opened the Bouvre house, but nobody came. I studied every car that came into town, looking for her face. While no one in the world looked like Andréa, there was one other beach-combing visitor who drove that same white Thunderbird. My heart sped up every time I saw it drive through, then it plummeted. It was exhausting. And for what? Another thirty-second conversation? A glance from her passing car?

* * *

All the Church Ladies, plus their bingo alternates, had celebrated their birthdays together since they graduated high school in 1898, and they'd now all entered their late seventies. Imogene and Pearl had a luncheon for them in the church rectory. Each lady received a plaque with her name in gold calligraphy: Joanie Mapes, Eunice Scovelli, Emma Whittle, Permelia Hinkle, and the McFall twins, who alternated playing as the sixth player. And Marge Covelli and Nanny Dewley, the alternates from Nehalem. Even Mrs. B, *Constance Beaumont.* The day of the big event, while I manned the store for Imogene, a woman wandered in, her face guarded by a straw hat and sunglasses. I stood up, my papers fluttering to the floor. She took off her sunglasses. Beautiful as ever.

"I'm sorry," I said, my heart swelling, "about your mother and father."

"Thank you… for the card," Andréa said. "It meant a lot. It's been a long year."

"It did?" I said without thinking. "I mean—"

"So," she said, "priest?" She opened the ice box and took out an ice cream.

I touched my collar like I'd forgotten it was there. "Yeah… it was so long ago—"

"A lifetime," she said. Her eyes met mine. "So much has happened."

Then she looked out the window and I panicked, afraid to lose the connection.

"You haven't sold the house?" I said.

"No," she said, laying down a dollar bill. I refused the money.

"I couldn't do it," she said. "Sometimes we just drive down for the day and I think every time that I'll open the house, stay for awhile. But then I just can't. Too many memories."

"Yeah, memories… I'm so sorry—"

"Everything isn't always about you, Theo," she snapped. "My whole family loved that house. We were happy there. And now, Mom, Dad, and David, gone."

"David?" I said. "Where's David?"

"You made it home from Korea, and I'm grateful for that, but he didn't."

"He was drafted?" I said. "I didn't know."

"How would you," she said suddenly stiffening as if I'd said something wrong. "Anyway, now it's just us. Selling the beach house seemed wrong." She glanced out the window.

"Us?" I asked.

"Yes, us." She continued to stare out the window.

"Andréa," I said, heart in my throat. "Andréa, look at me."

She turned back. Her blue eyes filled with tears. "I can't," she said, staring at my collar.

I started out from behind the counter to get closer to her. "I never stopped—"

Just then Bud crashed through the door like the town was on fire.

"Five-year-old girl from Portland," he said, "went missing from a campsite this morning about ten." He grabbed the phone and clicked for Lucy. "Neighbors found her brother who said they wanted to go to the river, but the girl hasn't shown up."

Alarm crossed Andréa's face. She darted a look to her car where a child sat inside.

"Yeah, Lucy, get my office would ya," he said, then turned to me. "We formed a posse of men on foot, and on horse, two helicopters from the Coast Guard, and cars driving up and down every street in Nehalem and Manzanita. We'll find her." He suddenly recognized Andréa and said, "Hey Andréa, sorry to barge in."

"Hi, Bud."

"What can I do?" I asked.

Andréa waved slightly, wiped her tears, mouthed *I'll be back next month.*

My entire body bristled with alarm. *Next month!* "No, wait—"

"I think it's Hansel." Bud said, his voice low and deadly serious, his hand over the receiver.

Andréa then slid out of the way, out the door to her car. *Next month.* I started to follow, but Bud's call was answered and I knew I had to stay.

"It's Grearson," Bud said. "I need deputies, guns, dogs. Got a missin' girl here."

Andréa glanced at me through the window as she pulled away. Her son waved from the backseat. *Next month* knotted in my gut; an impossible eternity. But what could I do? There was a missing child.

I closed the store, rushed home, grabbed my .38, and started my car. As I backed out, Bud ran to me and said, "Gun?"

"Got it," I said. "Heading up to Neahkahnie… look around the old homesteads." As I backed out, a sense of doom gripped me.

*   *   *

Around sunset, the little girl was found in Nehalem, not far from the river where she'd gone missing. She was sunburnt, crying, and hungry, but otherwise fine. She got lost, she said. Both towns took a sigh of relief; however, the Coast Guard felt Bud overreacted and wasn't too happy with him for "wasting resources." But Bud remained as convinced as Solomon that Genghis Hansel was back and our time of peace was over.

And though Andréa was gone again, at least we spoke—for the first time in six years.

Chapter 89

THEO

BY THE END of August divorce papers arrived in *my* mail for Imogene. It was Thomas's way of asking me to break it to her.

She tore the envelope open, didn't read a thing, and scribbled her name with vengeance. "I don't care," she huffed. "I just don't care anymore. Who needs a husband, anyway?"

"Well, let's face it," I said. "You don't need a husband… like Mamaí, you need a hero. But let me read those before you send them back."

Her tightened eyes relaxed. She grabbed a pack of Salems and headed out to her patio. I sat behind the register and read the documents. The papers were pithy and precise, like Thomas.

He had secured work in a lumber mill in Idaho and wanted to set her, and himself, free. He wanted only for her to be happy. He wrote, *There is no longer love between us, only pain.* I sealed the papers to mail and put that note in Imogene's coat pocket. She'd discover it when the time was right. And later I'd tell her Judge Madsen was paving the adoption path for Tula. I saw in Imogene's life the cliché about a door closing and God opening a window.

Was that hallowed cliché happening in my life as well? Along with the divorce papers came another piece of mail, a postcard from the Portland Rose Gardens that read, *I'm very busy selling Daddy's law firm. Will be in Manzanita by October, for a good long stay. —Andréa*

Chapter 90

THEO

THE MURPHY'S BOTTLE, still sealed with first aid tape, beckoned. But I'd been sober for almost a year now and felt strong again. I untied the string on the letters and splayed them out across my table, trying to find a way in, an opening, a plan of attack—where to start?

I thought about the Irish nun, who I simply called "Sister," and who we spent nearly six months hiding out with, how her vernacular was as poetic as any poet's I studied in college. There was rhythm to her language, which consisted of French, Korean, and English. Her voice was lyrical, composed but with a lament, as if she found joy in every moment, yet mourned the passing of all things in that same moment. She was the only Catholic I ever met who loved God with all her heart, all her being. And she was the only Catholic I ever confessed to. When I told her about avenging Kiernan when I was ten, she laid her hand on my head and said, "You are forgiven, my son." Then, with her hand still on my head, I knelt before her, she prayed the soldier's prayer, repeating, "May our cause be just."

In that dirt floor cave, surrounded by sleeping children and the waking bats, I experienced an inexplicable release of energy from my body when she said, "You are forgiven." It was the first and last time I cried for what I'd done all those years ago.

I wrote about her to Andréa, telling her how much Sister knew about the impressionists, the blue hour, and all the things Andréa loved. I wrote that she would have liked our erudite nun. I wrote that in one of the letters now spread across my table. *Which one?*

I remembered too, that in that same letter I wrote how the shadow of North Korea's army had turned to a pall of gloom over all Korea. How terror swept over the Southwest with the advance of the guerrilla units. How thousands of refugees fled. During the day we watched them in the valleys, along roads — the peasants, farmers, old, young; a tattered and weary string of black pearls.

We watched from a ridge high above, knowing we were safe for the time being, as long as we didn't make a wrong move. But wrong moves were easy to make, hard to undo.

Chapter 91

THEO

"**MORNIN'**," **OZ SAID** ducking to come through my front door. "Coffee?"

I pointed to the fresh pot on the counter as it gurgled to a finish.

"I ain't seen Sarge with his jaws clamped so hard on somethin' since the war," he said.

"Yeah." I laid a silver dollar shell into the aquarium. "He's like a pit bull with a bone when he gets a whiff of something wrong, and then he's about as good at enforcing the law as I am in the confessional."

"Oh, I don't know," Oz said with a mocking smile. "Some say you're just what the doctor ordered, for some vets anyways. Course, some say you're plum crazy."

"Anyway…"

"Anyway," Oz said as he drank and stared at my aquarium. The orange sunrise flickered off the glass. "Jeez, man," he said. "In Italy… this one time we hads ta hide under a building, in the mud with twenty guys." He took his Red Sox cap off his short, coiled hair. "Outside, more than a hundred a them cockroach Nazis. We hads ta listen to one a them beat a little Jew girl. It nearly killt Bud. I held him down with all my weight, hand over his mouth while that girl screamed. If we made a sound, we'z all dead. It was her or twenty men. I had Netty girl waitin' at home for me. I was returnin' from that godforsaken place no matter what. And that poor little girl, her whole family was gone anyways; best she'd just go with 'em, than stay in that hellhole. They finally shot her. Eleven times. But, better she not be a pretty girl in them Nazi camps. Don't ya think?"

I swallowed hard and said, "Well… I think war is hell, not just because of what happens, but because of decisions made and things seen… things that came home with us. We were twenty-year-olds makin' life and death decisions and then had no idea how to deal with who we were after those decisions."

"Well," Oz said as he descended the front porch stairs. "Don't know 'bout all that, but I do know if Bud sees that Nazi, Hansel, gets him alone, we ain't gonna find the body. No, sir! Not after what he done read in that new letter he got."

"What letter?"

"You ain't seen it?" Oz asked.

"No."

"Well, it's 'bout that Hansel character."

"What's in it?"

"Best you ask Bud." Oz jumped in his old pickup, started up the rumbling engine, backed out of my drive, and headed toward Nehalem River with his fishing poles bobbing in the back.

Chapter 92

GENGHIS

TORECK'S STUPID. I mean that was obvious from the get-go, but I didn't realize just how deep it ran. Still, he'd been useful through the months pretty much keeping his nose clean for once, staying out of sight in a two-room motel off I-70 near Topeka. He grumbled the whole while, but I did the things I wanted to do, one last time. Seen a Kansas City A's game, fields of yellow corn nearly six feet tall, hog races, smelled a summer afternoon full of cotton candy, ate my fill of the best bar-b-que in the world, and went to a good ol' tent revival where I made a new little friend, a girl who looked a lot like that pintsized Suzy Wu I *befriended* in Manzanita. But, with appetites satisfied it was time to get back to business.

We dug up my daddy's stash, money he'd hid from his preachin' days when, as any good preacher would do, he took tithes from his devotees, a good preacher, a good thief. He'd buried it behind the barn in a metal box. I had to return to retrieve my bequest. It took some doing, with the old barn torn down, the house burnt to the ground and the new owners building a new fancy house on our property. Had to "visit" the place three different times waiting for the chance to dig. I thought about taking that new family out but didn't need the heat. Did take their pretty little girl, Betty Jean's Bible, though, just a token from her frilly bedroom. Wishful thinkin'.

Now flush again, it was time to get busy.

I kicked the edge of the cot where he slept. "Pack your bag, time to get a move on."

"Move on to where?" He yawned and dropped his feet to the floor.

"Back to Oregon."

It was then I noticed he had a black eye and bruised knuckles, likely from his late-night run down to the truck stop tavern. "You gotta give up that life a crime your leadin'… develop some purpose, some sense of somethin' bigger than yourself."

"*My* life a crime?" he laughed. "Hell, I met you in prison. What ya in for, bein' a upstandin' citizen? Pretty sure you did some a them *crimes* yourself, old man." He lit a half-smoked cigarette from the ashtray full of butts.

I grabbed the foul-smelling ashtray and dumped it in the garbage.

"I don't commit crimes," I said. "I manifest destiny."

"Destiny," he laughed. "Shit man, whose? Mine? Yours? Them kids you like?"

"Pack your bag, Toreck. It's time to move."

"I'm not too keen on goin' back to Oregon," he said. "Not much there for me but the same ole people, same ole scene, same ole trouble."

"One more visit," I said, handing him a clean shirt. "Don't you want to know where that priest hid your family? Don't ya wanna maybe *visit* his pretty sister?"

"How much?"

"$2000," I said. "Here's your ticket." I handed him a plane ticket for the Portland airport, different time and airlines than mine. "We'll meet up in Newport."

"Why Newport?"

"Kite festival; kids everywhere."

"You ain't right, man," he said. "See you in Newport."

Chapter 93

Theo

IN THE MAIL was a large envelope with my name in bold block letters. I tore it open and took out a small, white King James children's Bible. Inside the cover in a little girl's practiced cursive, it read *This belongs to Betty Jean*. No last name. No return address on the envelope. The postmark was Missouri. I thumbed through the tissue pages and found a note: *It's time to put aside the deeds of darkness and put on the armor of light.*

I bagged the note to give to Bud for prints, and got dressed.

Solomon's ointment had inspired a large, purple-rimmed lump inside my hip, as if after all these years the bullet now wanted out. I rubbed more stench on, put on my coat, tucked Betty Jean's Bible in my pocket, and left, wondering who and where Betty Jean was.

It was a warm Indian Summer morning. The blackbirds on the wires took flight and dotted the carrot-colored sky, flapping their wings in unison, screeching and squawking. I felt the tin soldier in my pocket resting against the bullet in my hip; both constant reminders that there are real demons in this world. Like Bud, combat had taught me that. Maybe that's the fatal blow we soldiers receive—a glimpse behind the curtain of sanity, safety, and all things thought civilized, where we see transgressions that punch a hole so deep into our bruised psyche that from that day forth that's all we see.

I knocked on the door of Bud's sun-bleached boarding house, prepared for his "it's too-early" wrath. He yanked the door open so fast it startled me. "Come on in," he said. "Been up for hours." He closed the door. A blotch of blood-stained toilet paper was stuck to his chin and he was already dressed in his uniform. He marched down the hallway and past the living room, where a painting of Pearl and James on their wedding day hung above the fireplace. Down the hallway were grainy black-and-white photographs of her family from Korea and a large photo of Bud and James when they were teenagers. In the kitchen above the sink hung another picture of Pearl and James in Korea; she sitting on his lap, he in his uniform, both with broad newlywed smiles. Next to that was a window that overlooked her garden. The house was spotless… until we reached the dining room.

"What the hell?" I said, pointing to the yellow crime tape looped through chairs and tied to the curtains, blocking off the entry to the room on both sides.

"Crime tape," Bud said lifting it up so I could come through.

"But—"

"If I don't tape off this room," he said pointing at Pearl, "*That* cleanin' devil there comes in here and screws up this table with her dustin', cleanin', movin' things around to where I can't find 'em." He turned to her. "No cleaning here." He pointed at the table. "None. Off-limits. *Vamoose!*"

Her eyes tightened, lips pressed into a thin line. She turned and marched down the hall.

"And you say Imogene and I carry on?"

"Anyway, that detective in Missouri," Bud said, "sent me something he thought might pique my interest." He slammed a mug of coffee down on their oak table which was littered with files, empty coffee cups, Pearl's strange teas and herbs, a plate of half-eaten eggs and ham, an empty packet of Alka-Seltzer, boxes of ammunition, a .45 and a .38, and his wooden box of gun-cleaning supplies. He picked up a letter and said, "Look at this."

"The Reverend and Mrs. Hansel," Bud said, "were found murdered in their home twenty-some years ago when our Genghis was fifteen. And now…well, here, you read it."

The letter was from a Missouri police detective. Attached was an old newspaper article:

SERPENT-HANDLING PASTOR DIES OF SNAKE BITES

MO – September 1935 - A flamboyant Pentecostal pastor from Missouri died last week of over one hundred snake bites from his own copperheads. Reverend Hansel, known as "Snake," was infamous throughout the Appalachians for his roadside tent "hootenannies," where he slung snakes around his neck while preaching hell fire and brimstone. He was found seated in a chair in his front yard, dead. Next to him was Mrs. Hansel, a German Jew who had converted over to her husband's beliefs. She died the same torturous death.

The full-page article explained how, with all those bites, it would have taken hours for the venom to settle into their organs and that they died an excruciating death while their house went up in flames. They found remnants of a Bible open in front of them on a plate.

The letter then explained Hansel had served five years in juvie, but not for murder, since they couldn't really prove it. Instead they booked him for "mischievous conduct" for stealing their car and joyriding. The judge threw the book at him. Because he was a minor his file had been sealed for twenty years. The file also said he had over two hundred old snake bites all over his body, that it was a miracle he was alive, and that he had an unusually strong constitution.

"Hansel's returning," Bud said.

"I've done some research of my own." I explained that I'd searched newspapers at the library, and similar crimes with comparable topics.

"Here's one," Bud grabbed a loose newspaper cut out. "There was a missing child and the parents of that child were set ablaze while seated in their homes. Family Bible or a handwritten Bible quote on a table or stool in front of them."

"Sounds familiar," I said picking up the photographs of evidence found in Marge Hildy's place. Among those pictures was the photograph of that Bible quote Bud showed me before.

I read aloud, "The captives of warriors will be released. Plunder of tyrants, retrieved. I will fight those who fight You, and I will save Your children. And send them back to the House of Souls."

"Okay," Bud said, "I still don't understand that."

"Well, I can't figure out how this partial passage from Isaiah is connected to the murders," I said, "but he's combining a couple different—*very different*—beliefs here, and he's either confused about this phrase, or he actually thinks he's God's warrior."

"He's not confused... crazy, but not confused," Bud said.

"I've tracked some crimes cross-country," I said. "I think he's traveled back and forth leaving a trail of missing children, murdered adults, and no evidence, for several years."

"He's been captured. Escaped twice," Bud said. "Now he has little Toreck to help do his dirty work. He's a sick shit, but he's smart, I'll give him that. Looks to me like he has that thing called a *god complex*."

I set the letter down on the table, looked at him, and said, "What?"

"You're not the only one who reads, little buddy."

"Right," I said as I took the plastic bag out of my coat pocket. "Did Hansel have a sister? Maybe named Betty Jean?"

Chapter 94

THEO

AFTER FRIDAY NIGHT EVENING PRAYERS I was in the church office.

The phone rang. "So, Father Riley," the caller said.

"Hansel?"

"You're a pugilist. *A pugilist.* Fascinating. I read all about you at the Tillamook Library. Lots and lots of news clippings about your boxing years at Tillamook High School. That librarian, Miss Grimm, called you the 'boxing priest.' Now how cute is that."

"Who's Betty Jean?"

"Oh, you've figured some things out. Not bad. Not bad at all."

"Where are you?"

"Your mother was even interviewed. She's quoted sayin', 'I sent him to Tillamook High School for the sports programs.' What a smart and carin' mother you had, and you, a hometown hero, even then. I see li'l sister was just a wee redheaded lass holdin' your mother's hand while you, the big sophomore, held your boxing gloves up high and posed for the picture. Little campy, even for you, don't ya think, Padre? And those girls clingin' to your arms... Charmed life you've had. But now all you have is God, and in my experience He's just not much help."

"What's your game, Hansel?"

"I think it's more about your game, Padre. What is your game? I'm bettin' you just want your old life back. Are you a warrior for man or a warrior for God?"

"I don't see the point."

"The *point!* Well, gosh darn, shouldn't that be answered... I know I'd like to know the answer, how 'bout you, *Lucy?*"

"Me?" Lucy's whispered voice trembled.

"Get off the line, Lucy," I said. "What do you want, Hansel?"

"You can't answer that can ya, Padre?"

"You want absolution?" I said. "Fine, I absolve you."

"Too late to patronize me with your pious morality."

"Where are you? I'll meet you —"

"Isaiah said, 'Make ready to slaughter sons for the guilt of their fathers, lest they rise and possess the earth, and fill the world with tyrants.'"

"So… you're a son of a tyrant who wants to die," I said. "Why me?"

"How'd you get into that kinda fightin', Father Riley? Was it an Irish thing? I've heard you Irish boys like ta fight in the streets — Catholic thugs and Protestant rebels wantin' to be merciless angels of God."

"I wish more people took such an interest in religion and politics," I said.

"This here's your chance to be that merciless angel, Padre." He took a deep breath. "I'll have a taste of revenge on this world first, then it's your big chance to send a fallen angel home."

"So… a fallen angel who wants revenge?" I said.

The line went dead.

*   *   *

On the porch was a rock on top of an envelope; inside was a handwritten note:

Your night is nearly over. It's high time you wake out of sleep, be alert; be alive — put off the garments of that long night and the indulgences of its darkness, toss those loose robes of pleasure and flowing garments of repose; that festal bliss of the hours of darkness is not for the children of day. Cast off your deeds done in the shadows, brother. Your day of vengeance is nearly here. For my salvation waits at the tip of the Lord's bloody sword.

Chapter 95

THEO

BUD STUDIED THE ENVELOPE from Hansel's note. "Sounds biblical… *Garments of darkness? Your day is nearly here?* What's it mean?"

"Well, it's a distortion of the actual passage from Romans… It's really more of a threat to me, or who he thinks I am, anyway."

"A threat?"

"Remember I told you about the pen, that first time I met him. He called me a 'murderer priest.' He'd read the newspaper article about all the hero crap and came to some interesting conclusions. But then I came to some conclusions myself, and ultimately when he got around to asking for exoneration, in a way, well… I denied him absolution."

"Yeah, well, who wouldn't," Bud said. "But absolution… Is that a big deal?"

"To a damaged religious fanatic it is. Or if it wasn't before that day, then when I withheld forgiveness he turned his venom on me."

"Bit two hunded times," Bud smirked. "He's got plenty of it."

"Yeah," I said. "Well, he thinks he's a religious man who's been betrayed by religious men, most likely his father. He wants revenge and I'm his mark, which makes everyone I come into contact with, his target. And then, he wants it all to end. He's called me the 'gatekeeper to his salvation,' which means he has to get past me first. Whatever that means."

"We back to that silver bullet vampire thing?" Bud asked.

"Looks like."

Chapter 96

THEO

BUD MOVED PEARL into Imogene's temporarily, and then he spent the night on her couch. I sat up all night boxing shadows. I should have spent the night in deep prayer, rosary beads in hand, beseeching God to protect us. Instead, I cleaned and reloaded my guns, wanting to go hunt Hansel down for the justice his victims deserved before he could do more harm or create more casualties in his barbed quest for revenge, salvation, or whatever he was after. I'd waited too late before in my life. Not this time.

In Imogene's dim windows I saw Bud light his cigar twice in the middle of the night. He too watched those shifting shadows. When Solomon hit the bench in front of Imogene's in the morning, I went to the back porch and boxed out the energy that made me want to put on my soldier's gear and start tracking. I showered, said a quick prayer, sharpened my knife, and slid it back into my boot. Then I put on my collar and headed over to Imogene's with my paperwork.

* * *

The bench was now empty. Solomon was gone on his morning trek.

Imogene stood behind the counter folding three woolen blankets and a new flannel shirt for Solomon. "Look at that," she said, pointing out her window to the small white flakes that now drifted softly over Manzanita. "Pink snow in September."

It was bizarre but beautiful. I'd seen out-of-season snow in Korea once; another freak storm that combined with swirling cherry blossoms was a stunning sight. "Beautiful," I said, and planted myself at one of her tables with my paperwork.

Tula sat across from me with her cereal. Imogene plopped down on the bench next to her; as usual, Tula wiggled away, still keeping distance between herself and anyone but Solomon.

"Tula," Imogene said, "we should get you a puppy."

Tula's jaw plummeted. She leapt up from the table, rushed through the screen door and outside to the wet bench. We heard the unmistakable thump when her body dropped down on the bench and knocked against the register wall.

Imogene stood straight up. "What'd I say?"

"Let me take this one," I said as I grabbed Tula's hot cocoa and went outside.

I handed her the cup and asked, "Sweetie, don't you like puppies?"

She looked down the street, I assumed for Solomon. Then she sat back, held her cup with both hands, and blew the steam. "Puppies grow up to be dogs, right?"

"Yes... Is that a problem?"

She looked up at me with those big deer-like eyes. "I'm ascared of 'em."

"Why?"

She swallowed hard and focused her eyes on her cup, then said, "Mommy's boyfriend, Mark, tell'd me dogs lived under my bed and would eat me in my sleep." She slurped her cocoa. "Then he closed my door and locked it so's I couldn't get out."

Dear God! I clenched my jaw and said, "Love, we don't need to get you a puppy. Imogene didn't know. But, dogs won't eat you in your sleep." The moment I uttered the words, the image of her mother and Mark flashed through me like a bolt of lightning—the day I led the detectives there dogs prowled the crime scene, drawn by the stench of death and promise of a meal. "No dog will ever come near you in your sleep. I promise." I shook off the image. It was pretty gruesome for Manzanita—but then, righteous retribution is often an ugly thing.

"No dogs... unless you change your mind. Maybe you can talk to Solomon about dogs."

"Kay," Tula said with a heavy sigh.

"Okay, then," I said.

"Mommy never let me out when I banged on the door," she said. Then, as abruptly as Solomon and with as few words, she stood and went back inside.

I wanted to hit something, something named *Mark*, but instead followed her.

Imogene and Pearl played rummy and had a fresh deck of cards spread out on the table. Imogene's eyes bugged as she followed Tula, who carefully set her empty cup in the dish bin by the kitchen door, took off her sweatshirt, hung it on the hook instead of dropping it on the floor, took the shoe box with her mommy's red shoe and placed it in her toy box, out of sight, and then sat down right next to Imogene, real close. Imogene's jaw dropped slightly. Then she mouthed, "thank you" to me.

I shrugged my shoulders, not understanding Tula's sudden transformation. Then I realized that it was nothing *I* said, but that maybe, in thinking on how her own mother hadn't helped her, she was beginning to warm to Imogene, who she knew would do anything for just one of her smiles, and who certainly would have opened that locked door and set her free.

Chapter 97

THEO

IMOGENE'S SIGN glowed OPEN. I entered and said, "Afternoon."

Pearl nodded from behind the deli counter where she was chopping clams and onions for the Friday chowder. Mrs. B sat at a table and stared out the window, unresponsive.

"Where's Immie?" I asked.

"She *still* upstairs," Pearl snapped, as she scraped the fishy-smelling shells into the trash.

"Thanks."

I headed up to Imogene's apartment.

A buttery sunlight sifted into the dining room dusting everything with the smoky haze of a day ready to dissolve into night. Imogene, who sat at the table in silence, was so lost in thought she hadn't heard me clamber up the staircase. Her framed wedding photo no longer hung on the wall. Instead, Mrs. B's oil painting of a lone beachcomber on the sandy shoreline was placed prominently in the center, next to the window. In the dusky hues of the room, with her petite silhouette framed by the full-length burgundy drapes, Imogene, too, looked like a painting. There was something haunting about the way she smoked her cigarette—how it completely transformed her. She drank her coffee with one hand and held the cigarette with the other, carefully balancing her inherent baseness—making it look more like a virtue than a vice.

"Immie," I said. "Whatcha thinkin'?"

"Theo," she said blowing smoke, then dousing the cigarette in the bubble glass ashtray.

"You okay?" I asked.

"Just needed a break," she said in a near whisper, still gazing at the ocean. The tide was receding, grey-black clouds moving in. I studied her face. There was a dimension to her that never existed before. Her eyes once glimmered with a contagious joy and an easily sparked temper. But when I returned from Korea, that joy was gone. Now her eyes were like a bottomless ocean. After losing the baby and worrying whether I was dead or alive, somewhere between sorrow and fear, her eyes lost that sparkle.

Sometimes I'd catch a glimpse of her sitting alone like that, with her coffee and cigarette; it would send a shiver down my spine, frighten me that there was a hole punched in my sister's soul that I'd never begin to understand.

"Feels like a storm," she said tucking her cigarettes back in the baggy pocket on her dress. She stood, took a bobby pin from the same pocket, opened it with her teeth, and pinned back a curl of ginger hair. Then she glanced back out the window. "You know, just cold to my bones." She shivered and pushed through the swinging kitchen door. "And I'm tired. It's been busy today. How 'bout some tea?"

"Sure... tea," I said. "What were you thinking about?"

"Forgiveness," she said. "What it means... how it feels or if and when I've actually done it. How do you know if you've forgiven?"

"Ah, forgiveness," I said. "That's a tough nut to crack." I followed her into the kitchen. "What I can tell you is that when you withhold forgiveness, you tether yourself forever to that specific pain. So, cut that cord. Forgive and let go."

"So when do you know if you're successful?"

I paused too long.

"You don't know, *do* you, Father?"

"Just when I thought I was soundin' so priestly and all," I said with a half-laugh. "Well, I know that if you find you're not thinkin' about him, or hurtin' over what happened, and you've moved on with your life, then that may be the beginning of letting go. I know that much."

I noticed Bud's quenched cigar from last night in the ashtray on the counter.

"Him?" she said. "And you did sound a bit priestly there for a minute."

"Well, it's a start," I said, feeling the tin soldier in my pocket. "*Can* you forgive Thomas?"

The kettle whistled.

"*Can* we change the subject?" she asked.

"Okay... for now. Pearl's a little grumpy."

"She's been in a mood since Tula asked if the kids had daddies where she came from," she said, settling the bee-hive honey jar in front of me. "She'll be fine." She stared out the window again. "Definitely a storm. Feel it deep in my bones."

"Well," I said, "I think you're right about that puppy."

"But she said—"

"I talked to Solomon; he thinks a dog is a good idea. He'll work on it."

"So is this a plan?" she asked. "Replace my child with another, my husband with a dog?"

"Darn," I said, "you've busted us. Been planning this for a long time now."

* * *

I always thought Imogene took to Thomas because he was like Da; nothing nice to say and always brooding. She tried to save Da, but he was drowning too fast. There was no saving, no forgetting, no forgiving for any of us, not then.

As Da slipped helplessly into his grief—Irish whiskey blurring his view of the world—he clung to the past, while Mamaí was forced to forge our future alone. She resented his taking the luxury to grieve as if it was his grief alone. "It is my grief, too!" she shouted more times than one could count. After all, she'd remind him, "It was your fault!" Da crumbled under the weight of those four words, under the weight of the day that cracked our family in two and scattered us to another continent. It was too heavy a burden. Too much to forgive.

Her eyes bore the resentment, the unspoken, constant thought that it should have been Da who those McMurtry thugs beat to death. And it should have been Da who took revenge, not her ten-year-old son. No marriage, no two people could ever survive such a thing. Instead, Da died a slow, painful death—guilt ate him alive.

She never forgave him but also never left his side. Though Kiernan was then dust, and I skin and bone, to Mamaí I existed only as his shadow. She never saw me clearly again, and she never forgave Da, like she never forgave all of Ireland for the sins against her beloved sons. Forgiveness is not a family trait.

Mamaí endured her losses, her marriage, and other betrayals in the way a woman confronts a battlefield—rosy-cheeked, fists held high, and ready to fight to the death to protect her own. But Imogene, she was young, so she believed a lie. Like the lie I believed about needing to become a priest, she believed what most children of alcoholics believed—that she didn't deserve to be loved. When her baby died I think it confirmed that lie inside her; in that bottomless ocean, that lie was set in stone.

Mamaí often had that same stony look; both had lost a child, creating an empty space in them that, to me, would forever be as mysterious as forgiveness and as unreachable as Jupiter.

Would Imogene forgive Thomas for the many crimes he didn't commit? Forgive him for simply not being the man she expected him to be? Like Mamaí with Da, who fell so short in his husbandhood that to her, his crimes were against all humanity.

Forgiveness … a tough nut to crack. Could Andréa ever forgive me for believing lies when she knew the truth? And if she could, what then?

Chapter 98

THEO

SOLOMON CAREFULLY LAID one blanket at a time over his fire pit and offered the burning gifts to his deceased family to keep them warm in the coming winter months, as he did every equinox. I watched from the porch as he burned three blankets, raising his arms to the sky and chanting. Then he sat and meditated on the warmth those transported blankets would carry to his wife and their children in the heavens: still his family's provider.

When he was finished, he walked over to my porch and said, "You burn letters?"

"Not yet."

"Soon you climb Neahkahnie again," he said. "Burn them there."

"I can't climb anymore, not with this slug in my—"

"You will." He then took my porch blanket, a baseball, and one of my worn-out boxing gloves from the basket where I'd tossed them. "The dog will need to chew."

"Whose dog?"

"Frank's. He has too many to feed… Oz will bring the dog with big paws today."

"Where will he stay?" I asked.

"I solve this problem you ask of me. Now you solve *that* problem."

"Right."

* * *

"Mornin'," I said entering Imogene's. Bud had set up camp.

"Mornin'," he said. Imogene handed me a cup of coffee and went into the kitchen.

"So, is this our life now?" I asked. "Waiting for the next three a.m. call, the next move?"

"Appears it is," he said. He laid out a map, the notes from Hansel (now in plastic evidence bags), the white Bible, the Oregon State Penitentiary file, and two new reports from the Missouri detective, who was now as convinced as Bud that Genghis Hansel was on the move and that his 'Oregon Trail' was as dark and bloody as Jack the Ripper's.

"Did you know the Oregon Trail started in Missouri?" Bud asked.

"I'm sure I knew that at some point in my life… Is it relevant?"

"Don't know," he said pointing at a red line he'd drawn on the map from Missouri to Oregon. "Just that it's interesting when you map out some similar unsolved crimes, they're along the Oregon Trail. Check out the names of these cities and towns: Black Vermillion Crossing, The Devil's Gate, Parting of the Ways, and Farewell Bend. He's got a strange sense of humor."

"He's saying goodbye to this world." I said. "He believes he's going to cross over soon."

"Yeah… and look at this, his mother once lived in Oregon, over in Seaside. So there is a connection after all."

"Any living family?"

"None," Bud said shaking his head. "Nowhere."

"Well, the Oregon Trail ended in Oregon City, and his mother lived in Seaside, so Manzanita must be a compromise."

"I'm guessin' after your interaction in the pen," he said, "he changed his course."

"Been a moving target before." I said. "But once a man deviates from his path, he gets lost. Things get messed up. Manzanita has nothing to do with his original mission. His emotions have taken over. He's gonna make a mistake."

"Yeah," Bud said. "We can't leave our girls alone for a minute till we settle this thing. Though I don't think this guy'll do anything in broad daylight."

"I don't know. He likes to toy with people. He drives through town in a stolen truck, he comes to the church and talks to Imogene. He leaves red shoes, Bibles, and other clues we just can't make out. No, he's not afraid of broad daylight. He's not afraid of much, and worse yet, he thinks this is his last hurrah."

"Yeah, maybe more afraid of *not* being seen."

"That's why we're getting a dog."

"Dog?"

"One of Frank's puppies, for Tula, and as a bark machine."

"Oh, Imogene'll love that," Bud laughed.

"It was her idea."

"Was it her idea that a mutt like one of old Frank's Labradors who eats and shits and smells like hell, lives in her house? Cause that don't sound like an Imogene idea to me."

"We haven't worked out the details yet."

Chapter 99

THEO

SINCE BUD was firmly camped at Imogene's for the day—finally having a reason to be around her without having to explain—I walked the back streets, looking up and down for anything out of the ordinary. Many of the cabins and shanties were empty; with cooler weather, vacationers had packed up and left. The streets were quiet, smelled of chimney smoke. I'd come back at dusk, look for signs of squatters. Two squatters in particular.

After searching the streets I found myself at the foot of a spur trail. "Okay," I said staring up the west side of Neahkahnie. "Climb." I put one foot on Solomon's dirt path and then the other, trepidatious, imagining the sharp blaze of pain that would inevitably explode in my hip. But no blaze came. I picked up my pace and began to zigzag up the path toward Elk Flats, feeling just a pinch in my hip. I hiked through fallen conifers with wide root systems, trekked through the Douglas firs of my youth. The trees were so immense they looked otherworldly in this ancient rain forest. Soft drizzle fell over the mossy woodland. My lungs filled with life.

Then, a bolt of pain from my hip to my ankle dropped me to the earth. There I stayed, pressing on the spot. Angry, swearing. I had dreamed of making it to the top, past the ridge of Cape Falcon to stand two hundred feet over the surf where I'd hold my arms out and tilt my head back, winds caressing me, welcoming me back to my sanctuary, a place of bottomless primal understanding—no judgments, no obligations, no conditions. Just standing, heart to the sky, the mist of waves hurling against the cliffs, then settling on my skin. I pulled Andréa's face into my mind's eye. I imagined her sitting next to me, imagined our life, the life we would have had, then imagined her with her mysterious husband and their son. Another pointless dream.

As the pain in my leg subsided, I took in my surroundings. I was farther up the path than I thought I'd be. Neahkahnie Mountain was so similar to the lush woodlands of the Gangwon-Do region. The lakes and rivers, full of cuttlefish and pollack. I taught the children there, as Solomon taught me here, which plants were poisonous, which were not.

There exists three times in my life when I felt wholly right in my own skin or that I was in the right place, meant to be there, or do what I did. Three times: avenging Kiernan, loving Andréa, and teaching those children as Solomon taught me.

Chapter 100

THEO

THE SAINT MARY'S confession booth was no more than four feet by four feet on each side. The solid walnut walls were adorned with carvings of saints, the Bible, and Jesus on the cross. I ran my finger along the deep curved etchings. The church outside my thick red drape had been silent for over an hour.

Although these hour-and-a-half confession times were often boring, I sometimes took solace in the contrived anonymity. But this day was different. I sat on pins and needles listening to every sound. When I suggested to Bud that I sit guard with him, he said no, that if Hansel showed up anywhere it may be at the church. It was the first time I ever came into the church with a gun in my belt and a knife in my boot. I didn't feel very priestly, armed.

Soon Permelia opened the downstairs door and came in to set up for choir practice. The smell of her thick walnut brownies and coffee filled my hungry senses. It was only three-thirty. I had an hour to go.

The rectory's front door opened. I leaned forward and listened. Footsteps on the hardwood floor slowly moved to the altar, and sounds of a candle being lit reflected off the quietude. Who was it? The smell of beeswax filled the chapel. Footsteps again, but they were of a small person, not a six-foot-five monster. I relaxed as the curtain on the other side of the booth was pulled back, then closed. Through the thick mesh window I saw an unusually quiet Pearl.

I'm sorry to say I rolled my eyes, waiting for her to confess about killing slugs and spiders, or her bad thoughts about Mrs. Gandel, whom she didn't like. But today she sat quiet for a few minutes. I listened to her abnormally heavy breathing and rubbed my fingers along the scene of Christ carrying the cross on his back.

"Our world is far from the moon," she finally said, her voice low and lackluster. "My father say dat to me. I love him much… He say moon is friend who watch over me."

I recalled what Imogene said about Tula questioning Pearl about her father. Her round jade bracelet clinked as she ran her fingers along the white rosary beads on her lap. She took a deep breath and said, "Forgive me Father, I have sinned."

I leaned back against the cushioned wall and waited for her confession.

"I still see father… see face of smiling Japanese soldier who shot him like he communist criminal. My father was school teacher." She sat silent again.

I waited, not allowed to speak until she made a confession.

"Then soldier turn to brother. He shoot him, then mother… grandmother. I not so lucky. When finished with me, he throw me like garbage on pile of family's dead bodies. They burn our huts and destroy our village… I want to die… go with them." She took another long pause.

The only proper reaction was to reach out and give her a hug, but the consecrated wall that divided us dictated I sit still and listen.

"I stare into open eyes of my dead father. I pray, like he teach me. Nobody come. The full moon hide behind dark clouds… night come. No stars. The sky, full of sadness. I want to die. The moon not look at me. It pull clouds over eyes, ashamed to see me.

"Next morning American soldier, my James, lift me from pile of bodies." She wiped her tears. "He say I alive. My given name, Sook, mean innocent and pure. My father bless me this name. When James say I am alive, not in hell of ghosts and pain, I want to kill myself. James tell me I am reborn, like pearl from jagged shell, he say. He call me Pearl and soon he ask me be his wife. I move to America: Pearl, new woman, reborn August ten, 1946."

She wiped her tears and asked, "Is it sin to throw away Christian name? Because dat girl, Sook, died under moon of shame. Pearl was born. Was I wrong to let Sook go?"

"There's no sin here," I said unable to remain quiet any longer. "No sin of *yours*."

"Sook is dead," she continued, "but still in Pearl's heart is to murder animals who stole my purity and slaughter family. This is the sin in my heart. I want be in grace of God… but I cannot with ugliness inside."

"Listen to me," I said finally clearing my throat. "You are a devoted child of God. You are forgiven these thoughts. You are the victim here, let revenge be God's. Be at peace that he has already exacted what was due."

Pearl wiped her tears and exited her side of the confessional. It struck me how we were both victims of a war that never officially started and now wouldn't end. How we both wanted retribution but clung to what we'd been taught: *Forgive, let vengeance be mine*, sayeth the Lord.

She lit another candle at the altar, then the clatter of her footsteps and the closing of the heavy rectory door echoed through the chapel. My hollow words of forgiveness were an insult to her wound. Forgive? In truth, I didn't, *couldn't* grasp that kind of grace.

I stared at the saints carved in wood and felt ashamed. I once thought of the confessional as a sacred place to take one's most intimate thoughts. Now that I knew what kind of man may be sitting on the other side, I thought differently.

Chapter 101

SOLOMON

PUPPY WAS the same color as Imogene's chocolate pudding. It was good color. He whimpered all night but by morning was at ease with chew toys. He played on blanket outside my hut. He would be good guardian for Tula.

Theo sat on back porch in early light, same chair where his mother once watched the sun rise every morning. And where she set coffee on porch for me. Steam from that cup called me to her side. Together we watched a new day birth—for many years did this. Now, her son sits, wounded, confused, missing his mother's wisdom.

"Morning," I said.

"I see we have a new family member," he said nodding at the dog.

"Yes, he will be good now. First night is hard." I sat on rail. "You climb Neahkahnie?"

"I did," he said. "Well, almost anyway."

"Keep trying."

"I will."

"The storm comes now," I said.

"Okay. I'll order supplies from Portland today and get things ready," he said. "Bullets?"

"I was thinking more along the lines of water, food, gasoline, candles… "

"This storm is bigger than that… will need to be killed."

Theo sat in chair and said, "Okay… kill somethin'. Why's everybody talkin' about storms, anyway?"

"After storm, I will go."

"Go where?"

"My final journey is near," I said. "Wolf waits."

Theo's face dropped. He stared into rising sun and said, "Final journey?"

The sky was heavy and quiet, hard to read. Sunflowers leaned to ground in search of winter grave, trees were near bare and many birds had flown to next place. Osprey flew to perch above my hut, with tips of feathers spread like long fingers, clutching a fish. She landed and settled fish on limb at her feet.

"The Great Grandfather's world is beautiful place," I said.

"It is," Theo said. He, too, gazed up at bird of prey with her breakfast.

"I will be sorry to leave some things." I watched osprey pull at skin and swallow Mother Ocean's gift. "And I will be happy to see my family again."

"We're also your family—"

"Yes," I said. "And you must listen to me."

"I listen to everything you say. I always have, despite Korea, this collar, I hear you."

"Then hear me, my journey will end soon. All journeys end."

Theo's eyes burned red. He reached out, laid his hand on my arm.

"Do not weep for me at any grave," I said patting his hand. "I will not be there. I will be the wind, a thousand raindrops, morning sunlight on your face. I will stand on cliffs of Neahkahnie Mountain until the end of time, you and Raven come join me there, then go into the world and live your life. Feed the wolf who hungers most. These things are gifts from the Great Grandfather. Do not waste them. Your time of healing is ended. Your next journey begins now."

PART III

Chapter 102

THE DAY Toreck was released from yet another stint in the Tillamook jail—for treasure digging on Neahkahnie without a permit—the valley flooded like it hadn't in fifty years. Jetties broke, mudslides crashed down and closed the highway, winds gusted upward to sixty miles an hour, waves crested over twenty-five feet, and the Nehalem River rushed all the way up to Highway 101. Docks washed down river, homes and business were destroyed.

The morning after the flood, people were stranded in their waterlogged homes and flooded fields; bloated cattle carcasses and floating chicken coops spotted the valley. Many tied their rowboats to the roofs of their homes and then waded, rowed, and swam out to see what damage was done to their livestock. Chaos took hold of the valley. It was a miracle the waters didn't crest a half-mile away on 101 and come rushing downhill into Manzanita.

Ever the battle-ready Sergeant, Bud—with the aid of Lucy, who was able to call residents—organized everyone with boats, fresh water, and the emergency supplies he'd stored in the basement of their hotel for years.

While loading blankets into the back of Imogene's Woody, Tula asked me, "Is the world coming to an end now?" referencing a recent Sunday school lesson.

"No, honey," I said. "This kind of flood happens every few years around here."

Imogene rushed out of the store with a thermos of coffee and a bag of sandwiches.

"Here," she said. "Peanut butter and jelly." She handed them to Tula, who sat in the back seat with her now constant companion—the floppy brown-eared pup. She named him Solly, for Solomon.

"Why did God make floods?" Tula asked.

"Well," I said, "God's purpose in *the* flood was not to destroy people, but to expose and destroy wickedness and sin."

"I don't understand that," she said. "It's still scary. What are they doing?" She pointed out the window. The Church Ladies drove by like vintage queens in the Rose Parade waving a banner alongside the Packard that read "Daughters of Mercy."

"No need to be frightened of floods or them," I said and then winked to her in the rear-view mirror. But from that stern face there was no telling what was in her head. She could be *hoping* for floods, for all I knew. Solly laid his head down on her lap. Smileless, she petted his head and shook hers at the Church Ladies as they passed.

Tula gazed out the window as we drove up to Highway 101, about a quarter-mile from Saint Mary's. There we were stopped by the muddy waters that submerged the highway. Oz and Netty's place, the Sand Dune Café, was across the deluged road. Old Oz, in his army green chest-high fishing waders, piled sandbags in front of the restaurant. Thankfully he'd built the place up on the high ground of the lot and laid a tall foundation, knowing full well the valley flooded occasionally. Though this was the worst we'd ever seen. He waved. Netty, in her knee-high crabbing boots, rain hat, and coat, waved from the porch, where she gathered her potted geraniums up to safety.

Frank's gas station, the only one in the valley, was on the low ground of the adjacent lot and was mostly submerged. Frank sat on the top of his building with his cooler and boat tied to his chimney, looking like he was watching a parade. Holding up a can of Rainier beer, he waved and shouted, "What else can I do?" Solly's mother, Lulu, was in the rowboat tied to the roof.

"You got food?" I called to him.

"Yep!" He held up a loaf of bread. Behind him, a misty rainbow domed the sky.

From the parked car, Tula and I handed dry blankets and drinking water to people who passed in rowboats, and we drove rescued people and pets back down the hill to the church where the Daughters of Mercy had organized what they called "Rescue Central." Though the church was dry as dust, they all donned matching life vests and wore white caps and Red Cross swatches on their arms from when they trained as medical aids in 1939.

Emma Whittle and the twins wore white dresses and white shoes, but Mrs. Scovelli, who fancied herself a women under twenty-five, decided it was a good day to show off her bright red lipstick and a daunting low-neck sweater.

Imogene and Pearl made coffee and pots of elk meat stew and traipsed back and forth across Laneda keeping a continuous supply of drink, food, and dry clothing meant for the Goodwill. Mrs. B took a case of rum for those who needed to steady their nerves. And last I knew, Solomon and Tula went to his cabin to build a fire.

Imogene's car finally ran out of gasoline. I left it at the junction with the back open so passersby could take water, sandwiches, or whatever else we had left. I walked back to the church and started using my car to pick up people where Bud had dropped them off at the Woody. By the time I returned for the last time, the church was full: sixty cold but smiling people, drunk on rum. Finally, a friendly congregation.

Mrs. Scovelli flaunted around the card table like a saloon hall girl while the men tried to play gin rummy. That tight pink sweater on an eighty-year-old wrinkled chest was cringe-worthy; consequently, the men—who ranged in age from thirty to seventy—cast their eyes down, or up, or to the other side of wherever she stood, or even to the stained glass windows of Jesus while they played their hand and laid their bets.

Later, Bud and I took supplies to a family who was stranded in the valley. Dead animal carcasses floated in the water, a huge loss of income for our neighbors. Bud asked me to go because Doc Haydn was overwhelmed with patients, and I had *some* medic training. Two of the people in the house had been hurt trying to save livestock.

I set broken bones and cleaned wounds. It was a long night of rescues and dwindling supplies. By the next morning the entire valley was a muddy mass of destruction as the waters receeded. When we passed the boarded-up Bay City Restaurant, we saw several cars that had been carried away by the rushing waters. Beside two dislocated cars that had crashed into a boulder and were crunched into one another lay the long-missing black panel truck, windows broken out, back doors flung open.

Chapter 103

IMOGENE

DAILY SPECIALS

Red Wine, Elk Meat Chili with Corn Bread and Drink .75¢
Friday's Pie - Hot Apple Pie à la mode .50¢

The day after the flood a crowd of red flannel-clad hunters came in for chili, beer, and bullets. I grabbed the cookie jar, went upstairs, and plopped down for a smoke. Tula was at the kitchen table working on her alphabet. I set two Oreos on a napkin in front of her and said, "Here, honey."

She crunched her face, grimaced at the cookies, and looked at Solly, who was lying on the floor at her feet. She stared at the Oreos, then at Newt, who was in a bucket on the floor.

"What is it, sweetie?" I sat next to her. She scooted away. I finally asked, "Why do you always move away from me?"

"You stink."

"What? I bathed... deodorant, perfume. Is it onions from the chili?" I smelled my hands.

"No," she said. "It's them... you smell like mommy's boyfriends."

"Oh!" I said, quickly dousing my cigarette. "Honey, I—"

"They all *stinked* like them cigarettes." She looked down at her cookies and flicked at them with her finger. "You stink like them."

"Well," I said, wondering how many boyfriends her mommy had had, "I've tried to quit before. Maybe with your help, I can do it this time. You should have said something before—"

"House smells like 'em, too." She jumped up and ran to her room. Solly followed.

As she slammed her door I suddenly realized the times when Tula was more at ease were when we were outside. But here in my apartment, *our home*, she was always distant, almost angry. Could it be, all these months, just the smell of smoke?

*   *   *

For six months after Christina died the red walls of our apartment had closed in on me. The rooms spun, I gasped for air. The smell of her was everywhere—baby powder, baby lotion, clean jumpers, folded diapers—everywhere, an invisible army of sweet-smelling grief.

Thomas always told me to sit in the chair by the window so I could breathe in the ocean. He never understood that was where I held her the most—in that overstuffed, cozy chair. In that chair, the room closed in on me more than anywhere. Tears attacked, balls of fire blazing through enemy tunnels to the front lines. "It's just a chair," he'd say. Just a chair. He didn't understand we were locked in grief, a tapestry of bondage woven so tight it threatened my sanity.

I remember Thomas left for a two-week business trip. While he was gone I painted the kitchen and living room a light lemon chiffon. I gave that chair to a stranger who stopped by. His truck was packed with haphazard furniture, so I asked him if he needed a nice chair.

"Hell, yeah!" he said. "The wife kicked me out and left me with nothin'." After he loaded it into his truck, he tilted his cigarette pack my way and I took one. He offered me a light, took that too. I learned to smoke as his red taillights blinked at the stop, our green chair disappearing for parts unknown.

It was the only way. If I knew which neighbor had it or what house it was in, it would be too tempting.

I jumped up from the table and threw my cigarettes in the garbage. "Tula May," I called down the hallway. "What's your favorite color?"

It was time to paint again. It was the only way to get rid of the smell of smoke. I couldn't erase her bad memories or whatever she experienced with those tyrants, but I could get rid of reminders, and if I could start smoking I sure as hell could quit. How hard could it be?

Chapter 104

THEO

PEARL'S "MOON OF SHAME" kept me awake, kept creeping into my thoughts. It was often late at night with only the moon's light that we scoured for food on the north side of T'aebaek Mountain, outside our caves. We harvested alpine mushrooms for soup, even found a burnt-out farm where potatoes had survived the blazes of the North Koreans. We thanked that murdered farming family for their crop and other supplies: blankets, silverware. At Sister's insistence, we buried them beneath a moon that I imagined was not unlike Pearl's moon of shame.

My bedroom was dark. Only shadows, sounds, smells, and tastes that no longer existed outside of my mind. Then a car squeeled down Laneda Avenue. I jumped up, turned on the lights, grabbed my .38, and rushed outside. Searched the front porch, yard, out the gate, then across to Imogene's. Down the carless street. Everything was dark—no moon, only the one streetlight's vanilla glow and silence. He was a ghost. But he was there, like those Daubenton bats, veiled in some crevice, waiting. I searched up and down Laneda, staring into the night.

When I returned home there was an envelope tied to my mailbox. I yanked the rope free and went back inside, opened the dining room curtains so I could watch the street, and read yet another of his prophetic letters with my flashlight.

Your Manzanita is right out of the Bible. Demons, angels, holy places and heathens. Your old Indian, Solomon, like Azazel, climbs his mountaintop each day, a gathering place of demons, like Mount Hermon. Azazel was leader of the rebellious giants in the time preceding the flood; you know this stuff. That's what I like about you. Oh, and didn't you just have a flood? My, my, my, His wrath begins.

Azazel taught the art of warfare, made knives, swords, shields... taught his chosen ones secrets of witchcraft; led innocents into wickedness. Tisk, tisk, tisk. Weren't you once his apprentice? Isn't that young tulip now his little scholar? Innocent lambs to the slaughter...

Well, as you know, finally at the Lord's command, Azazel was bound by the feet and hands — Bound by archangel Raphael and chained to the jagged rocks, to abide in utter darkness until the Day of Judgment, when he'll be cast into an inferno, devoured by hungry flames. Amen! Amen! I say it twice to make it twice as nice. But you know all this, don't you, Father Riley. And you know I've chosen the perfect place for our final battle. Soon.

Chapter 105

THEO

"WHAT THE HELL is this about?" Bud asked.

"He's talking about the Book of Enoch."

"E who?"

"Not widely read... Anyway, in addition to wanting to *save* Tula, he's also after Solomon. This quest of his has become real religious warfare."

"So what is this *e*-noch?" Bud asked.

"It's an ancient book of text, not considered part of scripture to most, but his Jewish mother no doubt taught him bits and pieces of her ragged gypsy religion as she remembered it: confused, broken, twisted... not so unlike his father's snake-yielding creed."

"In my experience a religious nut is far more dangerous than your run-a-the-mill con."

"Yeah. Mine, too," I said.

"That's funny comin' from you. You know, the whole priest thing and all—"

"Yeah, I get it. Funny. Anyway."

"Well, I'd say you're more the expert on religious fanatics, so what do we do?"

"We need a plan," I said. "We need to anticipate his next move. It's important to not become the evil we abhor, to not react to him, or engage in his battle. We need to pull him in where we can get at him, because right now he's a ghost. And a ghost has all the advantage."

"I need to write that down," Bud said. *"To not become the evil we abhor.* Jeez, man, I need that framed and hangin' over my desk. Anyway, for now I'll hang posters of his ugly—"

"No, never telegraph a punch. It gives the counter-puncher an opportunity to create a good offense. Get them out discreetly. Don't look worried—he'll feed on that. We need to figure out what he's planning for this last stand, and where the hell he's hiding."

"So that's our plan… Be discreet, don't look vexed, don't upset him, and then figure out *every* next step he may make? Okay *Sherlock*, if you can do that, then I need you to come work for me. We'll have those pesky FBI Most Wanted thugs behind bars in no time."

"Again, funny," I said. "What I mean is if we generate a circus and scare everyone in town, it'll distract him. We don't want that. We need his eyes on me, or Solomon. If he's engaged in this imaginary religious battle, and we're the enemy he's focused on, we have a better chance of catching him when he trips up. And he will. But if he gets caught up in the thrill of scaring an entire valley, we won't know where to look. At least now we know where he's looking and will inevitably miss a punch or drop his guard. Using his own weaknesses we can draw him out."

"Always the counter-puncher," Bud said. "Okay, a defensive fight it is. So we'll rely on our opponent's mistakes to catch him. Discreet. I get it."

Chapter 106

IMOGENE

DAILY SPECIAL
Venison Cakes, Gravy and Biscuits and Drink .75¢

Another Newt *dead*. The moment Tula left with Solomon, we launched our clandestine operation: Pearl ran down to her house, plucked a live Newt from the bucket where Theo now stored one or two at a time, ran back to the store, and handed it to me like a hot potato. I inspected it to make sure it looked at least a little like her beloved slimy creature, then wrapped the dead Newt in newspaper and tossed it in the garbage. I dropped the new Newt into the bucket. It was the third salamander-swap maneuver in as many weeks.

"I'm gonna take a break," I said and headed outside to Solomon's bench which we had surrounded with carved pumpkins and bundles of hay.

The sun warmed the ache in my bones—bones that throbbed from two days of painting and bones in pain more than ever for a cigarette. My head burst at the seams from not smoking.

I didn't sit on the bench very often. Maybe I should. Maybe if I stepped out here and took in fresh ocean air instead of lighting a cigarette, I'd let go of the need for them.

After Christina I stopped going into Tillamook on Tuesdays to join friends for lunch and shop, because the ripple of gossiped whispers about "the dead baby girl" sent tremors through my body. Instead I'd return to Manzanita and sit on this bench and smoke.

For two years after her death Solomon came, sat by my side, and took my hand in his. We sat in silence. For those few brief moments he held not only my hand, but the brokenness in my heart—the relentless, stabbing agony that throbbed in my legs and the nightmares that woke me—and while he held onto those things that gripped me so tightly, I was free and at peace.

But then Thomas had lost his job and was home all the time. No more sitting in silence.

Solomon's red-tailed hawk swooped down from the tree and crossed the sky to his yard. A deep relaxation suddenly washed over me. I closed my eyes, leaned my head against the geranium box, and listened to the birds that titter-tattered, chirped, and flitted about in the fence line. When I opened my eyes, Solomon was on the bench beside me.

"Sol," I said sleepily, as if just waking from a dream. "I was just thinking of you."

He took a pack of gum from his shirt pocket and said, "Chew… all day." I took the pack of Wrigley's Spearmint.

"Then spit out your hurt and anger," he said, "Make room for love. It comes."

He stood and walked across the street. I unwrapped the foil from a piece of gum, set it on my tongue and felt the bitter sweetness unfold and spread.

As Solomon disappeared down Theo's driveway, the birds dove from the treetops to sit on their perches in his yard, close to their weary knight, as Mamaí called him.

Chapter 107

THEO

AFTER A FEW DAYS of waiting for the waters to fully recede, the roads to clear, and Highway 101 to open back up, Bud was itching to get to Tillamook and do some research.

We sat down at Imogene's for spiced cider. "How'd that truck end up in the parking lot of a long-closed restaurant?" he asked. "And who left it here in the valley?"

"We know who left it, it's more about when," I said. "Where was it all those months?"

"Don't know," Bud said.

"You gonna be here for awhile?"

"Yeah," he said. "Why?"

"I need to check on something."

I drove up the gnarled gravel road to Toreck Sealy's family cabin—a haggard shanty of a place. Bud was right; it didn't look lived in. But my knotted gut told me there was something.

I emerged from the car reluctantly and stood in the gravel, scrutinizing the property: no tire tracks, no footprints, and oddly enough, no birds in the surrounding trees, no animal sounds of any kind. Even the animals were put off by the wicked energy emanating from the cabin. The only sound was that of my footsteps on hard dirt as I walked toward the porch. On it were broken screens, busted chairs, fishing nets, rusted gold-digging equipment, and shadows. I stopped at the steps and looked up, scanned each window. Some broken, some boarded up. All dark and hollow like eye sockets on a skeleton's skull.

The Sealys arrived in Manzanita in 1935 from the Midwest in search of Neahkahnie's pirate's treasure. Old man Sealy was ruthless, Mrs. B said, and would send the children to school hungry, half-clothed, beaten. It was no wonder the last Sealy would be the likes of Toreck. No one knows what ever happened to his sister. Rumor was, something horrible and on this property. I looked around; the trees hunched to the ground instead of reaching for the sky, as if laden with sorrow. Did Toreck form his unholy relationship with Hansel because he reminded him of his baleful father?

I stepped on a wooden stair that led to the porch and froze, sensing something watching from behind the dirty windows. One more stair—it creaked. I took another step, reaching into my pocket to touch the Rosary. Superstition and history aside, the Sealy home radiated with malevolence.

Suddenly, distant tires corkscrewed up the gravel road. My skin prickled. I fled the porch and ducked behind a rusty oil drum by the barn. A silver Oldsmobile emerged out of the overgrown drive into the circular dirt patch in front of the house. The way the shadows hit its windows I couldn't make out the driver. Then, without stopping, the driver spun the wheel, did a swift u-turn, and sped back down the road. Gravel and dust flew everywhere.

Whoever it was saw my unmistakable blue De Soto, top down. Whoever it was now knew I was snooping around. Got that sinking feeling in my bones, the same one I got the day I looked into the eyes of Genghis Hansel, the same as when we found the red shoe—knew in my gut it was him in that Oldsmobile, and like a hermit crab this was one of his embezzled shells.

"Immie!" I pushed through her Dutch door. "Imogene?" I ran to the back, hoping they were on the patio. "Tula May, Imogene?" They were nowhere in sight. I yanked open the apartment door. "Imogene?" Darted up the stairs two at a time.

"Theo?" Imogene's voice came from the store.

I dropped back down the steps. "Imogene!" They'd been in the walk-in freezer. "Tula?"

"It's math day."

"Oh, right," I said, searching under her counter for the bat and gun.

"What the hell?"

"Listen," I said. "I went up to Sealy's place—"

"Why you go there?" Pearl snapped. "That bad place. You no go there."

"Well, I won't go again," I said. "Not alone, anyway." I reached down, grabbed the Winchester, and handed it to Imogene. "Keep this close."

"What?" she asked. "What did you see?"

"Did either of you see anyone, or an unfamiliar car—a silver Oldsmobile, maybe?" I asked. I'd captured part of the license plate—209—but couldn't see the rest through the flying debris. "It had a California plate."

"No," Imogene said. "Why?"

"Where's Bud?" I asked.

"He got a call."

"Call from who?"

"From Oz, he's just up at—"

"Stay here and call me at Oz's if you see anything," I said, flipping the sign to CLOSED and locking the door behind me.

Outside on Solomon's bench a patch of red caught my eye. It was a shoe, identical to Tula's mother's; a black satin ribbon wrapped around it.

Chapter 108

THEO

WE NOW HAD a *pair* of red shoes and absolutely no doubt who our killer was, but no idea *where* he was. While Oz and Netty were at Imogene's for dinner, Bud and I snuck across the street to my place so we could talk. We had explained enough to Imogene to keep her alert, but didn't need to upset her with all the gruesome details.

"Hansel's father was a fanatical pastor," Bud said. He stood by the dining room window and watched Imogene and Tula light the candles inside their carved pumpkins.

"Yep," I said. "Zealot, which makes sense, given the notes and phone calls."

"They used to put little Genghis in a box with snakes," Bud said. "If the snakes didn't bite then they felt the evil was out of him for that day."

Imogene and Tula went inside the store and turned the sign to 'Closed'.

"*Jeez,*" I said, then handed Bud a beer. "But, he was bit two hundred times?"

"*Reverend* Hansel," he continued, "was a hard old German, well known to the police because of his son's snake bites and all the reports from neighbors about a screaming child somewhere on the Hansels' five-acre farm."

Bud followed me out to the back porch. We sat and watched Solomon in his yard, carving totems into the side of the canoe he'd worked on for the last few months.

"That small-town sheriff," he continued, "said he never found any box of snakes or any screaming child. Guess'n he never looked. Hell, it was the Depression, nobody cared much about a child screaming somewhere else when they couldn't feed the ones at their own table."

"Monsters don't just happen," I said.

Solomon's golden fire blazed against the shadows of his yard and trickled over the stone fence like a slow-moving ivy. The smell of his burning herbs drifted through the night. A crescent moon rose high; its milky radiance lit up the porch with a shaft of light.

"He told Immie he'd see *you* again," Bud said.

"Right... Well, he saw me today."

Bud lit a cigar. "Looks like *again* is what time it is now." His cigar burned to life, orange against the black sky. He stood next to my boxing bag and watched Solomon, who took out the Frog Box, set it on the log, and began his evening incantations.

"We've got red shoes," I said, "a fat file, the black panel truck's been found, and now we have a new car roaming around with California plates. But how does any of that help us?"

"It's no help, really. It just all points us in a direction."

"Right, and that direction leads back to me, or at least to this town."

"I think Tula's caught his eye," Bud said. Moon shine shimmered off his badge.

"He mentioned her," I said. "Called her a tulip, which I took to mean ripe for picking."

"With each victim," Bud said watching the fire spit and hiss, "and I think there's about nineteen, he leaves a gift. Or at least what the FBI figured out later was a gift. He left Tula that red shoe all tied up in that fancy ribbon. That's a gift. He's marked his territory."

"And," I said, "from those distorted Bible passages, I think he believes he's rescuing innocents from evil. Kids from what he deems unworthy parents."

"Great," Bud said. "He's on a mission from God."

"Pretty much... and Tula's mom was... well, questionable."

"At best," Bud said. "What's the old man up to, there?" He pointed at Solomon's yard, which was filled with birds, fireflies, croaking frogs, and creatures gathered to hear the vibration of his deep voice trembling when he chanted prayers for his Ancient Ones. Solomon stood, tapped three times on the top of the Frog Box, and disappeared into his hut.

"He's preparing for a journey," I said. "A long journey."

Chapter 109

IMOGENE

DAILY SPECIALS
BBQ Elk Tenderloin Sandwiches and Drink .75¢
Friday's Pie - Custard with Walnut & Graham Cracker Crust .50¢

After lunch rush, well, not so much *rush* as it was only five people who came in, I set one cup out for Tula's cocoa, one for my coffee, and two for Pearl's tea on the picnic table.

"Here Tula, cookies," I said handing her a bowl of chocolate chip cookies. While she chose which ones had the most chocolate, I glanced out the window. Solomon was on his bench, ever our sentinel, and Theo stood in his window keeping an eye out.

Tula carefully set two cookies each on three plates and then one in front of Solly, who slept on the floor by the back door. "Two, four, six," she counted. Then she dropped down on the bench and wrote the number on her list of things she could count.

"Honey," I said picking up Solly's cookie, "dogs can't eat cookies."

Tula stared at Pearl for whom she had developed a budding curiosity— following her to her garden, planting seeds, watching things grow. Then she stared at Pearl's cups, one with hot tea and the other empty as always, and she asked, "Why do you use two cups?"

I shoved another piece of gum in my mouth—my fifth that day—and waited for Pearl to respond. She had never spoken of her need for two cups, though I was pretty sure I knew why.

When Pearl's eyes watered I decided it wasn't time yet and gently patted Tula's arm and said, "That's James's cup, honey. Now eat your cookies."

Pearl blinked the tears from her almond-shaped eyes and drank her tea in silence.

"But—" Tula started to speak. I hushed her again. Tula sat, looking bewildered about James. She stared at the green jadeite cup as though it might move. I figured I'd explain it to her another time. How someone could be gone from this world yet still live inside you, in your home, in your garden, in a chair, so alive.

"Cigarettes a habit," Pearl said to Tula. "You know, someting Immie like to do, become someting she have to do." She looked at me chewing like one of Gandel's cows and said, "Understand?"

"Yeah," Tula said glaring at me. "I know she's cranky since she stopped cigarettes."

"Well," Pearl interrupted. "My James, he like dat to me... a habit. Someting hard to give up. Understand. I make coffee and tea for him every day. Always James drink coffee in morning, tea in afternoon. Every morning in our kitchen he say to me what he always say to me, 'I'll have some too, baby.'" Her eyes pooled. "He call me baby. So I take two cups down."

Oh God, then my eyes started watering. I tucked my gum into my cheek. Tula stared at the cup and said, "So, his ghost lives in the coffee cup?" Tears rushed from Pearl's eyes. "Yes... James live in coffee cup now." Tula tore up from the table and rushed upstairs. I stood to follow her, but the phone rang. "Manzanita Market—"

Tula returned with her mother's red shoe and propped it up on its high heel right next to her toy box: a red leather gravestone smack in the middle of the store.

Chapter 110

THEO

WITH HANSEL still invisible, lurking, as Bud and I believed, we all kept a steady eye on Tula. Though life went on, we remained on high alert for two weeks.

Tula hadn't experienced what would be "normal" to other children— holidays, school, restaurants, new clothes—and had never played with others. Mrs. B felt a year of private tutoring and "gentle release," as she referred to occasional play times with other children, would be best.

"Hail Mary," I said as I entered a vicarage full of the noisiest children imaginable.

"Full of grace!" they shouted as they darted about, trading seats and tossing notes.

"The Lord is with thee," I said.

"Blessed art thou among women," they chimed.

"And blessed is the fruit of thy womb, Jesus." I settled my books and took off my hat. My ten regular scrub-faced early birds finally seated and sleepily awaited their lesson for the day. Tula was nowhere in sight. Did Imogene forget Sunday school class was before service?

"Has anyone seen the Miss McFalls?" I asked. The kids collectively pointed to the stairway with looks on their faces that told me the Misses were not just setting up cookies and coffee for after the service. "Open your Bibles to Genesis… I'll be right back."

I ducked under the archway and headed down the three stairs, opened the doorway to the basement, and there they were, backs to me. "Sibbie? Ibbie?" They turned, and there was Tula, red faced, lips squeezed tightly together, glaring at them as if she was ready to double her fists and start punching. Solly was at her side.

"What's happening here?" I asked. They all three looked like they'd been in a scuffle.

"Father," Sibbie said as she straightened her hat. "She cannot bring a serpent into church." She pointed to Tula's bucket. "And a dog."

Ibbie tugged her gloves back up over her wrists. "This child is—"

"*This child*," I said, "is late for a Sunday class that *you* are supposed to be teaching."

Tula stood holding her bucket. She glared up at the twins.

"Tula," I said, "come with me."

She triumphantly stomped past them. Solly followed. "Here." She handed me her bucket. "Can ya watch Newt for me?" she asked darting a glare at the sisters. "He's not safe here."

"You two," I turned to the sisters, "get yourselves together." Then I opened the back door and said, "But Solly can wait out here."

Tula nodded and headed up the stairs to class. Solly laid down on the back stoop.

"Well," Ibbie sighed, "that child's a handful—"

"If you treat her as such," I said looking into the bucket. The current Newt had expired—apparently Tula was right; he wasn't safe in church. "Sibbie, take this bucket over to Imogene's, would ya?" She took the handle as if it were a dirty diaper and went out the back door.

As I returned to the classroom a wild uproar surged from the far end of the room.

"Children!" I shouted. All of them huddled in the back, hushed in that instant and backed away from the fracas. There she was again, Tula, on top of eight-year-old David Mackay. I lifted her off and motioned for them both to go to opposite corners.

"Using your right hand," I shouted to get everyone's full attention, "touch your forehead." Their eyes were still on Tula and David as I walked to the front of class. "*Touch your foreheads!*" They all jumped. "At the mention of the Father,"I motioned, teaching them the proper way to perform the sign of the cross. "Then, the lower middle of your chest at the mention of the Son." Their arms and hands began to move with the actions they practiced the week before. Tula sat arms crossed in a chair in the back of the room, staring at the small stained-glass image of lambs in the valley. "And the left shoulder on the word Holy, and the right shoulder on the word Spirit."

They found their seating and the room fell quiet.

"Good," I said. "In the name of the Father, and of the Son, and of the Holy Spirit. Amen."

"Amen," They all shouted.

Sibbie and Ibbie stepped up the stairs in their floral dresses, straw hats, and white-gloved glory, calm as peacocks, looking like Church Ladies instead of street brawlers. They nodded to me, which I took as assurance there would be no more incidents. I stepped away from the pulpit and left ten innocent children with the two sisters and Solomon's angry warrior. In that ring, my money was on Tula.

Solly was asleep by the back door. I filled his water dish and spotted two huge footprints where someone had been standing at the church office window. Beside the footprints was a clove cigarette butt.

Chapter 111

IMOGENE

DAILY SPECIAL
Clam and Oyster Chowder, Corn Bread Sticks and Honey Butter .75¢

Tula crashed down on the bench where we had her milk and cookies waiting and said, "Don't like that place." She slammed her arms across her chest and huffed and puffed like a dragon, her lip tight as a fist.

"Why?" I asked. That instant outside the store, a silver car I'd never seen before screeched its tires and tore off toward Highway 101.

"Those Church Ladies wanted to take Newt," she said, and then relaxed, uncrossed her arms, grabbed a peanut butter cookie and said, "I think they want to eat him."

"Oh no," Pearl shook her head. "Netty say people die if eat a Newt."

"Good," Tula said, guzzling her chocolate milk.

"That's not nice, honey," I said. "Maybe try again next week, but leave Newt here." I looked again for that car, wondering if it was the one Theo had seen.

"I don't wanna. Them kids are mean."

"Did something else happen?"

Tula stared at me, then turned to Pearl. "Gonna see sunflowers today?" Pearl looked at me. I nodded. I'd ask Theo later what the heck happened.

"Yes," Pearl said. "We plant today." She stood and placed her S&H stamps into the Folgers can on the shelf where she kept her other odds and ends. She gave a nod to Tula's now ever-present red shoe, signaling to Tula to clean up her mess.

Tula jumped up, placed the shoe in its box, and shoved it under the table where we all agreed it would stay—a cardboard coffin. Still, its presence unnerved me, and Solly sniffed at it like he sensed… well, I don't know what, but whatever it was it gave me the heebie-jeebies. It wasn't at all like Pearl's two cups. James never *wore* that cup. I wondered if her mother had them on when whatever happened to her happened. Oh God, of course she did. My skin crawled, but it was important to Tula, so we dealt with it at breakfast, lunch, and dinner when Tula had it seated next to her like a stuffed kitty cat.

They hurried out the front door and walked to Pearl's, Solly trailing behind.

I was happy now Tula had become interested, no, fascinated in how things grow instead of how they die. Up until a month ago, Tula just walked down to Pearl's, stood with her bucket at the gate, and watched her work in her yard. A few weeks ago under Pearl's tutelage, she planted sunflower seeds one by one, ten inches apart. Now she rushed down there every morning to watch small green limbs reach up from the dirt and uncoil like tiny hands to the sun. Soon they'd tower over her, then the fence, and eventually they'd even tower over six-foot-two Bud.

Maybe Sunday school wouldn't work, but between Pearl's garden, Theo's aquarium, Solomon's mountain, and a dog named Solly, maybe Tula would get excited about her full life ahead. Maybe someday a full-on smile would spread across that sad face.

Chapter 112

THEO

BUD SHOWED UP in my backyard around six thirty, early for him. "Mornin'."

He stomped up the stairs and past me where I stood at my boxing bag, and went to the kitchen. I unlaced my gloves. I'd been at it for over an hour, beating my bag instead of writing the week's sermon. Those sermons were increasingly difficult to write. Something about standing in front of people I knew, who knew me, and lying.

Bud shoved the screen door open, handed me a cup of coffee, and told me to sit down.

I sat on the rail as he unfolded a news article with an attached sheriff's report.

"Look at this." He handed it to me and said, "There was another missing girl two months back. They found her last week, alive. She couldn't identify the man who took her. He told her he took her for her own good. I think you were right... he thinks he's some kinda savior."

"What about the girl's parents?" I asked.

Bud eagerly scanned the article with his finger and pointed to the page. "*Her parents cannot be located,*" he read. "She was staying with an aunt in Garibaldi when she was taken. Garibaldi's part-time sheriff didn't report her missing because her family tended to come and go; they were vagrants. The aunt has not seen the girl's parents in six or more weeks."

"Six or more weeks?" I said. "What kind of parents leave a child for six or more weeks?"

"The kind who don't deserve to be parents," he said. Then we both glanced at Tula's pink sweater on Solomon's log seat. "I think it's time we tell Immie everything."

Chapter 113

THEO

BUD STEPPED INSIDE the store and I followed, flipping the sign to CLOSED. I locked the door and said, "Immie, did you see the paper this morning?"

"What are you doing?" she asked. "I have customers. You keep closing me down."

"The paper?" I reminded her. "About that girl over in Rockaway."

"Yeah," she said. "It's awful… why?"

We sat at the table. Bud took off his hat and sat down.

"Well, just spit it out," she said. "And let me open my store."

"We think," Bud said, "these missing girls, murdered parents, stolen cars, red shoes, mysterious notes and all, are all the same guy… Genghis Hansel, like we told you a while back. But, I think he's been around longer than we know. He took the two girls, and probably Suzy Wu. The one they found last week keeps sayin' he smelled like Christmas or something."

"Christmas?" Imogene bolted straight up. Her eyes bugged out. "Cloves!" she said, and then cleared her throat. "He smelled like clove cigarettes."

"How do you know?" I asked.

"I told you. When that man came to church I ran outside after he left, after he was long gone. That was when I smelled his cigarette again. It smelled like cloves."

"Okay… cloves," Bud said writing it down. "We've got men covering Tillamook, Rockaway, and Garibaldi where girls have gone missin' and actual crimes have been committed, looking for clues. Maybe someone saw something. There's two men from the FBI who have at least started a file."

"Why are they reluctant to follow up on this information?" I asked.

"Like you said, it's like following a ghost," Bud said. "Even Toreck… hard to track his comings and goings. And let's face it, we have the murders of two petty criminals, a scary church visitor, footprints, clove cigarettes, and mysterious red shoes. Now, compare that to two missing girls and I guaran-damn-tee you the sheriffs are looking for them instead of trying to solve the murder of two people who, in their opinion, we're better off without, anyways."

Bud took Imogene's hand in his. "Now listen to me, I think he's set his sights on Tula."

Imogene's eyes widened and then flooded. "Tula?"

"It'll be alright, though," he said.

"We won't leave Tula alone at any time," I said. "Between myself, Bud, Solomon, and you gals, and Solly, there's no reason for her to be alone. Not ever."

"What's a man like that want with Tula?" she asked. "How does he know about her?"

"It's complicated," I said.

"Well, uncomplicate it for me," she said.

"He's a bad guy, Immie. He likes kids, okay?"

"Oh, shit," she said, glancing at her hands on the table. "Okay."

"Where is she now?" Bud asked as he stood from the table.

"She's with Pearl… " Imogene shot up and rushed out the screen door.

We followed her out to see Solomon standing at the end of the street outside Pearl's picket fence while she and Tula worked in her garden and Solly slept on the sidewalk.

Imogene let out a heavy sigh.

Chapter 114

THEO

WE ALL TOOK TURNS watching Tula and her growing menagerie. While I mended Mrs. B's fence, sleeves rolled up, Tula and Solly watched.

"What does that cartoon on your arm mean?" Tula asked.

"Well, it's not a cartoon, honey," I said. "It's called a tattoo."

"Bud has one of those."

"Sometimes men get them when they go to faraway places."

"What are faraway places?" she asked. "And why do they mark you like that?"

"These are good questions. Can you hand me the box of nails?"

She sat with her bucket on one side and Solly on the other, on the ground two feet away from me. She handed me the box and asked, "Why is your angel sad?"

"Well, when I first arrived in Japan, one of those faraway places, and before heading for Korea, another faraway place, some of us, my buddies, we got tattoos."

Mine was originally the image of an angel: strong, muscular, a Michelangelo's David-looking sort, with white untainted wings the full length of his body, his robust arms in prayer in front of him, eyes closed. Solemn, well intended, naïve.

"But why is yours a sad angel?" she asked. "Aren't angels happy?"

"Some," I said, trying to find an explanation for something I barely understood myself. "The angels here are happy, but sometimes angels in faraway places are sad."

"Why?" she asked.

"Well, faraway places can be hard to understand, but what matters most is you only have to concern yourself with happy angels."

Solly's head snapped up, then he jumped and ran after a squirrel, taking Tula's attention and rescuing me from the next, inevitable *why?*. As Tula chased

Solly, who chased the squirrel around Mrs. B's oak tree, I thought about my tattoo's alterations.

A year after Korea, after the children were killed, and after I had been shot and left for dead, I was shipped to a military hospital in Wiesbaden, Germany. I had one of the other soldiers take me in a wheelchair to a tattoo place in a seedy part of town. There, the German tattoo man exacted the truth from the image on my arm. He added a chipped, bloodied sword to David's praying hands and drops of blood, like tears falling from his white wings, and he opened the eyes of the sleeping angel and burned Sister's words into my skin beneath it: *May Our Cause Be Just*.

That altered image was closer to the truth. And having the truth was worth everything.

Chapter 115

IMOGENE

DAILY SPECIALS
Elk Meat Cheeseburger and Cherry Cola .75¢
Friday's Pie - Pearl's Rhubarb with Peach Ice Cream .50¢

Theo insisted we all change our routine schedules: Pearl came to work thirty minutes early one day, thirty minutes late the next, and so on. Bud spent two Sundays outside church, leaned against his patrol car talking with Solomon and scoping out every passerby, church goer, or day-tripper's car as if they were criminals. I liked to watch him work.

Lucy and I called everyone in the valley about the changes to the Halloween party, which was just a few days away. We'd originally hung posters in Nehalem, Wheeler, and Manzanita announcing the Halloween Jamboree. Announcing where we'd all be and when we'd be there. But then Bud said that was a "sitting duck bad idea."

Now the party was at the Grange Hall in Nehalem instead of the Bayside Bowling Alley. Netty invited Andréa, who was planning on coming down with her boy. I didn't tell Theo in case she didn't show up again. The brokenhearted look on his face was just too much. As always, an Andréa sighting robbed Theo of his soul for a good two or three days. Nope, not telling him.

"What is that?" Tula nodded toward the costume hanging on my bedroom door.

"That's my Annie Oakley outfit," I said, admiring my own work: the carefully frayed hem, the suede belt, and cowboy boots. "I think I'll look pretty darn good."

"I think you'll look pretty darned strange," Theo said as he came through the door.

"Me too," Tula agreed, looking into her bucket and nodding again as if Newt had thrown in his two cents as well. Dead or alive, he was her always-amiable sidekick, especially since I didn't allow Solly upstairs to knock over furniture and get into the kitchen garbage.

"Fine," I said. "At least I'm wearing a costume to the *costume* party."

Theo tossed his hat and jacket onto the bed and sat down. I appreciated that he'd been around every day the last few weeks. But I'd grown weary of him waiting, watching, and questioning every little thing. Thankfully, no one had seen or heard of Toreck or that Hansel person, and Tula was escorted by an adult or a dog day and night. Toreck wasn't smart or patient enough to be hatching some plan. They were long gone.

Tula asked Theo, "Can we go see Solomon now?"

"Yep," he said. "Let's go."

I listened as the downstairs door slammed and locked. Alone at last.

In the mirror I studied my hair. Maybe Bud was right—it looked better long. It'll be nice to have an actual Saturday night *out*. Maybe I could wrangle Bud into a twirl or two. I felt like a giddy teenager. Ridiculous, I know. *But so fun.* I even paid $1.50 for some nice silky nylons. Under a burlap dress! It was sweetly ludicrous. But giddy I was, and sweet it tasted.

Chapter 116

THEO

SMOKING SALMON hissed in Solomon's fire pit. He had nearly finished carving his fourteen-foot canoe, complete with elaborate etchings along the side of the red cedar. The depictions were the same as those on his totem that stood in his yard and told the story of his family. At the head of the canoe was the face of his old wolf.

The tiny Soul Box that Frog kept clutched between his limb and cheek was gone from its perch on the log. For the first time in my life, the box was nowhere to be seen. Then Solomon's door thrust open. There he stood with a feather headdress in his hands, small moccasins, and other items. I recognized that dress as the one that had been in a cedar box in his cabin since his ten- year-old daughter died of smallpox.

"Here, Little Mouse," he said and handed it to Tula. "Wear daughter's dress."

"Really?" Tula's eyes widened. "Can I put it on now?"

"Yes," he said. "Go inside."

She looked at me.

"Go ahead," I said then sat down on a stump, the heavy reality hitting me. He was giving things away because it was the end of *this* journey.

Solomon's lean body looked more skeletal. He stirred his fire.

"Sol, you feelin' okay?"

"I do not know what an *okay* feels like, but I am good."

"Right." I assessed his many projects: wood carvings, hide tanning, and what looked like the packing up of his things. "You goin' somewhere *soon*?"

Just then Tula sprang out of the door in full regalia. She twirled, holding out the caramel-colored buckskin where it was split and beaded up the side to reveal the suede pants beneath. Her hair was in jumbled braids with an eagle feather hanging loose from one tress.

"*Duh-HOOTS-nuh!*" Solomon said looking pleased. He placed a small necklace in her hand and said, "You wear first daughter's dress and necklace to your party. You will be strong warrior, Nancy Little Feet." He patted her head. "Very strong girl warrior."

Tula's face beamed with a pink glow and a half-smile. I pictured myself receiving the Eagle Feather, recalling the spark that blazed through me that day. That spark now burned in her. She began her spirit dance by the fire, patting one foot, then the other, chanting and wearing her outfit. She looked to her hands lifted in the air, then back to her feet, weaving her steps on the soft ground around the fire pit. She had learned her dance well. Her chant was rhythmic.

Solomon stood next to me and said, "They are gone."

"Who?"

"Children with dark eyes," he said. "Gone to their Ancient Ones. You let them go now."

I stared into the fire.

"Let them go," he said. "They are happy."

I swallowed hard and said, "You were only able to let Ruby go after you avenged her."

His strong profile did not budge as he watched Tula dance. He craned his head and looked at me; his eyes turned from hazel green to silver-grey.

"It was the right thing to do," I quickly added.

"And will you burn down a country of madness like you burned down a store? No," he said. "Let them go. Feed wolf who wants love and peace." He opened his door and said, "Yes, I will go soon," and went inside.

Solomon's fire burst into flames. Gold and red sparks spiraled to the sky.

"Come on," I said to Tula, and held out my hand.

"Solomon says you're like a son," she said not taking my hand but walking by my side.

"He was like a father to me, *us* when we were young."

"I bet he was a good daddy," Tula said and suddenly slipped her tiny fingers into mine.

"The best," I said blinking away a rush of tears. "The very best."

"He says I should stay close to you, Immie, Bud, and Pearl," she said as I unlocked Imogene's door. "He says I can trust you most of all." She looked up at me as if to assess with her disbelieving eyes.

"Well—"

"He says you were a good warrior."

"Well, honey that was a long time ago," I said locking the door behind us.

"That's what I thought," she said heading to the stairs. "Cause you're old."

"Well, I'm not *that*—"

"But Solomon says no, you're still a good warrior, you just forgot how."

"Right." I stood at the bottom of the stairs as she bounced up them in her Indian dress.

She stopped at the top, turned around, and pulled her hands to her hips. "He says you're a sleeping warrior who's gonna wake soon," and then she turned to go into Imogene's bedroom.

"Oh my goodness!" Imogene swooned. "An Indian princess."

I remained at the bottom of the stairs, running my finger along the worn edges of the sleeping tin soldier in my pocket.

Chapter 117

THEO

DARKNESS IS a difficult and shifting thing to grasp with merely the human eye. The candles in Imogene's pumpkins flickered golden in the night around the entrance to her store. I opened the dining room window wide to hear any sounds—rustling in the leaves, the trees—or footsteps on the pavement. I scanned the night for movement; studied shadows as I once did on T'aebaek Mountain. Identifying, taking inventory of every sound in the caves. Creaking bridges, cascading waterfalls, the children's sleeping noises, and those Daubenton bats. If Imogene's doors opened the new bells would ring, and her downstairs lights were on so I could see inside. And inside, Bud slept on the couch, and Solly by the stairs. Even still, something wasn't right. A brisk wind blew out the pumpkin lights.

The aquarium night-light clicked on. The clown fish prepared the sea anemone for night by feeding it, then laying their delicate bodies inside its fleshy tentacles.

With one eye on Imogene's, I dropped into my chair, repainted Kiernan's soldier's red band, and set the soldier in the window to dry. As the room darkened, the blue glow from the aquarium let the sea horses know it was safe to come out of hiding. The red angel fish disappeared into its night cave as the spider conch cleaned the sand and algae along the glass. The mossy green waterweeds drifted to and fro as if moved by a soft breeze floating through the water. It was how I imagined heaven must be.

Were the orphans in some floating hereafter with Sister? Did that heaven hold them as safe as my sea anemone held the clown fish? Every time my eyes rested on the aquarium, I dreamed of them there, finally out of harm's way.

I arranged the letters out on the table again. All ten were stained with drops of blood, sweat, and tears. These are the ones that made it through intact, and that's only because they had been held, *Return to Sender*, for me in Japan.

Several others had been carried across Korea, through the Karst Caves and into a chicken wire prison in a muddy outback near P'yong-yang. Those letters were taken by the NK guerilla soldiers, who opened them, thumbed through them, and then tossed them into a fire. So these letters marked *Return to Sender* were a treasure of sorts, a reminder of when things moved too fast to recall, when death was too frequent to mourn, and life too fleeting to stop, examine, and digest.

*   *   *

Soon citrus colors speckled through the curtains and settled on the aquarium glass. The night creatures scampered into the shadows—little vampires hit by morning sun.

Oz pulled his truck into the drive and shut the engine off. I opened the door and said, "Mornin'. Coffee's on."

"Sleep?" Oz asked.

"Wide awake."

"Oughta try some a Nettie's tea." He took off his cap. "Knocks big ol' Oz right out. And since I's watching little Tula today, she and all them questions, I needed my sleep."

"I'll try that sometime," I said. "And all those questions means she's smart."

"Oh yeah. She's a smarty, all right." He poured a cup of coffee.

"Stairs or shed today?"

"Shed's done," he said. "And your stairs'll be like new by the weekend. Y'all goin' to the Grange on Saturday night?"

"Yep," I said. "Imogene insisted."

"Well them girls thinks they's plenty funny... Think ol' Oz should be dressin' up like the Jolly Green Giant. *Jolly damn Green Giant!* That just ain't funny."

"No," I said, stifling a laugh. "That's not funny."

"I'm a fifty-year-ol' black man. A big ol' black man painted green just ain't funny. I would scare them kids half ta death. Jus ain't right."

"No," I said. "Not right." I looked in his eyes. "It's funny, though."

It took him a minute. Then his furrowed brows arched and raised high on his forehead.

"Yeah...," he said in his baritone voice. "I guess. Now Netty, she goin' as Sleepin' Beauty. Now that's funny. That girl don't never sleep." He laughed, placed his cup in the sink, and plopped his Red Sox baseball cap back on his head. "I'll get to them stairs, then."

Just as he opened the door, that elusive silver Oldsmobile sped down Laneda toward the Highway. We both rushed outside.

"That car ain't got no plates," he said. "That the one you seen up at—?"

"Yep," I said. "Call Bud."

I jumped in the car and sped out of the driveway. The Oldsmobile had already disappeared at the end of Laneda, but it could have only turned right, unless it drove into the ocean.

Chapter 118

THEO

AFTER AN HOUR of driving up and down the gravel-pitted dead-ended roads of Neahkahnie, all I spotted was two treasure hunters who saw me and hid in some bushes, leaving their equipment out in full view. I stopped next to the bushes where they were shushing one another, rolled down my window, and asked, "Seen anyone in a silver Oldsmobile?"

After a long silence, one of them moved a juniper branch away from his half-hidden face and said, "Yes." Then he stood and pointed to the south side of the mountain. "We've been here three days and have seen it twice. He goes over there somewhere. He's an asshole."

"Okay, how do you know he's an asshole?" I asked.

The other man stood up from his hiding place and said, "Cause he came into our camp, asked what the smell was. We showed him it was my wife's beef stroganoff heating over the fire. He punched me in the face and took the whole damned pan of food. He's an asshole."

"Yeah," I said, "well he's a hungry asshole, and maybe you should pack up and stop honeycombing this mountain for gold. Pack up and move on before he comes back. You may not be as lucky next time. I'm pretty sure your wife's stroganoff was just an appetizer."

* * *

Bud waited on the banister of my front porch.

"So," he said as I climbed the steps, "exactly what were you gonna do if you caught somebody, Father Riley? Pray?"

"I would have reported back to you, like any good citizen."

"You're not exactly like 'any' good citizen though, are you?"

"I'm a priest, Bud. Those days are behind me."

"The only thing behind you is that loaded .38 tucked in your belt."

"Backup." I said. "But, you're right, I won't go alone again."

"I just don't want you gettin' yourself killed, yet."

"Yet?"

He stood and opened my front door. "Let's figure a plan where the right people get taken down, not the wrong people. You were a good soldier, Theo. I need you to be one again."

"You forget, everyone I ever tried to help ended up dead," I said. "Like you said yourself, I'm good for nothin' but comin' in after the fact. Always too late."

"No fault a your own," he said. "But then you cleaned up, didn't you? Took care of business. What did Hansel's note say, something about Saint Michael, defend us, be our protection against wickedness and evil? Something like that. Well, I think he got that part right."

"I'm no saint."

"True, little buddy. But you're what we got. Now let's catch us a devil."

Chapter 119

SOLOMON

TULA PRACTICED her dance around my fire wearing new feathers and headdress.

"Solomon, when will you finish your canoe?"

"*Adzekl*," I reminded her. "*Adzekl* is word for canoe."

"I can't say that," she said scrunching her face like a fist. "Zekool... No, can't say it."

"Here, sit by fire, little one. We go soon." I gave her green apple.

"But when will you finish it?" She bit into it and made a sour face. "Where will you go in it?" She picked bitter skin from her mouth.

"When harvest moon passes through earth's shadow."

"Huh?"

"Here." I rubbed beeswax into etchings and pointed to pictures. "Here, see?" I pointed to Ruby and our three children.

Tula dropped to her knees at my side. "What are they doing?"

"They hold hands and walk in other world, wait for me to join."

"When will you go to them?"

"Soon."

"But... you won't *leave* me, will you?" Her eyes filled with selfish child tears.

"You are big girl now. You are strong now. You have Nancy Little Feet inside."

She started to cry, then wrapped her arms around my neck. I stroked the child on the back and motioned for her to return to seat on log. I sat down next to her and said, "I am old man now." Then I saw the face of my Wolf in the fire. *Soon*, I said to him inside my mind.

"So?" she said.

"You are young girl with long life."

"No," she whined like my first daughter used to. "I don't want you to go to them."

I smoothed her hair. "You have Theo and Imogene."

"I don't like him. I don't like anybody. Where's my mommy!?"

"Your mommy is dead, child."

Tula stopped crying and shut her mouth as if she had swallowed her tongue.

"Rounders are family now," I said.

I handed her a rag. She wiped her face.

"I gave you my first daughter's dress because you warrior now. She was brave. You have spirit like her, to live with kind heart, be good to people who care about you. Be smart, be safe."

She sniffled away her anger and asked, "I'm a warrior now?"

"Girl warrior," I said. "You will grow up to be woman… Woman warriors are strongest."

"Stronger than you?"

"Much," I said, thinking how Ruby survived death of our first two children to smallpox; she cried and released their spirits to the Great Grandfather. I could not let go. I remained angry and fearful for many years. To trust took much courage. Ruby was stronger and wiser than I could ever be. I lived long life trying to gather wisdom she was born with.

"What will *I* do when you go?" Tula asked.

"You will go to school, learn to read and write, live good life," I said taking her hand in mine. "Ruby and I watch down on you forever."

"Is forever a long time?"

"It can be."

It had been many summers without Ruby. Osprey swooped through the yard and settled on branch of oak tree. "When you see that Osprey there," I pointed. "That is Ruby. She is watching." Lightning shot through my chest.

Tula took a deep breath. "Really?" she said, and jumped down from the bench. "She's beautiful."

"Yes," I said. The deep tremble continued to vibrate through my heart and body. "She is."

Chapter 120

THEO

DURING THE NIGHT, Solomon finished his canoe. As the sun rose and while he was inside his hut, I walked down the porch steps and over to his yard. The canoe was packed with everything he wanted to take with him. Spices, feathers, and a few precious photographs, among them a picture of Mamaí in her powder-blue dress, and a young Imogene and me. My heart swelled like a balloon into my throat as I touched the smooth bowed side of the canoe. It had red etchings and drawings inside and out. It was packed full except for the north end, where he'd painted the face of his wolf.

His door slowly opened. Solomon stood on his stoop, looked at me, then stepped down and walked over to the canoe. He held his rib cage with one arm and carried his father's bow in the other; he looked pale. As he gently laid the bow inside the canoe, tucking it under an old blanket, I swallowed past the gorge in my throat and said, "Mornin'."

He patted the blanket with his hand.

"My mother's hands make baskets, blankets, and medicines." He leaned in and tightly secured the hundred-year-old basket lids, tying them together with a small piece of twine. "My father was shaman." He leaned down and took a jar from beneath the canoe. "But it was mother's hands make it so." He handed it to me. "This liniment… last time. Soon you need no more." He then opened the medicine bundle that was also in the canoe. "This," he said, handing me a purple crystal. "Keep in pocket next to bullet in your hip; as you walk it will be coaxed out of hiding."

I took the smooth gemstone and put it in my rosary pocket with Kiernan's soldier.

"This bundle," he said holding up the cream-colored suede bag, "must burn with me. It has my spirit power, and that power must travel with me to next world." He tightened the leather strap and tucked the medicine bundle inside the canoe.

"Solomon, I... of course," I said heavy with grief. "I'll do anything you ask."

He was gentle with the belongings of his Ancient Ones. Because I had once been a prying child, I knew that the medicine bundle contained all kinds of mysterious items: crystals, roots, arrowheads, horse hair, sage, animal bones, feathers, stones, even nail clippings and human hair. Not sure whose— someone he loved... *or someone he hadn't.*

"My own son," he said, "die same year you were born."

"I never knew that." I blinked back my tears. "I have always felt —"

"Yes," he said gritting his teeth and leaning to sit on his stump. Those gold speckles of light in his eyes grew dim. "You like son."

I quickly grabbed his arm and eased him down. A lifetime of emotion welled up inside me. I dropped to my knees in front of him and hung my head. His hand patting the top of my head felt as powerful as it did the day he gave me the Eagle Feather—like the hand of God had come down to soothe me.

"You are good boy, good warrior and brother," he said. "And good soldier who help children who loved you. Their love is strong. I feel it... You listen now, to Mother Owl," he said and pointed to her perch. "She bring medicine. She make you whole again." Then he pointed to Raven, who waited patiently on the sloping roofline of my back porch. "Raven's wisdom guide you when trouble come."

"Which trouble?" I said, "'cause it seems to be coming from all directions."

He looked north to Neahkahnie and said, "Mountain wakes." Then he stood and headed to his door. I followed him inside.

I hadn't been in his hut in months. It was beautiful in its starkness. Everything made of handcrafted wood. His bed still had the same blanket Mamaí gave him when I was in high school. His one cup, two plates, bowl, and three pieces of silverware were neatly set on their shelf. His incense burned in three different ceramic dishes, and his handmade beeswax candles were lit on the rustic wall shelves.

He reached for the dreamcatcher that had always hung in the small window over his cot.

"This," he said, holding it out, "for you now."

"No," I shook my head. "You keep it. You'll need it."

He grabbed my hand and forced me to take it. I relented. I had never touched the sacred porthole made of strings, feathers, and beads with a blue crystal in the center. I stood frozen, holding it in my hand as if it were the crucifix itself.

"Hang over bed," he said, "to capture bad dreams and let good ones fly free. But listen. Bad dreams are teaching dreams. They present themselves because they are teachers and messengers that need to be heard." He locked both his wrinkled hands over mine. "The children with dark eyes are free now. They wait for you... Say you have more children to save."

His words knocked the wind from my lungs. I'd always known he had some sort of communion with the departed, but never did it mean more to me than now.

"More children?"

"Teo they say," his craggy face cracked a smile. "They are with their parents, grannies, and aunties. They say you, too, will be happy soon."

"You heard them say 'Teo'?"

"Yes," he said. "Close your eyes." He reached up and put his hand on my face, then took a deep, labored breath. "They are safe now."

He handed me a basket of goods. "No time to make new dreamcatcher for Tula. She will need big one to catch her bad dreams. You make now."

"But, I don't—"

"Weave this blue stone," he said and reached into the basket to lift one up, "into web as symbol of Father Sky and dreams that lay with universe." He reverently laid it back in the basket. "Good dreams reside in blue stone. Tell Tula, visit them often. Hang in window. Bad dreams will catch in web and burn in the morning sun."

"I will," I promised, and set the items on his small table. "And don't worry, Tula's fine."

"She *will* be," he said with great confidence as he sat down on his cot.

He looked smaller; bones protruded from beneath his skin. "Let me fix you some food," I said. "Some tea, maybe." I opened the small ice box where he kept fresh berries, eggs, salmon and Twinkies. "Let's get you some chicken broth, and I'll go get Imogene—"

"Theo," he said, and laid his head down on his cot, stretching his legs. "No."

I stood lost in his world, one I once knew so well. His hut was darker than usual, with milky white light slyly peering through the worn creases in the curtains as though his world was a secret place it wasn't allowed to enter. Then I noticed he wore his rawhide pants instead of his jeans; his hunting knife was attached to his belt, and his father's spirit feathers were woven into his hair. His body sagged into the bed.

"I can't just stand here when you're ill," I said, knowing that getting Doc was a waste of time. Solomon wouldn't allow him anywhere near.

"Not ill." He closed his eyes and laid one bony hand over the other on his chest. "Need rest for next journey."

I let out a heavy sigh and gazed around the room. A rush of helplessness flooded over me. But I picked up the dreamcatcher and the basket and quietly opened the door. Arguing with him would be disrespectful and pointless.

"Theo," he said, eyes still shut. "Put nothing in adzekl… " He paused, moistening his cracked lips with his tongue. "Empty space at end of canoe, for Wolf."

"Alright," I said. "Do you want water?"

"The White Sea Otter," he said, "will guide us home." His voice was barely a whisper. "She will know you are my son, and she will give you her gift; she will let you see her… Go now."

My veins filled with cement, weighty with the realization of how transitory life was. Solomon's eyes closed tight. His breathing grew shallow. Life was leaving his body.

In the yard, his fire fought to stay alive. Mother Owl, Osprey, and Raven all remained silent on their perches. Mother Owl's head burrowed into her wing; Osprey stared intensely at Solomon's door; Raven's black eyes narrowed in on me.

Chapter 121

DAILY SPECIAL
Elk Meat Pie with Mashed Garlic Potatoes .75¢
Back in 5 minutes

Two days is an eternity when someone you love is in distress. But Solomon didn't appear to be in pain. He'd been in and out of sleep and seemed at peace so close to the edge of death. Of course, he'd been waiting to see Ruby for an awful long time now. I made an easy-to-swallow banana cream pie and took it over to him.

"Solomon?" I whispered. "It's Immie. I brought you pie." The sound of his deep breathing was reassuring—he was still here, yet completely somewhere else. I patted his cold hand and sat on the edge of his bed. I wanted to say *I love you*, but the seldom-said words were stuck in my heart.

"*Ts-ull-ULL-leel!*" His voice startled me. He reached his hand out, then collapsed.

I laid my hand on his forehead; he was fevered, so I put a cool cloth on his head. Solomon didn't move, but by the sound of his breathing he'd fallen back into a deep state. Had he saved any of his magic for himself, or had he given it all to us? Selfish us.

"It's ok." I pulled the blankets up to his neck, then put a fresh pot of hot water on his stove for moisture in the dry cabin. "I'll be back in awhile," I whispered, brushing the hair from his heavily lined face. He was off-color, but he always said fever was good for cleansing the body. That's what he was doing. By Friday he'd be on the bench waiting for pie, fork in hand.

"Blackberry pie on Friday," I said, then turned to leave.

"*Little ones!*" he whispered. "*Imogene! Tula May!*"

"I'm right here." I squeezed his hand. "And Tula's fine. You sleep now."
As I pulled the door shut, he again shouted, "*Neahkahnie!*"

Theo was outside in Solomon's yard, waiting with Tula.

"How is he?" he asked.

"I'm tellin' ya, he'll work it out and be fine by next week. It's just not his time yet."

"Immie, I'd like to believe that too, but—"

"But nothin'. Fine by next week," I said.

Tula and Solly were running back and forth, playing with a stick.

"I gotta go check on some things," Theo said. "Can you take her now?"

"Sure. Where you headed?"

"I'm gonna take a drive. Be back later. Tell Bud I'm on it."

"On it?"

"What's for dinner?" he asked.

"Do you know how much work I have to do to get ready for the party?"

"Then you better get a move on," he said.

"Left you a shepherd's pie in your refrigerator."

"Thanks, love," he said. "Now I'll see ya in a bit."

Chapter 122

GENGHIS

"THAT CLASSY BLONDE in the Thunderbird," I said to Toreck. "Who is she?" We sat in the parking lot of the Nehalem grocery store watching her park and get out of the car.

Toreck sat with his feet on the dashboard, sucking on a toothpick—one of his many habits from his repertoire of disgusting noises.

"You hear me?" I asked.

"Yeah, she's that snotty bitch used to live here when we was all kids, Andréa Bouvre." He said her name the way a ten-year-old brat would when mocking another kid on a playground.

"Is that a kid she's got there?" I asked.

"Looks like," Toreck said dropping his feet to the floor. "Yep, kid."

"Cute little feller," I said. "She a close friend of our war hero?"

"Friend!" Toreck said. "Shit man, couldn't separate them two since they's ten years old."

We watched her take the little boy's hand and go into the store.

"She musta dumped his ass though," Toreck said. "No other reason he'd a gone to that war, then come home a priest. Makes no sense."

"And if she dumped him," I asked, "when might that a been?"

"How the hell should I know?" he asked, then hocked a loogie out the window—*such* an expansive repertoire.

"Just try to think for minute, would ya?" I said. "I know it's hard, but when was it you last saw them together?"

"Just 'fore he left," Toreck said. "And it ain't that *hard* for me to think, just don't wanna, that's all. Don't see the point."

"Good to know," I said. "So ya mean before he left for Korea?"

"That's what I said, ain't it?"

"Not exactly, but it'll do."

We watched them return, her with a bottle of Coke, him with an ice cream bar. The boy had wavy reddish-brown hair. She chatted with some passersby, giving them directions, real friendly like. Looked like she was a good mother, holding that boy's hand, wiping his face… He was dressed nice, real clean. A happy child.

"So, war hero left for Korea about six years ago, right?" I asked.

"'Bout right, yeah," Toreck said.

"That boy's about five, wouldn't you say?" I asked.

"I'd say, yeah, 'bout five."

They climbed into the pretty white Thunderbird and drove away. She may be a good mommy, but a good mommy on her own, abandoned by the child's father, can only be so good.

Chapter 123

IMOGENE

DAILY SPECIALS
Elk Meat Lasagna and Green Salad .75¢
FREE Orange Halloween cupcakes!

It was finally Saturday. The evening sky was charcoal with a strange orange hue and a suffocating air. Tonight there'd be an eclipse: *perfect for a Halloween party.*

Pearl and I baked, frosted, and decorated one hundred twenty cupcakes for Halloween and made two pots of spaghetti and eleven loaves of garlic bread. Netty was making salads and scalloped potatoes, and Oz, his famous barbeque ribs.

"There!" I said, putting the finishing touches on Pearl's cowgirl outfit: suede dangly things from her shirt sleeves, red scarf tied around her neck, and her long scraggly hair in pigtails. "Cute as a button!"

The sun was setting and I hadn't begun to get ready. I'd stayed at Solomon's too long, but I'd never seen him sick before. It was probably a flu, like the Nortons over in Wheeler had. The whole family sick for weeks. Still, it was tough to take. Solomon wanted to be left alone, so we were all leaving him alone. Between baking, sewing, and decorating the hall, I barely had time to transform into Annie Oakley. Annie damned Oakley with a gun and some silky nylons.

"The guys'll be here in fifteen minutes," I called out, hurrying Tula. Then I checked under my curler cap. "Damn! My hair's still wet."

I yanked up the lid of my hair dryer, plopped down beneath it, and called to Pearl, "Go see she's really brushin' her teeth, will ya?"

The clock next to my bed read seven p.m. Theo had said seven fifteen sharp! *Shit.* I'd never make it. Men have no idea how much work we women put into making a nice party. I was already pooped! I plunked my feet up on the footstool. But when I saw my freshly painted ruby red toenails, I thought of Bud and felt an embarrassment of smiles across my face.

The telephone rang. Pearl ran back into the room and grabbed it. "Ha-ro."

"Ha-ro?" she repeated, then hung up. "Nobody." She went back to Tula's bathroom.

It was the third call today that nobody was there. I'd have to ask Lucy if something was wrong with my line.

"What are you doing?" Theo asked as he came through my bedroom door. "I said—"

I lifted the dryer off my head. "I know what you said." I looked him up and down. "What are you wearing?" I asked, then heard Bud in the hall. "You can come in Bud, I'm decent." He stepped into the room. "Now that's funny," I said, standing from my chair and assessing them.

They stood side by side. Bud was dressed in black slacks and shirt, and a tweed jacket, just like Theo's everyday wear, complete with a white priest collar and Theo's black fedora. Theo, who looked like he'd rather be anywhere else, was in a beige shirt, slacks, and cowboy hat, sporting a plastic sheriff's badge and toy gun, still wearing his real white collar beneath the shirt.

"That's funny!" I laughed. "You shoulda told me, I'd a made you matching capes."

"Okay," Theo's face turned even more serious. "Okay." He tapped his finger on his watch and said, "It's time to go. I just checked on Sol, and we promised Emma Whittle that we'd—"

"I know, I know." I pulled my bathrobe tight around my waist. "I just need to get myself ready now that everyone else is done." I shoo-flied them out the door. "You all go so I can have a minute of peace to get *myself* dressed. I'll drive up and meet ya in a little bit." I motioned for everyone to go downstairs. Then I pointed at Tula and whispered to Theo, "Watch her. She keeps trying to sneak over to sit with Solomon. I told her he'd be fine by Friday. Oh, and will you dump those two dead lizards I have in the kitchen before she spots them? They're rolled up in newspaper on the kitchen counter."

"I'll dump the deceased, but I think it's time to face some facts about Sol—"

"Not now, Theo."

"Alright," he said. "Is your hair still wet?" He rolled his eyes with the weary face of a brother who'd spent too much of his life waiting for women's hair to dry. "Cause if it is—"

"Don't be tellin' me to pull my wet hair back into a bun *again*… Now go."

"Come on," Bud finally said something. "Let's give Immie time to make herself even more beautiful, if that's possible. We'll leave Solly to stand, well, *lie* guard."

Bud was handsome in his suit. His tan skin next to the black brought out his blue eyes. They all shuffled down the stairs in front of him. He turned to me and winked as he descended the steps. I got a warm-fuzzy feeling inside, then that embarrassing smile. Was he looking forward to dancing as much as me?

"I'll be there in just awhile," I shouted. "Take the cookies!"

"I've got it," Bud shouted back. "Pearl has the cake and Solly's at the bottom stair."

The downstairs door closed. I flicked the light switch so the store lights would all go dark and went to my room to get ready. Tonight I'd wear the expensive perfume from Paris that Theo bought me years ago. I'd only worn it once.

With my hair finally dry, I took out the rollers, fluffed up my curls, and pulled on a silky slip so the burlap dress wouldn't itch. As I applied my red lipstick, I heard a noise downstairs.

"Theo?" I called. "I'm almost ready." There was no response. "Theo... Solly?"

Chapter 124

THEO

IN 1945 a mysterious fire started, one many believed was set by an incendiary balloon launched by the Japanese, then carried to Oregon by the jet stream. In that balloon's path was the Nehalem Grange Hall—an old box-shaped schoolhouse built in the mid 1800s, everything made of wood. When the fire burst to life, the schoolhouse nearly burned to the ground. It was rebuilt. But all these years later, it still smelled of a hint of smoke.

Feeling ill at ease, I lit a cigar and stood outside while Tula and the others had their party. For two days autumn's harvest moon had a shadow cast over it like a thick blanket, eclipsing the night's light. I felt alone when the moon was not watching over us. Was it Pearl's moon of shame? Does it know Solomon is deep asleep?

Tula made friends with one of the Sunday school kids. They both came as Indian Princesses. One outfit was store-bought; the other, priceless remains of a time gone by.

Orange paper pumpkins and white "boo" ghosts hung around the hall. The smell of pumpkin pie was thick in the stagnant air. Candles were lit on all the ten white tables, and everyone was in costume. The two girls danced to Mr. Gandel's banjo and harmonica tunes. Tula was actually having a good time without Solomon in her immediate sights.

I'd go check on him after the party. He was sleeping and breathing even deeper today. I closed my eyes and saw his image, one I'd seen a million times: Solomon sitting alone at the ocean's edge, his dark silhouette against the sunset. I smiled, feeling he'd always be there that way.

Earlier in the evening, after I'd put on my sheriff clothes, I stepped out to the porch to let him know I was leaving. There on his stump sat his young warrior self. Long black hair, bare back, sharpening his arrowheads. I froze. Mother Owl hooted loud and sharp. Osprey swooped across the yard, warning me to not step down from my porch. A loud "caw, caw!" came from Raven. I heard thunderous drums and the chanting of a thousand voices. I remained on my stairs, listening and watching as the skies darkened and our joining yards vibrated with the voices and sounds of both worlds harmonizing. All the universe guarded his ruminations. Then it all stopped. Silence fell over the yards. The skies cleared. The image of Solomon's young spirit was gone.

*   *   *

"Whiskey?" Bud offered a glass.

"Thanks," I said tapping my plastic sheriff badge, "but I'm on duty."

"Yeah," he said as he held up his glass in a toast. "Me too. Bible in my pocket." He downed the shot. "Where's that sister a yours?"

"Hair."

"She has beautiful hair," Bud said, then slammed his mouth shut as if he suddenly realized he said that out loud. "Look at Mrs. Gandel," he said pointing across the room, hoping to sway my attention. "That witch outfit—"

"Yes, it's nice," I said turning to face him. "Like my sister's hair."

"Listen," he said setting his glass down on the table. "Theo—"

"How long's it been goin' on?"

"A while now," he said and cleared his throat. "Well… I mean, there's nothin' goin' on, not really. I thought… maybe tonight, we could dance and talk—"

"I think that's a good idea."

"You don't mind—"

"Why would I?"

"Well, divorce… the church—"

"Damn the church," I said. "We've bigger fish to fry."

"Right."

Just then a group of teens from Nehalem burst through the door.

"Trouble," Bud said stiffening his spine. "That blond there, he's a young Toreck in the making." He marched over to them.

The Grange Hall was filled with about forty costumed neighbors, plus the five teens who didn't like what Bud was telling them. Pearl handed me a cup of punch and said, "Where Immie?"

"I'm driving back to town," I said. "See what's taking her so long, and to check on Sol."

"She here soon," Pearl said. "No worry, hair take long time."

"Okay." I guessed she'd know. "But—"

"And noting you can do for old man now."

Just then Bud grabbed the arm of one of the boys and not so gently ushered him out the door. In the large room with the banjo music and singing so loud, nobody really noticed. I went to the door to keep an eye out and make sure things were alright.

In the center of the huge hardwood floor, next to the stage, Pearl and Mrs. Gandel, along with the McFall sisters and the kids, were dancing to Mr. Gandel's broad range of Norwegian fishing songs. The only thing missing was my sister who, no doubt, in the revelation of her and Bud, was taking a bit longer to beautify. Pearl was right, I didn't need to worry. And for Solomon, there was nothing to do but watch Tula, as he requested.

Outside the scuffle grew louder. When I stepped out I saw that Bud had the blond boy bent over the hood of his car and was putting handcuffs on him.

"Can I help?" I asked.

"Runnin' him to Tillamook," Bud said and he guided the boy into the back of the patrol car. "Tell Immie I'll be back by nine and to save me a dance."

"I will," I said.

The boy sat in the back seat crying. Clearly no Toreck in the making. Hopefully this one run-in would do him some good. A night in jail could be a cure-all.

Back inside, Oz, who finally gave in and came as the Jolly Green Giant, and Sleeping Beauty Netty square-danced and loopty-dooed around the room. Thankfully Mrs. Gandel dragged a very drunk Mr. Gandel off the stage. Permelia Hinkle sat at the piano with her banjo-playing cousin at her side. The poker game was in full swing, and Mrs. B was successfully getting the Church Ladies drunk. There was an evil twinkle in her eye as she leaned on her booze-loaded cane. I stayed put on a stool at the door to keep an eye inside and out.

Right then Andréa's Thunderbird slowed near the parking lot, and that familiar lightning surged through my veins. When she pulled into the drive, I bolted straight up off the stool and stood like an anxious puppy at the door. *When would I learn?*

Pearl tapped me on the shoulder and said, "Look, Andréa."

"I thought you went to check on Imogene!" I said, watching the Thunderbird search for a parking place. "It's eight o'clock."

She looked outside at Andréa's car, smiled, and said, "Okay, I go, you stay wit Tula."

I handed her my car keys and thanked her.

Pearl, shocked I was giving her the keys, snatched them up and left. Hopefully Mamaí's De Soto would survive the break-slamming two-mile drive.

The Thunderbird finally parked. I forced myself to sit down and not look so fretful. I pretended to talk to the people just arriving and coming up the stairs, but really I was watching and waiting for Andréa.

Chapter 125

IMOGENE

CLOSED FOR Halloween Party 7-10 PM at the you-know-where!

Toreck crashed through the bedroom door. I froze at the vanity table, lipstick in hand, shocked to see him in the mirror behind me. *Why didn't Solly bark?*

"Toreck?"

He was barefoot. *Barefoot?* He wore green army-style pants, and his t-shirt sleeves were rolled up, revealing a tattoo of a snake on one arm and other marks I couldn't make out.

"Why, Miss Imogene Riley, you look mighty nice tonight."

He closed the door behind him, immediately suffocating the air.

I heard Solly outside my window barking at the building. "Solly?"

"Oh that mangy mutt'll do anything for a piece of bacon," Toreck said. "Now … Miss Imogene, all made up and smellin …," he took a deep breath, *"umm …* like a million dollars. Always wanted a million dollars."

My lipstick tube hit the floor. "I… you can't—"

He looked me up and down and said, "You Rileys sure like to tell people what to do, don't you?"

An ominous shadow of orange hues crept into the room.

My heart pounded so fast I heard the vibrations in my head. Just then the street light crackled and snapped ablaze outside my window. Solly's barking grew faint. I tried to stay calm, turned to face him and said, "Toreck, you shouldn't—"

"Shut up." His face hardened. His piercing gaze fixed on me.

With my back as close to the wall as possible, I inched my way to the window.

"No way out, *Love,*" he said. "Is that how big brother says it? *Love?*"

He dropped his cigarette to the floor and crushed it with his bare foot, his unflinching stare brazen as ever.

"Get out!" I shouted. "Get out of my house!"

"I don't think so." He ripped off his shirt. "It took too long to get in here."

An American flag tattoo waved over his left shoulder, a cross and skull over his right. I'd never seen so many tattoos or so much thick black hair from his belly-button down.

"Please, Toreck. Go."

"I don't think so," he said again, and without taking his eyes off me he locked the door behind him. The click echoed.

"What are you doing?" I asked afraid of the answer.

My feet wouldn't move, but when he took a step toward me something in my head exploded. "No!" I screamed. I ran to the window and yanked up, but it didn't budge.

"Glued shut," he said calm and undaunted. "I was in here just the other day."

My arms grew heavy and dropped to my sides. I stared at the lock. He *had* been in here. That night when I felt something was off… it was.

"You don't leave this place very often," he said as a twisted smile etched across his pockmarked face. "But when you do, I have a real nice time in here gettin' to know you."

Without turning, he reached behind him and pulled open a drawer. "In here," he said without looking, "you keep your pretty nighties." He slammed the drawer shut. I jumped.

"In here," he said and opened the next one. His eyes burned into me. "Here's those soft silky bras and lacey slips you wear under them cotton work dresses a yours. Nice." He smiled.

My throat swelled with the onset of tears and screams that couldn't find their way out. I glanced at my clock; it was only seven thirty. Nobody would come looking for a good long while.

He slammed that drawer. Every muscle in my body tensed at the sound. My stomach went queasy.

"And in here," he said as he pulled the third drawer open, "your nice little pink-and-white panties." He yanked it completely out. As the drawer crashed to the floor, all my underwear spilled out.

Tears overwhelmed my eyes. "Toreck, no…," I said, barely able to speak. "No… I—"

"You," he said, as he took a hunting knife from his belt and unbuckled his pants. "You nothin'."

"Just go."

"You always had the last say, miss princess. But now… "

"Get out!" I screamed as I backed away, inching along the wall to the closet where Thomas kept a baseball bat. Toreck's pants dropped to the floor.

"You! You stay away from me!" I shouted. I grappled with the closet door.

"That bat's gone," he said, his eager eyes fixed on my breasts.

I rushed back to the window. He watched me scramble for a weapon. But when I grabbed the vanity stool to throw through the window, he reeled, grabbed me by the waist, jerked me off my feet, and dragged me across the room, kicking and screaming. "Stop! NO! Theo! Bud!"

Toreck smelled of whiskey and cigarettes. He tied my hands to the bedposts with my new nylon stockings and said, "Keep screamin'." He gripped my face with his hand and said, "The first body through that door gets their throat cut." He ran the knife's sharp edge along my throat.

I gasped but didn't scream, now praying no one would come looking for me.

Then, slowly, he pressed the knife's steely tip into my skin. Tilting his shaved head, he watched like a curious child dissecting a frog. He pressed hard not an inch below my jaw. His flat, anxious eyes were transfixed, watching as he cut until he drew blood. A pernicious smile curved up the left side of his angular face. I grew dizzy with the sensation of the cold metal penetrating my skin.

Dear God, keep Solomon home, I prayed. *Please don't let him wake and come over here.*

Chapter 126

SOLOMON

COOL DIRT was beneath my feet. It was last time to feel this union.

"My name is Solomon, Great Grandfather," I said. I raised my arms to sky. "It is my time." In my fire was the face of my Wolf. "It is time," I said to him. I also saw Father's White Sea Otter and faces of my family. The voices of my Ancient Ones whispered through the pines, then grew louder as their bare feet danced around me. The ground vibrated with their chant. My heart grew full. We were once warriors of this great land—now was time to be warriors of another world. The Ancients whispered that before I pass over I will escort two dark souls to edge of night. That their journey here must end.

Chapter 127

IMOGENE

CLOSED FOR Halloween Party 7-10 PM at the you-know-where!

Toreck finally passed out. I lay naked beneath him listening to his breathing, searching—barely moving—for his knife. Then something startled him awake. His head snapped. He leapt from the bed to the window, looked down to the street and said, "Fuckin' gook!"

Oh God! Pearl?

The door downstairs shut and Pearl called out, "Immie?"

"Pearl, go away!" I shouted.

"Shut up," he said as he rushed to the door. He stood hunched, staring at the knob. His eyes dashed back and forth around the room. Then he stood up straight and sneered a twisted smile. "She's alone."

"Immie?" Pearl called from the bottom of the stairs. "Imogene!"

"Pearl, go away!"

"Shut up!" Toreck tugged his pants on, buckled his belt, and pulled on his t-shirt as she marched up the steps. He snatched the knife up from the floor, unlocked the door, and backed toward the bed, then sat down next to me on the bed and waited. His hand ran up and down my thigh. My wrists hurt from the nylon stocking ties, and my nose filled with blood. I struggled to get a breath. He stared at the door with the knife pointed at my throat.

Pearl pushed through the door and said, "Trick-treat!" Her face dropped. "Toreck!"

"You scream," he jabbed the knife at me, "and our girl, here, gets it."

Pearl's eyes locked on mine.

"Now," he said. "I worked myself up a little appetite here." He slapped my hip. I squeezed my eyes shut and struggled to not vomit.

"I think it's time for dinner, and if you're not a good gook, then you'll be dessert."

Pearl stayed cool and said, "She need help." Her voice was expressionless and firm.

"Shut up!"

"I get you food," Pearl said then pointed at me. "You untie her... *den* I get you food."

"Ah, she's just a little sore," he said as he tapped at my face. "We had us a good time, didn't we?"

"You no touch her!" Pearl shouted, taking a step toward the bed.

"So," he said. He waved the jagged hunting knife in her face. "You next?"

Pearl bolted back against the door and said, "No... jus no touch her."

He held the knife toward her, stepped away from the bed, and said, "Untie her hands," motioning to the knotted nylons.

Pearl quickly freed me. Electric shocks scorched through my arms as I lowered them to my sides. She covered me with the sheet and stood between me and Toreck.

"Now," he said, "let's fix me some food. I'll be needin' some fuel." He pointed the knife toward the door. Pearl grabbed my robe and wrapped it around me. I struggled to stand from the bed. Everything hurt. The scorching sting inside me was nothing compared to the rage I suddenly felt. He took my nylons and flung them around his neck like a scarf.

Pearl put her arm around my waist and guided me out the door. As we reached the end of the hall at the top of the stairs, Toreck kicked her in the back. She stumbled but caught herself on the handrail.

"No," he said. "I wanna eat in Imogene's *private* kitchen." He yanked my arm and shoved me in the opposite direction. Pearl followed us into the apartment kitchen.

"What's the special today, *Love*?" he asked.

Neither of us spoke. The kitchen was dark. Pearl and I stood next to the table.

"I said —"

"Clam chowder," I whispered. "In the fridge. And garlic bread."

"Get me a beer," he said shoving Pearl toward the refrigerator. "Now!" Then he pushed me into a chair and tied my hands to the table leg with my nylons.

Pearl turned on the stove light, opened the refrigerator, and gave Toreck a beer from a six-pack. "Here."

He guzzled it down and opened another. "Get me some fucking food!"

Pearl took the clam chowder and bread out of the refrigerator and wrenched the lid off the container. "Is cold," she said. "I heat up." Then she noticed the newspaper-wrapped lizards on the counter that Theo forgot to take out. While the chowder heated, and while Toreck wolfed down two more beers, I watched Pearl chop up some onion and a deceased Newt and drop it all into the frying pan.

Chapter 128

THEO

ANDRÉA FINALLY FOUND a parking place. My heart skipped a beat; I stood breathless at the top of the Grange Hall stairs. There she was, twenty feet away. Not running. Not backing the car out and squealing off. But there looking at me.

She emerged from the car in a calf-length skirt, a soft blue sweater the color of her eyes, a string of pearls, and high-heeled shoes. Her blonde hair was pulled back in a ponytail with bangs, her lips soft pink, her skin like poured cream.

She stood at the side of the car, and her eyes locked with mine. A soft incandescence to her appearance. She barely looked any different—maybe wiser and, if possible, more stunning. Then she slowly pulled off her gloves and tucked them into her handbag. She opened the back door and a little boy spilled out, wearing a Superman costume with blue tights and a long red cape. He handed her a pair of white furry rabbit ears. She smiled and promptly placed them on her head. As they reached the top step, she said, "Hello."

"Hello," I said, warmed by her eyes, the sound of her voice, just being in her presence. I forced a shaky smile. I was reluctant to take my eyes off her for fear she'd disappear. Crouching down to the boy, I asked, "And who's this?"

"I'm Teddy Jenkins," he said. "Teddy's short for Theodore, but I like Ted K."

My chest tightened. I looked up at Andréa; her eyes brimmed with tears. She dabbed the corner of one eye to stop a tear from falling, and looked at her son.

What wicked twist of fate was this?

"Alright," I said. "Ted K., How… how old are you?"

"Almost six," he declared, holding up six fingers. "This many. There candy in there?"

I stood back up, shaking, my heart in my throat, and asked, "K?"

Andréa's eyes were cast down to her son. "Yes, Teddy," she said in a whisper, "there's candy. Go ahead, honey." She motioned for him to go on. He ran off, his red cape flowing behind him. He ran right up to the food table, snatched a cupcake, and joined Tula and a group of children who began to admire his cape. "K is for Kiernan," she whispered, wiping a fallen tear.

My body trembled at the sound of his name: K for *Kiernan.*

"He's been wearing that cape for two weeks," she said, "with his pajamas, his school clothes, everywhere."

A costumed family from Wheeler ran up the stairs and whirled past us through the door, nearly knocking Andréa over.

"Right," I said, still fixated on Teddy inside. "I wrote you."

"I wrote you, too," she said.

"You wrote? I never—"

"I know," she said. "I just found a box with my letters to you, in my father's attic. All stamped, but never mailed."

I turned back to her and said, "Your father—?"

The Newtons from Nehalem arrived and hurried up the stairs to where we stood. "Are we late, Father Riley?" Mrs. Newton asked.

"No," I said as I held the door open for them, "Go on inside."

The porch fell quiet again as I studied Andréa's face.

"I wrote every day," she said. "And I asked Daddy's secretary, Anne, to mail them for me. I thought we were friends. Turns out we weren't. Daddy intercepted them. There was a letter on top of the stack from an investigator he hired in Dublin. Daddy thought I didn't know about your brother, the fire, and all. He didn't know we'd told each other everything and none of what was in the past mattered to me. He didn't understand that."

"*You married*—?"

"I was three months pregnant when you left. When I never heard back from you, which was his plan, Daddy convinced me to marry 'for the sake of the child.'" She watched Teddy.

"Daddy's eager associate, Robert Jenkins, married me on the courthouse steps, then received his reward: a corner office and a bonus. He's still with the company. Then Daddy arranged a quiet divorce when I was six months pregnant living in Paris with Grandma. It was all quite civilized. I was safe from scandal; Grandma doted on Teddy while I attended art classes, finished my degree. And most important, Teddy wouldn't be a bastard without a proper name."

"I went to Paris," I said, still watching Teddy. "Searched for you there." I looked at her and asked, "What about your husband?"

"He was my husband on paper for ninety days," she said. "He got his corner office and never spoke a word of the arrangement to anyone. Never saw him again till Daddy's funeral. But Teddy had a name, a home and family. Since I hadn't heard from you, and now we know why—but still, it was a difficult time to be alone. I had to make decisions for my... our son."

"Our son. Right," I said, taking it all in: her father's betrayal, a marriage, *our* son. "I see."

"I've been mad at you for years," she said. "But then I found your letters ... *you never knew.*" She shook her head, "And with those letters were news articles about you in Korea. He'd cut them out and saved them like he was proud of you. I don't understand him, never will. But I do think he forced me to do those things for my and Teddy's own good. I know that for sure."

"Ironic," I said, "that while I was in Korea trying to save children, you were here fighting for Teddy to have a dad. You did all the right things. It was me who screwed up by leaving in the first place."

"You forgive me?" she asked.

"Forgive *you*? Nothing to forgive. We were both trapped. We survived." I gazed into her eyes. "And now, here we are. What brought you back?"

"Daddy loved Teddy. He always said understanding where we were from was important to knowing who we'd become. He left the beach house to Teddy. I think he did that because in the end, he wanted him to know his roots... and maybe, unconsciously, his Irish father who went off and became a war hero. I think saving all those articles meant he was proud of you, in his way. He respected Mamaí, you know, and he did watch you grow up."

"I'm not the boy I was then."

"And I'm not that naïve girl."

"Father Theo!" Mrs. Whittle shouted as she ran up to us. "There's a call for you in the office. Tillamook sheriff's office. Urgent!"

"What? Um... Okay," I said, then turned back to Andréa and gently placed my hands on her shoulders. I gripped them more firmly and said, "Stay right here. Don't move. Please, *please* don't move. Don't run away from me. We'll work this out, I promise."

She nodded, her eyes watering.

"Everything's gonna be alright," I said, wanting to take her in my arms and wipe away all the pain of the last six years. "Nice ears."

She laughed, reached up to touch her Halloween costume as if she had forgotten they were there, and said, "Thanks." Then she tapped my plastic sheriff badge and said, "You too."

"Father Riley!" Mrs. Whittle shouted.

I rushed into the office and grabbed the phone. "This is Father Riley."

Chapter 129

THEO

"FATHER, THIS IS Sergeant Smith," he said. "Sheriff Grearson has been shot."

"What?" I said, thinking I misheard. "Where is he?"

"He'll be fine, but the hospital won't release him till morning."

"What hap—?"

"Well, I'll let him explain all that," the sergeant said. "For now, he'll be fine, but he asked that I call and tell you he won't be returning tonight and to keep an eye on Imogene and some kid, can't remember the name."

"Tula May, got it. Can't you tell me anything else?"

"Well," he paused lowering his voice. "There was a boy he arrested there in Nehalem—"

"Yeah, I was here—"

"Well," he said, "when Bud got here and took the kid from the car, the kid said hello to another kid who was hanging around the parking lot. That kid took out a gun and shot Bud."

"What?"

"Don't know anymore."

"Alright, thank you, sergeant."

How could the boy in Tillamook know Bud's whereabouts? It made no sense.

Imogene still hadn't shown up and it was nearly nine.

Andréa was at the door with a group of women gathered around her. Teddy was doing the Hokie Pokie with the other kids. It was surreal. Andréa finally looked my way, and our eyes met. I was torn, but I had to check on Imogene. Something wasn't right.

I motioned to the Jolly Green Giant, who stood with a child hanging from each arm like fruit from a sturdy tree.

"Oz!" I shouted. "Put the kids down."

"Where's everybody?" he asked out of breath.

"Listen, Bud's been shot," I whispered.

"What?"

"He's okay, but he's in Tillamook for the night," I said.

"Bud been shot before," Oz said. "But that was war... Who done it?"

"Well, we know who pulled the trigger," I said. "But there's something else goin' on here, just don't know what. So let's take a headcount and I'll go get Imogene and Pearl."

I rushed back to Andréa.

"Is everything alright?" she asked.

"No, it's not, and I need to go. But please wait, I beg you. Don't leave Manzanita."

Teddy ran up and slipped his hand in his mother's.

"He's almost six?" I asked.

"Almost," she whispered, and leaned down to wipe Teddy's face. "And yes, I'll wait."

"I'll wait too," he said with a broad smile. "Mommy, that girl is a real Indian."

"Hey," Tula said as she approached. "That Solly?" she pointed out the door.

Solly came running down the street barking. Where was Imogene?

Chapter 130

IMOGENE

CLOSED FOR Halloween Party 7-10 PM at the you-know-where!

Toreck sat six inches from me, knife at the ready. Pearl rushed to the table with a basket of garlic bread and said, "Here, eat."

He tore into the bread and snapped, "Where's that chowder?"

"Fresh clams, onion make it better," Pearl said.

She stood stirring the onions and Newt. They sizzled in a fry pan. We exchanged glances, then watched the frying 'clams.' Then watched Toreck knock back more beer.

I hoped the dead Newt hadn't lost its potency.

Toreck slammed his fists on the table and shouted, "Just bring it!"

"Okay," she said, and brought him a bowl of steaming chowder. "Eat. Feel better."

Toreck's wrist snapped up, pointing the knife at Pearl's face. "Fuck you, bitch. You don't care how I feel." His contemptuous eyes bore into her.

"She didn't mean anything," I said.

"I...," Pearl stammered. "I—"

"I-I-I," he mimicked and motioned to Pearl with his knife. "Fuckin' sit down, gook."

Pearl's face creased with fear as she searched for the chair beneath her and slowly sat. Toreck's caustic smell repulsed me. I turned away as he snorted and gulped like a pig.

He crammed a spoon of Pearl's bedeviled stew into his mouth while we both sat riveted. Pearl's eyes followed every bite as Toreck raised another to his mouth.

I hoped that the little lizard's deadly revenge would be painful.

I couldn't bear to look at Toreck so instead watched Pearl watch him. I realized that under the surface of the person she'd become since Korea was an unavenged war that raged inside her. Now she'd finally stumbled onto the opportunity to exterminate an enemy bigger than snails and spiders.

Toreck consumed several more pieces of Newt, swallowing without chewing, then slurped more beer and shoved bread into his mouth. God, the sounds he made were unbearable, but soon he grew calmer, slower.

As Pearl studied him, a shaky smile tickled her lips. He devoured all the Newt's lethal limbs, then pushed the bowl across the table and said, "More chowder, witch woman."

Pearl looked into the empty bowl and the tickle of joy disappeared from her face. Her eyes darkened as she reached for his dish. "Okay, more. I get more."

His hand slammed down on her forearm. We both jumped. Then Pearl yanked her arm away and calmly stepped back. I finally looked at his face—it was the ugliest I'd ever seen in my life. But Pearl and I watched as his eyes glazed over and his face suddenly drooped, stupefied. Tula's faithful friend was doing his job; a good warrior in his death. If my hands hadn't been tied to the table I would have grabbed his knife and stabbed him a hundred times.

He grew visibly confused and woozy, then he quickly stood, pushing the table over on its side, which lurched me forward to my knees. He shoved away from the bench, swaying back and forth with his knife still pointed at Pearl. She stood calm as a cucumber, eyes big as quarters.

He continued to sway. "Wha—wha—" He tried to form words, but none came. He reached his hand to his swelling mouth, where drool fell from the corners and tugged at his suddenly enlarged lips. Within seconds his face looked as if he'd been attacked by a thousand swarming bees. Pearl inched away from him and toward me.

The knife slipped from his hand. Toreck dropped to his knees on the hard linoleum floor. He swelled and swayed, reached for his throat, then grabbed at his stomach; vomit flew from his mouth. And with one last choking gasp for air, he plummeted face down into his own viperous puke.

A deep gasp of breath burst into my lungs. Pearl grabbed a kitchen knife and cut the nylons to free my hands. A surge of release rushed through me. Then dread.

"Toreck," she whispered, gradually creeping back toward his body. "You dead?"

She kicked the knife across the room, out of his reach. Then she took the broom that leaned against the wall and poked him hard. He moved. She raised the broom high above her head, ready to strike. She took another measured step, poked him again, then again. "You not dead yet?" She leaned down, checked his pulse and said, "You go to hell now." She jabbed his body with the broomstick. "Go!"

I braced myself against the table and stood speechless, holding my ribs.

Pearl gawked at his body for a long time. He wiggled and convulsed a couple more times, then he said, "Imogene," clear as day.

A scream boiled up inside of me and burst out, "NO!"

I grabbed the knife from her hand and lunged at him on the floor.

"You son of a bitch!" I screamed, then plunged the knife into him. I'd aimed for his heart but closed my eyes and missed—stabbed him in the shoulder. He moaned and finally fell silent.

"Oh God… What have I done?"

"It okay," Pearl said. "He die slow now. That better anyway."

"But what do we—"

"Put him in freezer," she said.

"How—?"

"Grab foot," she said taking Toreck's limp hands and nodding for me to take his feet.

I snatched a bottle of Mrs. B's rum off the shelf next to me, took a long swig, and said, "Okay," then took hold of his feet. We yanked and tugged him down the hall to the top of the stairs, leaving a trail of blood through the hall. "Now what?"

"Throw him down stairs," Pearl said.

"We can't throw a man down the stairs."

"Okay kill him," she said, "but no to hurt him?"

"Okay," I said, then gripped his feet with both hands and backed down the stairs. Pearl had his arms. He was limp as a noodle, but suddenly his head bobbed against the steps. As we reached the bottom, he mumbled, "Shit! What the fuck?" Then he vomited again and passed back out. Probably a concussion.

We dragged him through his vomit, nodding his head on the last four steps to the bottom, where we pulled him the rest of the way to the freezer.

I took a deep breath and opened the door. I looked around the dark store and grappled for the light switch. As I flicked on the lights, the phone rang louder than ever before, echoing through the room like a siren.

Chapter 131

Imogene

CLOSED FOR Halloween Party 7-10 PM at the you-know-where!

When the ringing finally stopped Pearl showed nothing, not even a flicker in her eyes. We continued to drag his body into the freezer. He woke briefly and grabbed Pearl's wrists. We both screamed, and I dropped his legs and grabbed the first thing I saw on the freezer shelf—a box-cutting knife—then stabbed him in the leg. He squealed and immediately vomited.

We slammed the door closed. The phone rang again, and I nearly jumped out of my skin.

The ridiculousness of it all welled up inside me. My nervous laugh—the same awful laugh I got at funerals—bubbled up from somewhere deep. It was low, then uncontrollable. I laughed out loud, too loud. I laughed, shaking my aching, damaged body, then reached behind the counter and tore open a carton of cigarettes. I lit up for the first time in months and took a long, slow drag. Pearl stood next to the freezer door in her cowgirl outfit looking at me like I'd lost my mind.

"The cowgirl and the lizard!" I cackled, hurting even more. I inhaled the bittersweet smoke, then leaned against the counter exhausted and in pain. "Think my ribs are broken?"

Pearl stared at me with eyes full of something. Fear? Shock? Pity? I couldn't make it out.

"Why are you looking at me like that?" I asked. "What?" I said as a deep burning sensation pierced through my lower half. I nearly doubled over.

"Immie," she said. "You sit down." She took my elbow and escorted me to the table. I could barely stand. "You sit now. I call doctor."

"No! What will we say?"

"You hurt, bad."

For the first time since it all started, I looked down. Blood had trickled down my legs and dried—a thick, red snake coiled to my ankles. "Oh, God!" I stared in disbelief at my own blood. Suddenly queasy, all I wanted to do was lie down and sleep away the bad dream.

"Here," she said, gently wiping my face with a fresh cloth. "You will be okay now."

The coldness felt good. My face swelled and the tears finally burst.

"You okay," she said sweeping the hair from my brow, face, and neck, assessing my injuries.

My hair smelled of him. My hands and wrists were cut and chaffed from being tied. I lifted my bloodied robe to see the marks on my thighs. It all came back, every hideous detail; the ugly whispers of a drunken monster.

The telephone rang again. I swallowed hard and said, "Should we answer?"

"No," she said, and then rushed to the window and peered into the moonless night.

My chest tightened. The phone stopped after the third ring.

Pearl grabbed Mrs. B's rum, the cigarettes, and an ashtray and set them in front of me. "You smoke now," she said. Then she took the mop from behind the door, rinsed it, and mopped up Toreck's vomit. "We leave him in freezer, he die soon."

"Then what?" I asked. "We cook him up?"

She stopped and looked at me like it was a good idea.

"No," I said. "We're not cookin' a man. Even that man."

"Okay," she said, then feverishly continued mopping.

I sat numb, feeling like I'd been hacked in two. Prickly sensations ran up and down my spine. I drank one, then two, then three long gulps of Mrs. B's rum. It was awful, but it burned a calming path through my stomach that emanated outward. I leaned back and smoked my cigarette. I'd missed cigarettes. My hands shook something awful, but Pearl was calm enough for both of us. I took another fiery sip. The sharp tang replaced the smell of his vomit. Just then someone pounded on the door. The bottle dropped from my hand and shattered on the floor.

Chapter 132

THEO

IMOGENE SAT at the picnic table motionless, holding a washcloth to her face. Pearl stood at attention next to her. The store stunk of vomit. "What are you two doing?" I asked.

Neither of them spoke, nor looked me in the eye.

"Why so late?" I asked looking Imogene over. Her hair was a knotted mess, her robe torn, her hands bloody. "What the hell?"

"Theo," Imogene gulped. "I… he…," she covered her face and sobbed into the washcloth.

"Where's this blood from? What happened here? Somebody say something, now!"

She started to cry so hard she couldn't catch her breath.

"Toreck," Pearl finally said, kneeling at her side and patting her hand. "He rape her." Pearl said it so matter-of-factly that Imogene stopped crying, took the washcloth away from her face, and looked up at me as if Pearl just said something she hadn't realized until that moment.

"What are you saying?" I asked. Then I saw Imogene's lips. Blue, swollen, cracked. Her eye was bulging and bruised, and purple fingerprints surrounded her throat. "Oh, God!"

I dropped to my knees and wrapped my arms around her. "Immie—"

Her body stiffened as she tried to sit up straight.

"Where is he?" I asked, looking around at the bloodied cloths, broken glass, and my sister's rope-burned wrists. "God help me, I'll kill him."

"I already try," Pearl finally said, then yanked the freezer door open. "He not die!"

"What?" I said peering inside the freezer. There he was on the floor, blue lips, puffed-up face and hands, and Pearl's foot-long freezer knife standing straight up in his chest, blood pooling around him.

"I feed him Newt," Pearl said. "I chop up, feed him Newt soup." She smiled at her own cleverness. "No worry, Theo—God already forgive me."

I stood speechless. "Is he—?"

"No," she said. "He not dead. He not die. Evil hard to kill." She kicked Toreck's bare foot. "We wait."

Toreck groaned, turned over, opened his eyes, and mumbled, "Padre."

I plunged on top of him, grabbed his neck and said, "I warned you to end this thing, you stupid son of a bitch." I gripped tighter around his throat. "I warned you."

He gasped, flailed his arms, arched his back, and finally took his last breath. His body wilted beneath me and sank lifeless to the floor. His blood coated my hands and knees, but I still gripped in rage at his throat. "You son of a bitch!" I shouted shaking his lifeless body. "You son of a bitch, why couldn't you let things go? You stupid son of a bitch!"

Pearl placed her hand on my shoulder and said, "It okay now."

I finally let go, sat back, wiped my hands on my coat, and said, "Good riddance."

"Amen," Pearl said.

"Amen," I repeated.

"Tell Bud I do it," she said. Her voice sounded far away, mumbled chatter in my head. I stared at my hands. The thirst for revenge was right there, gripped in my bloody fists. What good is a priest with vengeance in his soul?

Pearl yanked the knife out of his chest and said, "Is my good kitchen knife."

She wiped it off, grabbed the mop and towels, and without hesitation did the thing she always did when she was fretful—went to work wiping up the stain he was leaving on her neatly cleaned, organized, whitewashed world.

"I tell Bud I go coo-coo like he say all the time... I lose temper and just kill, kill, kill."

"It's okay," I said finally hearing her clearly. "I'll explain to Bud."

"Bud understand," she said. Then she poked Toreck hard with her finger. Then again, harder. "He dead. Should we say someting about God?"

"No," I said finally pulling myself up. "I'm not feeling very religious today."

She stood and wiped her hands, looking at Toreck's body. "Me too."

I ushered Pearl out of the freezer, closed the door behind us, and returned to Imogene. Her eyes were sunken deep into her bruised cheekbones, dull, red, and floating in pools of tears.

"We need to get you to the hospital," I said.

"No!" Imogene cried. "No hospitals." She sat staring at the clock on the wall. "It's too late," she said.

"Late for what?"

"We were gonna dance."

"You'll dance another night," I said remembering how excited Bud was to see her. "There'll be lots of dancing, but right now we need to get you some help."

"No hospitals, no doctors, nurses, neighbors, gossip... no more gossip." Tears washed down her cheeks. "I'm fine... I'll be just fine." She flinched, clutching tighter at her ribcage and dabbing drops of blood from her busted nose.

"You're not," I said.

"I've seen you patch yourself up plenty of times. Go get your kit."

"Immie, we need to get you some help."

"No!" she insisted, slamming her fists on the table. "No hospital. Get your kit."

"Doc Haydn's, then." I stood. "Pearl, grab her coat and some blankets, would ya?"

I tossed Toreck's bloody knife, cigarettes, and boots into the freezer with him and padlocked the door. I wished I'd killed him two years ago. I should have known men like that don't change; they just get worse. I should have known.

"No, Theo," Imogene cried. "I don't want anybody—"

"Nobody'll know," I said. "I promise. No gossip. No nothin'."

"We can fix her up," Pearl said. "She be okay. I a good nurse. Get your kit."

"Well... " I hesitated to agree but didn't want to upset her more. "Till morning then," I said. "We'll reassess after she gets through the night."

"Bud?" Imogene whispered.

"He's busy tonight," I said stroking her matted hair. I carefully lifted her from the bench. She sank into me like a ragdoll.

Pearl opened the door so I could carry her upstairs.

Imogene's body tensed as she asked, "Tula May?"

"She's with Oz and Netty," I said.

"Are you sure?"

"I'm sure."

Chapter 133

THEO

I TURNED OFF the lights in Imogene's store and slid out the back while Pearl taped up her ribs. I ran home to grab my medical kit and a bottle of the pain pills I was supposed to take but never did. When I got back to Imogene's I saw through the window that the freezer was open and the light was on. I took the .38 from my belt, turned the handle, and opened the door, expecting to see Genghis Hansel.

"Where the bloody hell is everybody?" Mrs. B shouted from inside the freezer.

I let out a sigh of relief. "B?"

"What the hell happened here?" she asked as she stepped out.

I looked around and said, "Are you alone?"

"Am I alone?" she blurted. "Of course I'm alone. Where's Imogene and Pearl, and who the hell killed that deserving bastard?"

"How did you—?"

"It's never locked," she said holding up a crowbar. "I panicked, thought someone locked them in. Now, where's my girls?"

"Don't get upset. Immie'll be okay—"

She took a deep breath and asked, "Toreck?" She nodded understanding my expression, and leaned on her cane like all the air had been let out of her. "Where is she?"

In Tula's room Pearl tended to Imogene, whose eyes were open but with that thousand-yard stare I'd seen so often in Korea on the faces of the displaced, tortured, and lost souls.

Pearl nodded; nobody spoke. I handed Pearl the medical kit, took one of the pills from the bottle, and placed it in Imogene's mouth with a drink of water. She smelled of soap, rubbing alcohol, and Pearl's herbal ointments. Mrs. B and Pearl were both red-eyed, looking like mourners at a funeral. They slowly sat down. Mrs. B passed her ivory cane to Pearl. We all three took a nip and silently watched Imogene drop into a deep sleep.

*   *   *

The lamp in Imogene's room was shattered along the edge of her rug; one nylon was tied to the headboard, and her drawers were all open, underwear on the floor. I stared at the nylon and a fireball of rage rushed to my fists, releasing in a punch through the wall. Pearl and Mrs. B rushed into the hallway.

I rubbed my knuckles and said, "I'll sit with her. Go get some tea."

They nodded and walked silently down the hall to the kitchen. I entered Tula's room. Imogene slept under the soft glow of the nightlight she'd bought for Tula. She looked small, like that day at Kiernan's funeral when I promised to watch after her.

"I was supposed to protect you," I whispered, kneeling by her bedside and taking her limp hand in mine. I placed Kiernan's tin soldier in her palm and closed her hand over it.

"Remember Mamaí's Gaelic," I whispered. "Kiernan studied it out loud. He said it was the language of the Irish heart. You wouldn't remember, but our big brother was a poet." I wasn't sure she heard me, but I kept talking.

"*Tá brón orm* was a word that stuck with me. He made me learn to say it. *Tá brón orm*. It's an ancient word with deep roots. Means 'I'm sorry.'" I squeezed my eyes shut. "'I'm sorry' and 'please forgive me' wrapped in one powerful word. *Tá brón orm*, Imogene, *Tá brón orm*."

Chapter 134

THEO

DOWNSTAIRS IN THE STORE I picked up the phone, dialed the hospital, and said, "Bud Grearson's room. This is Father Riley."

"Checked himself out, *against doctor's orders*," the nurse snarked, "and he—"

"Thank you." I slowly placed the receiver back in its cradle. There was nothing I could do for Imogene but stay by her side. What I wanted to do was wake Toreck from the dead and kill him again. I went to secure the lock on the freezer and opened the door to look at him. His mouth was swollen and green; his eyes still bulged open, and his hands clinched in fists. It was an appropriate death. I didn't cross myself, say a prayer, or close his eyes. Instead, I slammed the door shut and locked it tight.

I tiptoed back to Tula's room and sat in the chair next to Imogene's bed. She was asleep, her curls matted against her face. She opened her eyes and glanced up at me.

"Theo," she said.

"Yeah," I replied taking her hand in mine. "I'm so sorry, love—"

"You?"

"I started all this mess."

"No," she said and gently shook her head. "He'd had it out for me for a long time."

"What can I do?"

She opened her other hand, held up Kiernan's soldier, and said, "Put that back in your pocket for safekeeping, and... tell me a story."

In the lamp light the bruises on her face were more apparent. Why didn't Toreck come after me? His fight was with me. I guess in the end he knew how to throw the hardest punch. "A story, huh?" I said.

"Tell me about your sad angel." She tapped my arm where my angel lay sleeping under my sleeve. "You've never told me anything about Korea and those children."

I took a deep breath, sat back in the chair, and said, "Okay... Well, it was '51. You know, after Peters and I went missin'. We were lost in the T'aebaek Mountains. A lot of things happened, good and bad. One of the good things was that I got to know those kids, eighteen orphans. Anyway, cute kids. I read them your letter about that frying pan. They had no idea what I was reading, of course, but they listened with great curiosity. Then when I laughed, they all laughed." My eyes suddenly burned with tears.

"Oh Theo," Imogene said pulling her hand to her forehead. "Poor little things. You loved them. I hear it in your voice."

"It's a long story."

"Most love stories are," she said. "You talk. I love the way you tell stories, how you describe things. Please, describe everything. Take me out of my own head for a while."

"Okay, just a little more."

"Why sad angel?" she asked.

"Hmm... Couple reasons, really. Our nun explained to the children that I was an angel stricken from heaven to help them. It's corny, I know... And, well... the nun, who I called Sister, said I was a sad angel, hence the tattoo."

"Why did she think you were sad?"

"Because she knew I made a choice that cost me everything."

"Andréa?"

"You need to sleep," I said, tucking her blankets. "It's the best thing for you right now."

She struggled to keep her eyes open. The pain pills were finally taking hold.

"But—"

"I promise to tell you everything when you're stronger." I kissed her on the forehead.

"Check on Solomon," she said, her voice hoarse and weak.

"I will, love."

"And Tula—"

"Right now," I said as I opened the door, "you sleep."

I didn't mention Bud.

*   *   *

Pearl and Mrs. B sat at Imogene's dinette in silence.

I poured a cup of tea and said, "She's bein' nosy... that takes energy."

They both forced a smile.

"Good," Mrs. B said, pouring brandy from her cane into her tea, then offering some to me. I held out my cup and she filled it. "Nosy is good."

"Nobody going to miss dat man," Pearl said.

"I know," I said. "It's not him I'm worried about."

It was self-defense, but I didn't want my sister to suffer further by way of scandal.

"It's easy," Mrs. B declared as she downed her "tea." "I'm gonna get very drunk right now, and we're going to tell Bud that I got out of control and killed him." She grinned from ear to ear. "That'll do it."

"I love you, old woman," I said. "Not that anyone would dare doubt you could have killed him, but not this time."

"I know," she said.

"Who has Tula May?" I asked.

"We called Netty," Mrs. B said. "She's keeping Tula tonight."

"Thanks. I'll go check on Sol."

"I did," Mrs. B said. "He's awake. He wants to see you."

"Awake? Good," I said. "Will you —"

"You know perfectly well we aren't going anywhere," she said.

Before leaving I opened the freezer door and stared at Toreck's warped body. It'd only been an hour since I'd gripped my hands in tight judgment on his life. Should have felt regret, remorse; should have been on my knees begging for forgiveness, but instead, all I felt was relief that he was gone. But then I worried. With Toreck dead, would Hansel disappear or cause trouble? I locked the freezer again and headed to Solomon's, wondering if I should tell Bud or just hide Toreck's body? Already a dicey slope for a priest. Figured I may as well finish the job.

Chapter 135

THEO

IT WAS PAST MIDNIGHT and the Bouvre house lights were on. I resisted running to her and knocking on the door, deciding first to check on Solomon. He burned with fever, mumbled in his dreams, and breathed deeply but steadily. I held my hand on his forehead and said, "Be right back, old friend."

I left his hut and headed straight for her door. Andréa opened it wearing a long white robe tied at her waist, her hair down around her shoulders. She looked at me and whispered, "Theo."

"I saw your lights," I said grasping for a reason to be there. "Wanted to make sure you had your doors locked. There's been some trouble." Behind her was the staircase, hallway, and living room, camping gear laid out in the hall, but nobody else around.

"Teddy's sleeping," she said. "We're going camping tomorrow."

"So you're alone here."

"It's just us."

I stepped in, closed the door behind us, and said, "Just us?"

"Yeah," she said looking into my eyes like she did when she was mine. She smelled like heaven — jasmine to be exact.

"So," she said. "A priest? Was it your mother or because you wanted an escape?"

"Maybe both," I said. "But mostly because when I heard you married another, I knew if I couldn't have you there would never be anyone else."

Her eyes watered, and in that instant I knew nothing other than to pull her in. I wrapped her close and kissed her — the long, sweet kiss of my dreams.

As we held each other, I kept thinking it was a dream. But as I kissed her face and hands and touched her silky-smooth hair, she came to life. Was she feeling the same thing? No, it wasn't a dream. She was there in my arms, her hands feeling my face, shoulders, chest. Kissing me back. An immense joy filled me and I said what I'd longed to say: "I love you. You can't imagine how many times a day I dreamed of this; you, me, no war, no family coercions, just us. You're my life. You're everything."

"I love you," she said, holding my hands to her face, lips to my fingers. "Always have and always will."

I wiped her tears, cupped my hands around her face, lost myself in those blue eyes, and said, "Without you, I'm just a dead man walking. I never felt like I survived war until right this minute, until you."

"Mommy," Teddy called from the top of the stairs. "I wet my bed."

"I have to go to him," she said pulling away. "He's scared after losing his grandparents and scared of this new place."

"Of course," I said, reluctant to let go. "Tomorrow... we talk. And don't go camping tomorrow. Stay in town."

"Teddy will be disappointed," she said. "He practiced lighting lanterns and rolling his sleeping bag all day—"

"Here," I said taking my .38 out of my belt. "Remember when I taught you to shoot?"

"Yes, but—"

"There's been trouble. You may need this."

"Are we in some kind of danger?" she asked.

"No," I said. "Just being cautious, that's all. Tell Teddy he can go camping later. Tell him if he wants to learn how to catch salamanders, I can teach him."

She slid the gun into her pocket and said, "Okay. He'll like that."

"*Mommy!*"

"So," I said, "tomorrow."

"Yes, tomorrow."

Chapter 136

THEO

THE MOON, now visible, hung low; sadness filled the oppressive fog and settled damp on my skin. I hurried to Solomon's cabin. His yard was eerily silent. Osprey was roosted on her branch above his fire pit, waiting patiently, her feathered neck bright as a string of pearls on black velvet.

Solomon's fireplace was ablaze, but he lay in deep sleep. When I touched his forehead his eyes popped open, and he said, "Evil is awake." Then he slipped back into his trance. I didn't know how to tell him what happened to Imogene, or if I even should.

"*Ts-ull-ULL-leel!*" he said. "*Ts-ull-ULL-leel!*" Then he fell back into that other world inside himself. He was either healing himself or was on that final journey with Wolf. As much as I wanted to call Doc, he'd never forgive me. I'd made enough mistakes: some I didn't regret because I thought I knew better, and some for which I may never be forgiven. But denying him his death the way he saw it wasn't a mistake I was willing to make.

I sat and listened to him breathe, deeply and rhythmically like the sound of his chanting. I wanted to tell him about Imogene. Wanted him to jump up, grab his medicine bag, rush to her house, and make everything better. But there was nothing he could do for her now.

"*Ts-ull-ULL-leel,*" he whispered again. It was his word for flooding, or the tide coming in. Why did he keep saying it?

"Theo," he said, then turned his head toward me. His eyes bloated like the heavy lids on his Frog Box eyes. "I was wrong," he whispered. "Feed wolf who wants more than peace; feed wolf who wants to live. If life means battle, be warrior again. She has returned for you. She returns your life."

Then his eyes closed again and he fell back asleep.

His candle illuminated the kitchen shelves where he had two of everything he needed. Two of everything because more than two people, he said, was too many. But a life of only one was too few. I wanted to tell him about Andréa and Teddy K., but maybe he already knew.

Chapter 137

THEO

BILLOWS OF SMOKE came from the direction of Saint Mary's. I ran and arrived as the stained glass windows exploded. Oz's truck squealed to a stop at the driveway.

"We seen them flames a block away," he said. "Netty called the fire truck."

We found the hoses and tried to squelch the fire, but it was too late. By the time Nehalem's fire truck arrived, it was a total loss. Five gas cans were found inside the rectory.

"Arson," one fireman said. "Probably teenagers."

But I knew better. Watching a church go up in flames would be a dream come true to only one man I knew of.

* * *

Bud got to Imogene's a little before three in the morning.

"What the hell happened to the church?" he asked as he entered. His arm was in a sling.

"Arson," I said. "What happened to you?"

"Those boys said a guy with a crippled hand paid them twenty bucks each to get rid of me." He shifted his arm and cringed. "Luckily he hired local talent or I'd be dead. The fire?"

"Fire department says teenagers, I say Hansel." I opened the freezer and said, "But we have bigger problems."

"*Bigger!*" Bud exclaimed as he stepped into the freezer. He looked back at Pearl.

She put her wrists together, offering them up, and said, "You arrest me. I kill him."

Bud's jaw dropped.

"Pearl," I said lowering her arms. "Listen, Bud, I—"

"No, no," Mrs. B said. "It was me!" She poked me with her cane. "I got drunk... It was a drunken rage... Hated that bastard all his shit life I just couldn't take it anymore."

"There's more confession going on here than in church," I said.

"Come on, you two." Bud scratched his head, moving his hat back on his brow. "He's twenty-nine years old, and you two, well, B, you're what, eighty-five now, and Pearl, you're skittish as a cat about him." He looked back at Toreck's body. "He's stabbed, and... What happened to his face?"

"Now listen here," Mrs. B said, shoving me aside and grabbing Bud's good arm. "That was nothing but self-defense and nobody would think any different."

"Self-defense?" he said and darted a look around. "Somebody give me a full story here."

"If you ladies are done...," I said, then looked at Bud. "I killed him."

"*You?*" he said. "There's only one reason. Where is she?"

I opened the door to the apartment and said, "Wait here. I'll see if she's awake or if—"

"She'll see me." He pushed past and leapt three stairs at a time.

I stood numb at the bottom of the staircase. The clock chimed three times.

Pearl dropped into a chair by the register, wrung her hands like a dishtowel, and said, "He be good for her." Then she picked up a piece of chalk and the specials board and began to write. She nodded to herself. "He be good." She hung the sign in the window. *We close now.*

Chapter 138

IMOGENE

WE CLOSE NOW

Early morning sun sifted through my room like flecks of gold on soft velvet. The house rang with a silent hum that drifted in and out. The sounds outside of beach-combing children, birds, and the roaring ocean were muffled, distant from the emotional vacuum that consumed me. I smelled coffee and opened my eyes. What day was it?

My mouth was dry as cotton and my nose hurt like hell. As I raised up on my elbows, a shot of pain went through my ribs. I dropped back down and saw Bud across the room; his sweet blue eyes gazed at me. My old Bible was open on his lap. Why was he here?

He slowly raised to his feet. Suddenly the memory of Toreck raged through me—his hands... his breath. Tears burned, trickled, then a cloudburst.

"Oh, God... " I turned over and curled into a ball. "Go away. You can't see me now."

"Immie," Bud whispered. His body was warm as he lay down next to me. "Everything's gonna be just fine, honey." He took me in his arms, rocked me, caressed my hair, pulled the blankets up around me.

"We can raise Tula, ya know. We'll take her to church, if ya want. I'll wear a suit, even. We'll take a trip. Maybe California, that Disneyland place. She'd like that. You'd like that. And if you'd like that, I'd be a happy man, Imogene Riley, just to see you smile."

Chapter 139

THEO

THE STORE HADN'T BEEN that quiet since Mamaí died.

I spent what was left of the night in a hard wood chair at the base of Imogene's stairs, but since the time Bud had gone into her room there hadn't been a sound. Mrs. B had gone home around four in the morning; Pearl had curled up on a bench with a blanket. The Coca-Cola clock ticked at the silence.

Pearl snorted and smacked her lips while she slept. I stood, too much adrenalin to sleep, stretched my legs, put on the coffee, and opened the freezer door to look at Toreck's body again. Felt as much for him as the three dead McMurtry brothers—glad he was gone, but wondered what to do with him now, and wondered where Hansel was, what his next move would be.

Wondered too, if at the end of the oncoming storm I would be a man she could love again. Thought about that kiss. Andréa. Teddy.

At eight o'clock Pearl leapt from the table as if startled by a gunshot. She stood hunched, tight fists raised, and black hair looking like Medusa's snakes.

"Mornin'," I said.

She looked around, confused, her eyes puffy as a blowfish.

"Oh," she said, relaxing. "Okay." She dropped her arms to her sides. "How Imogene?"

"They're still upstairs," I said handing her one of her two cups.

"Then she good," Pearl said. "Bud here."

She took her cup, then James's empty companion cup, and sat down at the table.

"Yeah," I said leaning back against the counter. I glanced out the window toward Solomon's cabin and noticed there was no smoke from his chimney. A heaviness came over me.

Pearl turned to follow my gaze and her elbow knocked James's cup off the table and onto the floor where it crashed into pieces. We both stared at it in silence.

"Pearl," I said stepping closer. "We can get another one just like—"

"No," she stared, blinking her bloated lids. "Time to set him free."

The telephone ruptured the silence. I rushed to answer so it wouldn't wake Imogene.

"Hello?"

"Father Theo?"

"Yes, Lucy?" I stared at the freezer door as if she could sense what was behind it.

"I've been tryin' to call ya all morning. The Bishop's gettin' antsy that you haven't answered all mornin'. He heard about the fire."

"Shit!"

"Father Theo!"

"Sorry. I'll call him later."

Outside the clouds swiftly shadowed the sky and hung oppressively low— one shaped like a large spider settled over Manzanita. The abrupt darkness chilled the room and chilled me to the bone. Mrs. B was passing through my yard on her way home from Solomon's. She apparently went *there* for the night. She waved her cane to let me know he was still with us. There wasn't a car or another human being in sight.

Pearl took the broom and tenderly swept up the shards of glass. She placed them not in the garbage, but in a large fawn-colored envelope. She sealed it, wrote JAMES on the front, and set it on her shelf with her teas.

Bud finally descended the stairs.

"How is she?" I asked, then noticed fresh blood on his shirt.

He looked down. "Oh, I'm fine."

"How's Immie?" I asked.

"I gave her another pain pill," Bud said as he stared out the window. "They help her sleep. What about Sol?"

"Mrs. B was just over there," I said. "I'll go check in a bit."

Pearl grabbed the first aid kit, tugged Bud's shirt off, and tended his arm and rib cage.

"I'll go to hell for this," I said, "but we need to get rid of his body. If this gets out—"

"It won't." Bud motioned for Pearl to hurry up with the bandages. "I'll take care of it." He stood, then dropped back down into the chair, his face pale.

"You need rest," I said. "That's worse than you're puttin' on."

"It's nothing."

"That 'nothing' is bleeding through the bandages. " I said. "I'll take care of *things*... I'm just not sure how or if I should report—"

"Report nothin'. Take that damned collar off, Riley; you still think you're here for you, *your* soul or whatever. Truth is, little buddy, you and me, after all we've done, we have some splainin' to do to the big guy upstairs. So for now, it's not about us, it's about our girls. And that collar, it just gets in the way of doin' what needs doin'."

"*My collar*," I said. "Your trolley's off the track, Bud. I just killed a man last night, with my bare hands, *collar intact*. Now, we've had a tough night, but get this straight: I'm in this."

The phone rang. We left it be.

"Yeah, sorry," he said. "It *has* been a long night."

"We both know there's a huge gap between justice and what's just. And that gap's too tough to put in a report so we need to get creative in dealing with our Mr. Hansel."

"Right," he said. "So no reports. No religion."

"No reports," I said. "And the *report* I was talking about was the one for the fire... I'm sure it was Hansel."

"Where is that slimy bastard?" Bud asked.

The phone rang again. I grabbed it.

"Finally answerin'." Hansel said.

"Why, did you miss me?" I asked.

"Bet you hated bein' locked in that cell," he said. "No way out, them crazy North Korean bastards holdin' the key. Powerless when they shot them kids."

"You've been a caged man all your life, you know the score," I said.

Bud's face perked up.

"What was it, fifteen kids?" Hansel continued. "Execution style while you watched, hands tied behind you. Sad stuff, that. All under twelve, though, right? Cause younger than twelve means they just went back to the Guf. Thanks for your help, there. But there's still a few more needed."

"You've confused your Bible passages, Hansel... your daddy lied to you."

"My *daddy*," he seethed, "was a man of GOD, powerful in his RIGHTEOUS truth. No lies parted his lips, no bars caged him, no lawman trapped him—"

"Maybe," I said, "but he couldn't escape *you*, could he?"

"I have work to do, Padre." The line went dead.

"Hansel?" I clicked several times. "Hansel?"

"We gotta find him," I told Bud.

"Let's get everything loaded," Bud said, then tried to stand. He immediately dropped back to the bench, woozy from blood loss and no sleep. "Okay, you get everything loaded."

While I grabbed a box of shells from Imogene's cabinet, took the Winchester and set it on the table next to Bud, images of Korea stirred.

Sister's head was shaved, her eyes red, watery. My hands and feet were bound, my head gripped by soldiers. I heard the NK General say, "You want death. Death too easy." He shoved my face into the dirt. "You will see them," he said, and nodded to his soldiers. They dragged Sister, bloodied and beaten, past my cell into the shadows. "Karma," he said, "means drive you through universe as you reincarnate, learn your life lessons." He leaned down and studied my face. "This is life lesson, Soldier." Then he took his Lugar from its holster. "This," he said, as a burst of heat exploded beneath my skin. "This give journey through reincarnation a boost. You will see old woman and orphan rats soon enough."

I choked and gagged. Blood spewed out of my leg, soaking my pants and the dirt beneath me. The General stood calmly. "You are welcome, Soldier. You learn your life lessons at greater pace now. In karma, pain is good teacher."

I grew dizzy, then nauseous. "Where are they?" I bellowed.

"Not your concern," he said. "However, is your destiny I decide to make allies in United States." He lit a cigar. "I begin with you." He motioned to his militia and said, "Take him."

They dragged me to the far side of the cell, stood me up, and pressed my face into the bars. Outside were the remaining fifteen children and Sister, lined up and facing me. The young ones cried, "Teo!" The oldest fixed their eyes on me. I screamed, "No!" But then the shots—one, two, three… Bodies dropped. "No!"

Sister was praying, then another shot, and she dropped to her knees. Our eyes met and she fell forward. I screamed again, then blacked out.

Woke in a U.S. Army truck. They said they found me at the edge of their camp—no idea how I got there. They said I kept rubbing the scar on the palm of my hand, repeating, "A warrior owns his soul. No man can take your soul, poison your mind, or silence your heart. No man."

* * *

The phone rang again. I snatched it up and said, "Where are you, Hansel?"

"It's Tula May," Netty said, her voice high-pitched.

"What?"

"She was out front," Netty sobbed, "eatin' her toast with Andréa's boy. Then they's gone. They's done gone missin', both them kids."

"Where's Andréa?"

"Andréa and her Teddy come for breakfast. Teddy, he's playin' outside with Tula May. Andréa saw a car pull up next to 'em. She got worried, ran outside. When I looked out the winda', I seen Andréa screamin' in da street and them kids, gone."

"I'm coming," I said. I hung up, told Bud what she said and to stay with Imogene, and ran home for my car.

Chapter 140

THEO

I ARRIVED AT NETTY'S to Andréa and Netty waiting on the restaurant porch, crying.

"Theo," Andréa said, "find Teddy."

"I will," I said grasping her hand, "What happened?"

"I saw a silver car parked at the bench. The kids were gone, the car running," she sobbed. "I ran outside screaming for the kids. The car tore off. That's all I know."

I kissed her check and said, "I'll find them."

"Teddy looks like you," she sobbed. "He's brave like you. He thinks he's Superman."

My heart sank. *Superman.* "Then he'll make good decisions and stay safe," I said, trying to assure her. "You and Netty go to Imogene's. Everyone needs to stay together until we find this bastard and the kids are home safe."

As I headed to the car I said, "Alright God, I need a legitimate miracle here. No more of your jokes, your sick sense of humor…pure miracle. Nothing less will do."

Chapter 141

THEO

OZ STROLLED OUT of his work-shed at the side of the restaurant with two shotguns. He handed me one and then wiped sweat from his brow and said, "Crazy left ya a note on that bench." Then he took a piece of paper from his pocket.

It read:

Padre… And it came to pass, our God hath delivered into my hands, my enemy the destroyer. Like Samson fresh out of the prison house, we will make sport and then Samson must choose between two pillars.

"Two pillars?" I said. "The kids."

"That's wha' Netty figured," Oz said. "Where do ya think—"

"He's a hermit crab. Marge's place is an empty shell. Let's start there."

"We'll take my truck."

As we sped around the corner, the fog at the edge of Neahkahnie thickened. Oz forged ahead into the deep mist, his huge hands gripping the wheel. It looked more like dusk than ten in the morning. We scoured the streets for the silver car as we headed up Treasure Rocks Road and past four cabins with smoking chimneys. The air was thick with their smoke. We could barely make out the gravel road at Marge's old place.

With my hands locked on the barrel of the gun, my feet hit the ground before Oz even stopped the truck. I ran up the stairs and pushed through the door, shotgun aimed. The house appeared empty and cold. I rushed from room to room, each one colder and darker than the next.

I heard sounds coming from the bathroom and shoved the door open. The window had been broken and the room was full of pigeons. I slammed the door and continued to search. Outside, Oz called for the kids.

I saw something out the kitchen window. A rope swing hung on the tree, and something I couldn't make out sat on the swing. I walked outside toward it and called out, "Oz, in the back!" but the babbling brook muted any sounds. On the wooden seat was one of Tula's mother's red shoes.

"Oz?" I shouted, then grabbed the shoe. A ribbon had been tied around it like the first one we saw. "Oswald?" *Why wasn't he answering?* I rushed to the front of the house—he wasn't there. I tore back through the downstairs and yelled his name from the back porch. "Where are you? We need to go, now!" Something rustled in the brush. I scrambled down the steps and ran to the creek. Nothing.

Then, at the forested edge of the bubbling creek, not fifty yards from where I stood, was a wolf. Not any wolf, but Solomon's great Wolf. He looked at me with his stern eyes and nodded his head up toward the mountain; he dissolved into the mist, and I knew where I had to go.

The truck keys had disappeared with Oz. As I hurried down the hill, Mr. Forester drove past me; he reversed when he saw me, pulled over, and gave me a ride to the restaurant to get my car. But the keys were gone from the ignition. I ran to my house where the front door was wide open. There was a note lying on the floor inside with with Oz's truck keys serving as a weight. Seeing no one, I picked it up: *Lost your keys, Padre? Gimp. That's a hike down Neahkahnie. How's that leg feel now?*

I looked up, reached for my .38, and remembered I'd given it to Andréa. I grabbed my knife from my boot instead and headed to the kitchen. Someone clocked me out of nowhere between the front door and the dining room. I dropped to the floor, my face an inch from a pair of black snakeskin cowboy boots. One of them planted firmly onto my back.

I grabbed his other foot and tried to yank him down. "Where are those kids?"

"Sorry Padre, no time to chat."

* * *

When I woke, my aquarium was half-smashed. The anemone and cleaner shrimps were alive in the lower half of the aquarium, but most of my fish were dead and flung to the floor—except one. The tiny orange clown fish was safe in a glass of water on top of my Bible with a note that read:

Looks like those days of reckoning are at hand. But since I like you, I'll let ya choose one, and I'll keep the other.

I rushed down the hall, grabbed the rifle and spare set of car keys, ran across to Imogene's store and jumped into the convertible.

An acid burn tightened in my chest. With my hand on the gun, I drove deeper into the shadows of Neahkahnie, certain Toreck would have mentioned his family's abandoned homestead to Hansel. My throat swelled. How many people have to be hurt before I learn to do what needs to be done *before* it's too late?

Sunlight splintered through the mountain's tall oaks and twisted junipers. Gnarled bushes and broken trees scratched and clawed at my car. Grey clouds looked more like smoke settled on the pitted, gravel drive that spiraled up the half-mile hill to Sealy's tumbledown house, another empty shell. A perfect place for Genghis Hansel's "deeds of darkness."

Chapter 142

THEO

THE NORTH SIDE of the mountain was filled with hiding places. I closed in on the cabin. My jaw tightened. I gripped the steering wheel and whirled forward; gravel and dust filled the open convertible. A thin red line etched the bottom of the sky, then lightning lit up the clouds. *Storm.* Thunder crackled and camouflaged the crunch of my tires.

I finally reached the top of the hill and turned off the lights, then entered the foreboding homestead. My stomach climbed to my throat. I'd searched burned-out villages unsure of what I'd find: slaughtered villagers, children, and women, grandparents, blown to smithereens. I blinked those images away and called out, "Tula? Teddy?"

The rustic cabin was in the center of the lot. The shop and barn towered behind the cabin, though they were nearly engulfed by a thicket of pines and an old oak tree. The sound of rain was everywhere, hitting the tarps that covered remnants of cut wood, filling the otherwise quiet yard; a yard redolent with the lives of animals hunted and skinned on the ground where I walked.

Swiftly moving from window to window of the cabin, I stared into the darkness of each, shotgun poised and ready. Sounds filled my head: heavy breathing, footsteps on bamboo bridges. Heard them everywhere, like the ubiquitous sound of rain. I readied my finger on the trigger and squeezed my eyes shut—chased away another ghost.

An empty oil barrel drummed as the rain hit. I progressed toward the barn. The bushes on the left side of the cabin had familiar fabric hanging from them: a yellow sweater. *Tula's sweater.*

Across the yard and inside the barn was a dim light. A split deer, its hooves bound and dangling from a pivot the size of my arm, was suspended at the entrance of the door. I stepped through the blood-drenched ground that led inside but stopped cold in the doorway. There was a scratching sound behind me, inside a small trailer next to the oil drum. Something inside scratched to get out. I heard a growl. *Solly?*

I turned back to the barn. The rain battered the aluminum roof panels so hard that the birds frantically scattered from the beam twenty feet above. When I opened the door, the smell of rotting meat was overpowering. Bird droppings everywhere. I struggled to see through the shadows. Just then, a glimpse of something in the back, a flicker of light off metal. A gun? Knife? I ducked behind a barrel and watched. It moved again, then a match burst to life and a lantern glowed against the darkness. *There he was.*

Hansel stood in the yellow glow, two burlap potato sacks, large enough to hold one child each, lay at his feet. One was moving, the other was not. He poured gasoline on the bags. Tula screamed from inside one. The other, *Teddy,* didn't move. My heart dropped.

Then Hansel disappeared into the shadows of the massive barn.

I aimed the shotgun into the corner and said, "It's over."

"Not over," he said, not a hint of surprise in his voice. "Fun's just beginnin'."

I turned toward the sound of his voice—he'd approached quickly. Something slammed against my ribs, and my gun dropped to the ground, I to my knees.

"Just beginnin', Padre."

Chapter 143

THEO

HANSEL WAS BIG as a house. I rose and jabbed a right hook, then a left to his face. He was barely fazed. He swung. I ducked under his fist and rammed mine into his kidneys. He fought back; a massive blow to my ribs. I steadied my stance and snapped a fist straight up to his solar plexus with a hard impact. He flinched but struck back with a slam to the side of my head. He was no boxer, crippled hand and all, but he had it over me in sheer size and baffling strength.

Several feet from us Tula somehow wriggled out of the bag, then screamed, "Bear!"

"Nancy Little Feet!" I shouted, launching a left hook to Hansel's nose. "Get up! Untie Teddy! Run!"

Hansel's nose gushed. He appeared dizzy. I'd gotten him good, but would he drop?

"Nancy frickin' Little Feet," he laughed, gathering his wits. "She's a fighter, that one."

"Tula, run!" I yelled and struck an upper cut below his chin.

Just as I thought I may be winning the fight, he kicked me, a sledgehammer to my knee cap. I dropped to the ground right as Tula struggled to her feet and was tugging at the tie string on the other motionless bag.

Hansel went after her. I slid the EK from my boot and launched it into his back, smack in the trapezius. He stumbled, froze, but did not fall. He then plucked the knife from between his shoulder blades, tossed it to the ground, turned, and said, "Didn't you ever hear, boy?" A gallows smile crept across his face as he studied the blood dripping from the serrated blade. "PAIN," he shouted, "is the alarm clock of the Soul! Problem is, you don't know what time it is, do you?"

Shit! What was he made of?

"Time… yeah." I tried to stand, but what felt like a blowtorch shot through my knee. "I've got the time… It's time for your final battle, isn't it?"

"The Lord has tested my steel, trial by fire in a thousand fights. Ain't dead yet. Why ya think that is? One of them foes had to be a good man and yet they lost. You a GOOD man, Padre? You gonna be that thousand and ONE? Slim odds," he chucked the knife to the ground. "I am your redemption, WAR HERO, and you're mine. But you got one thing right… This here's the battleground of the end. Whoever lives is the better man. God's TRUE chosen son."

He gazed about the shadowy barn. Then, in a quick stride reached and grabbed Tula up by her hair. She kicked and kept screaming, "Bear!"

"Yep," he said, "be needin' a real nice sacrifice prayer for the one you don't choose."

"No choosing. It's me you want—"

"Oh, I've got *you*, Padre," he said, then pulled a .45 out of his belt and aimed it at me. "I've got you. And how's that pretty sister a yours anyway? We got her too, didn't we? And that classy blonde chick-a-dee? Didn't hurt her, seein' she's been as good a mommy as she could, given you deserted her."

"You son of a bitch." I staggered to my feet ready to charge.

"Now, now, Padre, such language. And that brat—he looks an awful lot like you. Guess he's sleepin'… Now, back on your knees. Hands behind your head." He motioned with the .45 for me to lower back down. I did.

Tula kicked him in the knee, then kept kicking. He tossed her like a ragdoll to the ground and said, "She's a mean little shit. Musta hit me with sticks twenty times 'fore I got her tied." Then he turned his face back to me and said, "Now, let's have that sacrifice prayer 'fore ya both meet your maker."

"Sacrifice," I said. Despite my adrenalin blast I calmed my tone and stared, hopeful, at that lifeless bag, trying to keep him engaged. "Sacrifice always involves transformation." I held my hands at the back of my head like I did as a POW. "It's what you want, isn't it? To be transformed from this human realm to the divine?" I watched Tula untie the bag and tried to keep his attention on me. "And you think killing children earns you that transport. But you forget, God hates murderers of children. He even stopped Abraham from sacrificing his own son—"

"Stop preachin', Padre… you don't understand *after all*. I have a vision. You're jus' a small biscuit in this here big picture."

"Okay," I said. "Well, this biscuit's arms are tired. I'm putting my hands in my pockets."

His grip on the gun tightened.

"So, what's that vision?" I asked before he could pull the trigger.

He watched, looking slightly confused, as I slid my hands into my pant pockets.

"My rise to heaven," he said with sudden clarity. "Sent by the violent and sinful acts of a fallen holy man... *that's you, biscuit.* I will rise as God kindles the fires of hell on earth. I will rise above those flames. My righteous task completed. Children delivered from evil. I will be hailed back into His eternal embrace. I see it. AMEN. I see it!"

"That's quite a vision."

"You mock God's angel?" he shouted.

"I would never mock God's angel. Just trying to understand, that's all."

The gun was ten feet away and with a .45 aimed at me, there wasn't much to do but cause a distraction, get myself shot, and hope the kids could get away on their own. That was no good, especially with Teddy's unknown state. I needed that shotgun. Needed that miracle.

Come on, God!

Then I spotted my bloody knife he'd tossed to the ground. It was close enough.

"You know what a bastard child is, Padre, don't you? A bastard in the eyes of God is tainted with the blood of sin... "

"Yeah, bastard. Sin. Got it," I said, one eye on Tula and the unmoving bag, the other on my trusty EK. "Now tell me about this vision."

"You don't give one shit about my vision, Padre." He grimaced from pain. *Stab wound finally sinking in?*

"Okay... You gonna shoot me, or what?" I asked.

"You don't sound concerned," he said. "A bastard infects the flock of the Lord. To his tenth generation, all are denied entry to heaven. In other words, no bastards in heaven. Sorry 'bout that."

"Yeah, your 'House of Souls'," I said. "The Chamber of Guf—I get it, but you don't."

"You know nothing!" he barked. "Nothing!"

Then Teddy slowly emerged from the bag, Tula tugging at him to come with her.

"Your religion's as twisted as your hand," I said, forcing his focus on me. "Your 'House of Souls' needs to be *emptied* before the Messiah comes back, not *filled*, you idiot."

"My daddy always said the minds of men would coil God's words into venom."

"I guess he'd know."

Teddy wiped his tears, then stood proud and pulled his hands to his hips like Superman, his red cape torn, but dangling behind him—his face was swollen and his nose bloody, but he was alive.

Hansel glanced at him but remained oddly transfixed on our debate. "That bastard child the reckoning of *your* sins, Padre?"

"Looks like that day is at hand for both of us," I said. "Now, DROP THE GUN."

"What about that prayer?"

"No prayers for you," I said. "Thought that was clear the *first* time we met."

"No absolution… Yes, I remember. But Padre, not one prayer for an ascending angel?"

He began to look queer. Desperate. Almost childlike.

All of a sudden I understood—he needed me. His choice, the way to his vision, was through me, his gatekeeper. "Prayer?" I said, "Sure, first drop the gun. Get on your knees. Let's complete that vision."

"You talkin' like you're the one with the upper hand here, Padre," he quipped, attempting to retain some standing.

"Yeah, it's a problem I have."

"I'd say you got several problems… Now, prayer," he said, aiming the gun at Teddy.

Teddy stuck his tongue out. Tula's eyes bulged at the pointed gun and she clutched Teddy's arm, yanking him toward the barn door some twenty feet away. Hansel's aim followed them as they hurried, Tula with Teddy in tow. He could have easily taken the shot.

"Well there's the little bastard now, running away like his daddy," Hansel said, his words beginning to slur from the loss of blood. He angled his head toward me and staggered to where the kids' empty potato sacks lay on the ground. He steadied himself by bracing his hand on a tool shelf. "So, which one do you choose?" he said. "God waits."

"Don't you hurt him!" Teddy shouted from the barn door.

Hansel quickly glanced at him, then back at me. It was enough time.

I dove for the knife and pitched into straight into his chest.

"Get out of the barn, kids!" I shouted. "NOW!"

Hansel's eyes bulged. The gun plummeted from his hand. He dropped to his knees on the gasoline-soaked burlap bags, clasped his hands around the knife, stared at me and said, "Prayer?"

"Okay, prayer," I said. "There *will* be a reckoning over lost innocents. *I*, not you, am His warrior today. *I* will avenge those whose innocence you embezzled, you son of a bitch. There's your prayer, Poet. In the name of the Father, and of the Son, and the Holy Spirit. Amen."

Hansel raised his hands in apparent supplication. Blood soaked his shirt. "Judgment day?" he asked in a low rasping tone.

"Yep," I said. "Looks like that day of reckoning is at hand."

"And my vision?"

"Oh yeah, flames." I tossed the lantern at his feet. "There's your vision."

The burlap bags exploded in gas-fueled fire around him.

"Not the prayer I had in mind," Hansel mumbled as fire crept up his body. "The flames," he said, "not the vision—" Then he fell forward, face down into his own inferno.

Chapter 144

THEO

THE BARN DOOR burst open and bright sunlight flooded inside along with Bud, gun drawn.

"Theo?" he called out.

"Here," I said. "I'm over here. He's dead."

Bud hurried closer and said, "Shit! What in tarnation?"

"Long story," I said. "Where are the kids?"

"Outside with Oz," he said, eyes on the scene in front of him.

"Oz okay?" I asked, as my eyes fixed on Hansel being engulfed by his own prophecy.

"*Someone* knocked Oz out," Bud said. "Left him with a lump on his noggin." He studied the flames and stepped farther away. "The kids ran right into us when they tore outta here. Tula's scared shitless, scratched up, but otherwise I think she's good. The boy looks to be beat up a bit, but more mad than anything else. One look at him and any fool could tell he's your kid alright."

"Are there no secrets in this town?"

We both stepped back from the growing flames.

"Only from you, little buddy... now this barn's goin' down. Come on."

Outside Teddy and Tula sat with Oz on the bumper of his truck with a now freed Solly at their side. When I came out they ran to me. Tula wrapped her arms around my legs. Teddy smiled and held my hand while he patted Tula on the back to comfort her.

"It's okay honey," I said. "He can't hurt you now." I leaned down, took her in my arms, and stood up, suddenly aware of the beating Hansel delivered me— and equally aware of the one the children were spared. Suddenly, I felt grateful. Very grateful for that miracle.

Oz said, "Let's let that one burn," and ushered Teddy and Solly into the back of the car.

"Where's Solomon?" Tula asked.

"Solomon's not here, honey," I said, "but he's proud... You fought hard, didn't you?"

"He says to fight the bear," she said, "so I fighted like he showed me, but—"

"And you won, honey," I said. "You won."

I held her close, checking her arms—beaten and bruised all over, but no broken bones.

"Take me home to Imogene," she said, her face buried in the crook of my neck. "Please."

Oz reached out, gently took her from me, and said, "You gonna be alright, darlin'." Then settled her into the backseat of Bud's patrol car with Teddy and Solly.

Bud scanned the barn and asked if I were okay.

"Been beat up before," I said.

"Yeah," Bud shook his head, "You seem to be makin' a habit of that."

Chapter 145

THEO

THE SUN WAS SETTING. Puffs of fog moved and settled throughout the streets as we coasted to a stop by Imogene's store. Bud and I quietly slipped inside. The pink light from upstairs trickled down the steps. Pearl was watching Perry Mason in the living room, but everything else was quiet. We carefully opened the freezer latch and tossed Toreck's stiff corpse into the back of the truck. As Bud covered the body with a tarp, I inched the back door closed so it wouldn't creak. Mrs. B appeared out of nowhere, glanced in the back of the truck, and said, "Good. Take out that trash."

"Shit!" Bud said. "Ya scared me."

"B," I said. "Tell Immie that Tula's fine, she's with Netty and Oz."

"She's sleepin'," she said, "and Solomon's still here for now." She tapped the truck with her cane. "You boys finish this thing."

"Yes ma'am." We said in unison.

While Bud tied down the tarp, I went back inside, grabbed Imogene's phone, and said, "Lucy, get me the Bouvre line, would ya, love?"

"Yes, Father," she said. "Is everybody okay over there?"

"We will be."

While waiting, I glanced at the stack of daily papers. Headlines of a rape, kidnapping, and vigilante killings, no matter how much the perpetrators were hated and wouldn't be missed, would bring an unwanted spotlight. I'd failed to protect Imogene from this attack, but I *could* protect her from reliving it over and over again through gossip and prying eyes.

Finally Andréa picked up and said, "Theo?"

"Is he settled in?" I asked.

"He passed out and slept for an hour but woke about seven o'clock. He's wide awake now, talking about how he should have kicked that bad guy, and how he tore his cape and scared Tula." She sighed, "I guess he's fine, better than me. I keep crying, thinking what could have happened... to you both." She started to sob and then sighed of exhaustion. "I've never been so terrified. Did I thank you? I don't remember anything other than you and Bud bringing him home."

"You thanked me... you thanked us both," I said noticing the clock—it was seven thirty. I needed to take care of a few things. "You going to be okay?"

"Yes, fine. You?"

"Yeah, since your little Superman saved the day."

"He did?"

"Yeah, if he hadn't shouted at Hansel, made him turn his head for split second, I don't know what I'd have done. But that split second was all I needed. So yeah, Superman saved the day. Tell him that."

"How about you tell him?"

"Okay, but first I have some things to do."

"We'll be here."

Chapter 146

THEO

SOLOMON'S BLEAK CABIN had gone cold, his incense out, the water kettle dried. The heavy sounds of his breathing had ceased, and the resounding silence drifted in and out of the space where he'd been. I sensed it—his mighty spirit had withdrawn.

He was ash grey, and his eyes were wide open, looking to the ceiling as if he'd seen something while taking his last breath. I bet it was Ruby—they'd waited a long time to be reunited. I was happy for him. And happy that he and his weary Wolf had completed their final journey and could finally go home. But in that happiness was a sinkhole of sorrow. I placed my hand over his open eyes and said, "Bless you… " I choked on my words, blinking away tears. "With every breath you've taken, you've proved real love never dies, but manifests in other ways. Go home now, Ruby waits."

Next to him was a small wooden box with Imogene's name burned into the top. I set it aside to give to her later. Bud came through the door and said, "Well?"

I swallowed past the lump in my throat and said, "He's gone."

Bud took off his hat and dropped into a chair. An ivory light shone through Solomon's window and illuminated his strong profile. I cleared my throat and said, "His final journey was to escort the evil spirits off Neahkahnie." I stood, opened the door, and looked at his packed canoe. "I've got a promise to keep."

"Right," Bud said. "Tell me what to do and let's do it."

We opened all of the windows in Solomon's cabin, letting out any part of his spirit that may have been confused or left behind.

"Spirit of Solomon Katata," I said. "You are free. Go from this place to the next world. Ruby waits." I lit a bundle of his herbs, and we wrapped his body in elk skins, then put him in his canoe with the things he'd set aside to help him find his way during his journey to the spirit world.

I took Kiernan's soldier from my pocket, tucked it inside Solomon's Medicine Bundle and whispered, "Return this to my brother, would you? Tell him I fought the best fight I could, but now, there's a little boy who bears our names; I'm ready to live… for both of us."

Chapter 147

THEO

BUD UNEARTHED his dilapidated wooden canoe from his garage, slid it up beside Toreck's corpse in the bed of Oz's truck, and asked, "You okay with this?"

"I have a lot of regrets and a lot of doubts," I said, "but this isn't one of them."

The moon cast a pearlescent glow over the wicked night. The eyes of God looked down on me—didn't know what to say, so I said nothing. Thought nothing. Pulled off my collar, slid it into my pocket, and drove in silence back to Solomon's with my late-night companion in retribution.

"Since all sins are not crimes," I asked, "are all crimes sins?"

Bud parked the truck in my driveway, looked at me, and said, "That's the kind of question that'll take a man a lifetime to answer. Don't ya think?"

I nodded.

* * *

Maybe God would understand we had no choice but to cover up the devastation left by Toreck and Hansel before more damage was done. I'd already lost one war and too many children. Maybe God would understand. Maybe not. Maybe saving Teddy and Tula was my one miracle in this life. If so, good enough.

We carefully lifted Solomon's canoe, with him inside, into the bed of the truck next to Toreck and drove the three blocks to the beach. Bud poured a can of gasoline over Toreck's canoe, shot a hole in the bottom so it would slowly sink somewhere offshore. Then he tied a rope—maybe six feet—to Solomon's sturdy ceremonial canoe so it would tow him out to sea.

We gently launched Solomon's canoe into the waves. The ocean beckoned with winds that stirred the waters. Then we shoved Toreck's boat into the water.

Thigh-deep in the tide, my hands shook as I lit the match that set Solomon's body free from this world. The great *a'sayahal*, Solomon's South Wind, kicked up and propelled his fiery release into the dark abyss of the Pacific Ocean. It was appropriate, poetic, for Solomon to escort a demon to the gates of hell, ensuring he would never return. We stood in the water as it rushed around us. I tossed another match into Toreck's boat. It burst into flames. The beach lit up like a yellow sunrise. As Solomon's canoe drifted farther, the rope yanked and pulled Toreck's into the dark sea. Solomon would meet Genghis at the gates of hell and make sure he, too, entered. Then he would reunite with Ruby and they'd move on to their next journey together.

I remained in the water as Bud walked back to shore and collapsed on the ground, the energy he'd mustered now gone. The canoes drifted toward the foot of Neahkahnie. Solomon's bright inferno glowed against the black sky with Toreck's boat, a low burning blaze, in tow until the rope snapped and they separated. Then, in a flicker of light, the White Sea Otter rose from the underworld up beside Solomon's canoe to guide him home. She allowed me a glimpse—a miracle from Solomon. And for a transitory moment I felt burdens lift from my spirit and stood rapt on that moonlit shore.

Chapter 148

IMOGENE

DAILY SPECIAL

Free Pie Today—For Solomon, Who Loved Pie.

At two thirty in the morning I cut off all my hair. By three thirty I had a short cut like Susan Hayward's in *Soldier of Fortune*. It was a start. I stared into the gold-framed mirror over my vanity. My red curls were cropped close to my face. I could hear Mamaí say, "Time to put the past in the past, Imogene."

I swept up the pile of hair that Toreck had buried his face into, swept him up as well, and tossed the whole mess into the garbage. Three days was all I was willing to give him. I went downstairs to the deli to bake pies. And though Solomon was gone, I felt him everywhere and I knew he'd be with me on this long journey back to myself. That journey begins now.

I pulled down the flour bin, took two tubs of berries out of the freezer, and tied an apron over my pajamas. It had been several days since I'd felt the softness of kneading bread, baking pies, and feeding sweetness into the ones I loved.

The feel of my hands kneading dough, mixing spices into berries, fingering flour onto the board, and shaping the pie crust just so with the wooden roller started to bring me back to myself. Five tear-stained pies later I was covered in flour and had berry stains on my fingers, arms, and apron. What a mess! It felt good.

As the steaming pies cooled on the racks, I wrote on my specials board: *Free Pie Today—For Solomon, Who Loved Pie.* I pictured him sitting outside on his bench, fork in hand, waiting, and knew I'd never make salmonberry pie again without the tang of salty tears.

I opened the box Solomon left me. Inside were ten gold coins, each the size of a quarter, and a note written in his shaky handwriting:

They say old pirate gold worth much money. Use this for you and to put Tula May through the schools, make her a happy home. It is time for love in your life. This will ease the way. Keep it secret or more pirates will come destroy our sanctuary.

Chapter 149

THEO

THE ANCIENTS SAY when a great soul dies, the winds are wild—grief strikes a hole in the heart. It was true, a great soul had died, and a mighty wind had raged through the streets of Manzanita for two days. The old Nehalem spirits were inconsolable. With Solomon's death, their time as a people had ended. The rhythmic dance of Solomon's good life would leave a hole in our spirits that no one would ever fill.

The last few days, as Solomon prophesized, had been biblical in scope. Innocent lives shattered, revenge exacted, bodies to bury, secrets never to be uttered in the light of day. It had changed us all, but for me? No regrets, except for what happened to Imogene. But other than that, I exorcised demons. No regrets at all.

* * *

Sometime after sunrise I rubbed Solomon's ointment on my hip where a strange lump had formed. It looked like a steel-blue marble under my skin. Then, suddenly, it broke through and dropped to the bathroom floor. There was no pain. A little blood, but no pain. I picked it up. The endless Korean War was knotted inside this piece of spent metal. I'd held it long enough.

* * *

That night as the Church Ladies stood hand in hand, eyes cast down in prayer next to Solomon's cold fire pit, no pomp, no circumstance, I sat at the dining room table next to my stack of letters to write two more. The first letter was to the news reporter, Hugh, whom I'd rebuffed last year. I asked him to do a story on Solomon and offered the obituary I wrote for our local papers as a starting point; offered him some notes about a real war hero and a story that deserved to be told.

OREGONIAN NEWSPAPER _ November 1957
Death of the Last Nehalem Indian – A WWI Veteran

Manzanita, OR – Solomon Katata died late last night in his home in Manzanita, Oregon. Born in Nehalem Oregon in 1862, his Nehalem Indian name was Sunnuct-chel, meaning *Double-Bladed Knife*. He was the son of the last Nehalem Indian Chief.

Katata was a notable veteran of World War I. After infantry training, he joined the 25th Infantry Division at Fort George Wright in Spokane, WA. From 1915 to 1918 he served in the Southwestern US, and spent the final eight months of WWI in France, where he was the First American Indian in U.S. Army history to receive the Distinguished Service Medal—he was 56 years old. It was later learned that his son was drafted. Katata, not wanting his young son to go to war, took his place. At the end of the war, Lieutenant Katata returned home unscathed from battle to his wife and their grown children. The family owned and operated a popular fishing and canning operation in Wheeler from 1912 to 1923, when his wife, Ruby, died.

In 1924, under the American Indian Citizenship Act, this native-born resident became a 'legal' citizen of the United States. Three days later he was arrested for burning his citizenship papers on the steps of the Tillamook Courthouse. He served one hour in jail and was given a ride home in a patrol car.

The Katata's three children have all since passed. Katata lived the rest of his days in his Ancestral home, known as the Weeping Cedar Tree in Manzanita. Though Solomon Katata's body has been cremated, there will be a plaque placed next to his wife Ruby's grave. Father Theodore Riley of Manzanita, a close friend of Mr. Katata's, tells us the plaque will have this phrase, said to have been spoken often by Mr. Katata:

SUNNUCT-CHEL 'SOLOMON' KATATA

1862 – 1957

Follow the way of the heart.
It is a hard way. It is a good way.

Chapter 150

THEO

THE SECOND LETTER was my resignation letter to Bishop Doyle.

I spoke with Andréa on the telephone last night while standing in my window, and she, across the street, standing in hers. Soft rain fell on Manzanita as we spoke and watched one another. I was elated just seeing her there—the Bouvre house no longer dark and cold. She said we could talk about what happened, years ago. She said she wanted to know all about my last six years, and wanted to tell me about hers. "Our divergent journeys have led us back to one another," she said as she placed her hand on the steaming window; I did the same and felt our eternal touch. Perhaps one season had ended and a new one could begin.

Clearly Teddy was my son, but not much else mattered anymore—not the past, decisions made, regrets, nothing. Just her, him, and me, if they'd have me.

But the past did need to be tidied up, starting with mine. There was only one way to purify my wound and exorcise *my* demons, so with the letters bound again by that bloody string, I climbed Neahkahnie to Destiny's Perch for the first time in years.

* * *

Pulled by the mystic gravity of Neahkahnie's bluff, I switch-backed through the tall grasses of the lower meadow and headed into the evergreen archways that overlooked Devil's Cauldron and Smuggler's Cove. Sun set on Neahkahnie's ancient rain forest with floors of fallen needles, the sweet smell of spruce, and ocean air. I climbed to the overlook that Andréa and I named Destiny's Perch, where the southern slope of the mountain spilled down to the beach. There, I built a bonfire, then read each letter; I finally let my tears fall. I honored that wonderful nun, Sister, and her Sisters of Mercy. Then each of the precious orphans, saying their names one at a time to the Great Grandfather, asking for blessings for them. Asking for their forgiveness.

In reading those letters I realized two things. First, I did do everything humanly possible to protect them. And second, the letters were never meant for Andréa's innocent eyes, but for mine and mine alone. Until now I hadn't been ready. Mrs. B was right, they'd been a container for my grief as much as Pearl's cup for James and Imogene's candles and garden.

For Andréa to have read all those ominous details would have caused her great distress, frightened her needlessly, and shown her a glimpse into war she need never see. No, those letters were returned to sender by divine grace. God's hand was in the returning of the letters to their rightful owner, not Andréa's disapproving father.

As the flames devoured the letters, I whispered Andréa's name, asked her for forgiveness, also. "Great Grandfather," I said lifting my arms to the midnight sky. "Release me from this agony. In the same way that bullet was purged from my body, free me from the crippling guilt and shame. I've been selfish, careless. Forgive me. Let Andréa forgive me for breaking *our* sacred contract. Now I know we have a son, a new sacred contract, and this bond will never be broken. Thank you, Father."

A cool mist settled on my skin. I looked across the flickering waters and then along the shoreline; the surface of the earth was neither completely lit nor completely dark. As the fire crackled, sparks flew to the sky, and I settled on a fallen log to watch the world wake. Sunlight filtered through the sapphire clouds, then that illusive light from the upper atmosphere burst through and scattered toward earth—a gift from the vaults of heaven.

It was twilight. Andréa's sacred blue hour. Sunlight radiated, illuminating the lower atmosphere with an ambient light, just like she described it. It covered half the globe as far as anybody could see. I stood from the fallen log and watched as the eternal light of God divided day from night, turned the shadow of death into the morning, and cleansed my blemished soul.

THE END